AMERICAN INFERNO

Bret Lowery

Copyright © 2011 Bret Lowery

All rights reserved.

ISBN: 1456575279
ISBN-13: 978-1456575274

For Ana, Jack, Lisa, and Ryan.

Another Death March In The Cold Driving Rain
Can't Come Soon Enough.

I

Nel mezzo del cammin di nostra vita...

I've been pondering the silence. I had no real issue letting go; the doing of it was a flick of a switch in my mind, automatic. Not a word, or even a thought; I just turned and left, like any exhale would. That was love.

Emotionally, I raged. I was selfish and angry and resentful and hurt. I grieved. I lacked all empathy. I understood the what of it, but facts are easy, facts are just math and logic and cruelty. This was not about facts. She believed in one set of them, I another. Disjoint sets cannot intersect; a union? Downright paradoxical. Uncountably full of points they were, points made and debated and rebuffed in their uncountable need to be unaccountably right, and all without word or comment or discussion. Interpretation and hallucination. False. The truth made untrue. I raged. That was love.

She'd said nothing, formulating, counting, observing, ever the scientist, constructing her theory in absence of me. Like all good philosophy, it was indefensible; like all good theories, relative. Perception was reality; just when it became such, I never knew. And God how she perceived. When the theory was explained to me, by only her eyes and a few terse words of fear, I learned the truth. Such a truth it was. Although they said it shall, it did not set me free. Liars. Judgmental ones, at that; her eyes, I mean. So beautiful, and afraid, needlessly, perceiving my lacking in their lack of perceiving. To her, this was *not* love.

Forgiveness is a chimera, a kind of superior selfishness. "I forgive you" clearly conveys the direction of power. Done correctly, with feeling, with gusto, it can suck the will to live right out of its target. A bulls-eye on one side, the eye of a bull on the other. After all, as long as one is judging the other lacking, how much letting go can there be? When two people argue, give and take, take and give, that is love.

Love, and that is all of it. We are without any limit to our thoughts and feelings in life and can create any reality we choose to focus our attention upon. I chose her. I chose the pain. If unjustly accused, do not let innocence settle on the horizon. Do not let your case vacillate and meet its demise in the sweet but sinister embrace of apathy, dumb and numb, because innocence is elusive. Elusive, like love.

In silence I stood at the door, turning away, from her and her eyes. Back then, I had raged as well, but for far, far different reasons. THAT... that was the problem. Plain vanilla, had-ta smell-ya, god damn ignorance. She didn't know. She had no way of knowing. She'd never know, and I'd have to live with that, knowing her eyes spoke of her ignorance and the thing that drove her away as a result: just her goddamn conscious ignorance, and fear.

But that was all months ago, miles away, mountains between.

Now I am allowed only the precipice on which I stand, facing the wind. My precipice has a name: the Jumpoff, two miles as the crow flies east of Newfound Gap along the Appalachian Trail, in the midst or thereabouts of the Great Smoky Mountains National Park. I stand on the edge of a sheer drop of a thousand feet, nothing compared to some other drops, but enough to do the job. I feel… fear, and the humidity, and scorn, standing here, on the edge, toes firmly grasping the nothingness, heels barely in contact with the Anakeesta. A rare blue sky and gentle wind with a feel of late April surround me with nearly two hundred ten degrees of kindness, from the Balsams in the southeast to Mount LeConte in the northwest, burning not my skin but this moment in memory, evolving me, planet into star, creating this damn universe in my head, Bang style. I close my eyes and rock ever so slightly forward, upward, a tenth of a millimeter at most, a heartbeat away from no heartbeats at all. I am separated from the next by the last, the

Alpha from the Omega. Somewhere in the middle is the mu of me, finite and not like pi unending, unlost but in intent to lose myself, forward, backward, one and the same, disconnected, with a pastnowfuture identical, full of the meaningless symbols of existence we create for ourselves and our sanity. Far off the noises of the world retreat.

A poem unbidden comes to mind:

In dark times
The eye begins to see
At the edges of the morning
The scents of the dew
Carried into this tomorrow
From yesterday's memory
The rocks forming outlines
Taking shapes of ancient beasts
Groaning under their weight
Silently, gray and dark
They awaken without thinking
Never having dreamed
As I have dreamt of them
Yea, they have haunted my steps
But still I chose them
They have been my lovers
Surrounding me with cold comfort
Such comfort as can mindlessness
Muster ancient from this earth
The trees with yellow-gold leaves
Dream their colors in their Fall
But discarding them aside in Winter
Forget their past and give away their skin
The stones never knew color
Never known what I have known
The trees may tell their tales well
But they disown what they know in sleep
The rock is more constant
And seeking verity
Forgetting myself

**I have turned gray as well
Being no tree.**

"Goddamn it," I mutter to no one in particular, except perhaps the bobcat 50 yards or so to my left and slightly behind me. He responds with yet another low, soft warning *grrrrul.* He says, *I won't bother you if you don't bother me*. There is silence for a moment, then wet, chewing sounds. The cycle of life in action.

I sniff the air. Here on the ledges, there is space, a sense of scale. On the open ocean, one gets a feeling of overwhelming vastness and emptiness, a mote on the surface of a sphere as beyond us as we are to the motes crawling on our own personal surfaces. At sea, you are nowhere, you are nothing. The woods engender the same dissolution: you are pressed in from all sides, by mighty trees swaying in the waves of the wind, an ocean full of statues, tall and silent. You are surrounded by a crowd of impersonal onlookers, cold and distant gods. They close in with hoots and horns and howls. The trees are thick with presence: eyes, webs, thorns, teeth, tongues tasting, mouths mouthing, feelers feeling. Raw. Ominous. Wet, chewing sounds. Your pace and pulse quicken and you push on. Persist, and with courage, with effort, you reach the cliffside, and the woods open to an ocean of air, and you stand on a beachhead of stone against the open blue, and cease to sense the difference between the sea and the wood and the sky. You realize the scale is all the same, and the silence, and how far you've come, and how far, how very, very far, you have to go… if you go, or rather, choose to go on, to face the press of the wood, the pulse of your heart, and long, long loneliness.

The image overwhelms me and empties me simultaneously, and I feel suddenly tired, and once again I am bereft of all purpose and desire. I am not entirely human, not anymore, anyway. I am a laborer pausing in the dust and heat. Thus, I test myself on the mountainside.

I have failed again, I think, and step back. I had not yet seen my last evening; but… there was hardly time to turn about. Another day, another dollar. A sudden rustle of disturbed brush, and my feline friend is gone. He too has failed; I wonder why.

Then, the reason: a stumbling clack of stones and Southern accents suddenly emerge from the scrub with cursing and other loud guffaws of laughter – not thru-hikers. "God *damn* it," I mutter again. An unfortunate iatrogenic effect, these things on the trail with me. In sympathy I experience an intense itching somewhere, from a fungus for which there is no cure. I scratch, to no avail.

They emerge from around a corner, discussing the apparently unexpected and still questionable results of a last-season Vols game; locals, strangely enough. Surprisingly, they seem surprised to see me. A "Howdy" escapes me, obligatory in these parts even if usually prescribed with a more friendly, less Lamont Cranston-like tone. I head in the opposite direction, not waiting for the response, not caring, away from this crowded place, back to the Trail, to the north, to my goal, to solitude, to anonymity, to freedom, to the end, the end, two thousand miles or slightly less as the crow flies. To Maine.

Why Maine? Because of her. Because of those eyes. Because the breath of my being dissolves at night in the cool air, a white vapor present even in summer when it is still crisp in the evenings at altitude. A white vapor, like a ghost; a ghost, like what remains of my form. Still in motion, so not gone, not yet. Still in motion, to Maine. One direction is as good as another when the whole world is your trail, but some trails are better than others. Wild ones, where the woods press round. North, to escape. It sounds sad and pathetic, really. All because of *her*? Well, of course not. There was also the other her, and the *other* her, and… well, you get the picture. But then why tell the truth for free when you can sell the property around it for a fat profit? Or, better yet, disappear into it for a nominal fee?

The locals are already out of earshot, like the bobcat, and unlike the wind. I pay my fee with silence, and continue.

II

5280 feet, 1961 miles to Katahdin

"Closely Control Children," the sign says, assuming an irresponsible idiocy in its readers. I laugh, and look over the scrag to the empty air. I sit on the Bunion, Class II Precambrian metamorphic, pack half empty, trying to crush two days' worth of clothes back into a stuff sack space of an hour's worth. An act of chiropractic cleromancy: the lump pressing into the back of my left kidney had annoyed me for the last time, and I was looking forward to the Sawteeth and a painless night at Peck's Corner. Charlie's Bunion to Peck's Corner to Tricorner Knob to Cosby Knob to Davenport, then out of the park, across the interstate, and onward to Snowbird Mountain, then Max Patch, Spring Mountain, Roan Mountain, mountain mountain mountain.

Why do more people visit the beach than the mountains? Because these mountains require work. As Danilo Dolci said, words do not move mountains; exacting work does. To me, it is no drudgery; I love this work, as so few of us do, therefore I come out of love, to these mountains I love, away from the people I don't. Many would see only toil; I see a step, just one, followed by another, just one, a simple thing. Addition. One plus one plus one plus… well, you can count as well as I. Addition, not multiplication; the million steps still before me do not exist. That's just how it is. Here, I am a slave to pattern and a slave to no one, not anymore. Free in adding to this time, each moment another step, each step another to the next moment. Always adding, never subtracting. Even when and where the trail descends, there is no subtracting, not in my knees anyway. They ache. I've had enough of subtraction. Less is more they say; but for whom? Accounts Receivable? All has been taken from me; I have no balance left with which to buy my way. So, I have left the marketplace of existence or what passes for such in such a civilized society as ours, prim and proper, and I barter for time, north, to Maine. Adding to my pointless motion. Always adding, because these mountains require work.

I should vomit. I should rehydrate more often. Instead, I do neither, and drink the view on this rare, royal aquamarine of a day as I shove everything back in my Gregory.

Posttraumaticstressdisorderisananxietydisorder...
...thatcandevelopafterexposuretooneormore...
...terrifyingevents...
...thatthreatenedorcausedgravephysicalharm...
...itisaseverandongoingemotionalreactiontosevertrau...

Stop.

...aumasuchasthedeathofalovedoneathreattothepatient...
...oralovedoneslifeseriousphysicalinjury...
...orotherlifethreateningconditionoverwhelming...
...normalpsychologicaldefenses...

"STOP," I command myself, becoming absolutely still. I close my eyes and focus on the wind. My pulse and thoughts begin to recede, albeit slowly.

...butschizoidpersonalitiesdifferintheirneedanddesire...
...tobealonewhereasmostpeopleprefer...
...andindeedneedthecontactofotherstheschiz...
...earstheintimateemotionsofthe...
...ortherevelationofinnermostemot...
...innermostemot...
...innermostemot...

Then it was gone, thankfully. Damn I hated that. Damn autostreaming. Damn eidetic memory. Damn damn damn.

"Storm's comin'," says Virgil. "Best git movin'."

"I guess so," I say after a moment. It's hard to decide, really. I look around at the jagged, smashed rock face, at the graffiti, at the stupidity and temerity. The stove finds its resting place in mid-pack. The view continues to impress. Pluses and minuses in staying here. I can only guess about the moving part. Should I, or shouldn't I? I know at some point I have to, but…

A minute more passes while I play at debating, in reality merely breathing. "Storm's comin'," repeats Virgil. Ever the coach, Virgil is. I finally secure the overflap with a strap, and poke the midsection to ensure the lump is gone.

"You know," I venture after another moment, "you're not supposed to be here." I realize after I say it that it sounds like a threat, but I didn't mean it that way, and I don't apologize. Virgil doesn't say anything. He understands.

I pick my Gregory up and throw it over my shoulder; luckily, it doesn't keep going and carry me with it. I fiddle with the lifters, secure the chest strap. A hawk cries out to my left in the clear air past the Bunion.

"Shit," says Virgil, freezing.

"Don't worry," I tell him, "I'm right here."

"Shit, shit, shit, best git' movin." says Virgil. So we're off again, after standing up and a final belt tightening, down the trail. Enough of problems. We round the northeast face of the Bunion and head down the Sawteeth.

The Sawteeth: five miles of 24 inch wide, billion-year old Anakeesta slate with the occasional sheer drop-offs on either side. Without a doubt, the most lethal place in the Smokies on a moonless foggy night with no light. Here in the day the route seems painted atop nothing more than a vast aggregation, as if a protolithic meteor shower in misty aeons past rained an evil hail of soapy flat stone down on my track, a track which somehow over time retained and even improved its slickness, able and willing to pitch the even momentarily unwary backwards, forward, or off into the blue on either side. I imagine this to be a fuck of a walk in January.

But for now, the blue daytime remains, clear, crystal, a dream remaining awake with me, with my awakened mind. But I failed the test at the Jumpoff; I remain what I have always been. Self-involved. I shall have neither soul nor spirit; I shall not be permitted to come up from the depths. Luckily, neither will be needed for this task.

I walk, and admire a delicate white and grey lace here, adorning the brush and spruce, a spidery white web, parasitic; some sort of moss, perhaps. It's everywhere, this elevated form of kudzoo. It does not laugh at my joke. I imagine it holding the snow, briefly, while its task is done, making spores or seeds or something that can sprout again in the spring when the weather warms up to fifty degrees or more, here what passes for passes in the Smokies. It is beautiful. It is flimsy and fleeting. It is life. Presence does not require permanence. Ebb and flow are in their nature in all that is natural. The leaves fall; the leaves spring. In all of this remains only all of this. Truly, there is no greater miracle. No snow nor storm nor smoke can undo it. Year in, year out, death comes, and life comes. Both spread together, a tangled loom of tendrils, a delicate lace in the wood.

There is the smell of scat on the wind here, too. Lace, and scat, a disturbed combination for which I am certain there is a website, and more disturbingly, regulars. This time, I laugh at my joke, or rather my depraved sense of humor… and cut it short at the sharp increase in the smell. Bear? Deer? Skunk? I imagine a bear chasing a buck chasing a skunk down this foot-wide balance beam I hike on. Be my luck.

I round a sharp turn; a mushy lump lies in the trail, already attracting flies, and stuffed with berries. Black. Large. Bear. Large black bear. I wonder how many times I'm going to cuss today, or worse, how often Virgil will, drunken disorderly sailor that he was.

There is a crash of brush off to my right; a large object descends rapidly. Apparently I disturbed his Happy Private Time. "I know how you feel," I call out, as if it would help to empathize at a time like this. The smashing and crashing continue, running sometimes, tumbling sometimes, down the steep mountainside. Very quickly, he/she/it is an eighth of a mile away, and going strong. "Sorry," I try half-heartedly, after my failed attempt at empathy. "SORRY," repeats Virgil, loudly and triumphantly, and *that* makes me laugh. What a jerk.

"I bet you enjoyed that," I say to him, laughing. "You should have more respect for the wildlife."

"SORRY," he says again to me, though this time I know he doesn't mean it. We pick up the pace. Very soon the silence returns, except for the occasional, superfluous "sorry" from my adroit friend.

As the day slowly wears on, the events of the day slowly wear off. Soon I forget bear and bobcat and find my thoughts drifting back, back to when I entered the park, some five days previous. I came up out of the North Carolina wood to cross the enormity of Fontana Dam on a morning of fog and gray skies. The mist on the still waters of the Little Tennessee merged with the seventy-year-old stone of the largest dam east of the Mississippi. "Shit," Virgil had remarked, and then done so, as if to emphasize the point. Who could blame him? We crossed the rampart in silence, broken by a few sudden gusts of wind as the cold front moved over us, collecting the mist on our things as we went. A mist is almost worse than a full-blown downpour; at least with the latter you know you're wet, rather than feeling it come on slowly like a cold cancer. Later that night at our first shelter in the park I'd opened the pack to find my change of socks so meticulously dried yesterday into wool jerky turned into wool thirsty instead. My sleeping bag was not slept on that night, but it hung by the fire to dry, though lower than the food, lest bears come. That night, Virgil and I sipped dreadfully delicious of cold poverty.

It was only after I'd finally managed to drift off that I'd dreamt a strange dream. I was already in Maine, but it was many years ago, and I found myself thinking solid, carved thoughts, as if I was someone else, but also myself, both, and neither, but something else entirely. When I awoke, I remembered words, as if dictated to me, or from me: *Some part of the beholder, even some vital part, seems to escape through the loose grating of his ribs as he ascends. He is more lone than you can imagine. There is less of substantial thought and fair understanding in him, than in the plains where men inhabit.* That morning I found my reason dispersed and shadowy, more thin and subtle, like the air. Vast, titanic, inhuman Nature had me at a disadvantage, and screwed me. She seemed to address me directly, with archaic scorn. Virgil didn't speak to me for the whole day, and ate all the granola. Maybe She told him to. The grayness of the lake had followed us, even as the skies had opened up into their current clear currents. My soul remained cold and dissolute, hence my stop at the Jumpoff.

Despite it all, my boots continue: *plod, plod, plod...* I am still the Crusader, even if judged faint-hearted by those who do not love the Crusades.

Suddenly, I remember a time that Harlan Ellison rode in my ugly green 1974 Monte Carlo, sometime back in '84, or was it '85? He was giving a lecture – a term I'm sure would make him snort if he heard me say it – at my university, and a group I belonged to was charged with showing him a night on the town, such as it was. A girl I liked rode in the back, someone I would not speak with for another, oh, twenty years or so. I vaguely remembered that he was typically, unapologetically brusque, and that after we got out of the car, we were nearly run over by a guy fleeing from The Man and wearing handcuffs on one arm to prove it. He'd made a lucky escape, and stared at us like a feral cat, heaving, gasping, and sweaty. Other than that, I've completely forgotten the rest of the evening. Memory is strange. There I was, with personal one-on-one time with one of the great if acerbic writers of the latter half of the twentieth century, and all I remember now was the guy wearing the handcuffs. Strange. No wonder I never learned anything. I find myself wishing some alter ego would call me from my apartment and tell me that I'd screwed up and that he was taking over my life: my own personal *Shatterday*. Ha ha. Too bad there was no cell service up here on the A.T., seven miles from the nearest road.

No, wait: I remember thinking that he liked "my" girl, and that I hated him for that. Sigh. He'd commented on her eyes, how they were like... like... some Greek classical reference something. I wanted to....

I stop walking. After all this time, all these miles, *this goddamned thing* was what I was thinking about. I had – *had* – to get the past out of my mind. That was the whole point. That was why I was here, finally, inexorably. Damn eidetic memory. Damn damn damn. I couldn't get to Maine fast enough.

I close my eyes and the ceaseless words form again, streaming sentences of pseudo-psychobabble:

...theamountofdisassociationpresentafteratraumaticvent...
...isindicativeofanincreasedriskforPTSD...
...peoplewhodisassociateaftersuchevents...
...areatsubstantiallyhigherriskforPTSD...

"Well no duh." I say to no one, out loud. Funny how the thought of *her* and those words went together. Free association kicks in. Like cops and donuts. Like ham and cheese. Like anchovies and stink... well, now at least I was thinking of food, and that was a relief. Food always takes precedence on the trail.

I had a ration of chili all made up while I'd restocked in Gatlinburg, a Redneck Riviera if there ever was one. Mostly white beans, a few red beans, a few black beans, with some ham and bacon fat thrown in; Gatlinburg I mean, not the chili. The latter was spicy and exotic. I'd enjoy it on a cool evening at Peck's Corner, now just a few miles ahead and a quarter-mile off the trail to the right. My thoughts of camp and campfire faded again into background noise, becoming static in my skull, a waking dream-state, as my consciousness retreated into silence and my feet started moving again of their own accord.

It was sometime in those last few miles, somewhere on the Sawteeth, sometime when I was lost in unthinking thoughts, that the mist moved in, and the world changed.

I didn't notice it at first, deep in the fundamental state of movement as I was. It was Virgil who first mentioned it, without saying anything. He just started to whistle nervously, a sure sign of trouble, I'd learned. I didn't even notice that at first, until I noticed he wasn't stopping. Then, I stopped, and looked up. The day had gone from blue to white, a close-aboard blanket of fog, very unusual for these mountains in its eerie warmth, not cold at all. This wasn't a typical condensation of cold downdrafts hitting warm, tree-covered stone; this was, well, *weird*.

It bothered me that I'd never noticed until it was full on me. "Thanks a lot," I said to Virgil. "You could've said something." He just looked around and kept whistling, softly. For a moment, I had the sensation we were falling, into some deep place where the sun was silent. But no, there we were, standing on the same sandstone and slate.

Just as suddenly, there was the sign: *Peck's Corner, 0.3*, with an arrow pointing to the right. Following orders, I turned, and Virgil with me. The trail descended steeply down the wooded hillside, becoming more of a gully than a trail, given the steepness of the slope. I pushed hard into my Lekis, trying to spare my knees of the stress. I slipped a few times on the way down, but caught myself quick, although it did prompt a few complaints and random swearing from Virgil. The mist closed in tight, thicker and thicker. It would be another cold, depressing night, despite the chili. Virgil kept complaining all the way down. Shades of the day at the dam. Shades and ghosts.

Then, we were there, the shelter appearing out of the mist on the left of the trail, which continued down the ridge to the valley far below. As I cast my headlamp on the shelter to see better, I saw graffiti on its side, unusually large graffiti, and read:

Abandon All Soap, Ye Who Enter. Beer?

I laughed despite the desecration, but as I did so, I thought I heard words, from someone under the porch of the shelter in the ever-present dark that seemed to cling to them. Almost a "Hello," but somehow not in English, as if saying something to be understood from intuition, not cognition. It was followed by more faint words, almost a chant of sorts on the wind, speaking of ancient days and other places. I stopped, but then out from the blackness stepped a giant of a man, dark, Asiatic, with small horn-rimmed impenetrably-black glasses, bare arms, an open Lexan bottle of some dark liquid in his right hand and whatever remained of his dinner prep wiped from his left on a maroon cloak with a (silk? here?) brocade just before he extended it in greeting, a strange admix of culture and savage. Imagine a man who could not be portrayed by the handsomest leading man in Hollywood, Bollywood, or any other wood. He seemed to be of the stuff of giant Egyptian stone pharaohs: smooth, perfect, seemingly pupil-less, faintly and humorlessly smiling, communicating indifference, raw power, and oddly, compassion, all at once. I had a weird sensation that he'd sprung from the mountain around us. I could not avoid him. I did not shake his hand.

"Padma, Padma Sambhava," he said, peacefully. His lip curled into a bigger smile when he realized I would not shake his hand. He withdrew it, then offered the Lexan bottle in the other.

"A tea of sorts," he said. "Herbal." There was a pause; I stood there like an idiot, staring. I did not want him or his attention or his damn tea. Finally I walked to the shelter, leaned my poles against the wood, took off my pack. Virgil sat on the bench without comment.

"Suit yourself," Padma said. He took a swig, then, cryptically: "Soma." At least that's what it sounded like. He glanced sideways at me, seemingly expecting a response.

I popped the top of my pack open and began unpacking my stove and food. There was no one else at the shelter. *God damn it,* I thought. The sun descended behind the ridge, past the thick trees, into someone else's tomorrow. The shade began to creep in time with the fog. Dinnertime.

He put a small pot of water on his stove, turned up the white gas, hit the piezoelectric. The sharp hiss of gas burst into flame; he cut it down immediately.

"Fire," he started, "was not always warm. A story goes that the sun god brought it down cold from heaven, but the snow leopard was jealous of its beauty, and took its cold away, to the mountains." It was a strange statement, forcing me again to look at him. "Some people are like fire," he said, looking at me. It felt like an insult.

Enough of this. "Durant," I said. "My name's Durant."

"And your companion?" he asked, gesturing at Virgil, who was now sitting on the wooden bench just inside the shelter.

"That's Virgil. Say hello to the gentleman, Virgil."

"Hello," said Virgil, as if trained.

"Mr. Virgil," the man said, bowing slightly. Then, he began digging around in his pack. "Some men are like the snow leopard. Ah, here is my soup." He pulled a Ziplock full of dry mix from his pack. "What sort of man are you, Mr. Virgil?"

Virgil of course said nothing; he was preoccupied with the bits of old crusty things and dislodged splinters of wood on the bench.

"Ah, an individualist, I see. And you, Mr. Durant, " he said, turning to me again as he pulled a large spoon from his pack. "What sort of individual are you?"

A goddamned philosopher, I thought, meaning him, not me. I removed my boots, one at a time, slowly, to enjoy it. It was going to be a long, tiresome night. "Just passing through," I muttered.

"Aren't we all," he said, a statement more than a question.

A few minutes passed in silence, thankfully. Silence is something so many take for granted; or, never know at all. Silence is more filling than sound, a stew to the other's soup. The wind blew, cooling, stronger. We turned into cooks, except for Virgil, who always expected a chef unless he came across the fortuitous berry, which wasn't infrequently. Steam and smells rose from our gear, mixing with the early evening's mist. I found my eyes had closed.

"Sleepy?" Padma asked. "It's a late road, but an early evening. Local, or headed further north?"

"Maine," I said, not opening my eyes.

"Impressive," he said. "I'm just passing through myself. Interesting place," he said. I got the impression he was looking around; I kept my eyes closed.

When are the other hikers going to show up? I thought. *This is the most visited national park in the world, and I'm alone in Spring with an extrovert six miles from the closest road, eight if I stayed on the trail.* I focused on my attention on the sound of my Jetboil, simmering softly.

"Very well then, suit yourself." he said, seeming to finally give up. "No harm intended."

"None taken," I said.

"Really? And why is that?" he asked.

That was it. I'd had enough. I opened my eyes and locked them on his. "Are you going to analyze my every word all night?" I asked. "If so, at least I get a chance to analyze you back."

"Excellent!" he said, and he stood up and actually bowed. *Jeez, where are the OTHER hikers?*

"I should think we shall have an excellent night, " he said, "as I rented the shelter for 12 people." Then he laughed.

The whole fuckin' shelter? Shit. Shit shit shit. The guy was a certified licensed Class I psycho. I stood and backed up a step, reached for my hiking pole, expecting the knife to come out at any second.

He immediately got my look, and stopped himself. "Oh, no harm intended at all, Mr. Durant. I assure you. I am here only for the journey, just as you are. I am quite sincere." He bowed again.

I relaxed slightly, but harrumphed. "Sincerity?" I asked warily. "Sincerity is just one person's truth at a local minima."

"I don't follow, " he said, although in a manner that suggested he did.

"All it takes is an application of emotional energy to roll the ball up and over the slope into a new realm of truth. I can state my belief any time I like, but it may not be my belief tomorrow, and I reserve the right to contradict everything I've ever done or said."

It almost made me sound almost smart, which was my intent. Too bad my comment turned into a can opener. He considered it, then…

"I still don't follow," Padma finally said, baiting me although I didn't realize it.

"Reality," I said, dumping the worms out of the can. "We are psychological beings; when we deny that, we deny ourselves." I found myself agitated, and tried to calm down. *Exactly*, I thought. "It doesn't matter how I feel; what matters is what I do about it. When we really believe the two are identical, when we are being *sincere* and *honest* and *open*, we are never lying more to ourselves. *I love you* and *I hate you* are the two most interchangeable statements in the world." I immediately wished I hadn't said the last sentence.

"Hmm…." he said. "Elegant words are not sincere; sincere words are not elegant."

"I suppose so," I said, processing his quote, "if you don't equate beauty and elegance with truth. Many mathematicians are Buddhists," I added, guessing at his personal proclivities. *Relate to the crazy*.

He smiled slightly. "Ah, I see, local minima…" He took another swig from his Lexan. "So…" he continued, "words… words don't mean a thing."

Well... I... I felt myself begin to sputter, kept my mouth shut. A long moment passed in silence as I began to realize just what was in the can I'd opened. This guy wasn't some schmuck. He was... quick. I pondered strategy for a moment, then offered a rook.

"I'm running away," I finally said, giving up. "That would be the way you would put it. I apologize for my anti-social behavior."

"Very sincerely put. No need to apologize." He took control, smiling. I felt embarrassed. "I regret anything negative I've made you feel."

Now *that* was a grab for power. "*Made* me feel? But we've just met. I assure you there's nothing of that sort," I said. "I really don't feel…" and the words just left me.

"Feel?" he asked, prompting.

"I'm… just not in the game tonight," I admitted, offering him the other rook. "I'm not in the mood for being contrived or artificial, and forget about spontaneity. It's all so worn out these days, and I'm tired. I'm just here to detach, OK?"

He hummed for a moment, then ignored me and went too far. "I want to venture something. You've been damaged and realize it, and realize the damage's effect, yet allow the effect to, ah, affect you."

That was over a line. "Can we just eat?" I said, annoyed and letting it show. "Is this really necessary?"

"What are you afraid of?" he asked. "It's just conversation. Words don't mean a thing."

"Words make all the difference in the world," I said. I felt a pit open inside of me, full of all of the things I'd said or left unsaid. Damn eidetic memory. I couldn't escape my past even if I wanted to, short of… short of….

"Right speech is to be admired," he said, apparently agreeing. "But what of right action?"

"Oh, WHAT is *this?*" I asked angrily. Fuck this guy. I didn't spend all day to get here and be stripped like this by some stranger.

A long silence passed and he seemed disappointed, then turned back to his gear, working it. The silence became unnerving. Finally he spoke, softly. "I beg your forgiveness if I seem a bit forward and direct, Mr. Durant. I assure you that you owe me nothing. You owe others... exactly what you believe you owe them. As for yourself, it's what you owe yourself that's what matters now."

That was more unnerving. Evidently I was to be psychoanalyzed, and like it. Part of me bristled, pissed. *What else is it that I must apologize for?* On the other hand, I was trapped. I wasn't hiking out at night to get away from this doofus. No; I'd have to use my wits, play along, game the gamer. What choice did I have? *Relate to the crazy.* So, I chose a tack, and hoisted sail.

"That's where you're wrong." I corrected. "I have everything to apologize for… well, many things. We all do, but we rationalize it. Out there we have to. That's why I'm here. I'm done, finished, with rationalizing my life."

"Ah, I see," he replied. Another silence mixed with the night fog on the ground outside the shelter. He seemed genuinely uncertain for the first time, something I found strangely disturbing, yet comforting. *Maybe if I act crazier than he is, he'll leave me alone*. Maybe not. He stirred his soup, then stopped.

"So… you're on a Quest," he said.

Oh puh-LEEZE. "Label it as you see fit. Call it a Quest or call it Christmas. Call it honeysuckle and moonbeams. Call it selfishness or pride or narcissism or depression. Call it long distance. It doesn't matter." *That's it; stay in control, act the boss.*

He seemed to ignore me. "And what is it that you are finding?" he said. "A rock? A tree? The next turn in the path? It leads only to another turn, another tree, another rock." He stirred his soup. "But of course, you already know that."

"I am finding myself," I said, defensively and reflexively.

At that, he bellowed in laughter for nearly a full minute. "Finding *yourself?"* he finally managed. "I have news for you." He leaned close and whispered. "*You... are... right... here."* Then, he backed off, stared at me incredulously like the moron I was, and bellowed again. I felt ashamed and looked down as he howled, laughing at my expense. What a son-of-a-bitch.

"Thanks," I said finally when he stopped. "Enjoyed that. Anything else you'd like to know?"

"Yes," he said. "What is it about you Americans and your... inconsistency, shall we say?"

I was lost. "I don't follow," I said.

"All you damn Americans and your damn *enlightenment*. What burden is it that you carry anyway that requires *lightening*? Your own belly fat? I've never understood what it is that drives Americans. You all have a thirst that is never quenched, as if you are each of you always smoldering, ready to burst into flame at the slightest personal or international provocation. Things are a Pilgrimatic black or white, or a cynical materialistic gray. One minute, you all act like little lost Protestant lambs needing a Good Shepherd or a good buzz or a good time to guide you along or off or onto the path you yourself have already lain. The next, you are all Crazy Generallissimo Bushes needing to exploit and take and consume and mark-up and distribute and commercialize and advertise and *sell sell sell*. You are a dangerous combination of Abrahamic religion and ubercapitalistic politics, walking hand in hand. You are childlike in your beliefs about the universe and your fellow man and your own egoistic individuality; children, but with adult appetites. The rest of the world is justifiably frightened. What will be left for them, for their children, for their appetites? Something that you will either out-compete, or failing that, that your next generation of smarter bomb could certainly take out in a microsecond. American enlightenment is always purchased at a fat profit. What do any of *you* know of suffering?"

I was taken aback: a rambling speech, about America? OK, he wants to go off on that tangent, off we go. I tried responding with sarcasm, always an excellent choice after rant-filled rambling speeches.

"I thought the Buddha taught that *suffering* did not exist, but tell that to the families who lost loved ones on 9/11."

Whammo. He stopped smiling and his serious demeanor returned. "Well, " he said, clearly remeasuring his responses, "he was wrong, but he *was* just the Buddha, after all. He never had to philosophically contend with weapons of mass destruction. War and death were more... *personal* experiences in his day."

It was nice to get a punch in. I gave it a moment, but then he broke it.

"It seems you've had more than mere honeysuckle and moonbeams. Perhaps the moon has turned you into a lycanthrope."

Odd word to use, that. Not a word one encountered on the trail very often, the stuck up little prick. *Do I pass the test, Teach?* "Maybe it has, or maybe I'm just hairy. Not a lot of opportunities to shave out here," I said, through gritted teeth.

Smiling again. "Maybe," he said. "Maybe you weren't... ready."

That was an insult. I showed my annoyance again. "Aw, come *on*. Ready? Who's ever *ready*? Whoever says they're *ready* is either ignorant or bluffing. I'm neither. Are you *ready?"*

"Is that a threat?" he asked.

Oh no you don't. We are SO not going there. "You know what I mean," and I knew he did. "Readiness doesn't come into it. It is what it is, that's all... and yeah, you're right about us, us Americans. What's fulfilling about it all? To, what did you say, *sell sell sell* day after day? At worst I just wasn't... wasn't... fulfilled, I guess." *Actually, I knew: no guessing required.*

A softer tone now. "*Ahhhhh*, fulfilled. Yes, a much better word than *enlightened*. *Full-filled*, measurable, predictable, quantifiable, analytical, number-driven, very American."

He paused but I said nothing, then he prompted with what was recognizably a koan: "What requires filling? An empty vessel."

"Or a practically emptied one," I said, still annoyed. *Sometimes there is much truth in sarcasm.*

He reached out and touched me, and my muscles seized. "I am sorry for your loss," he said. A moment passed, then he resumed stirring his soup. We listened to the winds and the owls on them for a few minutes. I relaxed a little, breathed; maybe he wasn't a whackonaut who rented out the entire shelter just to chop me into bacon strips. But I reasoned I needed to keep his mind occupied, lest he do so. For some reason I couldn't begin to understand, I felt I had momentarily gained the upper hand. I decided to trust instinct and up the ante.

"Purpose," I finally said. "Purpose requires filling. It's a void requiring pressure to achieve its shape, and maintenance to keep it."

He considered that. "Yes," he said after a while, "yes, you may be on to something there. Pressure creates purpose."

"Evolution," I continued.

"Yes," he said, considering.

"Evolution is in every moment, if we choose it," I began. "We can choose purposeless alternatives—drugs, alcohol, ritual, ignorance, sex..."

"Hiking?" he asked, feigning innocence.

I stopped for a second, then laughed, finally breaking my own nervousness, much to my intellectual surprise. "Yes, I suppose so. Hiking.... But, in MY case, my purpose is Maine." I laughed again, this time for effect. *Let him think my guard is down.*

He waited until I finished, then: "Why?" he asked. I had no answer. I acted like I wasn't paying attention.

"We can choose a purposeless life, but then, pressures come from the outside rather than from within. We are blown by chance. When we create drive, with our petty American adult appetites as you put it, within ourselves, we are driven. It's the difference between being a balloon or an airplane. Which are you more confident will get you to exactly where you want, exactly when you want?"

He smiled. "*Touché,* I deserved that. You are saying that you Americans are the pilots."

My how his mind jumps around. Yes, let's get it back on the American thing, good. "I'm saying *someone* is always the pilot. Right now, it's us Americans. The Sumerians, the Egyptians, the Romans, Chinese... well, there's always been a pilot, and they change from time to time."

"Only now, your planes go anywhere, everywhere, with whatever mindless payload you choose to deposit on the foreign landscape. Technology."

I shook my head. "Evolution," I corrected. "Can't be helped." *Rock on*.

Again, he leaned forward. "*Reaaaallly?*" he breathed. "The simple inevitably leads to the complex?"

I thought, almost said *No,* then said, "Yes, but not necessarily in the form and time intended."

He jumped up. "Now THAT I'd call enlightenment!" he said. He removed the boiling tea from the Whisperlite and cut all his stoves off. "So you Americans are the highest form of evolution, eh?" He poured his tea into a titanium mug.

I almost bristled, but realized: *Actually, that is what I think.* I said so.

He sighed, then, "Ah well, so much for enlightenment."

"Shit," Virgil agreed.

Padma looked at him, as if for the first time, judging. "He's a strange companion," he said. Virgil ignored the invective, just like I knew he would.

"None stranger," I agreed. "but he probably agrees with everything you're saying." *Imply he has an ally*. Then I caught myself: Virgil, an ally. Hah.

"Really?" Padma laughed. "What do you think?" he asked Virgil. Virgil just stared at him. Padma laughed again. "Well-met," he said, complementing my taciturn brother.

"He's probably the most enlightened of us both," I remarked, honestly.

Padma turned back to me, nodded his agreement. "So, if everything's so great *there*," he said, gesturing grandly all around, "why are you *here?"*

Another long silence. "Don't you already know?" I finally muttered. I suddenly felt lost again.

He smiled. "Evolution 'not in the form and time intended.' Yes, I like that, very much. That sums it up. You're finding yourself by losing yourself… or something like that." he said.

I ignored the last sentence. "Sums what up?" I asked, now really feeling lost and defensive.

"Oh, a few things, including that American ego of yours. It's not all a collective thing-a-ma-jig *out there*." He said *thing-a-ma-jig* slowly and carefully, liked he'd learned the placeholder recently. "Even now," he continued, "even now, you are one of them, and you are not one of them. Finding and losing."

That hit me hard. I held my breath for a moment, then, "The world is what it is."

"Which means?" he asked.

"Men who are nothing, who allow themselves to become nothing, have no place in it." The words came from me almost automatically, though they weren't mine.

"Except here?" he asked.

"Except here." There, we finally agreed on something.

More silence, then, "So did you become nothing, or allow yourself to become nothing?"

"What's the difference?" I asked. "Don't I have free will?"

"Maybe," said Padma. "Maybe not. What do you think?"

"You tell me," throwing it back at him.

"I think you have the will to be free, but not necessarily free will." He smiled like a cheap plastic Buddha at a bad Chinese restaurant. *Crazy philosophical whack.*

"Words," I muttered.

"Words make all the difference in the world," he said, grinning ear to ear.

I yawned. "Now you're boring me," I lied, but he was too good for that.

"If that's your choice. Are you *really* nothing? Can't *you* just be the pilot of *you*?"

Excuse me? I looked up at him. I guess we didn't agree after all. "I choose to be a balloon." I said. "Let the wind blow me where it may."

"Despite you will to be free, you've allowed yourself to become nothing," he said. It sounded like a conclusion.

"To everyone I ever knew, yes," I finally gave, exasperated. "I understand my lot because I choose it. Experience has taught me well. Besides, how many Americans go on an actual spiritual journey these days?"

"Understanding *is* the internalization of comprehension," he said. "Experience is the aggregation of conscious events…"

I recognized the quote instantly; for once the eidetic memory came in handy. "Theosophy?!" I started. "Now you're giving me theosophy? I'm too tired right now for Madam Blavatsky. Next you'll tell me that there is no religion higher than the truth."

"Is there?" he asked.

"God only knows," I said, truthfully.

A low deep grumble floated through the air from somewhere to our general left. We looked and went silent. Another bear, maybe a hungry one. But three or four minutes passed, and nothing. Finally Virgil broke the silence.

"Sorry," said Virgil. Padma and I both looked at him, then each other, and laughed.

"HE gets it," Padma remarked, meaning Virgil. The he told Virgil, "One can be saved from foolishness by another if one is receptive. But the real question is: should they be?"

Since he'd clearly just called me a fool, I ignored that one; after all, it was true, no escaping it. We ate then, saying nothing. The chili I'd prepared was spectacular, or at least I deemed it so. A few moths fluttered in on the night wind, including a gigantic luna moth, pale greenish-yellow against the dark wood. It landed near Virgil, which would normally have gotten it an automatic death sentence. He regarded it slowly, hypnotically, almost as if he appreciated it. It sat and slowly opened and closed its wings for a few minutes, before finally fluttering off.

"Who *are* you?" I asked after we'd eaten, unable to stand it any longer.

He smiled. "Me? I'm just… a virtuous pagan, one might say. I experiment with the truth…" He seemed to want to say something else, then think better of it.

Well, he has an ego at the least. "Gandhi said something similar of himself," I pointed out.

"Ah, you're well-read I see. Here I was thinking that you were just another American. I suppose then I'm in good company... one virtuous pagan to another."

I assumed that was a joke, so I ventured one of my own, testing his limits. "Perhaps you're the Comte de Saint-Germain."

For the first time that evening he wasn't amused, and showed it. "No, I'm not, and I'm not Ahasuereus either."

Smarty pants. "Well, you don't look Jewish, despite your wandering."

That seemed to return him to an amused state. "More wondering than wandering, but enough about me. I think I know who *you* are...."

No way are you going to finish that sentence. I jumped in. "Me? I'm more of an atheist than an artist. Just flirting with rapture."

"You don't say," he said, producing cocoa, judging by the smell. Funny, I hadn't noticed him making any. I waved away the mug he offered me. "You still don't trust me, do you?" he asked.

"Trust? Trust is just two people's sincerity at a local minim...."

He raised his hand to stop me. "I get it already. But do you?"

I regarded him carefully. He still had his sunglasses on. His skin was absolutely perfect.

"No," I said slowly. "I don't get any of it at all. Not a syllable or a season or a smile of it. It's all the same thing it was on the day I was born: a mystery. Every ounce of my being and experience says that my intent seldom matches the results, or that my intent was all I ever really had. Goalless experience, with no end. Therefore, I hike: the goal, the end. Simple."

"Simple? Well then, perhaps it will lead to the complex, and not in the form and time intended." he said. I shrugged; who was I to argue about the future? There was a long, slow wind then through the shelter. We listened to it, then as it died, Padma said: "It sounds like purgatory to me, or perhaps worse."

"What requires filling?" I reminded him.

His smile left him then, and he said: "Yes, I think I understand you," then he quoted: "'Of all pains, the greatest pain, it is to love, but love in vain.'"

That broke me. I looked down, tearing up. Of course I knew the quote; that one was just high school English, for Christ's sake. "Enough. Stop," I said, shedding a tear. God DAMN memory. God damn love.

To his credit, he stopped. Nothing else was said. We cleaned up, put our things away, hung our packs on the cables, away from the bears. I pretended he wasn't there, crawled up on the bunk inside the cocoon of my bag, and eventually, after a long time spent tossing and turning, went to sleep.

During the night I had another strange dream. It was of a 4th of July parade on some Main Street in some pastiched, stereotyped red brick-and-glass-diner-front world that never existed. A strange marching band consisting entirely of sousaphones and glockenspiels pounded out a surreal Schoenberg-like, aphonic march ahead of me. Flag girls waved dozens and dozens and more dozens of American flags in, around, and sometimes through the band members, the onlookers, and the… elephants? Men in universally black suits and fedoras with women holding babies circa 1944 applauded fervently from the sidewalks, with both hands… without dropping the babies. Everyone, including the babies and the sousaphone players, was smoking. I found myself confused and lost in an enormous black convertible with impossible chrome tailfins 50 feet high, sitting above the back seat, inexplicably naked. As my car passed, the once-vociferously-cheering-and-applauding crowd stopped as one, staring at me, coldly, dispassionately. Perhaps there was something written on the side of the car, on the banner that hung there, but what it was, what it said, I couldn't see, didn't want to see. I was sure it described me perfectly in three or four words, words I'd never know, didn't want to know. As I passed, behind me, a clone army of blonde, buxom baton twirlers, perfectly in sync, impossibly perfect in their smiles, tossed their flaming batons high in the air, and the crowd erupted in their mindless approval again. I tried waving, then standing up and waving. Suddenly though, my car stopped, and dark, smoking men in dark black suits with dark black ties rushed my car, climbed over and in, grabbing my arms, legs, and hauled me out onto the pavement, all screaming in a cacophony: "*Sir, you're coming with us now!" "Surrender now, sir!" "Where are your PANTS, sir?!"* I tried to pull away, couldn't, and began screaming, screaming: "No! Stop! It's my parade! My parade! Mine! Mine! *MINE! MINE!...."*

In a sweat, I awoke to a masked morning sun more like a candle surrounded by cloth. The previous day's mist was blowing away, a smoke of burned bridges from the past. With only the near shore remaining, I sat up off the cold bench, rubbed my eyes. Virgil sat near my feet, half covered in his blanket. He regarded me balefully, saying nothing. Padma and his belongings were nowhere to be seen.

I sighed; at least, we'd have a normal breakfast: muesli with cranberries and some hazelnuts I'd roasted a few days before, and a decadent smoked Gouda. Virgil picked all the hazelnuts out of his portion and ate them one by one. The cheese was all mine. We ate quietly, assessing events.

"What a weirdo," I finally ventured. Virgil cocked his head to one side; said, "Weirdo," agreeing.

"Yeah, flame-broiled. I guess we best git' movin'." I responded. "Best git' movin'," agreed Virgil. He was being particularly agreeable this morning. I guess he was as weirded out by our evaporated shelter guest as I was.

After breakfast, I cleaned up and packed up our belongings by in the Gregory. I picked the black North Face shorts to hike in, as they accented my white legs, zebra-style. You'd think hiking somewhere on the upside of 250 miles for not quite a month would've produced a better tan than I had, but apparently Mother Nature had something else in mind for me, like what happens to whale carcasses after they've been ashore for oh, say, not quite a month: that beached, bleached bone look, where the flesh has been picked clean. At least I was lean and trim and losing weight as I went.

On the contrary, I wasn't a whale out of water; I was where I belonged, in my element: air, earth, water, and, if lucky and properly stocked, fire. I felt particular energetic this morning, ready to face the day after the previous night's excesses. The trail's wearing weariness hadn't set in yet. I put my hat on, grabbed my hiking poles, got Virgil up and going, and took two steps towards the step out of the shelter.

That's when I saw the note. On brown, almost burlap-looking paper, like ancient papyrus dried for many days in a desert sun, and held down by a rock. The writing was very strange and organic, like something I shouldn't understand but did anyway, the letters overlined, old, ovoid, and odd. It reminded me of that almost-song I heard when I first approached the shelter. It said, or seemed to say:

I should like, if I could, to leave a humble gift. You will come to seven shelters. In each you shall meet a guide. Each guide shall provide you with a map. Each map will point the way. So it is wanted there where the power lies.
–P

I read it, then read it again. What the fuck? The guy was a total whack-job. If I saw him again, I'd be certain to get away before he saw me. I'd have to hope that his comment about "just passing through" was an accurate one, that he was no thru-hiker headed in my direction.

I hiked uphill back towards the A.T., just off the crest above; carefully, not just due to the ditch of a trail, but the real possibility that Braveheart was waiting in the brush with his face painted blue, ready to strike. "Watch out for the weirdo," I warned Virgil. "Weirdo," he said, acknowledging the task at hand. But we reached the A.T. uneventfully, and I turned right, towards Canada. The next goal: Mt. Guyot to Tricorner Knob to beyond, around the original Cosby, Tennessee area, a beautiful stretch of high country, highly wooded walking.

The previous day's mist had disintegrated into nothingness. After the dangers of the Sawteeth, the trail had widened back into a decent path hugging the side of the ridge, just off the state line on the very top. This was Smokies hiking at its finest. As the morning wore on, the first mile passed by, and as my cardiac system began to get back into its groove, I felt my usual body warm-up complete, and I stripped off my morning long-sleeve without braking. I was unusually up-beat, energetic, the weirdness of the previous evening fading into silence. I felt the second mile slip beneath me, then the third. Today would be a good day, mileage-wise. I checked the map; at this rate, I'd make Davenport Gap tonight, a sweet 20-

mile day. There was no sign of Mr. Sambhava. Relief gave way to the void and normality of the trail.

As usual, my head emptied, sentences replaced by vague and indistinct proto-thoughts, as a rhythm of ligaments and muscles directed me down the talus. I enjoyed, relished, my emptiness. I found it odd in an indirect way that my emptiness was itself not that, but an experience of something, and therefore not empty, rather a formless thing. Was I emotionally disturbed, populating my mystical world with fantasies based on states of mind not found in the real word? Or, was I perceiving something real? I thought of my dream my previous night, the weird melody oompahed-out by the thousand marching sousaphones, and imagined I was explaining it to a non-musician. "There's no melody," he'd complain. "Yes there is," I'd respond. But what was different? What was the melody I heard that others did not? Where was it? Is a melody real, or something only imagined, a state of mind? I reminded myself that melodies were mathematical, describable in waves and patterns, sinusoid, finite. Even so, some doubted the reality of math itself. Plato had his indistinct forms on the cave wall, I had the shadows of the wood. Words *do* make all the difference in the world, I thought. Without them, there can be no faith. Without emptiness, no words to fill it. But, whose discrete math would describe it, and as what? Without faith in shadows, I marched in time and relished my emptiness, Plato be damned.

I suppose that despite it all I almost believed in God. Here amid Nature, it was easy to believe that Nature does not operate by chance. It was easy to assume that every event, past or present, happens because of laws which are part of a threaded web of consequences. Everything, living or not, is put together from basic building blocks which may or may not be evolving towards consciousness, of one higher form or another. I realized that I *was* thinking like a theosophist, and laughed. What would Padma think? I kept walking, not stopping to ponder or care. He and Plato and Blavatsky could have each other.

Virgil kept up, in silence, occasionally whistling. We tended to ignore each other while moving, if only to pay attention to our surroundings, appreciate them like yet another mysterious female. I sipped from my Dromedary, the tube conveniently placed over my shoulder from its source within my pack's bladder compartment. The water was vaguely warm as usual but I never cared; any colder and it would have given me stomach cramps. Luckily this time of year there was no need for an insulated system. Birds unseen passed overhead and around, sometimes in flocks headed in the opposite direction, the definition of a "harbinger", although given the time of year these were late to the party. The ever-present juncos chirped softly and jumped about like mice in the undergrowth.

Suddenly, there was a sharp, very fast, very loud *shk-ka shk-ka shk-ka shk-ka shk-ka shk-ka shk-ka shk-ka* in the path just in front of my feet. Virgil and I stopped dead. There, in the rocks, was a timber rattler, blended into the rabble, absorbing the day's heat but obviously expressing his displeasure at my nearly treading on him. *Don't*, he pled, flag-style. I realized my right foot was within his strike zone, I pulled back, slowly. I'd come very, very close to being bitten, and deservedly so. I walked the long way around our newfound friend and left him complaining and coiled. As the sound of his rattle faded behind us, Virgil suddenly challenged him with a loud "WEIRDO." The he looked at me, said, "Hungry, weirdo."

I took us another thousand yards down the trail and the slope. At the bottom there was a large, flat rock in the sun with a great view to the southeast, just where the trail turned back up before traveling too far down the ridge. I unlatched my pack, threw it on the rock, where Virgil joined it. I leaned my poles against its side, opened the top pack and pulled out lunch. Virgil ate some apple slices, I had some recently-purchased smoked turkey and the rest of the Gouda. We both drank a lot of the water.

As I looked around, the trail seemed different somehow, which was odd since I'd hiked here many times in the past. If any of it was known to me, this stretch certainly was, or should have been. Still, it felt like a shy new lover: unfamiliar, if not entirely wrong. Even the rock we sat on seemed almost misplaced, or stranger still, placed, deliberately. Then I noticed the stones in the path: ordered, like tiles, leading uphill and around a switchback. I thought I heard something, and looking south, far south, imagined I could almost see a large white pagoda, then a series of them, with long, multi-colored streamers in the wind, hugging the top of the mountainside, impossibly sheer and tall. Then, the sound of a distant, deep, ringing bell, without any strike accent: *ooooom, ooooom, ooooom* it rang, sinuously and slowly. Suddenly an inescapable sleepiness assaulted me, and I felt my eyes close, and I fell back, falling falling falling…

I bolted up, in early evening. I was strangely upright, walking, steeply downhill. I wondered if I had sleepwalked, but found my pack on, my poles in hand, and Virgil close by. Ahead through a falling mist was – Davenport Gap shelter. I had lost all memory of the last twelve miles or so: couldn't remember Tricorner, couldn't remember the rescue helipad, couldn't remember Cosby Knob shelter. But I recognized Davenport: only two miles from the park perimeter road, it was the site of many a good time.

Little did I know *how* good.

III

2600 feet, 1941 miles to Katahdin

Elissa Francesca Tipton had but one goal: to be full of passion, full of life, full of experience, full of knowledge, full of sensation, full of dreams, full of joy, full of everything and anything… and anyone. Willing, breathing, she sought to find ecstasy, to empty herself into it, to be blessed by miracles, to explode into orbit, to cease to be by becoming. She sought to die; the little death, *la petit mort*, over and over in a cycle of being/flowering/arriving/dissolving, to die and die and die. To fulfill every urge, every desire. Then, the ultimate part of her, the core, the place where a soul might have been once long ago, would be filled with a heat, a heat without light, a fire first of friction and smoke made to smolder then burst into a consuming flame. The heat would burn, would awaken, would descry, define her: her, or her inmost being, her true self, exploding into rapture, born again and again and again, amen. The Great Secret would take her on its waves to its bosom, and she would ride and ride and ride, dying each time, and rising again, Savior only to herself. Day in and day out, she crucified herself on a cross of arms and legs, twisted, angled, pretzelline, and held there firmly as she or he or they thrusted and grunted. Sometimes they called out her name, if they remembered it. Sometimes, she did.

It was for all these reasons that Elissa sat on the bunk at Davenport, and waited, for men.

Men. Men men men men men men. Hard, strong men. Men who had worked and strained to get here. Men who would be dirty, smelly, manly. Men. Men she could use; torment, fervent, ferment. Men who were animals to her. Men, to whom she would ascend as an animal. Or, an occasional woman, to whom she would descend, man-like. Didn't matter a whit to her. Elissa tried her very best to put the *suck* in *succubus*.

She opened a pink Nalgene full of Fresca and vodka, took a big swig. She'd mixed it at her cabin in Cosby, just down the road. She'd get up in the morning, shower, shave, usually coming in the process. And it was never enough. She needed more, needed men, needed needed needed. A Trinity of sorts; though less saintly, more savage. She'd put on a tight pair of pink shorts and a tank top, or a cutoff T-shirt, which exposed her to the point of near-arrest. No underwear of course; it'd just be a waste of time. She'd go outside and get in her '92 Dodge Ram and drive to the A.T trailhead on the park boundary at Davenport Gap and hike up the two miles to the shelter. On the way, she'd probably come again, just from the friction of her shorts and thighs, rubbing deliciously. Once at the shelter, she'd sit, and wait. Sometimes men would already be there, and she'd act the coy, shyly smile, ask them what they were up to, as if there would be a large variety of answers that might actually be interesting topics of extended intellectual conversation. After all, one must warm up the oven before broiling the bird.

But usually, within 15 or 20 minutes, the kissing would begin, followed by the heavy petting, followed by whatever the stones and structure that made up the shelter could absorb shock-wise. Once a jock tried to impress her by hanging from the cabin roof beam while she sucked him off. She in turn was impressed by him, in several ways, some of them making her sore, some making her scream, some both at once. She remembered what's-his-name quite fondly, whenever she thought of him, which was never. He wound up with gonorrhea; untreatable, resistant, it ravaged his groin, turning him into ground chuck, though that wasn't his name. Elissa had done every antibiotic there was, thrice; unfortunately for him, his immune system had been a virgin when they'd met, unlike the weapons-grade bacteria she'd carried. If she was anything, Elissa was a giver. On another occasion, a young man and his fiancée were hiking together. She wound up doing the girl while the boy jacked himself, but when she started on the boyfriend, throwing herself on him like an avalanche, the girl started crying, and cried and cried all while the boyfriend moaned and moaned. When they'd left, they left in opposite directions. No matter to Elissa; she followed the girl down to the road, tried to comfort her, and would up doing her again back at her cabin in Cosby, for a couple of days. She recalled that the girl had tasted like strawberries and kept wanting to call her mother. Too bad the phone was out of order. The boyfriend called the state troopers after a week of binge drinking on his part; when they found her finally back in Gatlinburg, she was broken, vacant, dissociative. She spent the next several years back with her family in Nashville, going to church every Sunday and Wednesday, working at the local Walgreen's and calling it a career, and avoiding eye contact with everyone. Of course, Elissa had no way of knowing this, but if she had, she would have focused on the lingering strawberry taste in her mind, the feel of the girl struggling helplessly beneath her as she tried to deny both of their passions, and remembering her mastery and control, Elissa would have smiled, and masturbated to the memory of it.

*****

I hiked down to the shelter deep in doubt and concern. Something was very, very wrong. Maybe I'd had a stroke, a not-unheard-of thing on this trail for someone at my age. I simply couldn't recall how I'd gotten here. And that bit about the pagodas! My encounter with the nut-job had clearly affected my subconscious, enough to conjure two dreams, one sleeping; but one waking? I probably needed to hike out to a hospital. From here, the closest one would be Sevierville General, nearly forty miles away thorough heavy tourist traffic. At my age, stroke was beginning to be a low-probability option; and after so many weeks of travel, the sheer wear and tear only increased the likelihood.

I stopped at the edge of the building, unhooked and dropped my pack, throwing my poles down. Virgil knew the drill, and sat as well. I sat hard, stared at my boots, facing outward. I was scared; me, after what I'd faced, lived through, run away from! When it was my decision at the Jumpoff, I'd considered it without fear. Now, I was scared I'd just drop over dead in the middle of the woods from some fated, uncontrollable aneurysm, like some kind of… what? Hobo? Wild animal? Was I, one who had seen so much meaningless death, in such fear of meaningless death after all?

First things first. I was breathing harder than normal, from the stress. I caught myself, tried to slow my heart down by closing my eyes. I reached for my water, took a swig. A cool rush of evening air swept in, lowering my temperature but not my concern. I checked my watch and watched my pulse drop from 120 to 70 in about thirty seconds. Still, though, I could hear breathing; if anything, getting heavier. I opened my eyes, looked down at my chest. That's when I noticed that the sound wasn't in sync with my… wait a minute, what the….

I turned around, looked in the shelter and… *oh... my... god.*

"Do you want some of this?" said a deep woman's voice, referring to what her fingers held.

"No thanks," I said shortly, whipping my head away back to the trail.

"Aw c'mon honey," she said, shifting her position from the sound of it. "I won't tell Mama, I promise." A laugh like hailstones from clouds of cheap cigarette smoke fell.

"Please stop," I asked, not really asking. This would require immediate insistence on my part. I'd had enough and I was mad as hell and I wasn't going to be taken advantage of twice in two days.

"Baby, I'm just SOOOOO…" she cooed.

I whipped around to face her. "STOP IT NOW," I ordered. "ENOUGH."

She froze, looked at me for several seconds, then a very insulted, "Well, if you're gay you're…"

"I'm nobody's fool!" I shouted, walking straight up to her. "Let me make this as clear as it's clear what you are. I'm not your fool or plaything or *thing* in general, nor will I be made one or become one or be seduced into one or *whatever*. I can assure you to the depth of my innermost black cold uninterested soul that I am *neither* a puppet nor a puppeteer. Put your pants on, shut up, and either leave me alone, or get lost." I disturbed an owl on the roof, who hooted his disapproval in the early evening, filling the space left as the echoes of my outburst died away.

"Well shit," she said eventually, quietly.

"Shit," repeated Virgil, predictably.

"Aw shut up!" she snapped at him. That did it; I jumped at her, grabbed her by the wrist, making her yelp in pain. "Speak to him again like that and you'll be speaking to me about something else!" I yelled right in her face. "Now *PUT YOUR GODDAMN PANTS ON AND SHUT UP !"*

The owl flew off, startled and scared, heavy wings quickly beating the night air, racing away. I released her, turned, strode over and grabbed my pack, then slammed it down again without looking at her. Wasn't I the gentlemen? Gentle, and such a man. There was a long, long silence this time.

"I'm... sorry," she said, mutely. Rustling sounds of fabric indicated I was getting what I wanted. I said nothing. "I didn't mean..."

"No, but you don't care if you did," I retorted loudly.

"I don't understand," she said, with the beginnings of tears in her voice, and louder, faster rustling. "I thought... I guess I thought that..."

"You weren't thinking," I said. I looked back towards her, but left my body facing the trail. She had a leg in, and another going in. Still topless though. Damn she was pretty. *Crap, I'm so full of crap I should have a toxic waste warning tattooed on my left pectoral.*

"Thank you," I said in an effort to produce something harmonious, turning back to face the night and anything else other than a random crazy naked girl. I took my boots off as if pretending I had something better to do. Ironic that this was the point at which I chose to disrobe, even if it was just boots coming off.

She managed to get her shorts on, then a t-shirt. She stood up, uncertain, walked over to me. "I'm sorry," she repeated, almost sounding sympathetic. "I don't understand."

"I'm not interested," I insisted, equally lacking in sympathy. "If my tone was harsh…" I stumbled, trying to find a way to avoid apologizing. I finally came up with: "Look, I'm not well, OK? I just want to eat, sleep, and get down the trail. Fair enough?"

"Oh… OK," she said, strangely dazed. She had the look of a child whose favorite bunny was just run over by the lawn mower. "I…" she tried gamely, smiled, but came up with nothing, frowned, got an embarrassed look, finally turned back, and sat down on the shelter's bunk.

She has nothing to say. She's embarrassed because if she isn't seducing or being seduced she has nothing to say. I felt a strange, uneven pity; not much, just enough for me to notice, not nearly enough to do or say a whole lot about it, or care much tomorrow. A pair of red squirrels suddenly darted out of the gathering dark, tore across the floor, back and forth at each other, zipped around in a few high-speed pointless circles, then tore off back into the evening, oblivious to either of us. It was a slightly amusing antithesis.

I pulled out my gear, got up and put my pad and bag on the bunk, a few feet from her. It was then I noticed that she had no equipment of any kind.

"Isn't it a little late to be out here day-hiking?" I asked, trying to fill the awkward silence with something resembling conversation, albeit sarcasm.

"I… I guess so," she said, looking down. "Usually..," then nothing; I understood exactly what she meant. She didn't have a flashlight, let alone anything else. She didn't plan on leaving until morning.

Well, great. I'm stuck with her tonight. Just grrrrrreat. "You can have the bag," I said to her. "The pad's mine." Virgil would come out on the short end of the deal, but being short that wasn't too bad for him, and he always left the responsibility of all the decision-making with me anyway.

I dumped out my pack without grace, set up the usual dinner suspects. Tonight I was dining on, ironically, fish, a vacuum-sealed teriyaki salmon. I put on my headlamp and walked out behind the shelter, looking for… yes, there they were: ramps, a kind of wild onion or leek, in finer establishments with tablecloths and indoor plumbing referred to as an *ail des bois*. I picked a few for cooking, perfectly legal in the park when used for personal consumption. Virgil hated them; too bad, they'd be all mine tonight. I rinsed them off outside, then brought them back to the bench for chopping.

The girl got up off the bunk, walked over to me, sat down. "What's that?" she asked, still wiping tears from her eyes.

"It's a wild onion," I said, not looking at her, chopping.

"You can eat those? My daddy used to mow over them," she said, attempting conversation. For some reason, the statement moved me finally to pity; somehow, the way she said *daddy* implied a lot of things: alcohol, beatings, prison. I was probably just being judgmental, but still… I wondered how many times her daddy had mowed over her.

"May I ask you a question?" I asked hesitantly.

"Sure," she said, still sniffling, wary.

I thought the better of it, then: "Never mind. Would you care for some salmon?" I didn't have enough for two, but in my growing guilt I could endure my hunger. I tossed the granola to Virgil, who promptly began munching. She moved in close to look at the fish; turned up her nose and made a face. It was funny and sad. I could smell her now; perfumed, beautiful… but a danger to herself and others.

I turned; she was right there. "Durant," I said. "My name's Durant. I'm sorry." *Oh damn it, why did I apologize?*

"I'm Elissa, Elissa Tipton," she said, taking my hand, pretending to shake it, weakly with a weak smile.

I almost actually asked her, *So, what's a girl like you doing in a place like this?* How we men react to beautiful women so predictably, despite it all. She didn't move, and her hand releasing mine wrapped itself around my midsection. That snapped me back; I turned back to the fish, threw the ramps in, watched them wilt almost instantly.

"Please don't," I asked her this time, very quietly, not looking at her. "I'm sorry about before, but I'm damaged goods, and I can't take any more damage." From sideways I could see her look at me, close-up, then she touched my shoulder. "OK," she said, releasing me, removing her arm. I stirred the fish as it began to break into pieces.

Change the subject. "Tipton," I said. "That's a common name in these parts. Some of the original area settlers were Tiptons."

"Yes. My great-great-grandpa moved to Cosby from over in South Carolina, to get away from the war," she said, faking surprised interest, wiping her eyes. "How'd you know about us?"

"Oh, I used to live around here… well, over in Wear's Valley. Had a cabin up near that back entrance to the park. Just a vacation place; my home was down in Atlanta."

"What do you do, hon?" she asked, still acting the seductress to the city boy. *She doesn't know any other way*. My pity grew; my mood softened. Then she added, "Are you a preacher?" and I almost laughed.

"I… I was a doctor, " I answered. "ER doc up in Buckhead. Lots of car accidents, people accidentally Cuisinarting themselves, things like that." She smiled slightly, vacantly; didn't have the slightest idea what a Cuisinart was, didn't care. She was focusing on the "doctor" part. She had that look women get when you instantly become far more attractive than you actually are due to the sudden magical appearance of relatively prodigious amounts of cash.

"So you're not a doctor anymore?" she asked, fact-checking.

"Well, technically, yes, but… I've decided to… take a very long vacation." I said, stirring my stir-fry. *To say the least*.

"Uh-huh," she said, with a look. I knew that look, the look that women got that said to their mothers, sisters, and other rivals: *I've got me a doc!*

"Beautiful weather today," I said, to say something. "I have some other munchies, if you're…"

"I'm not hungry," she said. "I'm… not usually hungry. I mean, I don't eat much."

No wonder she's so thin. "OK, if you're sure." A cool breeze floated in from the evening, and I saw her shiver slightly. I reached in my pack, pulled out the blue stuff-sack, opened it and pulled out a light fleece shirt. "Here," I said. "It'll be big on you but it will keep you warm. Sorry about the smell," I added, meaning the fleece.

"No problem there, hon." She slipped into it, smelling it on the way in. It was sexy and disgusting at the same time. I watched her put it on, watched her slink into it like a snake reversing its shed.

"So," I asked after remembering to breathe and failing to come up with anything better to say, "what do you do?"

"I'm… I sell nutritional supplements over in Pigeon Forge, to tourists mostly. And I have a web cam," she said, smiling, still coyly, faking shyness. It made me nauseous, then I realized, *No; that's the smell of burning ramps.* I cursed and cut the heat down, added some water. A hiss of steam rose from the pot.

"You have a girlfriend?" she asked. *Still focused on the doctor thing I see.*

I answered honestly for a change. "No. I've traded one set of feelings for another set," I said, "What sort of… supplements?"

"What? Oh, just vitamins, herbal crap, you know, crap like that."

"Ah." I replied, as I began to eat.

"My web cam's where I make my big bucks," she said, moving closer to the warmth stove, now deprived of its pan. I cringed at the web cam comment: *please don't let her go on about…*

"I do teases, solos, or an occasional two-fer or three-fer with the guys I meet here," she said, unfolding and warming her hands over the stove.

Yeah, I figured that one all out on my own, thanks. She went on about her shows as I ate. She was of some notoriety on the Internet I gathered; an early adopter, as the techies would say. She went on about her techniques, talents, and the hikers she met here and seduced. I felt a frost of glass grow in my mind, and my thoughts detached, began to run, skate across the ice, glide away farther and farther. My thoughts began to race, and for once I was glad at my ability to disassociate and lose myself.

AChristian'sheartislustfulwhenvenerealsatisfactionissought...
...foreitheroutsidewedlockoratanyrateinamanner...
...whichiscontrarytothelawsthatgovernmaritalintercourse...

A moment's reflection remembered the reference: the Catholic Encyclopedia, probably something I'd read during my marriage classes since she'd been Catholic, after all. Then I was lost again on the waves.

...wheneverthereisadirectconscioussurrender...
...theguiltincurred...
...isalwaysgrievoushoweverwhenthereissome...
...impuregratificationforwhich...
...butsimplyhadpositeditscauseandhadnotdeliberately...
...consentedthesinisconsideredvenial...
...theamountofflagitiousness...
...flagitiousness...
...flagitiousness...
...flagitiousness...

My waveriding stuck on the odd word like a 60's 35 on a 70's Panasonic. I blinked and my thoughts skipped a beat as a brain cell double-checked the accuracy of my memory. It was right of course; it always was. Damn eidetic memory.

...flagitiousnessdependsupontheproximatedanger...
...ofgivingwayonthepartoftheagent...
...thethingsdonetobringaboutvenerealpleasurethissinapplies...

"You OK, hon?" she asked, her hand on my leg. I wondered how it had gotten there, but the action had stopped my thoughts dead cold. I sighed. *La race toujours maudite par les puissants de la terre.* Hers or mine? Perhaps both; both used in their own ways by the *puissants de las terre. De las terrible.*

"Yes, I'm fine, it's just a little... flagitiousness" I said, provoking an utterly blank look from her.

"You sick babe?" she asked.

"No," I answered, which was about as far from the truth as Tucson. "I'm just...."

"Tired and damaged," she said, running her fingers through my hair. She rubbed the ends of it between her fingers, eyeing me like a cabin Cleopatra, Taylor-style. I could see how she got what she wanted, and why she was here; that look would make the lowliest of foot-soldiers feel like Dick Burton marching legions across the Rubicon, and this path offered a lot of foot-soldiers. *Whosoever looketh on a woman to lust after her hath committed adultery with her already in his heart.* Guilty as charged, officer. No need for the dickalyzer test. I tried and sentenced myself then and there. I felt a punishing electrocution in my future; or was it my present? Whatever it was I was feeling, it was definitely electric.

I remembered something else less crude, more erudite... ah yes, *le fleurs de mal*. More French; after all, it was *la langue de l'amour*. Her hand began running lightly up and down my leg. *La langue de la bave.* Suddenly my defenses kicked in; my electricity shorted in my own drool and exploded like lightning, and words began to spew from me almost uncontrollably:

Wandering a wasteland at high noon,
where only ashes echoed my lament,
to leafless nature, whetting as I went,
the dagger of my mind against my heart

I pushed myself away from her. The action made my memory skip a few lines.

Had I not seen among that crew,
Nor was the sun unsettled by this crime,
The queen of my heart; I recognized those eyes,
Laughing at my pain with... *with... with...*

Just as suddenly as it came it had gone, thank God. I turned back to her, breathed. I tried to explain. "It's... it's part of a poem, French. *The Flowers of Evil*, Baudelaire, 1857. We get the word *bawdy* in its modern use from him." She stared blankly. "I'm sorry," and for the first time in months I felt genuine, and acutely embarrassed. "When I get... well, I tend to lose a certain kind of... nerdy self-control."

"I know *jussssst* what you mean, hon," she said, walking up to me, putting both arms around me. "That was real *purrty*," she said, purring. Her leg began to rub against mine. "Ain't nobody said no poetry to me before."

I held her shoulders, bracing her. "Maybe someone should," I said. "Maybe what you're missing is the poetry in life. There's beauty all around, beauty in the barest breath of sunshine. Maybe you should... should…."

Then I realized I was dictating, giving advice, going back to my old ways. Why did I speak these words? The human heart has not yet fully uttered itself, let alone mine. Who was I to act? I meant to do justice, and to speak the truth, wherever it led, whatever the cost. But I showed neither mercy nor compassion nor reverence for... what? I tried to remember, and for one brief shining moment, the words escaped my memory. After all, I was a man, she a woman. Memory be damned at a moment like this, when there is only truth in the lie of a beauty perceived. For the first time in a packful of evenings, I drew a total blank, and it was the most restful moment I'd had on the trail yet.

Then the moment passed and pernicious memory returned, and I remembered another woman, a woman with hair of copper, eyes of sapphire, and a heart of diamond-ice, who'd believed me evil, who believed the worst of me, the worst in me, despite my innocence. I'd left her, left others before her; hell, even left her before her. I could leave this one too, couldn't I? What was she to me, given her, and the rest? All the falsity that was in me returned, and a light mist of rain that began to fall with the evening outside turned into another mist, another rain, in my mind and heart.

That rotated into another memory. I remembered a time of light rain and evening mist long ago when I'd first sat up all night with that girl, talking. I remembered how she looked that night, in copper and sapphire. How could I forget? I'd tried for so many years, then in a moment of weakness I'd tried to regain just one moment close to what the years before had been. I'd tried, and through no fault of my own, failed. Failed, like I did at the Jumpoff. Failed, like I had so many, many times before. Yes, I'd rather be a balloon; free on the air, for then, none of this, none of it, not a bit, would be mine, or I, any part or parcel of it. I'd turned and left, like any exhale would.

All of this took perhaps three seconds to process.

"But I can't tell you what to do. I'm just a fool. Do what thou wilt," I said, feeling thelemic.

"You sound like a preacher," she said, warily.

Ha-ha, a preacher of thelema. "It's nothing, never mind. Are you warm?"

"I'm fine, hon. You *sure* there's nothing I can...."

"No, nothing," I said, and resumed eating. She watched my fork head to my mouth, then back down. It was full on dark now, and I knew she must be hungry. I reached over and grabbed my other Lexan fork, the one I'd usually prep with.

"Here," I said. "You must be hungry. Try it and you may like it."

She looked at the fork, the a long time at the fish. "*Mmmmmm*," then she took the fork, poked at the fish. "What did you say this was again?"

"Salmon," I said, "It's sweet. It's good, trust me."

She took a bite, hesitantly, then with a look of surprise, ate faster. After two minutes most of my dinner was gone; I didn't really mind.

"Don't you think I'm pretty?" she asked suddenly, putting the fork down and wiping her mouth.

"Yes," I said, "but... I'm just not…." There I was, sputtering again like a schoolboy.

"Can I have a drink?" she said, coyly. I handed her a small titanium canteen I carried with water; the metal always seemed to keep the water colder than Lexan did.

She drank for a long time, then set the canteen down. Her eyes met mine, held them. Her mouth was wet from my canteen. Her lips glistened in the light of my lantern.

"Don't you think I'm pretty?" she repeated, touching her hair.

"I want to tell you a story," I said, standing up, backing up. "I want you to understand why I cannot do what you want me to." I bumped into the shelter's post then, braced my back against it, as I started.

"I was born well in a well-to-do family, although my parents had known hunger and poverty as children. They made sure I did not. Childhood was uneventful. But then came an awakening that was dreadful and marvelous. There was a girl who played flute in the band and had gray eyes, another with long dark hair who flirted with me coyly, another who told me she liked me even though I'd never really paid attention to her. I didn't think of myself at the time as the cause, and I didn't know what the price for speaking to them was, let alone how to. Then there was college, where I found out the truth of it, and paid the price, with interest."

"A girl?" she asked, seeming to keep up.

"A girl like you. Golden, strong, intent. A girl not like you. Copper, vulnerable, owned a tent. A girl I loved, who did not love me."

"Oh, I'm sorry, hon," she said, hugging me. *It was just an excuse, meaning her, and I knew it.*

"I'm the one who is sorry," I said, "Sorry I ever knew her. Five agonizing years I could not let go. Five long, agonizing years I wasted until she left. I was a goddamn robot. Then she left for work, then I left, for med school, met my wife, married her, still in robot mode."

"You married, hon?" she asked, pulling back.

"It doesn't matter," I said. "If I was married you'd never know it now; if I wasn't married you'd know it from knowing me, and be wrong. I'm not a better man because of it, despite how hard my wife tried. I failed, and that's that. I was just a man, and I failed, on both counts. Guilty and guiltier."

"I don't understand, baby," she said, pulling back a little more.

"Believe me, if I did, I'd advise you better, I promise." I was losing control and I knew it. "I'd sing you a country and western song about it. Maybe my coon dog would die and my porch would collapse. My woman done left me. Unfortunately, as I have no idea myself what really happened, I can't explain it any better than you could guess. I was there; I know. I just can't accept it. I'm still in the denial phase, so to me it's still just a river in Egypt. No, wait; denial is much, much more, in the hands of an artist. Is that not perfect?"

She did not answer. I was talking over her head now, up in the heights of existentialism. Her thoughts were lower down in her body.

"No, I suppose not," I said. "Let's just say that I am no longer anyone's slave, nor is anyone mine. I can't give you what you want, or I'd be right back to square one, when I've come this far and left the rest of the chess pieces behind. I can't play the game. I won't play the game."

At some point I'd begun tearing up, but I couldn't remember exactly where. I thought I'd lost her, but then she said something that caught me completely off guard.

"You're still in love with her, ain't you, poor hon?" she said, pulling me back.

I could feel the cell doors slam shut inside me, the klaxons going off, the raid sirens blaring. My heart skipped four beats. I blinked wet eyes, couldn't see. *Hell hon, I'm still in love with ALL of them.* Ha ha ha. *And all of them, every single goddamned one, hates my guts.* "Is that not perfect?" I managed to whisper.

Nevertheless, after a moment, I found myself talking. "I spent twenty years married, twenty years in happiness and sadness, hope and regret." I wondered who was saying the words. "Of course I still love her." It couldn't possibly be me. "But it didn't matter, and it doesn't matter. Freedom is the sincerest form of flattery. It's like Sting says: if you love someone, set them free."

"I like that song," she said, reaching around and holding me.

"It's a truth," I said, letting her hold me. I allowed it, and the inexorable, unavoidable truth of it all, and the tears that sprang from it came instantly. It was always a hard rain to bear, and this time no less than all the others.

"Aw, don't cry hon," she said. "I don't wanna hurt you. In fact, I'd love to *help* you…." So coy and plying. Unfortunately, I know exactly where this leads, and exactly where it ends. It's a playground of broken glass promises. How can one sleep at night, and love?

I stood back away from her. "Please, don't."

She seemed to suddenly reach a conclusion. "Oh now, I *know* what'd make you feel better." The she went over to the bench, sat on my sleeping bag, and proceeded to... start the entire encounter over again the same way she started it when I arrived.

What could I say? I'd tried; I said what I had to say. It wasn't me, I knew; it wasn't about me, it never was, or would be. It was about her. Of course I was just an object to her; hell, she was an object to herself. All I could do was stand there and watch, listen. After all I'd said, how many different ways I'd said *No*, there she was, doing what she wanted to do all along. I might even have felt sorry for her, if I wasn't so flabbergasted, annoyed, tired, and angry all at once. Oh, I was a good boy; my walls went right back up, and I kept my composure, feigning interest, occasionally actually being interested. I ignored her occasional comments and their ilk. Nah; she's got a ticket to ride, and she definitely don't care.

I sat on the bunk next to her as she shifted into second gear. Was it just me or was it getting cooler? Yeah; night was definitely settling in. I always reflected at night. I learned something new on every step of this path. I've seen a waterfall cascade like diamonds down from heaven over the stones, in winter turning to quartz and frozen crystal, a chandelier reflecting the sunlight in a million prisms of color. I've seen distant heights, heard their birds singing, wondered at the moon that rose over them, and the sun reawakening them and their sky, silver into gold, black into blue. I've become aware of the visible, of that which is heard and seen, and heard and unseen, the invisible, that only dwells where those of old said saints resided. I've come home. I've forgotten the rest, heard no other, lost all homes and memory of that which was false, growing deaf to deceit. I've relearned how to trust, and lost all the trust I've had, finding no need for it out here. I existed essentially, finally. Why, I watched a bobcat eat a rabbit just the other day, I wanted to say, but such a joyous message would be lost at a time like this. Beautiful and lovely though she was, lost nonetheless. Unlike her, I was not searching, but finding. The finder's fee I'd paid in silence, at the Jumpoff. Oh, I'd lost something alright, something fundamental, and something fundamentally wrong, and oh so right.

There was a third gear she found then, though the clutch was grinding. Man, was it ever grinding. Round and around now, sigh. At this point she made so much noise that I could no longer distract myself, so I let myself listen. Thankfully, it didn't take much longer.

Pow. There went the transmission. A few minutes passed as she coasted to a stop. Thank God there had been no overdrive. Formula One, she wasn't. Formula 409, maybe, but nothing drivable on the European Circuit. Still, I had to admit she was Nascar material; better performing than the street-legal average. "You like that baby?" she finally asked. "I know I sure did!"

She laughed, not waiting on my answer, since it didn't matter anyway. Other people's feelings were merely rhetorical, after all.

I walked over to my pack and dug out the trail mix. Funny how I felt like a couple of nuts right now. As I dug in my pack, I asked her, quietly, "Why did you do that?"

"Aw hon, didn't you like me? It made you feel better I'm sure," she said, with homegrown certainty in her voice.

"No, it just made me feel, that's the problem. No more hanky panky, OK?" I looked at the handful of nuts I'd retrieved in my hand, then for no apparent reason threw them out into the night. I sighed, and retrieved some more.

"Baby," she asked, with a slight whine in her voice, "what's *wrong* with you?"

I turned, facing her, angry again. "No means no, right? Ever said no? Ever been raped? "

"Baby, *everybody* likes sex," she said, with the same low excusive whine, as if she was speaking to her father.

"Ever say no?" I repeated, firmly, harshly.

"Well... no, baby. I never say no."

"Ever been raped?" I asked again, very quietly.

There was a long pause. "I... well…." She slowly pulled the sleeping bag around herself, tight. I didn't think she was even aware of it. I wanted to say, *It was your dad, right?* But I wasn't here to make a point or prove anything. Rightness has no value in the world of the loins, let alone among the dust of the trail.

A few bats flew into the shelter then, and all hell broke loose. She started screaming. She began thrashing, yelling for me to *Get 'em*! and *Do it*! It struck me as interesting how alike terror and ecstasy were. The vocalizations, the word choice, the self-centeredness of both. I laughed out loud; yep, they're practically the same. Of course, like the last set of orders she'd given, I'd ignore this set as well, being a terribly disobedient private in this army of two. She pushed back against the back wall of the shelter, as the bats ignored her and flitted about the roof, undoubtedly checking for bugs, maybe even mice, a common nighttime inhabitant of these simple huts. She screamed again. I doubted that they could hear her at all, but sure as skunks the rest of the mountain could.

I thought about providing comfort, but... well, she'd ignored my requests, so what did I owe her? *Maybe when she starts crying* I thought; then she did. Damn. *But if I'm a gentleman, I'll be taken advantage of afterward.* I sat back down on the bunk, munched my nuts, watched her scream and cry and thrash. Virgil sat unmoved, unmoving, ever the stoic. Honestly, it was funny. I was more concerned about the bats finding a good meal than her. I felt vindicated, enlightened in the best sense; my load, lightened. It was funny. I laughed again, and she gave me an eat shit and die look, but kept on screaming and thrashing. In my laughter I started choking on the dry cashews. Virgil in disaffection started watching the activity on the ceiling.

I couldn't decide which act in this drama I liked more, the love scenes or the monster attack. As I was considering, the bats left just as quickly as they'd arrived. I kept coughing from the nuts. She wiped tears from her cheeks, shaking.

She grabbed my trail map off the bunk and threw it at me. "You ain't no gentleman!" she said. "Those things could've gotten me!"

"They're harmless, like you," I lied. I finally washed down the cashews with some tepid water. "Nothing to be afraid of. They're just bats, only here for the bugs."

"I don't like bats," she insisted, pouting and crossing her arms.

"Well, they don't like you either," I said, and she started at that as if it were a real insult. "You're in their home. You should have more respect for the wildlife." Virgil whistled his agreement.

She looked past me out the front of the shelter. "I don't like it here at night. I get scared. At home I turn on a light. It's too dark out here."

Then that damn compassion thing kicked in again; she was afraid, and I understood fear. I gestured to her. "C'mon," I said, "let's clean up and get ready for...." then I stopped, in dreadful anticipation of the next word. "... to go to sleep," I edited. She looked disappointed.

I got up and cleaned up the mess kit. I'd get water in the morning. I automatically reached in my pack and pulled out the stuff sack with my clean clothes, but turning and seeing her, it hit me: I have to change, *in front of her*. Great. Just *grrreeeaaat*.

I decided to announce it, set the ground rules. "I have to change," I said. "No hanky panky. Do you mind?"

Suddenly the incident with the vampires was entirely forgotten. Let The Next Act Begin. "Hmm, not at all, hon," she said, looking me dead in the eye with a smile and not turning away one teensie-teensiest littlest bit. Sigh. Apparently my disrobing was going to make up for my lack of flying rodent chivalry.

Normally, a shelter is very much a community place, a return to communal living, with everything that implies. Half naked and worse strangers are par for the course, and believe me, it's *always* worse. A few less bodily secure people might walks outside around the corner to change, but normally, after at most a few days of roughing it, nature overcomes nurture, and a kind of natural morality sets in, and in its nature, naturalistic. Social nudity becomes something actually social for once. Besides, nobody looks good; the handsomest big screen muscle man turns into a Grizzly Adams wannabe within a few days away from hot showers, shaving, and porcelain. Starry-eyed starlets become startlingly starving starklets. As a result, one just stops caring about the things that never really mattered in the first place, like looks, for instance. You don't even want to stare; nobody, but *nobody*, remains pretty for long. Trust me, you don't *want* to look.

Unless, of course, like her, that's what whizzed your cheese.

I took my shirt off, sat, removed my boots and socks. I stood back up, reached for the shorts. A long, low *hmmmmmmmm* escaped from her. She wore a big smile. Suddenly I felt annoyed again, just like with Padma, for the same reason. Here was someone else trying to take something for their benefit, with no regard for me. But I saw the thief in the night, and saw the coming theft for what it was. Very well, let the thief have her take. The most she could really have was what her eyes stole, and I was no busker.

I dropped my shorts, asked her, "Well? Do you think it needs more cowbell?" She just stared, and smiled. It was cold now; I shivered slightly. Her hands began moving under the sleeping bag. Annoyance turned to anger. I walked over to her on the bunk.

"NO MEANS NO," I said. "Whether touching me or yourself, it's exactly the same. Stop it."

To her credit, she stopped. "OK," she said, looking down, "I guess you're a real gentlemen."

"No, I'm not. But some of us are *damaged goods.* OK? I just can't, and I've already explained it, and *that's it*."

She smiled a weak smile, said, "OK, hon. No hanky panky."

"Thank you," I said, then I went back to the pack, grabbed my shorts to sleep in. "Nice ass," she editorialized as I put them and my nightshirt on. I stowed my gear then, ignoring her. I went out, hung the pack up on the bear cables, walked back in, and sat down next to her. She put her arm around me.

"You're a big meanie," she said, pouting for effect now.

"Which is why I gave you my bag," I said. She didn't seem to be able to argue with that; instead, she put it around us like a blanket.

"Well, I can give it back," she said, snuggling close under the down.

"No hanky panky," I said. "I mean it."

"I know," she said, "You're kind of weird, but I know. No fun stuff." She gave me a little squeeze anyway, and Little thankfully only reacted a few seconds after the fact. *Yeah, I'm kind of weird.*

So we tried to sleep. I'd grabbed my pullover to wear for warmth, but since she was sharing the bag, I gave it to her as a pillow instead. "That's not what I want," she whispered, snuggling up to me, putting her head on my shoulder and throwing a leg and arm across me. For a moment I wanted to slug her, but you know, it actually was nice.

We lay there for a long time, listening to the deep silence punctuated by hoots and chirps and the sound of leaves swaying in the wind.

"Still scared?" I asked her.

"No," she whispered back, then she actually asked, "Are you OK with this?"

"Yes," I said. Maybe she had learned something after all; maybe respect would lead to self-respect. Funny how life was like that.

A deeper silence descended then, while the moon shone finally, coming up across the ridge. The ghost light lit up the trees. She squeezed me. "Yep, you're a genuine nice guy," she said. "I don't get many nice guys."

That was one I could live with. I'd been called worse than nice. *Wu wei.* Action through nonaction. There was great truth in the Taoist philosophy. Teaching through denial. Gandhi used to sleep with his female admirers, to test himself. Well, I was no Mahatma Rice, let alone the Mahatma. I could feel her leg flex, stretch, as she shifted. She finally brought it up high, and ran into an old friend of mine.

"You're hard," she commented, giggling.

"*NO... HANKY....* " I started. She just chuckled, and brought her fingers to my lips, stopping my words.

"Hush," she said. "No hanky panky. Besides, I like you too much." She wiggled a bit as she said it, wiggling me and Willie in the process.

"You like everybody too much," I reminded her.

"What's not to like?" she asked, with another squeeze.

"Like, *too much?*" I asked, not helping but to laugh. She said it in time with me, laughing too. She kissed me on my chest, laughing.

We tried to sleep then; I tried not to think about Willie. But Willie was talking to me, suggesting things. To distract myself, I tried coming up with a tongue twister. A few brain cells were evidently post-processing the earlier French thing, so *French* came up as a starting word, then I needed a word that rhymed... ah, *finch. French finch,* good start. Then I had *fifth French finch*, finches have *feathers*, feathers can be *fringed*, so after a moment I had it: *The fifth French finch's fifth frilly feather's fringed.* Pretty good for a guy with a hard on, a beautiful sex-starved girl, and no appreciable stores of reserve body fat left with which to resist anything. I imagined myself saying it five times fast: *The fifth French finch's fifth frilly feather's fringed. The fifth French finch's fifth frilly feather's fringed. The fifth French finch's fifth frilly feather's....*

"What?" she asked.

I realized I was speaking out loud. "It's a tongue twister I was thinking of," I said, repeating it out loud for her.

"The fifth French finch's fifth frilly feather's fringed," she said, in one bolt, no errors. I was impressed.

"Yeah, but can you say it five times fast?" I challenged her.

Boom. "The fifth French finch's fifth frilly feather's fringed the fifth French finch's fifth frilly feather's fringed the fifth French finch's fifth frilly feather's fringed the fifth French finch's fifth frilly feather's fringed the fifth French finch's fifth frilly feather's fringed." It was perfect, seven or maybe barely eight seconds long, every syllable distinguishable, even if in Southern.

"Holy shit," I said, in genuine shock and amazement. She laughed hard. "OK, so you like THAT?" she asked, poking fun at herself. I understood, laughed, and she laughed with me, and for no reason at all I spontaneously turned my head down to hers, and without thinking, kissed her hair.

Dead silence. I started to pull back, and at first she didn't react. "I'm sorr.." I started, then she suddenly pulled up and her lips met mine, and we kissed like the moon itself was going to fall. We kissed and kissed, and everything that was wonderful about life, everything that made anything and everything worthwhile came back to me, and for a moment I had the illusion of a genuine connection, purpose, a root cause, a ground underneath me. I felt my arms go around her, wondered at it, felt her slide on top of me, felt her pushing into me, felt felt felt. For the second time, out of a clear black sky, she'd made me feel....

MADE me feel. Made me feel. Made me feel. I stopped, pulling my head away. MADE me feel. She froze. "Now I know I've got to run away, I've got to get away." I said. "Tainted love," I said, not laughing or chuckling, but that lower, darker thing there is no word for, when you're ashamed, overwhelmed, and the cynicism comes to the surface and takes your feelings back down like a homicidal lifeguard to drown in the depths of the heart. I touched her lips. "I'm sorry," I said, meaning it, meaning something for the first time in a long time. "I broke my own rule. I took without asking."

"I don't mind," she said softly.

"But I do," I answered. "I... I *cannot*," the word wrenched from me. She looked at me for a long time, but in the darkness I could see nothing. Then, her lips pressed very very softly into mine, ever so gently, and she said, "I don't want to hurt you, and I won't." She waited for a moment for me to say something, but I was past words, or maybe they had passed me by. Then there was an even lighter kiss, so light, and every muscle in my body trembled.

She pulled her head back down, rested it on my chest. I stared upwards into the blackness, seeing nothing. I listened to my own heart pounding in my chest. She gently ran her fingers across me, and we descended into whispers.

"You're not like the other guys I meet."

She'd said it so... plaintively. I answered as best I could. "I'll take that as a complement. We all need the poetry in life."

"Yeah," she said, brightening, then, "Tell me some more."

I thought for a moment, and said:

The east wind sighs
A fine rain comes
Beyond the pond of mountain trout
A noise of thunder diminishes
An old toad waits by the sandstone
Empty of all wants and desire
I feast my eyes on this wonder
I can't believe how overcome I am
I have lived in the wrong age completely
And I have loved the wrong love foolishly
If the Goddess of the River ever
Thought of this hungry fisherman
Let her laugh, deservedly so
And let her keep her banks of wildflowers
Unopened in the Springtime.

She was quiet for a long time, then there was a long exhale. "You wrote that, didn't you?"

"Not really," I admitted. "It's just a few lines from some old Oriental poetry, spliced to fit my mood. Best I can do under the circumstances."

"It's beautiful," she said.

"Words don't mean a thing," I said, and I thought the earth would fall from under me.

"Now you stop," she said, then, "Thank you."

"For what?" I asked. "I've done nothing."

"I said stop," she said. "Night, hon."

"Good night," I said.

I slept a dreamless sleep then, or my dreams left me, and perhaps ran with hers somewhere, wherever dreams go. But they were only dreams, the least of commodities. I awoke once, in the middle of the night, to find her softly breathing, still around me and on me. I realized my arm around her had moved, that my hand lay under her shirt, on her breast. It was soft, warm, smooth. I wished I'd never met her. I moved my hand.

The morning sun rose, becoming a sky of rose. Of course, it was impossible to catch a glimpse of it from anywhere near the shelter; it was too sloped and wooded for that. Just south of me, the campers on top of Mt. Sterling were enjoying a spectacular sunrise from the old fire tower, at almost 6000 feet. I'd seen the sunrise there a few times, lost myself in it. I envied them; but that's why it was a rationed campsite. Here at 2800 feet in shade and shoulder, it would be a warmer, though slower, start to the day.

She hadn't awakened yet. Still, her head was snuggled just under mine, arm and leg thrown over me, sharing the warmth against the morning chill. I wondered what made her, her; what had happened to make her choose this place, this time, this life. I wondered if she had chosen it consciously. Is Hell given to us, or are we given to it? Do we own it, or does it own us? Anywhere a man abides, there lies the end of the path that led him there. I wondered if she was still trapped; but did she? I recalled Padma's words to Virgil; he was right about foolishness. Whether I or anyone else could, *should*, save her, wasn't up to us. What we could do was refuse to play the part the darkness wanted us to play in her drama. I'd refused, and she'd glimpsed… well, I could never be sure what she'd understood, now could I? Had she seen the path out of her Hell? Perhaps; but had I?

"I've chosen mine," I muttered to no one. Just as I'd chosen my sins. They were as much a part of me as my lungs. I breathed my sins, in and out; I reeked of them. A gust of wind blew in then, and I thought I heard the vaguest tint of laughter on it, Asiatic, mocking.

I thought about sitting up, rubbing my eyes. Instead, I stroked her hair. She was so beautiful, so fragile, but damaged goods, the beauty and fragility a lie, though to just exactly whom, I wasn't sure.

Suddenly she woke up, opened her eyes, looked at me. "Hi, lover," she said sleepily, squeezing me.

"You know that's not true," I said. She didn't respond.

Perhaps I eventually got up, made us breakfast. We might have chatted a bit, sipped hot chocolate, watched its steam mix with our breath. I may have touched her face, she may have kissed me, I may have let her. We might have kissed for a while. It might even have been nice.

But at the end, it was the end. I cleaned up, dressed, packed, and finally made ready to go. It was the right thing to do. To stay entwined in bliss is bliss, yet folly; and we'd known only the latter. She'd save her bliss for someone else that day, someone who wouldn't care, someone who'd use her, and be used by her. I knew it, and felt only sorrow, for her.

I almost left without saying goodbye, but against my better judgment, I caught myself, looked at her. She was looking down, mumbling a tune. I couldn't quite catch it at first, but then I heard:

"It hurts to set you free
But you'll never follow me
The end of laughter and soft lies
The end of nights we tried to die…"

At the word *die* she looked up at me, and stopped. The look on her face was… was… I turned away. I found myself saying improbably, "Change motivated by pain leads to more pain. Change motivated by desire leads to

more desire. Only change motivated by choice leads to more choices."
What a pompous psychopomp I was.

Survival is almost always the act of an individual. What we can save we can save; what we can't must save itself. That's how I left her, at the shelter, disheveled and dirty, maybe unable, probably unwilling to save herself, and headed out of the park, towards I-40, and Maine.

I was at least a dozen miles outside the park before I realized that she was still wearing my fleece. I laughed. My, my, my, how the ladies affect us.

IV

6275 feet, 1803 miles to Katahdin

One cannot turn chaos into a place that is named. Chaos is to be feared, a place we flee from. The woods are lovely, dark and deep; but in that depth, we drown. To prevent such deaths, the authorities create borders, rules, limits, to limit and rule that which cannot be. They draw lines on maps, then color inside the lines, being good children; usually some shade of green meant to convey a preserve, a natural, untouched state. But it is a lie, for the drawing of such is not a natural growth, but a man's definition of growth, and its green color on the map akin more to the color of money than of moss in both lay and lie. The lines they draw create places, places given names, as if nonesuch existed before such lines and the men who drew them. But the lines they draw around unboundable chaos, the names they give, the place they "create", creates not the wild, but merely, a "park". The word conveys a Disneyesque facade of smiling faces and comfortable safety. One halfway expects maudlin cartoon characters to emerge and offer to autograph your cheaply manufactured yet kingly priced t-shirt with a convenient and cheaper permanent marker. Alas, we have forgotten what lives in our roots: that it is the wild, not we, who preserve the world. It is we who are inaccessible, not it; it is we who are separated from the wild by the lines drawn, not the wild constrained out of chaos from such pointless marching in circles. A circular path ceases to be one, leading forever down into stagnation. In treading the straighter, longer path, we find the truer path in ourselves. Thoreau said, "It's from instinctive memory, from the wilderness of the imagination, from a mindfulness forever wild, that Art starts." In America, Thoreau's Art is a lost art. In America, *shallow* and *hallow* rhyme for a reason.

It was in this state of mind that I was glad to flee and be freed of the park and its people, a hundred-fifty-odd miles in the past and a million years distant, and return to the wild whence I'd come. Neither it nor I could be kept in our respective cages. It is spring, and the sky is blue uprising, surprising. I am free. In fact, I put the park and its experiences out of my mind. They were distractions, contaminations, perturbations. They added up to hallucinations. Stress, was all. I needed out, to go farther, to get out of the 12 million visitor a year goddamn park and get alone, alone and lost down the trail, so I could return to the real trail inside.

It took about three hours to get to the top of Roan Mountain, Tennessee, location of the highest shelter on the entire A.T. It was a hard hike, through a steep, narrow gully acting as both trail and creek bed, lined with thick bushes. Several times Virgil and I found ourselves crawling over boulders and pulling ourselves up by grabbing onto the trees.

I passed one of the summits of Roan, pausing only briefly to reflect on the heights that would be covered in flame azaleas three or four months hence. Virgil was chatting incessantly about the weather; he'd yakked and yakked all damn day, completely out of character for him, when we'd already worked the topic to death the previous day when a warm light rain had carried us firmly back into Volunteer country. I had no idea what had gotten into him; bad granola perhaps, or those muscadines we'd gorged ourselves on just outside Erwin, at that Nolichucky hostel. Maybe a few had fermented into a backwoods burgundy, or worse, gotten the ergot. At the least, Virgil sure was high on life today.

The mountain with its 7-mile-long, 1000-acre grassy bald has one of the thickest stands of coniferous forest in the southern Appalachians, and "the world's largest natural rhododendron garden," or so proclaimed the books. If there was an Almighty Pantocrator, here was the evidence of Him, here in the trillium and the bluets and the sarsaparilla, the latter just beginning to bloom. Above 6000 feet again, I was alive in the rarity of the cool upper air, incomplex, without bounds.

Then, there was the sign. It pointed off the trail up a narrow path through the bushes. We climbed to an old fire warden's cabin. It was a real building made of real stone, with four walls and an actual door: a Sheraton of shelters. I opened the door, went in. It was dark, musty; it had a dirt floor. A ladder in the corner led up through a hole into a second floor. There were windows, real windows, made of real glass. "Shit," said Virgil, and I completely agreed: the place was a freakin' Shangri-La.

Then the moment burst; there were sounds coming from upstairs: movement, laughter, loud. The smell of… burned meat. "Shit," Virgil said again. "It's nothing," I reply, "just hikers like…" I almost said *us*, then noted the sparsity of the gear on the ground. Strange gear, very light. They weren't thru-hikers.

Suddenly and without warning, a large vicious dog attacked us from out of the darkness of the corner. I leaped back towards the door, inadvertently closing it behind me in the process; Virgil screamed. Then, just as suddenly, mid-leap, a chain around its neck stretched taught, whipped its body, slingshot its torso sideways, its nose inches from me, my back against the door. *Wowf wowf wowf wowf wowf wowf wowf wowf wowf* it howled at us, deep and horrible, straining with all its strength against the shaking links. I was trapped; I couldn't open the door and get out without moving forward. My hand reached for my Bowie knife in my pack's right side pocket.

"Aw, shut up Kirby!" shouted a loud male voice from upstairs. The beast stopped yelping, started growling instead, but the chain didn't give an inch of slack. "I said, SHUT UP!" the voice hollered. At that, the dog jumped back as if hit, whimpered, slunk back into the corner.

"Don't mind ol' Kirby, he's just our old coon dog, come on up!" shouted another man.

"Yeah, come on up!" yelled another. "Bring yer meat!" came from someone distinctly a woman, then laughter from all four.

I dropped my pack and poles on the floor by the door, out of reach of the dog, now slumped in a corner whimpering dejectedly. I detached the top pack with the food and stove, and Virgil and I went up the ladder, and when my head went through the hole, it beheld a singular sight: three men, huge, like lumberjacks that had eaten both their lumber and their jacks, and a woman, thin, in white angora, sipping a large fruit-topped drink from a gigantic tiki mug shaped like an Easter Island *moai*.

"Hello," said the woman, "come on up, there's plenty for everyone." She handed another giant *moai* to one of the men; some dark frothy liquid sloshed out as she did so, and she and the man chuckled.

They were sitting on what appeared to be, improbably, coolers: large plastic coolers. I wondered how the hell these enormous men had gotten these coolers up to the top of Roan – then remembered that a state road crossed over the mountain through a gap I had yet to come across. Still, it would be a hike of two or three miles to get these coolers here, and these guys… They just didn't look like the hiking type, let alone the type to hike with any burden of any kind.

One of the men stood up, turned to me. He was wearing overalls over a red t-shirt, and the overalls were stained with something resembling, what? Barbecue sauce? Then he extended a half-eaten something that resembled a chicken leg in greeting, gesturing and talking while chewing.

"Name's Merle," he said. He pointed his food at his brothers. "This is my brother Earl, and my other brother Burl." "Yehp," said Earl; Burl just grunted at me. They were all eating, a meat of some kind. Chunks of it, in their hands and hanging out of their mouths and parts lying on the floor. It was revolting.

"Well *hey* there sugar puddin'," said the girl, handing me a giant mug. "My name's Pearl, and these here are my bothers. It's so very nice to see you. Come on in, have a sit, we sure have got enough to go around." I blinked. *Sugar puddin'? Did she actually call me sugar puddin'? Oh my God, she's speaking to me in Hee-Haw,* I realized. *Real genuine Hee-Haw.* They all laughed, through wads of meat in their mouths. Burl stopped short and started choking, until Earl whacked him on the back. Burl grunted his thanks, and never stopped chewing.

God give me strength was the first prayer I'd said in years.

*****

Merle Chiacco was the best used car salesman the Tri-City metropolitan area had ever seen. His fantastic feats of financial fecundity were fruitfully and faithfully festooned across the fertile fields furrowed along Ford Street. Simpletons in single-wides, scarecrows, suckers all, stood in single-file to be swayed by the soothing sounds of simple, sweet, and sycamore-shaded Southern straight-talk. A lullaby of legalisms he laid on the laypeople of the land, loving them, and their lovely, lovely loyalty. Generation after generation, God-fearing goons, guffoons, and grandmothers graciously gave of their hard-earned, sometimes hard-of-hearing hands; intransigently, with interest. He'd possess their pumping hearts and pump their pocketbooks for pocket-change, growing plump in the process; at least, until he perniciously, painfully repossessed them. But then, when the greed and gluttony and Golden Age finally gave, when the economy of the Earth entered its evil, egregious eclipse, when Merle's lot overflowed with milk and honey and inventory, he found himself penniless, pale, and packed, primed to post bail and bail out with his brothers.

His brother, Burl, was no better; a builder of barns in Bristol as a boy, he banked on his burliness, which became by-the-by brown, bulky body fat. Now, he was in mortgages. Mortgages meant made money; more and more and more made, magically, mysteriously, at the margin. As his grant grew geometrically, his gross of gross -- his appetite for appetite -- grew gigantically, grotesquely. He commissioned a chef compensated with commissions to create *crèmès de cholesterol*; morphed those margins into marvelous mounds of margarine. And when the markets melted, melted like so much margarine in a malarious Myanmar manhole, Burl, beside himself, became manic, mangy, myopic, misanthropic, malodorous. As adjustable rates acceded in Asheville, as his always accelerating alms announced their abatement like an abscess, some sort of abhorrent, anaemic abortion, as the abstruseness of it all ate at him, he abandoned his abode, adjoining his fat ass with that of his always accepting family.

Earl too was an esplendent eatery. He was also the titular triumphal triumnivarate -- himself, and his two chins -- for a treasured trail of title pawn places from Tazewell to Tobaccoville. Jalopies and junkets juiced with joy, generating generously. Many of Merle's most magnificent meatpies were with the inevitable ebbs of the economy Earl's eager, educed, de-electrified eels in the end. But just as Merle and Burl had blossomed, blown up, and burned out, so too had Earl and Earl's ego enlarged, eclipsed, and elapsed. Banks never pawned the cars they carried, and Earl, entering the economic evolution's *extremis*, corralled his corn-fed carcass by cohabitating with the other Chiaccos.

Possession is by definition an evil spirit lurking within. In The Year of Our Lord Two Thousand Eight, the exquisite exorcism began, thanks be to God. First America, then the world. Finally, after years of greed and double-digit returns everyone knew wouldn't, couldn't last, with no real tangible wealth created in the process, the heavens and those theoretically in it could stand it no longer. The raw, unchecked supergod of Possession begat its inevitable demon spawn Repossession, which like Cronos ate its own. The real estate markets died, securitized debts died, the credit markets died, the stock market died, and in that genocide died all those in debt, whether by chase, choice, or chance, fair or foul. *In sickness and in health* is only a saying, words one mouths knowing the oath is an old-fashioned one, when one is expected to follow the fashion lest the social graces be denied. Can a man dying of thirst refuse the water that is given him? No; hunger and thirst follow their own course, refusing oath and social grace alike. By the following New Year, Two Thousand Nine, only Death came to its fireworks and feast, and feast the circling carrion did.

After all, you are what you eat.

*****

"Not really," I was answering. "People always think all doctors are rich, but after malpractice insurance and med school loans, most of us whose parents weren't rich get by as best we can."

That prompted a lot of noise from the group. I couldn't call it laughter; it was more like a cacophony of train horns, designed to grab one's attention to the danger through sheer volume and discordance.

"Yehp," Earl finally managed, "they always stick it to the little guy." That prompted nods from the other two. "Sure you don't want some of this? Best barbecue in Bristol, I'm tellin' ya."

"No thanks," I said, still disgusted. No way was that crap held at the proper temperature, and the last thing I needed up here was the runs for a week. "I've got my own, anyway," I said, unpacking on the floor.

"Yehp, them and the dang *guv-ment*," Earl said, slowly with clear noxious hatred emphasized at the per-syllable level. "Takin' and talkin', talkin' and takin'." "Yehp, always the same shit," said Merle. "Same shit," Virgil agreed, then more cacophonous laughter.

Merle straightened up from his slouched consumptive position, arching his back, as if preparing to be louder, a goal he subsequently achieved, remarkably. "So what do *you* think of this *O-bam-a* guy, Dr. *Dee-ur-ant*?" Guffaws from the other two, at mentioning Obama or at his deliberate mispronunciation of my name, I couldn't say. "Bet you voted for him," said Earl. Burl grunted his agreement. "Yehp, well, let's let the *Doc-tor* give us his two cents, eh," replied Merle.

"Well," I started uncomfortably, "frankly I was never very political, but he seems intelligent at the least…."

Merle's spine contorted to the full vertical as his voice and ire rose together. "Aw, come *on*! The *last* thing we need to present to the world as our *leader* is some softie *LEF-tist LIB-er-al in-tel-LEC-tu-al*." Hums, hmms all around. "*Told* you he voted for him," muttered Earl at the floor, but Merle continued. "I mean, the guy said when he got elected," then a mocking high-pitched feminine tone, "*This was the moment when the rise of the oceans began to slow and our planet began to heal.*" Guffaws, knee slapping all around. "Who does the guy think he is, *Moses* or somethin'?" "Yeah," Earl added, "fuckin' Moses?" Merle came up out of his seat completely, "YEAH, fuckin' MOSES ?!!"

Suddenly Merle shot floorwards, propelled from behind by the hand of his sister on his large, porcine shoulder. "Now boys," she said, like a pull-the-string plastic June Cleever, "you know what the doctors told y'all about your *stray-yess*." Stray-yess, two syllables. Moans and groans from "the boys", like mating, pneumonic wildebeest. "Now, now," she said, more matronly this time, refilling their mugs with something from a large plastic jug. They were all clearly drunk, and had been for some time.

"Well, he AIN'T no fuckin' Moses!" Merle said, still angry.

"Well now, no he's not, now is he?" said Pearl. "Sure you don't want any, sugar puddin'?" she asked, meaning me.

"No thanks," I said.

"Aw, ain't like you're on duty," said Earl. "Whydncha try some?" *Whydncha?* Oh, he means.... He leaned over as if to whisper to me, but he was too drunk to realize he was still yelling. "It's made from real...." Pearl stopped him with a hard whack on the head. "Ow!" he cried out, flinching. "Now Earl," she said with saccharine sweetness, "the doc already said he didn't want none, 'kay?"

"He's a fuckin' MUSLIM, that what he is," Merle was continuing. "A fuckin' Muslim who went to fuckin' Muslim school with other fuckin' Muslims." I felt a cold wind go through the room, even though the window was closed. "Moses *killed* fuckin' Muslims." Thankfully, he resumed eating his disgusting meat product at that point. I didn't even bother to correct his Mideastern timeline, let alone try for the rest of it. *Schoolin'* was still considered with superstitious suspicion in parts of these hills, and the Chiaccos had clearly traveled well within them. What a fertile crescent it was.

Pearl interjected with her Sunday school opinion. "Hon, it was Joshua that knocked them walls down, 'member? Moses never got 'cross the River Jordan." She smiled, filling Burl's mug up from the jug, with some sloshing, red liquid. Strange; it almost reminded me of….

"Aw; Pearl, I *know* that. I meant them Egyptians. Them Egyptian Muslims got killed by them plagues," said Merle, and Pearl just shrugged.

And *gluttony kills more than the sword* I thought, watching them suck it down. "So you sell cars?" I said, trying to distract the kids off the Muslim killing thing.

"*Sell* cars? Nah Doc, I *am* cars." He thumped his chest, then thumped his brother. "Earl there's in the title loan business, and Burl's a mortgage broker, poor Burl." Burl's head sunk in dismissal, or was it nausea?

"Guess times are pretty bad," I said, testing. Moans and groans all around.

"Ehhh doc, things are terrible. Used to be a man like me could break a few thousand, skim a rube or two a week. You know how much I made off of the twenty, twenty-five percent interest rates I offered on my *personally* financed loans? They'd be payin' double what I paid!" He sighed, a dreamy creamy lover's look on his face. "I'd throw in free oil changes, but my guys always found something wrong under the hood," and he laughed long and hard at his cleverness. "Grandma and grandpa were always grateful when we'd find that problem with their brakes, and save their grandkids' skins!" More laughter. "Yehp," said Earl, "THEN, if they got in trouble they just pawn that piece of junk with me, and I'd charge 'em forty or fifty percent." They both laughed, shoving each other. "Yeah, the good ol' days." said Merle.

But Burl interrupted the history lesson with a loud expulsion of gas, and everybody laughed. Pearl grabbed him by the nose. "Burl, don't you go gettin' *dis-ten-ded* again," she said with a sweet smile, and Merle and Earl just laughed the more. "Yehp, *dis-ten-ded,"* said Merle. I just looked at them. *Could he be more distended than he already is?* I wondered; then, a historical note came to mind as a sulfuric smell spread about the room: *this must be what Hitler meant when he said Germany needing 'breathing room'.* Ironically, Burl threw a salute back at Pearl in response, unable to speak for the chewing motion. *Zeig heil*. "Aw, damnit Burl!" said Earl as the wave hit him.

That's when the fight almost began. Earl smacked Burl upside his head with the turkey leg-ish carcass he was holding, which pushed Burl over into Merle. Merle swore and hit back with his left hand, squarely connecting in an outside punch around, under-over, with Burl's jaw. Then he slipped, backwards and sideways, into Earl's shoulder, pushing him back with a surprised *Woooah!*, right off the cooler on which he sat onto the floor. Cursing and shouting began; Burl turned to hit back at Merle who grabbed his arm, Burl grabbing back at Merle's beard, and Earl swearing like a sailor on steroids and struggling to find the inner strength and mathematical capability to deduce a loophole in the law of gravity that would allow him to lift himself to join the frackus with a minimal expenditure of energy.

"BOYS!" shouted Pearl, and all three of the appropriately-named children froze. I had backed myself against a wall of the shelter, out of the boxing ring. Virgil hadn't say a word, just huddled by the gear. We'd watched this spectacle of the idiotic unfold, not needing spectacles to perceive its idiocy. Pearl looked at Virgil and I in obvious embarrassment, like a mother about to attempt an explanation as to the history of the unexpected baggie of homegrown and nudie mags on her usually pristine kitchen table to a group of surprise visitors in Sunday-best from the neighborhood Pentecostal. "Well..." she started, as if underground hydrodynamics had a thing in the world to do with it. Then, she thought better of it, slouched, but on seeing a half-opened small can on the floor, picked it up and offered it to me with a bright smile and two words I did not expect at all: "Vienna sausage?"

I blinked. A small corner of my mind was rolling on the floor, laughing hysterically. But my mind, or at least the part that analyzed everything, was trying to tie the two words she'd just said into some sort of comprehensible narrative. *Ergo,* from "Vienna sausage" came the thought: *Austria.* Austria conjured memories of Julie Andrews, leading more improbably to an improbably-singing Christopher Plummer, then yodeling, then quickly to rappelling; rope, hanging, the Wild West, six-shooters, shooters, shot glasses, whiskey, DUI, the police, Sting, double bass, Shirley Bassey, *Diamonds Are Forever*, space lasers, *Star Wars*, Wookies, cookies, cookies-n-creme, ice cream, ice, polar bears, black bears, honey, Winnie the Pooh, the Hundred Acre Wood, innocence, experience, William Blake, watercolors, gouache, goulash, Hungary, Austria-Hungary, back to....

I blinked again. A few raindrops appeared on the shelter window. Maybe I should have let the brain cells that wanted to roll around laughing on the floor go for it. Instead, I tried sensibility as an offset to this absurdity.

"No thanks," I said. "You folk come here often?" Sure, it sounded lame, but sometimes plain milk toast makes for a balanced breakfast.

"Neh," said Earl, who finally regained his perch on the cooler after a strong heave off the floor that in itself had nearly killed him. "Neh, I think we're…."

"We got lost, o-KAY, *Doc*-tor *Dur*-ant, o-KAY? We were trying for the Nash'nal Forest," said Merle, wheezing, still in ass-whoopin' mode.

"Yehp," Earl went on, "we wuz tryin'to go huntin' today." "*HUN*-tin!" interjected Burl, for no apparent reason. "Yehp, score us a big buck or two," said Merle. "Yehp, a BIG ONE!!!" said Earl, making horns on his head with his fingers. They all laughed, pantomimed, making big horns. They laughed, resumed eating. Funny, I hadn't noticed the rifles in the corner before. I sure as hell had now.

After a pause to swallow, Merle shifted forward, looked long and hard at me. "Maybe, we're gonna shoot us a buck up here, Doc. Now... you ain't gonna *rat* on us, right?" The other two hmm'd, huhh'd on that. "RIGHT, Doc?" Earl emphasized.

I looked at each one it turn. A marquee flashed before my eyes: *Deliverance II: Die Doctor Die*. Pearl looked at me and smiled, utterly oblivious, as she kept refilling their *moai*, as they kept drinking. Smiling, drinking, eating, laughing, choking, fighting, threatening. They were, each of them, despicable. I realized *milk toast* had been the wrong breakfast to serve for these assholes. So, I went for it.

"Oh, fuck you all," I said, quietly, shaking my head. There was a long moment where they just stared at me, with Pearl pouring, overflowing Burl's drink onto the floor. Yep, it did look a lot like blood.

Suddenly, Earl and Merle burst out laughing, howling, slapping each other. *HA HA HA HA HA HA HA HA HA HA* they went on, dropping meat as they went; but Burl just continued to stare at me, emotionlessly; or was it nausea? Pearl, finally noticing her spill, quickly ran for and produced paper towels, mopping up in servitude to these useless creatures.

"You know, 'gainst my better judgment, I LIKE you, Doc," said Merle, leaning over and slapping me hard on the arm, dropping more meat on the floor. *Jeeeeezus.*

"No, I mean it," I repeated, with heartfelt honesty. "Fuck you all." But that just produced more laughter. Lord how I wanted them to shut up, but it was not to be.

I saw Merle put on his game face, and sighed. "So tell me, Doc, do you happen to be in the market for an automobile?"

Are you shitting me? "Not much call for one up here, now is there, Merle?" I asked.

"Aw, you could always *driiiiiiiiiiive* to Maine," he said, slapping me again. "You know you don't have to walk!"

"Yehp, what's up with that?" said Earl. Burl just kept staring at me, but at least had resumed drinking.

"Why, I think it's a real treat to have a real man here with us," said Pearl, refilling. "Don't you pay these boys no nevermind." They just grunted their disapproval.

"So, how far you walkin' again?" asked Earl.

"About two thousand miles or so," I said.

"*Sheeee*-it," said Merle, "How much of that you got left?"

"That is what I've got left," I said. "I've already done about three hundred seventy or eighty."

They paused in brief shock, then resumed eating. "*Sheeee*-it," said Earl; Burl whistled, finally looking down at his plate rather than at me. Merle just smiled, then: "Aw come on now, son, surely you need some fine luxury wheels to get you there *quicker*."

"But fine luxury wheels would take the fun out of meeting fine luxury folk such as yourselves," I said.

They laughed again. "Don't listen to him, Doc. You'd be wantin' a Beemer or Lexus or somethin' he ain't got," offered Earl, nudging me hard. *Where did these people get this need to shove everybody?* "Shit," said Merle, frowning and looking down, "I got so much shit in inventory right now I don't know what I got... except... *a great deal with your good credit!!!"* Good recovery, that one. I had to hand it to him… except he probably wouldn't be able to lift it.

"No thanks," I said.

"So how you gettin' home, sweet potato?" asked Pearl. She pronounced it *sweet poh-tate-ah.* Real genuine Hee-Haw, damn. *Deliverance II: Die Doctor Die: The Wally Cleaver Cut.*

"Anybody got a banjo handy?" I asked. They stared at me for a second, then nodded no, confused.

"You play, Doc?" asked Earl, still confused. My inner child howled.

"Aw the doc just plays *golf*," responded Merle, punching him again. "He's pokin' fun at us," he observed, turning a bit sour with his first real insight. *Nah, not me: you're doing just fine with that yourselves*. But I'd picked up on Merle's comment about his inventory, and decided to go for a vulnerable spot.

"So nobody buyin' cars these days, Merle?" I said, slapping him back, attempting to get him back to his unhappy place.

"It's a shithole out there," said Earl. Burl nodded, slouched forward, looking down at his feet. "Yeah, a real shithole," continued Merle. "Half of Bristol is boarded up, ain't nobody buying nothin'."

"Yeah, fuckin' Muslims," said Merle.

"Hunger *is* the Great Equalizer," I said with hope, but then a quote from the Koran occurred to me, so I smiled and added cheerily, "After all, God helps those who persevere!"

"Well, we sure as hell ain't got a problem with *hunger!*" said Earl, and they all laughed. "Show him!" Merle said to her. "Yehp, show him Pearl!" said Earl. Pearl shook her head, but then sighed, and opened a cooler to show me meat: piles and piles and piles, a cooler-full, shredded and chunked, red and brown, fatty, but strangely gristled, and with large bones in the back that almost, almost looked like....

Suddenly Pearl was right next to me, whispering in my ear. "Here Doc," she said, quietly, "have a drink," and I found a large *moai* full of the same frothy liquid in my hand. *How'd she move that fast?* I glanced back at the cooler, but it was closed again.

Before I could ponder, the weirdness of the moment was totally eclipsed by another, altogether different class of weird moment. Without warning or fanfare, Burl stood up, swayed back and forth drunkenly, and grabbing Earl's shoulder for support, launched his bulky bulbous destroyer into the ocean blue.

"Liberals as a rule are all filthy mouthed uncivil scum!" he shouted. "The damn media are all filthy mouthed filth peddlers and the fact that you are a liberal means that you have to lie about the Republicans. The liberals have screwed up everything, *EVERYTHING!!* Liberals have killed everything they touch, they gave North Korea the *your-ay-knee-um*, the Clinton Administration gave North Korea the okay and a *bareback* to build a *nu-cue-lar* reactor, so they could turn our precious *your-ay-knee-um* into weapons grade shit for the bombs. It was all Jimmy Carter man!" Hmms, hummms from the others, nodding their agreement, as they chewed vociferously. "Fucking JIMMY CARTER and his Syrian homosexual lovers gave those fucking godless yellow commies all our FUCKING *YOUR-AY-KNEE-UM....*"

Earl belched, loudly. Pearl rolled her eyes while Merle applauded. "Earl..." she started, but Burl would have none of it. He was on a roll: a big fat buttery yeasty one by the look of him.

"President ROOSEVELT! THERE was a fucking cripple liberal for you! He couldn't stop the Germans, he didn't have the courage or the balls to stop Hitler, so they sneak attacked us and millions were killed and Bill I'll Fuck Anything With Any Cigar Handy Clinton just did the same fucking thing with 9/11!"

The he rose to his toes, and got *loud*. By loud, I don't mean the thing he'd been, they'd all been. I mean a best approximation to a word that there is no word for in the English language because no one ever needed a word to describe something never experienced in human history save the occasional supervolcanic eruption or megathrust earthquake that killed every member of its audience in the process. If it was a color, a poet might have invented a word for it, something non-marketable and ludicrous like *uberdecibeleen* or *mondotransphonue*. But *this* was no shade, but a sound. How can one describe a level of volume never produced by a human larynx before, at least one without a million dollar stage show complete with towers of rare earth superconducting magnet speakers, throwback thousand-volt tube amps, and the reanimated, rejuvenated *The Who* as their backing band?

"BUT BUSH HAD THE NERVE TO STOP HUSSEIN IN HIS TRACKS! THERE'S A GOD-DAMN MAN FOR YOU! THERE'S A MAN WHO WON'T STAND FOR JUDGES WHO WON'T FOLLOW HIS AGENDA OR SCIENTISTS THAT WANT TO HUG THE CLIMATE AND THE FROGS AND TREES AND THE FROGS IN THE TREES AND WON'T PUT UP WITH C.I.A. WIVES WHO GO TO NIGGER AND GIVE OUR YOUR-AY-KNEE-UM TO THEM YELLOW BASTARDS AND DON'T TAKE CARE OF THEIR HUSBANDS LIKE WIVES WHO LOVE THEIR HUSBANDS SHOULD DO (*he's crying*, I realize) AND NIP IT IN THE BUD JUST LIKE WE NIPPED THEM FRENCH IN THE BUD WITH OUR FREEDOM FRIES AND JUST LIKE WE NIPPED HUSSEIN INSANE IN THE MEMBRANE *TWICE* I'M SAYIN' *TWICE*!"

"Nip it in the BUD!" shouted Merle, but sounding pathetic in context. "Nip it in the FUCKING BUD," shouted Earl, slightly more convincingly.

"...NIP IT IN THE FUCKING BUD," Burl preached on, "AND GOT RID OF THAT FUCKIN' MUSLIM MADMAN! GODDAMN LIBERALS

LET THAT GODDAMN MUSLIM MADMAN GET OUR YOUR-AY-KNEE-UM AND THEM HOMOSEXUAL SYRIANS AND JEWS AND YELLOW NORTH KOREANS BUILT HIM A GODDAMN WEAPON OF MASS *DEEEEE-STRUCK-SHUN* TO FUCK *US??? US??? US???* FUCKIN' LIBERALS, FUCKIN' MUSLIMS, FUCKIN' JEWS, FUCKIN' FRENCH, FUCKIN' LIBERAL FRENCH, FUCKIN' JEW LIBERALS, FUCKIN' LIBERAL MUSLIMS!!!"

"YEAH," shouted Merle, jumping up, "FUCKING LIBERAL MUSLIMS!!!!"

"FUCKING *LIBERAL MUSLIMS!!!!"* they all hollered, if not in unison.

There was the brief pause for breathing's sake. In that moment, perfect, unstained, I imagined I saw a glorious bald eagle, golden and white and resplendent in its apogee, soaring, sweeping, approaching the sun, almost outshining it, straining to reach, higher and higher, the last kiss of air beneath its Olympic wings. And in that moment, then, and only then, at his apogee, Burl hurled loudly and prodigiously on the floor.

"Oh, goddamnit Burl," said Merle, sighing and shaking his head. *Couldn't have said it better myself*, I thought. When he was done hurling, which took quite a while, Burl sat down, unwaveringly triumphant, as if illuminated by the heavens with a halo all his own. Except, in this case, his halo was made of drenching feverish sweat, with a few bits of rebroadcast, remotely identifiable mystery meat about his face.

Well, that was enough for me. On rare occasions, I enjoyed fishing. Fishing is a delicate art, like lacework, beer pong, or cosmic bowling. Large mouth in particular made interesting targets in such cases, and such simple prerequisites needed for the task: a line, a hook, and a worm on it. I prepared all three for these large mouths, and cast.

"What interests me," I began, as Pearl scurried over with the paper towels again, "what interests me is this economy we're in now. Don't you think that the Asian economies, and their emphasis on stringent currency management in the late 90's, after the Asian market crisis you know," I said, winking at Merle, "when they started to promote exports and build reserves backed by the dollar, don't you think that lowered U.S. borrowing yields, and Greenspan *being Greenspan*," with a *big* wink at Burl, "kept the rates artificially low, so asset volatility and yields dropped, so banks and funds that had too *little* leverage were swiftly punished by the markets since the NPV of their future liabilities got bigger and bigger as interest rates dropped and stayed low, leading both hedge fund assets and securitization of debt to increase as the banks and funds sought to offset those liabilities with above-market returns?"

You know those cartoon scenes where someone expects a sound, but only hears a lone owl hooting in the distance and crickets chirping? The moment was like that. The moment was just like that.

"Well, that and Saddam bin Laden," I said.

"GOD DAMN RIGHT!" said Merle, slapping me again.

"And," I said, feeling the bass tugging at my line, "the fact that all us fat lazy Americans couldn't be satisfied with a reasonable rate of return on our homes; *nooooo*, we had to hold out for twenty or fifty or a hundred or two hundred percent profit, like Nimrod Neighbor got, so we all screwed each other's pooch until nobody could afford their payment anymore. But who needs to pay? There's always foreclosure."

Silence descended again. More crickets.

"Yeah, we pretty much did this to ourselves. Oh, we can blame the SEC or the FDIC or MAJESTIC-12 or NAMBLA or some other acronym; the government for doing something or not doing something, or in general play the blame game, but, at the end of the day, everybody who walked away with a big fat paycheck for only a few month's or year's investment in their house, they're to blame for this. You, me, all of us. *We* fucked ourselves, and we deserve what we got."

Crickets with jackhammers. Crickets with megaphones. Crickets launching Space Shuttles in a hurricane. *Deep Impact* crickets. Brave, patriotic, flag-waving, drum-and-fife-playing crickets giving the order and pushing The Button; megaton-MIRV crickets. Crickets, crickets, crickets.

"Or," I added thoughtfully, "maybe it *was* just poor monetary policy, really an adjustment to global resource allocation, ignorance of asset bubbles due to old dinosauric fears of inflation, and the financial *innovation* that led to creative ways to solve those problems... problems viewed from the selfish narrow perspective of the individual, family, corporation, or portfolio manager. I mean, why should anyone put the world before their own leathery hide?"

Not even crickets. Crickets chirping in sign language. Crickets performing mime on the streets of Paris after a power failure, hailstorm, *cafe au lait* shortage, and Ebola epidemic. Monk crickets who took a vow of silence. Underwater crickets. Crickets in space. *Dead crickets.*

"Hurmm.." said Merle, finally, clearing his throat, "that sure is a lot to think about," declaring his steadfast resolve to do no such thing.

"So subprime debt goes insolvent. As a sound businessman, what do you do? You say, *Oh my! Where DID all these liabilities come from?* and dump like a truck driver with cholera at a Darfur landfill. Later at the bar, you wonder why you spent all your cash to keep from being an attractive, marketable, acquirable asset; but, the rate of return you could get! Emphasis on *could*. Who could blame you? You had huge health care premiums to pay, an aging workforce, a burdensome pension plan obligation from twenty or thirty or fifty years ago, competition from Tzikistan, and that sharp little Beemer you had your eye on for quite some time, which after all you deserve. So suddenly, your balance sheet full of securitized debt is immensely vulnerable, and people get reminded that leverage comes from the word lever, which can tilt the opposite way when big fat market forces push hard on the other side."

"More, hon?" asked Pearl, having again snuck up by my side, with her pitcher of mystery fluid. I looked down at my mug and saw that it was empty. Funny, I didn't remember drinking out of it, and I remember everything. It didn't matter, as she started refilling it anyway.

"OK, OK, so we want to fix this mess, right? Right. Bailouts? Delay foreclosures? Make smores, hold hands, and sing *Kumbaya*? Fuh-*get* about it. OK. Every single loan application has the names of the people that 'worked' on it, right? Right. It has the broker, the underwriter, the appraiser, the lawyers, whatever. So spend a few bil to go through all of the foreclosed home loans and making a record of the people involved." Earl and Merle looked at Burl, then each other. Burl was head lowered, in bucket, recovering. "Think a lot of the same names, the same shady hoo-hah's won't pop up? The ones who signed off on the outrageous ARMs, neg-ams, no-docs... get *their* names, and the names of their bosses and bosses' bosses all the way up to the top of the agency. Then take *their* cars, homes, boats, jets, clothes, furniture, kids' toys, vacation cottages, jet skis, and have a fire sale. Burn baby burn, RICO inferno."

Burl's head popped up from his bucket long enough for him to say, "Now, wait jes a minute there...."

I looked at Merle. "And the automotive manufacturers? Bail *them* out? They've had thirty years to get competitive with Japan. Thirty years! Hunger is the Great Equalizer. Let the market fix the problem once and for all. Like Aptera, for instance, or Tesla. Why couldn't Detroit do what they're doing? The minds in Detroit don't deserve a dollar."

Merle leaned forward, "No *Detroit*? Bahhh... how's the little guy like me supposed to get by? Average Americans want *average American* cars."

"So the rich folk are buying the Hyundais, Merle? Anyway, who cares? You're just a middle man. You take, mark up, and sell. Where's the wealth creation in that? Anybody can be a middleman, no skill involved at all. You don't add any *value*, Merle. Better off without."

I looked down in my mug, Merle seething and squirming. I noticed it was empty again. How the... I looked up at Merle. He caught it, and laughed loud.

"Aw, it looks like our *Doc*-tor is just drunk," he said, laughing. "Well, you really had us goin' there, Doc."

"Maybe so," I said, still staring at my mug, beginning to wonder what was going on. I did feel a little weird. Almost as if....

It was only then that I noticed a thumping coming from the other end of the room, a strange muffled thumping, seemingly distant and disturbed, like it was underwater or buried. Kirby began growling downstairs; he'd heard it too. "Shut UP, Kirby!" shouted Merle and Earl. Burl stirred at the sound, looking less nauseous and more nervous. Pearl inexplicably grabbed a single large boot someone had removed, and beat the cooler in the back with it, twice. The she seemed to catch herself, looked at me, and smiled, all Fifty's TV Mom Stereotype again.

"Hey," I started, "what's…."

A prepared plate of meat product showed up in my lap, with Pearl squirreling away back to her corner by the time I noticed. Rain began to streak the windows outside; the sound of stormy weather played against the walls of the shelter, and not the calm, easy listening 1933 version. It disgusted me. I didn’t dare bite.

Merle broke in. "Ehhhh, Doc, this damn bail out has us ALL pissed. Who knew that the nanny state was going to step in and force changes to signed legal documents? Who knew they would take two trillion dollars from people that have their own mortgages and bills to pay and use that money to pay for people that don’t feel like paying? Who knew that our damn *guv-ment* would step in to take money from people who WORKED to earn it, to give it to people that made bad financial decisions?"

Earl looked at his brother as tears formed in his eyes. Merle looked back at him, astounded. "That was beautiful," said Earl, losing it. "Jes *beautiful*." Merle just rolled his eyes.

I thought it needed a better response than that. "What do you expect people to do?" I asked. "Not try to provide for their families based on the favorable terms *given* them? Who *allowed* this to happen? Who *enabled* it? The hawks and raptors attacked the vulnerable, the crows and carrion feasted on the kill. I see both in front of me. Where's *your* house Earl? Is *your* house payment in the twenty percent of monthly income range? What about you, Merle? Maybe the better people should get the houses and landlord the fiefdom into vassal-like submission? Sure people should read and understand a contract; but who's the voice of conscience and sound financial reason at the closing? *Everybody's* at the table to make money -- THAT's the real problem. If equities give you five to ten percent but property nets you fifty or a hundred, what would any sane person do? A train running downhill off the tracks onto ice at full throttle with no brakes isn't a train, it's a *bobsled*, and you don't haul coal and corn and condoms and the rest of your economy from here to the future in a fuckin' *bobsled*. The market created the problem, *we* created the problem, but there were no brakes anywhere in the market to control it, prevent it. *Nobody* said *no*, but that's *human nature*, and that's free-range *capitalism*. Merle, sure, people bought houses they shouldn't have, but *that's* human nature, and *that's* capitalism. You can't spank a hungry monkey just because it steals a banana! You have to keep the bananas locked up in the first place because there are goddamn hungry *monkeys* around!"

Wow, that was the most I'd said in one breath in months. What *was* my problem?

Earl snarled like a bear in a trap. "Some people would have taken a second or third job to make things work, but not anymore!" he answered angrily.

"*What* jobs, Earl? Where are they? Are you really asking the thirty or forty percent of homeowners near or in foreclosure to get some nonexistent job at the WalMart or delivering pizza? Or do you just foreclose on 'em? Shit Earl, suppose the jobs existed and everybody took them. What would the cost be to everyone's health? To their wives and husbands? To their free time? To their lives? Their children? Would *you* want to work two jobs, Earl, let alone do so?" I remembered my residency, the 80-hour weeks, and what it had done to my young marriage. "My point, Earl, was that if *we* drive prices up, *we* have to drive them down again to recover. We *have* to regulate. We *have* to investigate. We *have* to lock up the fucking bananas."

Merle spoke up loudly with only a partial *sequiter*. "SORRY, but the ONLY way to get the REAL value of these homes is to let the free market work. If the *guv-ment* artificially sets the value of home prices by spending a zillion dollars, then you don't have the REAL value of the property!"

"Well I don't really disagree with you there, but only because it's way too late for anything else." I said. "I guess if people made fifty or a hundred or two hundred thou a pop in the good times, they should expect to lose fifty or a hundred or two in the bad. But that's because there's no real *wealth creation* involved. Oh, you can create more houses for more people as population increases, but it seems to me that just saturates the market eventually. People can't drive two hundred miles to work every day; there's a limit to how big things can get. We just ran into it. Nah, times have changed: folks are going to have to produce something and add value to make money from now on. People won't be making millions overnight chucking option-ARM loans to mathematically challenged borrowers over the phone. There isn't going to be some magical industry where fast food workers and people with high school diplomas will be able to make big six figures, *anymore*."

Burl interjected again by suddenly standing up, walking to the corner with his bucket, and applying more vomit to it, thankfully in that order.

"Of course, for all of you," I said, looking at the ceiling, "even if you stopped your gluttony, it's too late to pay back what you owe. You've gulped so much down your throats, you had to steal what wasn't yours."

Inside the shelter there was only the sound of wretched heaving, slowly dying in the night air. Outside, the wind began to howl, like fell wolves in desolation. Thinking it so as well, downstairs Kirby began to howl in answer. Merle was shaking.

"OK, Doc, that's enough outta *you*," he said, threateningly.

I stood up, defiant. "Or you'll what? Shoot me?" I eyed the guns in the corner again; when I looked back at him, *maybe I will* is what I read in his repulsive, ignorant face.

Then there was Pearl again. "Aw now Doc, here I was thinking you were a gentleman, *calling* you a gentleman! Maybe you just need another drink," she said. I looked at my mug; again, it was empty. I suppose I had enjoyed it.

I ignored her as she poured and I felt the floor began to tilt from under me and the room started to slowly spin counter-clockwise. I was definitely drunk, but... something else too. Suddenly she was back across the room again, laughing. It strangely attuned itself to Kirby's howl, to the wind and the hounds on it. It had strange overtones, ninths on top of sevenths modulus elevenths, making the glass in the windows vibrate, slowly twisting the old nails in the wood, making my insides slide sideways. Now *I* wanted to vomit. I sat back down, before I fell down.

"Aw shit, I tell you no more and I no longer answer you," I said, because I didn't want to, and because I couldn't.

"Good, cause I'm gonna tell you like it is," said Merle. "These same people that *didn't know what they were signing...*" (in finger quotes) "...are going to have NO trouble finding out how to work the system and get their free money from this *guv-ment* bailout. Do you think the *guv-ment* is going to stop at one or two trillion if there are some *poor, hard working decent people...*" (more sarcasm and finger quotes) "...that didn't get help? Come on, name one *guv-ment* social program that hasn't had a budget overrun!"

I didn't bother trying, and he didn't bother waiting for an answer. Honestly I didn't know of any.

"This situation is a mess, but *guv-ment* intervention is only going to make things worse. Not to mention that it sets another dangerous precedent as well as being a slap in the face to every responsible person in this country. This should piss off all the parents trying to raise their kids properly...uuuurh..." (*belch, continue*) "... parents who actually take the time to raise self sufficient children with personal responsibility are in the minority now, so their voice no longer carries as much weight. Too many in the *meddle class...*" (*fq's again, clever boy*) "...looking to *guv-ment* to solve all of their problems."

"Damn liberal *guv-ment* Jews!" said Burl, from the corner, weakly but wanting to be a contributor.

"Jews AND Muslims," I managed, feeling terrible: dizzy and disoriented. "Hmm. A strange Illuminati. Controlled by OPEC and the Boca Raton Chamber of Commerce, no doubt. Well, thank Rosencrantz it's *somebody's* fault." Then, *Damn! Memory error?!* Rosencrantz? Billy Shakespeare.

Rosen*kreuz*? Danny Brown, doing business as Humbert Eco. As drunk and screwed as Barnardine at an Opus Dei rally? Dr. Durant Allegheny.

But Merle was trudging on, ignoring me. Interestingly, sparks of light began to come out of his hair as he spoke. I looked at Virgil, to gauge his reaction. Virgil, I noted, was turning purple. I watched him slowly begin to pulse as Merle went on.

"TARP: what a joke! A tarp's somethin' you throw over a car in your yard! So let me get this straight… the *guv-ment*, Wall Street, and all of these supposedly smart fucking people didn't see this coming for five or six years, but they can figure out how to fix it in two weeks of *meetings*? What they should have done is let the system work itself out, and WAIT and see what needed to be done. We are burning through billions and trillions of dollars at about the same rate Paris Hilton burns through shoes. When are people going to learn that *guv-ment* has not ONCE budgeted for anything accurately in the past hundred years I love it how people are so upset when banks that got bailout money take clients out to nice resorts and nice meals because they are in the *money* business so to court people that still have money they have to go someplace nice trust me it is hard to get somebody to invest millions at your bank if you are taking them to fucking *Denny's* for a Grand Slam after a night of partying at the Red Roof Inn if you don't like it don't buy stock in that company if you are just envious well shit you just start studying for college so you can go to biz-ness school and start working your way up on Wall Street THAT is the beauty of this country you can do whatever you put your mind to just find some way to add value and stop fucking complaining!"

Virgil fascinated me. He began to sway in reds and purples, oozing time like a cobra. I heard a weird music play: a humming like a god of bees, and a drumming of hail on the roof of the shelter. A background of Pearl's weird laughter, gale-force winds, and dogs, dogs howling. More heaving from the corner at times of melodic climax. A *Moment Musical* in magenta and mimosas. Time and space combined in octahedrons to make sense of the long sentences and fluids that filled the spaces between the atoms, atoms made only of sunshine and tiny bits of grey matter. A thinking space we filled, thinking all around us, throbbing veins in tempo to this Music not only of the Spheres, but also the Pyramids, and the Spirally Shapes. Merle was still reciting his one long sentence, as my mind refused to admit the reality of punctuation anymore. I opted for the optical instead, the auditorium and the audience one and the same, projector and projectionist uniting with the projection.

"*Salvia divinorum*," whispered Pearl in my ear, refilling the devilish ambrosia, then scuttling away, with more laughter that came out of her mouth in what I noted was a cascade of soft shiny green fur. I had no idea she was Roman.

Apsychoactiveherbwhichinduces...
...strongdissociativeeffects...
...itisaherbaceousperennialinthemintfamily...

"The first round of bailing out the banks only led to every other fucking business segment wanting to latch on to the *guv-ments* teat. Why not? I mean the economy is bad for everybody right? So if momma *guv-ment* is going to throw out a boob, why shouldn't you cop a feel too?"

$X^N+Y^N=Z^N$ where $N > 2$ has no solutions in non-zero integers X, Y, and Z. Well, of course, *except* for....

..thespecificnameofsalviadivinorumwasgiven...
...duetoitstraditionaluseindivinationandhealing...
...itliterallytranslatesto...
...diviner'ssage...or...seer'ssage...

"A gentle conundrum," said Virgil, in yellow words that sounded like sour apple and Botswana. "It seems, Madam, the funeral's baked meats do coldly furnish forth the picnic table… but I know not *seems*. I am a puffed and reckless libertine! To be fair, it is often said by critics of Shakespeare that Hamlet often spoke as if he intended a separate meaning or words that he was not expressing in another play really written by the Duke of Earl." The he began chanting slowly in a deep *basso profundo*, a throbbing Motown bass line: *Duke, Duke, Duke, Duke of Earl, Earl, Earl, Duke of Earl, Earl, Earl....*

I had no clue Earl was a Duke. I'd swear he'd never mentioned it. Earl a Duke and Pearl a Roman! Never would have guessed.

...whichisapotentkopioidreceptoragonist...
...SalvinorinAisuniqueinthatitistheonly...
...naturallyoccurringsubstance...
...knowntoinduceavisionarystatethisway...
...Salviadivinorumcanbechewed,smoked,or...
...takenasatincture...
...toproduceexperiencesrangingfromlaughter...
...tomuchmoreintenseandprofoundlyaltered...

Interesting, I heard the punctuation in that one. Burl spew blue flame from his guts and out of his mouth.

"Alas, poor Burl; I knew him, Durant, a fellow of infinite jest holding his fancy schmancy skull in his hands." said Virgil. "He bored me a thousand times, and now how abhorrent in smell he is! His gorge rises at it!"

"Act five scene one. Hush already, you show-off," I told him, or imagined I did.

"Why not give small business a tax break and let the guys in the miniature golf or arcade business start a Frisbee golf course if there is money to be made? Course fuckin' Frisbee golf ain't allowed by the Taliban!"

Pearl grabbed me from behind, turned my head to hers, and kissed me. She was bare-breasted. Our mouths melted into quicksand, hot lead, heavy, like warm fudge pudding. There was an interesting mole on her....

"To be, or not to be," Virgil recited, turning tangerine orange in the corner of my eye. "Is *this* a question? There's the point; not to sleep, to dream, aye there it goes Mary Mother of God! For in that dream of death, when thee we wake, and born before an everlasting Judge, from whence no passenger ever returned... wouldn't that just *suck???*"

"Who *would* fardels bear !?!?!" I imagined asking him, breaking the kiss, as Pearl grabbed my fardel and began bearing it. Virgil answered, "Those who grunt *and* sweat under a weary life!" He shook his traffic cone colored head sadly. “But you, Durant, have pulled off an excellent play within the play, a reverse-Hamlet: you flew to others you knew not of, rather than bear those ills you had!"

"I never thought it would come to the point where big businesses would act like welfare queens grabbing at free money. I guess my theory on laziness is correct: if somebody else will give it to you for nothing, why would you want to work for it?"

Her family gathered around the bed. "I'm sorry," I'd said to them, "there was nothing that could be done." Without a helmet on I-285 at rush hour, doing over a hundred, the police said. I'd gone through the motions with my team: intubation, norepinephrine, paddles. The blood was replaceable, but some of her brains were no longer with her, and where they were I couldn't say. She was fifteen. Her mother wore red to match her daughter. Her father wore black to match her mother three days hence. The memory was a blazing iron of fire, red and raw.

nothing that could be done
nothing that could be done
nothing that could be done

"The new stimulus bill? Somebody needs to explain to these fucking politicians the difference between creating jobs and creating work I heard they gave some idiot nine hundred thousand dollars for a Frisbee golf park that creates *four jobs* What the FUCK is THAT Why is the *guv-ment* using taxpayer dollars to get into the Frisbee golf business And it needs to be clarified that building that course creates WORK for four people, not jobs What are they going to do when they finish building this course I can't imagine it's more than a few months to get 'er done Then what WHAT do they do with their new *job* that was created Oh that's right it WASN'T a fucking job to begin with Sorry but at a cost of nine hundred thousand that is a lot of Frisbee golf that needs to be played to break even OH YEAH *guv-ment* never has to worry about adding value I fucking FORGOT...."

...Thestemsaretypicallyangledlikeothermembersin...
...Theflowersareproducedinspikesracemesorpanicles..
...andproduceashowydisplaywithcolorsrangingfrom...
...bluetoredwithwhiteandyellownotas...

...corollasareoften...clawshapedand...
...aretwolippedwiththeupperlip...

The fifth fifing French father filches Freddie's fifth friend's five filthy fingers! HAH!

"Greed is GOOD! And can't be no GREED with no INTEGRITY!"

No integrity. No integrity. No integrity. More kissing, on my neck.

That just meant a flower dissolving in alcohol at the Academy is more stressful than whatever white collar country club Milken got to hang out they have to live somewhere to buy homes that they can afford with REAL fixed rate mortgages at debt-to-income ratios that are in line with historical norms and a lot of the same names same names that 'nobody' saw coming to a REAL market value of property if there is a BILLION dollar payday waiting for me when I get out in line with what rental incomes will dictate in that very same flower. *Ipso facto*.

Zebras? In Tennessee?

Orgasm. Pearl's laughter.

No, not zebras; pelicans!

(No, just Virgil.)

Some have beds in their jail cell, some have jail cells in their beds. Who is the real prisoner?

But there can *be* no weakness in Sparta! (How I'd howled at that. Funniest thing I'd seen in a long time.)

I managed to focus my eyes. Pearl was shrouded in light, *was* all light, an angel. She stood behind Burl. "Well Doc, thanks for coming and playing our game tonight. We have some *lovely* parting gifts for you!" With that, she raised her arm, and in her hand she held what looked like a long, thin knife. Down her arm came, hard, deep into the back of Burl's neck.

A fountain of blue. Warm tropical water rained on the dirty worn wood floor. Burl gurgled, sounding like Daffy Duck as she peeled a long slice of his neck off from the side. What a maroon! *Abba-bee abba-bee abba-bee, that's all, folks!*

Pearl held the blade up to her face, looked at me out of the corner of her eye, smiled, and licked the blade. "You see, Doc," she said, quietly, smiling, "there are hells, and *then* there are hells."

I found it odd the neither Earl nor Merle seemed to notice the shower of blue water from Burl. Earl was slumped, staring at the floor. Merle was still going on about the markets.

"The eight-figure bonuses and golden parachutes for the high level execs that didn't do squat to add value are not good for business or perception. But my answer to that is don't fucking whine to the *guv-ment* about it, just readjust your portfolio! The system ain't perfect, but if the board and shareholders of the company agree to it, then that is enough for me. *Guv-ment* intervention almost always...."

Pearl walked beside him, grabbed him by the arm, spun him around to face her, the she drove the knife deep and very slowly into his abdomen.

"Fucking Muslims!" he said as the blade sank into him. "Fuckin'... goddamn... Mus... Mus.. *Mzzzzzzzz....*"

She dug around in his abdomen for a minute, slicing in circular motion. I noted her technique needed work, and perhaps a sharper blade. I wondered where the anesthesiologist was; what a derelict, not attending during the surgery! Probably out playing golf, I mused, or driving his leased Maserati down the A1A with his twenty-something "niece from Cleveland".

Presently, she held a large organ in her hands. Lobes proper shape, size, placement; color, check; membranes, check; falciform ligament, check; but not enough of an inferior vena cava left for the transplant… hey! Wait a minute.

Then I experienced a *swooshing*, like a hard dry wind off a sand dune late at night, driving invisible crystals and grains hard into my face. They stung my eyes, choked me. I managed to look at Virgil, who looked normal again, except that he seemed awfully concerned about something. I had a sensation of being sucked in, down, back; I discovered gravity again, or it rediscovered me. Weight was administered, weak and strong forces reengaged, the electromagnetism in the air abruptly powered off. I fell backwards, onto the floor, involuntarily shutting my eyes and crying out.

"Coming out of it so soon, Doc?" said Pearl. I heard her laugh, then... wet, chewing sounds. The cycle of life in action.

My head pounded, my heart was racing. Some part of me slid into gear then, and I forced the clutch, feeling it give. *Salvia divinorum*, she'd said. Salvia! The most potent psychedelic plant known to man, but also the shortest-acting, known to last for only five minutes, give or take.

Then, without my asking or wanting it, those five minutes rewound themselves and replayed to the singular audience of my reenabled mind, and in dawning abject terror I opened my eyes.

Merle lay on the floor dead, blood all over it and him, a hole the size of a grapefruit in his exposed abdomen. Earl was slumped over, his throat ripped out, his chest plundered. Burl was sitting, leaning back against the wall, and Pearl.... Pearl was nude, painted aboriginal in blood, and busy slicing his tongue out. The cooler in the back of the room was thumping and shaking, loudly, and Kirby howled and growled downstairs with the hurricane outside. I was frozen, fixed, my heart running a million miles an hour and me not moving at all.

"So, what do you think Doc?" she asked me as she went about her work. "Do such words and thoughts and actions nourish the soul? It is not by bread alone that you are sustained. Keep in mind what it is that truly feeds you." With that, she ate Burl's tongue, and turning to look at me her eyes suddenly blazed like twin neutron stars of white fire.

Just then an impossible bolt of lightning seared the sky just outside the window, and with that I flashed as well. In one motion, I dove to Virgil, grabbed him and my top pack, and made for the hole downstairs by flying. I heard only insane, demonic laughter and the reverberating *BOOOOM* of the bolt as I pushed Virgil ahead of me and we fell rather than climbed down to the floor below. We landed on Kirby, who seemed to be trying to climb the ladder. I punched him a few times in sheer reflex and he yelped and snarled, but we'd hurt him bad in our landing. Before he could react, I'd pushed us both to the door, throwing it open as I grabbed my pack and we made for the shelter of the storm and black impenetrable hills.

We tore through the pouring rain, Virgil and I, running as fast as we could go, leaving the horror behind. It couldn't be. It *couldn't be*. Lightning exploded around us, wind whipping the thunder in with the raging brush and trees on the summit, wracked in turmoil and anger. We ran, terrified, seeing only in frequent flashes of light less or more distant, with raw survival instinct, back down the short connector trail back to the A.T., then automatically stumbling to the north, towards the road that crossed Roan Mountain up ahead, two or three miles maybe.

Perhaps I could flag down a passing car, try to explain the unthinkable thing I'd witnessed, beg for help, pray or pay for rescue. I tried to formulate a plan as we ran across the heath and stone topping Roan. Luckily the slope was nearly flat, with some downhill. It *couldn't be*. We ran, ran, emotion in motion, churning, heaving, rain-drenched, breath harder and faster, gasping, all plans leaving me, succumbing to primal fear. We ran, in abject terror, away from death, and towards it. I stumbled on the wet rocks, skinning my knees, jumping up and running only to crash again. Thunder, raging noise all around, the cannons of hell. Total darkness, then blinding light. We were as likely to be electrocuted on the exposed ridge as anything, or run right off a cliff and fall to our deaths. I kept grabbing Virgil, screaming and flailing just as terrified as I, to avoid losing him. We ran and ran, feral beasts gasping for air, sweating and soaked. *Boom.* I stumbled, and a tree crashed over to our left somewhere. Virgil screamed again. I, we kept running. *Boom.* It couldn't be. It COULD NOT BE. *Boom.* We ran and ran, until I could run no more, until the weight of my pack and my swollen throbbing heart felt ready to explode in agony.

Suddenly the path dropped from under me, and I fell back onto my pack, hitting the ground, sliding down uncontrollably, creating an avalanche of mud and stones and paraphernalia as we went. A branch caught my leg, stabbed me; I yelped and twisted in pain. A rock hung in the pack's hip belt against my side, tearing my flesh. I screamed, not knowing where we would end up, expecting to be airborne at any moment and dead the next.

Then with a painful thud I hit an unnatural flatness, and skidded to a stop: the road, at last. But my revelation lasted only a moment before the avalanche of rocks I'd brought down crashed down on top of me, with murderous bloody impact, and with a final flash and crash and cry of both light and darkness, I blacked out.

A truer Night fell then, a night that crashed in a rain of fire within which there was only a dream, a ghost-image, of remembrances and resigned dissolution. There was a meeting of the minds in my mind, and there we found mocking anonymous laughter, and a profound pool of ink I dared not look in or think about. In it swam beasts of scale and scale; one, reptilian, the other, grotesquely grandiose, cosmic in size and slink. Around the pool was a mirror, circular, reflecting only the darkness I could not look in but swam in nonetheless. I wondered that I did not lose breath and sink in it, heavy as it was, a salten sea, but then I realized I was one of the beasts therein; that I had become less than a man, a mere fish, sucking and gasping in the dark. I pondered in my sea of decisions, their consequences reflected in the mirror surrounding. There, I saw only myself, a primitive creature of the caverns, repeatedly left to my own devices, my own whirlpool of insensate choices, digested into muck. Deep inside, some part of me sought in vain for some appendage, some tentacle I could reach with, release with, to grasp at the surrounding solidity, to escape and evolve into a thing breathing the night air in the real world, to crawl away as best I could, trailing my mucus behind. But I had not the strength nor steam nor stem to brace myself against the current and fight for a new survival on the alien landscape that solidity, true earth, would bring. No; my nightmares ruled me, and I had become them, a fish-man, with bulging protrusive eyes staring only at what-had-been and what was and without will at what must be. Then I saw my twin, my reptilian conscience, the other in the muck with me, and I realized we were one and the same, and as the devourer in me approached to destroy the fish-man soul left of my memories, as impossible jaws opened wide filled with teeth and fire and slime I screamed and screamed and....

I shuddered awake, gulping for air, hypnopompic from the Golden Dreams of Dostoevsky. Twice two made four without either of our wills. No, we were true givers both; our wills gave away our possessions to those we left behind, left standing above us as we were lowered, deeper and deeper into the hole, towards hell, away from the heavens, but yet away from the crying eyes, few or numerous, no matter. The body and the spirit, separated, one above, one below. Lost and found, but mostly lost.

I lay there, shaking, shivering, recovering for nearly a full minute. The storm still raged, lightning flashed, water fell harsh like sharp-bladed saw grass blowing in the wind. I remembered the time when I read the divorce papers, her response to my filing. I remembered the way time compressed itself and how my temples throbbed and my joints hurt. I remembered the piles of past-due notices and bills on the floor, a haphazard throw, to cushion the impact of it all on my feet on the few occasions when I actually got up. I remembered ordering a lot of pizza, and still losing weight. I remembered how whole weekends would pass on my couch, the cheap one bought with the last of my credit, before all the credit in the world stopped, as I had already. I remembered how I stank. I remembered feeling like a fish in a whirlpool. I remembered and remembered and remembered.

Then I remembered running, and falling, and why, and the fullness of the past hour hit me like a train without tracks, and I realized that here, almost six thousand feet above the shores of the sea, I was drowning still, still a fish, still in the whirlpool. The darkness of my dreams had evolved into the darkness of my waking memories, the darkness of deep water soaking my soul in this storm.

The road was a lot, lot closer to the shelter than I remembered. No wonder I'd run smack into it. I could not stand. My professional diagnosis was major concussion, possibly a skull fracture. I lay still on the pavement, knowing no cars would be passing through this pass at this hour, in this weather. A throbbing entered my awareness, dull, then sharp stabs of wincing pain: my left side, my right thigh, my right elbow, both ankles mangled. I was bleeding from at least four places, two of them seriously; unnatural warmth poured wet and fierce from my right leg. The cold high-altitude rain washed my face, fell into my eyes, stinging them, and my cheeks. But, as I tried to move and stench the bleeding, a grayness bloomed, neither consciousness nor unconsciousness, and on some detached intellectual level located near my left kidney, I recognized that I was going into shock. Raw images entered me then, blown in by the wind which took my reason with it, sparkling lights in my head like stars in a sky nearly free from them at the moment, burnt into me by the stabbing electricity that skewered the heavens. In my last effort I rolled over onto my side to put pressure on my bleeding leg, knowing I was passing out. Then, finally, blissfully, a sudden sensation of total warmth, utter calmness, and the void took me down into a grave of somber silence.

*****

The next day began as a long grey day, full of mists and clouds that grazed along the ground. Blacks and whites intermingled, producing shades of colors that were not colors: the colors of stone, lichens, and patrol cars, full of sheriffs and rangers. Sheriffs who listened to the mostly fictionalized story I told in silence, then full of doubt but yet their duty climbed up the path to the shelter to see for themselves. I already knew what they would say. I knew that words could not express the inexpressible. I knew these mountains, and they knew me. Neither of us were strangers to each other, unlike the strangers all around me now, and the strangeness that seeped in the fog like a slow ataxic virus eroding my will and my memory. I knew, *knew*, it could not be, so I knew what the verdict would be, before they said it, before they went, investigated, and came back. *Nothing*, they said, muttering amongst themselves, spitting their tobacco, turning to look anywhere but at me, but all serious, all knowing, judging, perceiving. *Nothing*, they said. I knew what they'd say, even as Virgil and I had been found by the early morning motorist passing through Carvers Gap, followed closely by a ranger on his morning rounds. Within an hour the sheriff and ambulance were there, bandaging my head, my back, my arm, and stitching up my leg and head; but for my eyes, for what they'd seen, for my soul, they could do nothing. I knew I couldn't tell them everything, tell them what had *really* happened, in the ranging tempest of an evening now gone from this reality. I didn't given them names, or details, or anything else. So I told them... enough, barely, in a daze, dazed as I was, just enough to get them to go, to look, to return, and report the inevitable reality that was *Nothing*.

I was questioned for what seemed like an eternity: who I was, where I'd been, why I was here, where I was going. The fact that I'd shipped my I.D. on ahead of me to Damascus didn't help matters, although I had of course memorized my driver's license number, insurance group and member IDs, hair color, eye color, weight, height, and anything else written down in my wallet on some scrap of something. One after another redneck with a badge asked me the same questions, cleverly rephrased, nuanced, enhanced, in the practiced ritual of investigative rite. I insisted I'd seen a violent argument, and left; but, all they found was a titanium pot (mine) and a Whisperlite (also mine), left behind in a hurry. Oh, and some strange coarse animal hair and a few odd worn places in a post downstairs, as if a chain or rope had been tied around it, which only one very young deputy seemed to really think anything of. He seemed to be the smarter of the bunch, to my initial apprehension, but the others quickly shut him down by virtue of their professional rank, political posturing, and physical girth. He skulked over to his car, and never really stopped eyeing me. I avoided him as much as I could. Virgil played along, played the fool, silently, admitting zero of consequence.

Turned out that rolling onto my side had probably kept me from bleeding to death and saved my life. The medics checked me over, stitched my leg where I'd punctured a major artery, field dressed the more vicious-looking wounds, gave me a pill for the throbbing ones, checked my pupils, my blood pressure, my electrocardiogram, my drug use history. I answered all of their questions, concurring with a concussion, and reminiscing wistfully about college and our mutual drug use history while the cops were off comparing stories and radioing back to headquarters. I made it a point to exaggerate the romance and thrill of it, and that along with my professional background helped me bond with the young, liberal medics, which in turn gained me one or two basis points in the eyes of the law. If there's two kinds of people white folk trust, it's doctors and cops. Maybe I wasn't a total whack job after all. One of the medics, a pretty lady from Puerto Rico with dark hair but the blue eyes of her Virginian father, took a shine to Virgil, who was never one to refuse a lady. They checked him over carefully, gently, and he let them, shaken as he was, poor little guy. I made us some oatmeal from my battered pack while we sat there on the pavement, and he ate gratefully, and slowly. The youngest and most fit of the bunch walked up the hill and collected my hiking poles and the rest of my gear I'd strewn behind me on the way down. Amazingly, I'd managed to actually bend one of my titanium Leki's around a old fallen oak, a truly stupendous feat of physics, given that it should have come apart in sections rather than bending. Very luckily, other than the one hiking pole of the two, nothing was seriously damaged. Gregory really does make the best packs in the world.

Truth be told, I knew better than to think we had escaped relatively unscathed. I had escaped from the harshness of my old life down a path perpendicular to it, way back at Springer Mountain in Georgia, at the A.T.'s head. Now, here I was, three hundred eighty miles later, bruised and battered, shaken and stirred, broken inside and out, and only beginning to realize my reality had turned tangential to the path I hiked on, out into the void. The Earth turned in its orbit, staying close to the fire; I had shaken free of its grip, and was headed like a projectile towards a distant emptiness. Still, the gravity of the situation compelled me, and escape, with its velocity, now required all my energy to achieve it.

Getting there was work. Luckily, I happened to be a trained expert. I'd seen confusion, hallucination, trauma aplenty in my practice in Atlanta; in twenty minutes I had them convinced I'd hallucinated the whole thing due to my fall, and that I was beginning to realize it now ("Definitely feeling better," I kept repeating.) Although the medics wanted to load me up and ship me back to civilization; the sheriffs just wanted my head, for making them hike a whole mile, uphill no less, to check on my delusion. None of them had ever hiked to more than a Dunkin' Donuts from its parking lot by the look of them. The rangers were in much better shape, a quiet, stoic lot, as rangers were wont to be. No, the medics were my real problem now, but there I had them; I knew my rights, among them to refuse treatment, for all my sicknesses, past and present. And refuse I did. Oh, a lot of hand-wringing occurred, from concern and deep doubt, both. But I kept on insisting I was fine, and by then they all knew I was a real doctor, and I knew all the tricks of patient management. I would not be dissuaded from my course. We argued at length, while I cleaned up our breakfast and repacked from the horrid job the investigators made of my pack's contents in their search. The cops almost refused to give me my knife back, and it was only when I said that I understood and offered to let them keep it that they grudgingly gave it back... like I knew they would. After all, what crime had been committed with it?

So it was that in the end, almost four hours from the moment I'd awoken in the morning on the road with my own blood adhering me to the asphalt and the blaring horn of a Jeep Wrangler gently requesting that I remove myself from its path, that for right or wrong, good or bad, I finally regained the trail on the opposite side of the road, leaving the experts to their mystery... and their expert opinion. The cops would of course begrudge my waste of their time, calling me various names in the retelling; a few would wonder, that one young kid in particular, whether I knew more, or hid more, than I had revealed. But it was no matter: I was gone, down the trail, out of their city, county, state, responsibility, holding cell, inbox, filing cabinet, judicial docket, and lives. The old ones would file minimal paperwork; one or two might, *might* call their cousin or brother-in-law or fishing buddy in Damascus or Wytheville or Shenandoah to keep an eye out for me, just in case. But by then, I'd be just another dirty, smelly, hairy thru-hiker, just like all the others. By then, my limp would be gone, my stitches absorbed, my scars well-concealed behind a facade of false *machismo*. Virgil was more problematic; if they mentioned him, I'd be certain to be spotted. No hiding Virgil; he stuck out like a juicy peach in the Gobi. My best hope, our best hope, was to stick to the plan: escape, and anonymity.

Into the woods/to get the thing/that makes it worth/the journeying. So I went back, into the woods. But what thing made this journey worth... this?

An hour from the Gap, we stopped at the Stan Murray shelter for lunch, and was tempted to stay and recuperate. The picnic table and flower petal-littered ground was very inviting, but it would've meant a ten-plus mile day tomorrow. I continued on, through fir and fern, damp in the grey wet air. I walked for a long time, I don't know how long. The day passed by with the miles. The throbbing in my leg waned and waxed as the hours traveled under me. I refused thought and pain alike, like I had refused proper medical treatment. My goal was Maine, nothing else. Stay the course. Virgil bore it well, ever the stoic.

Eight and a half miles later, after a solid four hours of painful downhill walking, I came across an old red barn in a pretty valley, otherwise known as the Overmountain Shelter. It lay along a Revolutionary War historic route of the "Overmountain Men", five hundred colonial militiamen from west of the Appalachians. The fought the Loyalists at the Battle of Kings

Mountain, with guerrilla "Indian" style tactics; due to the slower-loading muskets of the day, the colonials took the day and the mountain, killing one hundred eighty Loyalists, but losing only twenty eight of their own. The British commander was killed when trying to escape through the battle lines. I remembered reading about it seven months ago, every word, every fallen body. It was a beautiful valley in the early evening sun, peeping out from the clouds, clouds now headed east to the sea.

But sanity had turned orthogonal to my state of being, crosswise to my purposes, detached and remote as polar ice, just as cold, and hard. My leg had started bleeding again; I'd have a bad scar, no doubt. I didn't care. I had scar tissue aplenty.

Nevertheless, I tended it carefully, washed it with some sterile saline provided free of charge by my new medic friends, and put pressure on it until it stopped bleeding again. I gently applied some antibiotic ointment, and replaced the gauze bandage, also freely given. God bless the medical profession and the people in it.

The barn was greater concern. It reminded me too much of my previous evening. I walked up to it slowly, quietly, but heard nothing. I yelled at it, asked if anyone was inside, as I dared not go in myself. Nothing. I asked Virgil, "YOU want to check it out?" He just looked at me with his head cocked to one side like I'd told him to remove his own head and eat it. Yeah, fuck that. A pretty stream flowed through the valley to one side of the shelter, and there were two fire rings there, a picnic table, and a nice flat spot free of rock and tree roots, a good place to sleep. I unpacked my tent, and resolved to have a night under the stars; to hell with the demon shelter.

Afterwards, I made us a fire, and we ate. I produced my harmonica, played a few blues numbers, which Virgil always liked to dance to. Only tonight, we weren't in the mood, for dancing, or talking, or doing much of anything except wonder what the night would bring. Would it erase or confound our experiences? After the second number, I found myself out of all energy, exhausted. Virgil was already nodding off, so I got us into the tent and lay on top of the sleeping bags, too sore and spent to even crawl into them.

My dreams fermented in the open air, becoming a noxious poison when I slept, when my guard was down. Vigilance: that was the key. Cognitive flagellation. Beat it out of yourself, with every strained pull of a tendon and every ache of overworked ligaments. The strain of the body replaces the strain of the soul. If I was Catholic, I would have belonged to Opus Dei; if I was Protestant, the Southern Baptists. Guilt as a lifestyle choice. Pressure creates purpose. But my religion was the trail, and a godless religion it was, with nothing in the sky above me but the moving clouds that marked time ticking away. And yet….

Now that I was still and silent, my thoughts returned, and I found myself recalling the events of the previous night. What had happened? It *could not be*; yet, it was, I was certain. My memory never failed me, ever.

Posttraumaticstressdisorderisananxietydisorder...
...thatcandevelopafterexposuretooneormore...
...terrifyingevents...
...thatthreatenedorcausedgravephysicalharm...
...itisaseverandongoingemotionalreactiontosevere...
...traumasuchasthedeathofalovedoneathreattothe...
...patientoralovedoneslifeseriousphysicalinjury...
...orotherlifethreateningconditionoverwhelming...
...normalpsychologicaldefenses...

...thefifthfrenchfinchesfifthfrillyfeathersfringed...
...thefifthfrenchfinchesfifthfrillyfeathersfringed...
...thefifthfrenchfinchesfifthfrillyfeathersfringed...

I screamed then, to stop the incessant flow of thoughts. A primal scream, and finally my feelings acceded to the same wind that had sustained my delusions. Virgil bolted awake, and shook visibly, cowering away from me. I felt terrible, and apologized profusely, reassuring him, but realizing I wasn't going to sleep tonight. I waited the long minutes until he finally fell asleep again, then quietly got up out of the tent, unzipping the fly, and walked out to the embers of our fire and sat down, to stay up and watch the stars, finally visible again in the clearing night.

The good thing about emotions is that they, just like dreams, are transient. Too bad the truth lasts forever, rebrewing them on a whim. *Mobilis en mobile*; yet, *verum est*. I could only hope that sheer physical exhaustion would numb me, the way it always did. Thank God for endorphins, my only treatment for the intoxicating nature of my obsessions. Endorphins, caused by my effort to translate the handiwork of fortune and navigate through it, or at least up to the next ridgeline. And endorphins were chemicals, and chemistry was physics.

Physics, at the extreme. That was the only explanation. The stars in their fusion around me ignited the thought. Ghost production of muon-muon pairs outside of the apparatus. Higgs decays to a pair of taus or photons, 4.2 inverse femtobarns' worth for every three hundred trillion collisions. Decays of unknown particles in the GeV range, unexplained by the Standard Model. Ektopyrotic membranes, in collision. Warped Calabi-Yau manifolds, exhibiting loop quantum gravity, where time is not fundamental; it emerges from the aether of the equations. A mystical clan of secrets, building sand castles, generating microscopic black holes between Switzerland and France; ironically, like people, decaying with time. The High Religion of tomorrow, whose deity deigned to reveal Her secrets only to the Bavarian Illuminati, now headquartered conveniently in Bavaria, Illinois. Her own priests still sought to understand Her. Being no priest, I only knew what I read, understanding little, but knowing forever.

I knew electrons have the right to produce photons by the process of *bremsstrahlung,* but never in a vacuum, never alone. No; a companion nucleus was required, something generating an electric field of its own, with which it could interact in passing, losing energy. Or, a Hawking virtual pair: one disappears forever into the black hole when the other escapes into the emptiness. The same was true of people: even if you just pass them by, they can suck the life right out of you, and worse if any real bond is made. The physics didn't lie. At every scale, by any measure, being alone maximizes our energy, protecting us. Passers-by, acquaintances, friends, lovers: all only take, from the subatomic level on up. We all have rights: the right to exist, free, unperturbed, in trajectory both straight and narrow, and believe in whatever beta release of reality we believe in, whatever it takes to get us from point A to point B.

I had the right to lack both a religion and sanity, for instance, yet believe in physics at the extreme. I had the right to refuse treatment for either, for all, and just continue. I had the right to both believe and disbelieve, to ignore the man behind the curtain.

As I pondered this inconsistency, a voice entered my consciousness; a familiar voice, a real voice, and just like that man, a wizard of sorts. A voice I'd somehow known all along would be there, from an innate knowledge that had prevented me from sleeping this dread evening and brought me out to ponder stars. A voice I'd ridiculed, denounced, but denounced out of that place of fear we cannot speak of lest we recognize openly the coward in each of us. I could see that: could see around the corners, could see myself and the coward within. I feared to face that coward, and face him, but then he came around my corner, or rather the corner of the barn, with his wizard's voice, and with him came my fears to face me whether I willed it so or no.

"So," he began, "it's just physics, is it?" I knew he'd know, know what I was thinking. I knew, like I knew my answer to the question didn't matter for one attosecond.

"You tell me, Padma," I said, acknowledging him, turning to look, and there he was, all cold stone with featureless eyes, and his diabolically faint smile. He regarded me for a moment, looking the same, dressed the same as when we'd first met. The he slowly walked over to the embers by the stream where I sat, and sat down next to me.

"When the snow leopard took the cold of the First Fire away to the mountains," he began, slowly and softly, "he did so because he thought he was doing the right thing. Even his act of selfishness resulted in unintended good: by doing so, he gave man the means to warm himself, cook his food, light his nights... and he gave the mountains their inestimable beauty."

I absorbed this in silent reflection, looking up at the hills around me. I swallowed my fear; I resigned myself to whatever his next words would bring. I waited for him to speak again, for that was the whole point of this moment... wasn't it? To be mocked by... what? Or whom? I didn't know, and was too terrified to ask. I turned back to the night sky, now full of stars.

"Even when we are alone, we are never alone," he continued, watching the stars with me. "There is always something more, something the senses and the animal in us perceives only subjectively and dimly. Something simultaneously created and creating. Ignorance refers to it as *mysticism*. I won't call it religion. The religious say that God is beyond man's power to conceive, yet ask you to believe anyway, without question or consent, to please God, whose pleasure or indeed need for such is an odd *non sequiter* at best, a doubtful artifice at the least. Doesn't sound reasonable, does it? The more enlightened look for the truth in the math, in the ground, in the seas, in the skies. In their intent and methods they lie closer to the truth. Yet, the mysticism remains, and for a very good reason: *to show you your fear in a handful of dust.*" He turned to look at me. "I do not expect one such as you to understand this... *yet.*" I swallowed, hard. "Fear is a product of the animal in you, of your senses and perceptions, of your mysticism and ego, genetic, and acquired. Fear creates lust, greed and gluttony, laziness and selfishness, anger and sullenness, heresy, murder and suicide, betrayal and treachery, and worse. Are you afraid, Durant?"

I forced myself not to look at him, keeping my eyes on the fixed stars. "I am terrified, but it doesn't matter." The sky seemed a great well of possibility and absence, an opening I would fall up into at any moment. "If I feared you, what would it matter? It would accomplish nothing. I am powerless: that is what you are trying to say."

"Brave, but incorrect. On the contrary, you are no such thing," he responded, softer than before. "You have all the power in the world. You said it yourself: you chose to be a balloon, to let the wind blow you where it may. So, where exactly has it blown you?"

I thought about it for a moment. "To you," I said, beginning to understand.

"Not quite. I'm just a vessel, or a vassal perhaps; either description will do. We all serve, whether we choose to or not."

I laughed gently for a moment from the irony of it. "Free will again," I said. "Damn free will. Sometimes I wish it could be taken from me. Is that what you are here for, Padma," I asked, looking at him, "to take the fire from me? Are you the snow leopard? Will you take *my* coldness away? What are you here to do, save me, or damn me?"

He was silent for a long time. Finally he spoke. "You *are* brave, whether you think so or not. As for what I am here to do, the truest answer would be to neither save nor damn, because neither option really exists outside of yourself. Do not regret your free will, Durant. Your ability to choose, to choose the cold, to choose pain, or love, or hope, or fear, or happiness, or sadness, or anything else -- to choose this trail -- your ability to choose is the greatest of your talents and abilities."

"But it's all so... *unbearable*," I said, choking the word out. I suppose I wanted to be damned; why not ask him for it, to do to me what I'd already done to myself.

"Why is it unbearable?" he asked.

"Why? Why? Of all the... because it is, because it has been! *Why?*" What was this? Wasn't it Judgment Day? Didn't he know? Who was I to explain such to... to....

"All right, if you say so. Then, reason with me a moment. Suppose I were to say this: suppose you were absolved of all responsibility for your actions. Would that suffice?"

"Of course not," I answered. "I've done such... *wrong*. The wrong exists, whether I feel responsible for it or not."

"So why do you do wrong? Is it because you want to?" he asked.

"No!" I said. "Once I thought... that maybe if... maybe if I tried harder…."

"Are you trying your best or aren't you? Surely, you would know."

Such simple questions. "It depends! Not always! Sometimes! SHIT!" I was agitated now, beyond terrified at this line of questioning. "I don't know!"

"Ahhh, doubt. There is always doubt, and stubbornness. If there is always doubt, and you cannot know if you are trying your best, then how can you know if the wrong you claim to have done is really your fault or not?"

I had no response. The doubt was what it was. I shook, from fear and not the cool spring evening.

"So the possibility is open that you have not really done anything, not been sinning at all," he said, very, very quietly.

"Sin!?" I said, wondering at the implications the word, and his use of it, meant. "You mean, as in *God?*"

He pointedly ignored the question. "Or is it that you don't regret you sins so much as you fear punishment for what you have done? Is all this talk of free will and responsibilities mere shadow? If that's true, why don't you just ask God not to punish you?"

I inhaled, then burst out in nervous laughter. "Shit! I doubt *God* would grant such a request," I managed after a moment.

"Really?! You don't say! *You* know what God will or won't do, eh? Well, suppose that despite your ego you were granted a special dispensation: henceforth, you may sin as much as you like, no matter what, and God will never, ever punish you for it in the least. Would that be enough to talk you off this mountain?"

I stopped laughing, looking at him sideways. I could see the stars reflected in the darkness of his ever-present sunglasses. What did his eyes look like? What did they really see?

"No thanks," I said. "The wrong would remain with my guilt, regardless. I'll remain a balloon here, if it's all the same to God."

"What if God removed you *abhorrence* of sinning, so that no matter what you did or didn't do, all of your guilt and negativity was erased, immediately, as if it never was? A magic pill, if you will; the ultimate antidepressant, anxiolytic answer to everything."

"Balloon, please. The knowledge of what I've done remains."

"So, you decline my offer of a guilt-free, pain-free life?"

"Yes," I said warily.

Without warning, he turned, and grabbed my arm. "What if I *commanded* it!" he shouted at me. "You MUST accept!"

"STOP!" I cried out, pushing myself backwards on the ground.

The moment froze, then he laughed at me, all impenetrable smiles and calm again. "Hmmm... seems your free will comes in pretty handy after all."

Motherfucker. He'd cornered me. I stayed where I was, in the meadow grass where I'd stopped. He turned back to face the stars again, dimly lit in reds by the glowing coals. "Imagine the bind you put God in," he continued. "If He gives you free will, you suffer; if He takes it away, your past suffering remains a scar on your soul, or you proceed to harm one another blissfully and cluelessly with no end in sight. There is no right answer."

"No wonder gods and men anger one another so often in... *literature."* I refused to say *history*. Faithless is as faithless does.

He feigned shock. "But what could God have done?"

"Not given us free will in the first place, perhaps? God hands us a contract, a contract we never sign, never see, never agree to, then *He* expects us to live up to it." Pure trite bitterness.

He looked down, then back up at me. "But you already know what the alternative would mean, and you've no desire to be a philosophical zombie. A sentient being without free will is an impossibility, a metaphysical absurdity. But let us try this. Suppose God were to create a new you, in a brand new universe, a brand new spacetime continuum. For all practical purposes, this new universe and your copy in it will be exactly that: a clone, a doppelganger, except that right now God has the choice to create the new you with free will or not. In fact, God has carved His choice on a tablet of adamant, unbreakable stone, immutable and irrevocable for all time. The choice has already been made, by God Himself, and you have no input or responsibility for it, but its consequences are yet to be; yet, being omnipotent, He knows the consequences already, and therefore the blame lies entirely with Him, and all good or evil that comes out of that choice lies with Him as well, does it not? Now, the question: *how do you hope God has chosen?*"

The moon glowed overhead, full and soft, rising with the hours. The was a long distant howl of a lonely coyote far away, then, a thrice distant answer, barely audible. Were the two adversaries marking territory, or lovers in search of each other? Was there a real difference? Did it matter? *Well, shit, Sherlock.* "I see your point," I said.

"Good. Now, that's enough bullshit about free will and sin, right? Right."

Bullshit about...? "Are you Satan?" I asked, unable to take the tension. "Are you here to tempt me? Is that it?"

He grew genuinely angry, or so he seemed. "Why do you persist with such foolishness when the answer is right in front of you? Tempt you? How can He tempt you if God created you the way you are, knowing what you would be and do and not be and not do, yet allowed you to be who you are, here right now, with me, anyway? Merely to test? Merely to damn? Do you think God a mere puppeteer? Do you think God would be so wasteful with His souls that He would create and build such a paradise as *this,"* he gestured around, "yet spiritually destroy for all eternity so many of the beings He created and built to admire His handiwork in the first place? Do you think God and Satan are one and the same? Do you think them both frivolous and unforgiving spendthrifts who waste their limited resources only to dispose of their investments with endless, eternal cruelty and malice? What could you, a lone human, possibly do in thirty or fifty or seventy or ninety years' time, that would merit punishment, not for ten times that time, not a million times that time, not a million billion trillion quadrillion times a million billion trillion quadrillion times that time, but *forever? Who* is *God* to be so unendingly *cruel?* And *who* are *you* to think yourself or your actions or your tiny slice of time here on this rock so... *important?"*

The breeze blew hard for a moment, finally turning from cool to cold. Even now, in spring; even now, with the very fires of Hell at hand. Or was the cold a sign that hell was somewhat different than the masses expected, a sign that Padma was right?

"I have a joke for you, an original like yourself," I answered. "A hen, a djinn, and a Finn walk into a bar in Norway. The bartender asks the hen, What's your pleasure? The hen says, I'll have a Cock. The bartender produces a rooster, and the two of them go at it until they both fall over dead. The bartender asks the djinn, What's your pleasure? The djinn says, I want a Bottle. The bartender hands him a fifth, and he drinks it and every other bottle up in the place, but falls over drunk into one of them, and gets stuck in his stupor. The bartender asks the Finn, What's your pleasure? The Finn says, I need to borrow a pen and a piece of paper to write you a note that will convince you and all of your people to give me Norway. The bartender is incredulous. You're going to write me a note that will convince me and all of my people to give you Norway? he asks. What makes you think you can do that? Because, the man answers serenely and confidently: *the Finn is mightier than the fjord*."

Padma looked at me for a second, the reared back and laughed: long and hard. "That..." he finally managed, "that... was the strangest, worst joke I've ever heard."

"Thanks," I said as he continued to chuckle. "It's all in the timing. Hear a lot of good jokes, do you?" I knew he didn't, just like I now knew he wasn't human. *Nobody* ever laughed at that joke before; at least, no one who didn't want something from me.

He stopped laughing, but kept the shadow of his smile. "I take it your fear has left you then? Have you decided to face what you must?"

I sighed, and reattached. What choice did I have? I got up, walked back over to the fire, sat down next to him, and paraphrased Frank Herbert. "When the fear has gone, only...."

"You *and* I will remain," the mind-reader finished.

I turned to look at him. "If I left now, and hiked down and went home…."

"Then you would go home, back to the life you had, knowing only the memory that remains, the disquiet you have felt, the strangeness you have known. In a few years your own mind would wrap itself in a protective cocoon of the familiar and comfortable. Eventually, after many many years, you would deny all of it, yet it would eat at you, a sinuous cancer of your mind, a fire that would never die until it consumed you from within."

"Because *I cannot forget!*" I cried out. "I never forget! Words, people, names, faces...."

He took hold of me again, but this time gently, but firmly. "*That is why it must be you*," he said. "*You* would *never* forget the lesson... but the real lesson has yet to be learned." He let go of me, then stood up, looking down at me. I waited for him to say something, but all that passed was the night breeze, gusting a little harder now along the cliff face.

"I have the free will to refuse," I said.

"And the free will to remain," he replied instantly. "If you go now, you will remain in an unceasing limbo of doubt and questions, and in time deny what you have experienced. You will choose to empty yourself of it, and find you cannot do so. You will remain a balloon, here or there no matter, pressure creating no purpose. Evolution will *not* occur in the form and time intended. You will remain trapped by your past, a prisoner of the passing days, until the hours in them accumulate one after another after another until they finally piledrive helplessly into the singular whimpering period at the end of the very last sentence you utter on the day you die."

I choked on his words, felt them stab me, tear at me, and I felt the aches and pains in my body flare up, and I suddenly imagined myself old, alone, with this same pain now and forever, shoving back the tears at the thought and the knowledge that he was right. "I will go on as I am now," I said. "As you are now," he answered. Of course, I'd known the truth of it all along, but the trail was a forgetful place where the truth dissolved with every sunset. I'd become more alone than solitary. Alone, and yet....

"*Who ARE you?"* I whispered, hoarsely.

"What answer could I possibly give that would satisfy you? Suppose I said I am God, I am Ganesh, I am Jesus, I am Thor, I am Satan, I am Mohammed, I am Buddha, I am an alien, I am a delusion, I am you, I am all of them, I am none of them. What would you believe?" He knelt back down next to me, face pressed up close to mine. "Look at me, and you tell me: what do *you* see?"

"I... I don't know," I said, my voice shaking, as I stood up, to get away, run way, to get anywhere but here.

"See? To you, words *don't* mean a thing. Perhaps ignorance is the thing you should ask God to free you from," he said, standing back up. "Perhaps ignorance is the real damnation. Perhaps Hell is the place where knowledge and physics dies and the mysticism wins out. Perhaps free will exists to provide you with a limited-time opportunity to free yourselves from your own intellectual blindness, from the animal and fear within. Ask yourself whether the dream of heaven and light and splendor should be waiting for you in your grave, or whether it could be yours -- yours, theirs, anyone's -- here and now and on this earth, in *your* life. Perhaps that is what God really meant when He said... *LET THERE BE LIGHT!!!*"

Suddenly his voice boomed, and his words became rolling thunder. Lightning flashed across the open sky, the stars ignited with a sudden jeweled radiance of a trillion suns, the moon exploded in blinding silver flash, as he removed his glasses and looked at me with eyes that were twin neutron stars ablaze with white-hot searing fire, as I cried out, falling backwards, down on to stone that instantly melted into a searing dark whirlpool of formless cold lava that dissolved into nothingness, opening up under me, and screaming mindlessly into the depths I fell and fell and fell and fell and....

V

Somewhere along the Appalachian Trail

A large wet eye regarded me balefully. I blinked; it blinked back. It angled slightly; up, down, diagonally. Whiteless, inky, it rotated a quarter-turn, blinked again. It seemed neither friend nor foe, but an interim indeterminate breed of hesitant curiosity. I felt neither fear nor fearlessness from it; nor it, it seemed, me. I also felt a cold stickiness, mucosy, on my nose, and an ever-so-slight pressure, like tiny rubber shoes, gripping. Above the eye, a lone cloud in the background, thin and near transparent, and the color of scattered sunlight on a still spring day. I reached up, slowly, very carefully, and plucked the misplaced salamander from my face.

I sat up and opened my hand, looking at my new passenger. His red spots offset his slick black body, impossibly tiny. I looked up, forward, then behind me. I was in the middle of a trail, *The* Trail I suspected. I leaned over and released him carefully in the mud, near a warm puddle, so he wouldn't dehydrate and dry out like so much salamander jerky.

I knew who I was. I knew what I'd done, where I'd been, who I'd been, and what I'd seen and heard. What I didn't know was everything else.

It is said of the Maelstrom that the sailors caught in it could see all the way down to the bottom, where the crust meets the cold, and see the other ships wrecked there, wrecks full of the silent sated. Those dead had also seen the bottom, also seen the land of the dead, before they were swept down to join it in their mutually quenched thirst for death. It was also said that for all those who saw that land that it was too late, past the point of no return, and there was no escaping. This was known, a sailor's fact taught in no school of the Queen's, like the dragons at the end of the world, like the isles of beautiful half-naked natives strewn across the Pacific like pearls on a silk string, like the treasure and gold and adventure that awaited even the lowliest deck hand, before their first voyage at any rate when it was still a youthful naive dream boasted about in the docks or inside a rundown dockside tavern. It was known, true, unassailable; yet, how anyone actually knew it, when everyone who learned of it by definition died in the process of learning it, was itself unknown. Unknown, like how anyone actually avoided being eaten by the sea monsters at the end of the world, or why it was that no one ever returned with gold or plunder or beautiful girls of their own, save an occasional captain or more likely their noble patron; yet, still the young men were driven by dreams of hopeless hope to attempt and tempt the unknown nonetheless. Most sailor's facts were like that: a seasick mélange of the illogical, irrational, impossible; the known and the unknown, bitter in taste, rough in texture, hard to swallow, and harder to keep down. I'd never been a sailor; hell, I'd never even learned how to swim. But I knew the Maelstrom, and the kraken, and the unreachable chest of treasure. I even knew of an unreachable chest or two. I knew the tales. I'd sailed my ship through those tales... all the way to their bottoms, to the land of the dead. Which, I imagined, was where I was now.

My jaw hurt. My feet were damp and cold. I had to pee like a racehorse.

An enormous milk thistle greeted me to my left. I found myself automatically fact-checking: introduced species, native to the Med and North Africa, toothed and thorny and spiky to discourage foraging (effectively so), fully of milky sap from whence its name derived. An extract, silymarin, is used to treat liver disorders: hepatitis, cirrhosis, drug damage, and certain poisonings, especially from the death's-cap mushroom, *Amarita phalloides*. Early settlers, bringing seeds unwittingly with them across the sea, had used it as such, on rare occasions when someone was stupid and/or drunk enough to avoid or ignore the teachings of their elders and consume the *Amarita* in the first place. Thistle even protected the liver from long-term exposure to really bad things like toluene, though the settlers had never found such in these hills. No; us Latter-Day white folk schlepped in the toluene with our saturated, hydrogenated religions, and the rest of it.

I stood up to take a leak. That's when I noticed Virgil. He was sitting low in a tree right next to me, regarding me quietly. I unzipped and peed in his general direction as I said good morning. My head felt like a used punching bag filled with baloney and rainbows. I wondered what would go better with baloney: the thistle, or the mushrooms? The mushrooms would go with the rainbows, at any rate.

I'd been saved, Virgil with me, but it was a strange salvation, like a cure from which one gained addiction. The incessant pills of modern psychiatry seemed tame by comparison; but I guessed that *psychiatry* in a manner of speaking was the whole point of this. Behavioral therapy. Play acting to resolve cognitive dissonances, dissonances in the clashing keys of *Be* and *See*. Only, this time, there was no play, nor was there acting. I had to see past the inkblots to their inner Atlantean meanings. If I'd carried some aluminum foil with me, I would have made a hat of it; but somehow, I knew the microwavability of my head wouldn't matter a whit. Too bad, Brad; everything I had left was polyester and nylon, nothing to block the NSA's mind-control microwaves with. Maybe a wet towel around my head would work, like it did for Schwarzenegger in *Total Recall*. Damn, I wished Sharon Stone was the one chasing me. *That* would be ecstasy. Instead, this was more akin to St. Theresa's adventures, just relocated to Mars. Some ecstasy, this. Who or what was sending me these visions? Allah, or Iblis? Satan, or God? A tumor? Space aliens? Is this what Paul experienced on *his* trail to Tarsus? Was Padma my Fatima? Or, was I just bloody Birmingham bonkers?

"I don't know about you," I said to Virgil, "but this looks like a job for the Masked Avenger." No comment, just a stare. *Not a fan*, I guessed. Oh well, neither was I. I finished my business then reoccluded the Mahdi.

I was wearing my pack, hip belt unattached, chest strap undone, but shoulder straps on. It is probably more accurate to say that I was lying on my pack and got up with it on. It felt packed and balanced correctly. That was totally at odds with my last waking memory, a memory of fear, fire, and falling. There were words that burned in that fire, a brimstone hail. Truth was a harsh mistress, one who would ride you hard and long, talking and taking as they say, only to leave you empty, penniless, and alone. Only now, I wasn't alone; I had Padma, or whatever he, or she, or it, was. I guess one can't escape the Truth after all. The Mistress always returns, in a changed form. If I was a balloon, I was a child's balloon, tied on a string and carried from one amusement to another. The wind only blew me as far as that string would stretch; I might strain to fly away in a breeze, but that was the extent of it. Someone else, some... *thing* else, was in control. Maybe he/she/it had always been there. Maybe I had only recently attracted he/she/it's attention. It didn't really matter. What mattered was the knot in the string that held me, the Truth of it, the Mistress. Metaphors, mixed, with sweat and stone and sky.

So, time to pick a direction. North was the correct one. But, which way was that? I didn't carry a compass; this was the Appalachian Trail for God's sake, not some bushskirting ecotour for spoiled rich hipsters in the Pantanal. Heck, the whole trail was originally conceived as a place where people would live and make stuff, like a big, long, skinny arts and crafts festival that never ended. Even without the hippie dream, as just a trail, it was like hiking up I-95 from Savannah to Bangor: a thoroughfare of trails, with plenty of offramps -- and never, ever more than nine miles from the nearest road, Maine excepted of course. At least, it should have been that easy. Now, it was a trail to someplace else.

Then it occurred to me: *how do I know this really IS the Trail?* Maybe this was a simulacrum, a vision, a simulation. In that case, one direction was as good as another; the plot would find me. Or, maybe it was part of the test, and I had to use my wits. Or maybe I *was* bloody Birmingham bonkers... but, if it was a simulation, or a hallucination, or any other kind of nation, it was a damn detailed one. But such detail could only mean one thing: I was meant to believe, to have faith; to circumambulate the Kaaba and Ishmael and Mother Hagar and Abu Simbel; to Hajj for Hajj's sake. The purpose of ritual is to reinforce the idiot in us all, compulsiveness as a control mechanism, to implant and chant and never recant, with the added magics of gilt and gold, Latin and Shahadah, frankincense and myrrh. Magic, and stupid simplicity; like a big doobie, really. We know the world is made of magic, but we fear it. To soothe our shaking, we assume there is a magician behind it, and go through the motions meant to appease Him or Her or It or Them. Just another sailor's fact, another tale about the unknowable Maelstrom. I had always assumed that the world's magic lacked a Magician. I had assumed there was no man behind the curtain, and paid no attention, per instructions given Dorothy. But, you know all about "assume": it makes an ass out of me and....

Well, me, at any rate.

Yes, it was damn detailed. I noticed the dew: on the thistle, on the tree Virgil sat on, on the grass around the edges of the trail. Dew and light meant morning. The sun was to the left down the valley. Bingo: I was facing south, and north was behind me. Why face one's yesterdays? I gathered up Virgil, said my goodbyes to the salamander, turned towards my qibla, and proceeded north.

As we walked I began to notice certain interesting bits of flotsam. My boot laces were tied; they'd been undone when I'd walked out of my tent to sit by the fire. Heck, half my pack was strewn about last I remembered it; yet, here it all was, an ultralight monkey on my back. My socks were damp, but not from water: sweat, as if I'd worn my boots all night, which I imagined I had. I was wearing the same clothes, but they were clean. Did somebody bathe me in them? I looked around at the terrain. The ridge I was sideswiping, and those around me, were no more than a few hundred feet high. If I was still on the Trail, still heading north, I was at least in Virginia already. Then I made a slight turn around a hill I was rounding and caught a glimpse of larger ridges ahead, a few thousand feet maybe. Within five minutes my feet confirmed my eyes; I was headed up again. I knew it wasn't the rugged hills of the Cherokee National Forest, the Nantahalas, or the Smokies further south. The salamander, plant life, humidity, and altitudes suggested Virginia. I kept moving.

As I began to climb, as my breath ran short, for some strange reason an impulse to whistle came over me. I'm not sure why. I'd never really whistled in the past. I mean, I whistled, but not as a rule. I mean, I didn't have anything against whistling, but I never really... had much to whistle about. I didn't really know any songs. I mean, of course I knew some songs: every damn song I'd ever heard I knew, even all that kill-me-now Christopher Cross suburban-mall-elevator-ride tripe that stole the Album of the Year from Pink Floyd's *The Wall*. (*All* four major Grammy awards? No, seriously: *all* four? Were the Grammy judges all out *Sailing* on Quaaludes that year or something?) What I mean is I didn't know any whistling songs. I wondered if there was such a thing. I imagined a late-night cable advertisement for some lousy compilation album: *Top 100 Songs That Are Normally Associated With The Act Of Whistling And Not Heard Otherwise Arranged.* I pondered what was on that album, and came up with nothing. No wonder it wasn't flying off the shelves. The closest I could get was those damn Magic Pan Flute albums that were all over TV in the 70s and 80s. Thank God that fad had lived its day and died, just like Christopher Cross, or his career anyway.

Then, an official white blaze on a tree: we were still on the A.T. or its reasonable facsimile for sure. A brain cell devoted to finding something to celebrate the event with came up with a bouncy number that prominently featured whistling: "Always Look on the Bright Side of Life". Ah yes, a little Monty Python. I recalled that Pink Floyd often interrupted their studio sessions to watch *Monty Python's Flying Circus*. As I processed that, I found myself singing and whistling.

> *Always look on the bright side of life...*
> *(Whistle whistle, whistle whistle whistle whistle)*
> *Always look on the light side of life...*
> *(Whistle whistle, whistle whistle whistle whistle)*

And so Virgil and I ascended the ridge, singing and whistling as we went. Virgil started whistling too, although he clearly didn't know the words, or the key, or how to keep a beat, or much of anything else. To each his own.

Damn, my head was all over the place today. There's no accounting for some things, and not enough for others.

Perhaps that's why I climbed: to see farther. But what was it Padma had said? *And what is it that you are finding? A rock? A tree? The next turn in the path? It leads only to another turn, another tree, another rock. But of course, you already know that.* No, he was wrong; I really didn't know anything. I knew it was dark and raining somewhere and that I was blind. Was blind, and did not see. I was just another point on an evolving wave function whose very objectivity was debated. When did the collapse occur? Was it gravity, God, or just us guys? Who was the Observer that did the Observing? My position was probability, my momentum absolute. But knowing both to certainty was impossible. Why? I guess certainty was as impossible to engineer as deathlessness. Which implied God has His limits. Interesting. Taking the limit to infinity, was there an integral that provided an answer? I doubted its very derivity. It seemed falsity was bred into the nature of things. A power series might converge to some truth, but I sensed orthogonal polynomials instead. I had no solution, just an unknown, an argument. X to this f(X). X was blind, f(X) did not see. No, I had no idea why I climbed, because I saw no further now at my f(X) than I did at my original X. All I knew was that Padma was one helluva function, an improbable combinatorial, a diagonal slash not in any set of mine. My set was an empty one, containing only me.

One thing only comforted me: that life now seemed a hyperbola, no longer elliptical and predictable and repetitive and ho-hum and redundant. It had achieved trajectory, its curve slope, its vector direction and tensor. Hyperbolic hyperbole here in Hyperborea. The collapse of the function no longer seemed possible, likely, or even desirable; objective reality from such a collapse had become a thing of the past. Even the past was in doubt; if the present could not be relied upon, what could? Relied, as in *re-lied.* Again and again and again. Einstein had been misquoted as saying all was relative, but maybe it was, or maybe he really said it and had been mis-misquoted. Or maybe, maybe, maybe, maybe. Maybe the wave function had yet to collapse, and we were all along for the ride in a sea of probabilistic unresolved illogical irrational superimposed multiversal nonsense waiting for the Observer to open His eyes and give a shit enough to force us into a single state of objective resolved logical rational coherent universal sanity in one big *whoosh* of Rapture and/or Armageddon and/or Ragnarok and/or whatever it took to beat us into submission. Regardless, I soared, on the wings of obtuse angels, on this rocket trajectory, up, up, and away in my beautiful, my beautiful balloon... and I had yet to collapse into a damn thing.

So there.

I imagine a contessa in Palm Springs or Palm Beach or someplace overbuilt with consciously-placed palms becoming aware of these facts. I imagine her sitting by a fire late on a rainy night like this one, alone, lights out, sipping her *Côte d'Or* not realizing it's really a mere *Languedoc-*

Roussillon, or, My Hand To God, a *Sangria Chilean* bought at auction by her well-meaning but senseless buried fourth husband. Then, suddenly, a thought, and another and another, and out of nowhere a genuine Buddha-scale enlightenment occurs. She drops her glass, the crystal splaying in high frequencies complicit with its collision with cold marble. It would be like a fluff poodle suddenly realizing that the moon was there.

Ah yes, that must be it: why God did not reveal Himself to us. We'd explode, our frail assumptions shattered, our delicate balances unbalanced, the biological, illogical myths that support us and insulate us from the awful cold replaced with a colder formal proof: *Here I Am, Here I Remain*. A few, maybe, close to the truth, would survive the change, but most of us, most of our beliefs, would lack hospitable accommodation, without even a lowly manger in which to swaddle. The Southern Baptist, the Al Qaeda terrorist; the rich atheist who voted for Bush, the poor animist who lived in the bush; the believer, the disbeliever, the nonbeliever, the transbeliever; the butcher, the baker, the candlestick-maker: *all* could not possibly be right. No; for most, revelation would mean revolution, the light bringing a personal darkness. All the religions of the world said so, anyway. A few called the process *enlightenment*. Most just called it Hell. A staunch believer in democracy, I assumed the majority were right. The Second Coming would bring only chaos, pain, and death, regardless of who or what it was that came that second time. Perhaps the just thing was to make it a First Coming instead, the arrival of some *One* completely unexpected, and damn everybody. That, at least, would be democratic. God as humans viewed Him never made sense to me: what sort of well-intentioned Creator would damn most of whom He created? Where's the sense or justice in that? Either we were wrong, or He was nuts. *Ego*, I had hoped we were alone. *Ergo*, I had hoped we were not. I still feared, wanted, needed both. Stupidity as comfort food. Ignorance as bliss. There is another world which our senses only dimly perceive, being dim and all. Being dim, we require dimness, the Light turned low. Otherwise, if He came, He'd bring everybody one helluva sunburn.

So why couldn't He have made us more... resilient? Adaptable? Capable? Endurable? Accepting? Intelligent in the deeper sense? Deeper in the intelligent sense? Maybe... maybe that's what all this was. An education of sorts. Trial by fire. Surviving the crucible, silencing the voices within that would have possessed us. Evolution... in the form and time intended? Or, not so much? Light and dark, making shadows. Children believe in their own rightness, from their perspective of utter callousness and self-absorption. *What do they know?* we ask. *Someday*, we reply to ourselves with pained but knowing nods. And if we look at children as blissfully, innocently, demonically ignorant, what must a god, not even our own species, not even corporeal, think of little ol' *us*?

Maybe... God had to learn too, how to be God. Maybe He had to grow up. Maybe He had to change, had changed. Maybe it wasn't over, maybe God was still evolving, maybe God *would* change. Which made for a *really* terrifying thought.

Enough. I had to stop and drink for a bit. I was tired, it was hot, my mind was on overdrive. I was use to hiking thoughtlessly, not this endless exuberant terror and existentialism. Blah blah blah.

As if an answer to my prayer, I came up and out onto the ridge top, and pavement. It was an old two-laner, with a low stone border betraying its origins in the Great Depression and the New Deal. It wound itself out on the top of the ridge, paralleling the Trail, both of them headed up, entwined in bliss. I admired the views into the valleys below. I kept walking, and after a bit I saw a sign on the road. I bravely bushwhacked off the trail, a few feet at most, and saw the sign proclaim that this was the Blue Ridge Parkway, confirming that I was in Virginia.

The Parkway was an engineering marvel and an ecological disaster, running four hundred fifty nine miles from Oconoluftee, just inside the Great Smoky Mountain National Park in North Carolina, to Swannanoa, Virginia and I-64 at Rockfish Gap, where on the other side of the interstate it turned into Skyline Drive, the main drag leading into Shenandoah National Park. It was a tortuous serpentine route, a hundred twenty miles longer than needed, just to get in all the views and provide sufficient work for the work teams of unemployed and, later, conscientious objectors that had build it. It had taken fifty-two years to complete; I even remembered the opening of the last segment all the way back at Grandfather Mountain in North Carolina, twenty-two years ago. I'd been there, at that event, with a girl of copper hair and emerald eyes. We'd driven it in her struggling blue Toyota Tercel on our graduate-school budgets. I looked at the pavement.

We'd been here, right here, all those years before. I'd never hiked this far up the Trail, but still my heart had been here. Now my heart was like the road: old, bleached, and cracked. After a moment, I sighed, and releasing both heart and eye, I returned to the trail and the incessant hike.

We didn't have to wait long. After a short walk back down the lee side of the ridge, still close enough to hear traffic, a shelter appeared. *Cornelius Creek Shelter*, the sign said. My brain went into search mode. It flipped through the list of trail shelters while I stopped and pulled out the map. I located us simultaneously in both paper and perception, placing myself back in the real world: I was somewhere between Buchanan and Snowden, Virginia, a few days from Shenandoah itself. I passed the shelter and kept walking.

Well, that was a quick…

…OvermountainShelter8.7milesto
AppleHouseShelter9.3milesto
MountaineerFallsShelter9.6milesto
MorelandGapShelter7.9milesto
LaurelForkShelter8.8milesto
WataugaLakeShelter6.8milesto
VandeventerShelter6.8milesto
IronMountainShelter7.6milesto
DoubleSpringsShelter8.3milesto
AbingdonGapShelter10milesto
ThePlace9.6milesto
SaundersShelter6.4milesto
LostMountainShelter12.2milesto
ThomasKnobShelter5.1milesto
WiseShelter5.9milesto
OldOrchardShelter5milesto
HurricaneMountainShelter6.7milesto
RaccoonBranchcamp2.4milesto
TrimpiShelter10.6milesto
PartnershipShelter7.1milesto
ChatfieldShelter7.2milesto
DavisPathShelter11.3milesto
KnotMaulBranchShelter9milesto

ChestnutKnobShelter10milesto
JenkinsShelter14milesto
HelveysMillShelter9.8milesto
JennyKnobShelter14.2milesto
WapitiShelter8.4milesto
DocsKnobShelter15milesto
RiceFieldShelter12.5milesto
PineSwampBranchShelter3.9milesto
BaileyGapShelter8.8milesto
WarSpurShelter5.8milesto
LaurelCreekShelter6.4milesto
SarverHollowShelter6milesto
NidayShelter10.1milesto
PickleBranchShelter13.6milesto
JohnsSpringShelter1milesto
CatawbaMountainShelter2.4milesto
CampbellShelter6milesto
LambertsMeadowShelter14.4milesto
FullhardtKnobShelter6.2milesto
WilsonCreekShelter7.3milesto
BobbletsGapShelter6.4milesto
CoveMountainShelter6.9milesto
BryantRidgeShelter5milesto
CorneliusCreekShelter5.3milesto...

hmmm... at least 380 miles further for what I assumed was a single day (but there I went, assuming again). By all rights, it would be late May; no, early June. But the flowers/the water/the smells/the bird calls/all of it said.... I sighed. I could never be sure.

But for now it was to be the politics of the Maelstrom for me, the land of the dead, the Mistress, the *Amarita*, the cognitive dissonances, the Atlantean inkblots. It was the chaos of Schrodinger's frickin' feline; I was both alive and dead, simultaneously neither and both, needlessly complexified. My my my, I was *all* over the place today. If *this* was the gift of free will, Padma could have it right back. I laughed at him. If he'd read Pynchon, I would tell him to go absquatulate *this*.

I was back up by the road then, and two Porsches zoomed by on the Parkway, honking as they passed, a young twentysomething girl's laughter pureed in its trailing turbulence. It sounded like someone was having a good time. I wondered if it, or she, was real. Then, about forty seconds later, a park ranger followed at a slightly faster pace, with lights churning but no siren. Hah. That seemed real. Up they all went to their respective fates.

Then the trail rounded a sharp turn all three had taken, and suddenly in front of me was a long slow rise, another eight hundred feet or so, over it seemed three or four miles, as the trail moved away again to the left of the road. At the top would be Thunder Hill Shelter, at 3960 feet, nothing like the Smokies, but a hard climb nonetheless, here along Apple Orchard Mountain. I'd spend the night there, at what I knew was the top. It would be a steep descent down tomorrow to the other side, to a valley at 835 feet, then another climb back into the 3000s. A steep descent, downhill all the way, as they say, until it wasn't. Up and down, down and up, like everything else. I watched the Porches and the ranger appear and disappear around the twists and turns, farther and farther up, smaller and smaller as they went.

I didn't stop, just offered the water to Virgil. He'd been completely silent all day since our attempt at whistling, not a word or a note since. Usually this was the time of day when he and I warmed up, both literally and figuratively. But we'd fallen through a rabbit hole into a warren of a Wonderland, and the tunnel led up, and on, and who knew where. What would be waiting for us at Thunder Hill? Would someone be waiting for us there to slice and eat *our* organs?

That thought made me stop. I looked up the trail warily. It was lit up in sunshine now, post-rain, bright, full of life. But I was pressed in on all sides, by mighty trees swaying in the waves of the wind, an ocean full of statues, tall and silent. It closed in with hoots and horns and howls. I closed my eyes to rid myself of the image, finding it inside my eyelids, a projection of my mind and the fear that ruled it. I had free will: Padma had assured me of that. I could leave the trail, maybe hitch a ride on the Parkway, back to civilization and its sanctuary of sweet smiles and sincerities. I could end this. I cocked my head and looked at Virgil, and it hit me. "I didn't bother to ask you," I said. "I'm sorry. Do we go on, or should we best git' movin'?"

"Best git' movin'," my always confident partner voted.

"You sure about that?" I questioned. "Might be a storm comin' up there."

"Storm's comin'," he agreed, but then reaffirmed, "Best git' movin'."

Like the drivers in the Porches, our fates were sealed. Free will was funny like that. Cause; always, always followed by pernicious effect. Virgil was right, as usual: there was a storm coming, but wasn't there *always* a storm coming? It's how we define ourselves as a species. The present of time is the present itself. Our presents open up to the future, every day a bright and shiny Christmastime, full of tinsel and splendor. And when you live like I do, when every waking moment is remembered with every waking moment, you realize the scale is all the same, and the silence, and how far you've come, and how far, how very, very far, you have to go... if you go, or rather, choose to go on.

I chose, we chose, to go on.

OK, the next number in sequence please: six. *The sixth....*

Suddenly there was a loud, fast, sharp *shk-ka shk-ka shk-ka shk-ka shk-ka shk-ka shk-ka shk-ka* in front of me, in the path among the stones. I knew that sound, and stopped. "Hello," I asked the timber rattler. "Would you be the Serpent in this Paradise?"

I half expected an answer, or perhaps even a question, something Eastern-y, full of sonic content, lilting and musical but with little in the way of semantics or practicality. Instead, there was only a hissing added to the rattling.

"BEST GIT' MOVIN'," insisted Virgil, shaking. For once he was right about something, but....

"Just a moment," I insisted, softly, leaning ever so slightly towards our trailmate. "Mr. Rattler, should you be someone else, or something else, or something symbolic of something else, or someone else, or otherwise be from somewhere and/or somewhen else, or are or have been or will be in any regard anything other than that which you appear to be simply and as-is, let me say this: I have no quarrel with you, nor do I want one, nor do I or have I or shall I wish one, unless of course I am predestined or foreordained or are otherwise useless or powerless or defenseless or helpless or otherwise less than that which I would want to be and want to be and shall want to be and...ummm...." At that point I'd lost my train of thought. "Oh, fuck it," I said. "Look, Mephistopheles, I know these contracts people enter into with you have to be air-tight or else really really bad things happen, but I want no bargain with you, OK? No deal. Fuck it. Don't even bother," I said, then walking around him, added, "I mean it. Fuck it. Fuck that. Fuck you."

Suddenly the rattle stopped, and the quiet wood returned. That was *not* normal rattler behavior. *Oh shit.*

"OK, well, I... I..." I stammered after a few seconds, "of course I mean no offense..." I turned away, but then back, adding, "And, I'm not judging you, OK? I'm certainly in no position to judge. I mean, you did what you believed was the right thing to do from your own personal mind-set...."

The violent rattling instantly resumed. I jumped back, startled, waved my hands and Lekis in front of the Beast, backing away as I continued up the Trail. "OK, OK," I said, "we can discuss it later if you really feel that strongly about…."

That's when I noticed my Lekis, the ones I was waving around at the snake, the one I'd bent around a tree or a rock just the other.... *Shit.* It was the same pole. The *same* pole. Not a scratch or a dent from my slide into near-oblivion on Roan. I'd bent the titanium thing into a permanent two-o'clock position, and left it with the medics to dispose of. Yet, here it was, straight as the Pope's mother, *Il Mama dell'Papa. There* was the place I'd scratched the logo on the Wonderland on the slopes of Rainier, and *there* was the place I'd cut the hand straps off when I bought the pair at the NOC in Wesser. It was the same pole. It was *the same* pole.

The power to reverse entropy? Shit. Shit shit shit.

OK, so, somebody cared about me, because they cared about my poles. Or, an impossible facsimile thereof. Hmm. I looked back at the rattler, refocused, gritted my teeth. "I don't know what you are," I said, "but *no deals*." After a moment taken just to be sure there would be no response, turning my back on God-knows-what, heart hardened like a bare-chested Yul Brynner, I headed uphill. *For he shall prove but mine instrument in the devising of such wonders, that he himself hath not imagined.* Behind us, thankfully, the rattle faded into silence.

After a minute of climbing, I said to Virgil, "We're not stopping until we get there and face whatever it is we're supposed to face, OK?" He didn't respond, and I appreciated his quiet determination. My thoughts drifted then, returning to the Trail and the act of walking and breathing. Finally, I relaxed, resigned, as ready as I was going to be. My boots disintegrated into their rhythm, my breath in submission to it, and up we went with the afternoon.

*****

A large, rare behemoth made its way slowly up the Parkway in the golden Virginia sunlight. It was, undoubtedly, the most outrageous recreational vehicle ever constructed by man: the Swyftbyrd Volange Plutonium Prime. The entry steps were made of rare lapis lazuli streaked with golden pyrite from the Kokcha River valley itself, bullnosed by the Swyftbyrd resident stone artist P. Pfeiffer Puffins. The risers were hand-made Murano crystal with embedded flowers shaped like little tires and spark plugs. The ceiling and AV cabinet were covered with rich Corinthian leather and tasteful platinum-and-diamond stud embellishments. The veneer on the dash and steering wheel was redwood burl from Merced. The helm? Equipped with an Illudium Q-36 global positioning system with real-time traffic and weather alerts. The *sálon* featured a custom giraffe (farmed) leather sofa with quadruple electric recliners, and a special *de rigeuer* liquor cabinet covered with more redwood veneer and stocked with signed crystal glasses by Coupures Facilement in Geneva, and decanter from nearby Cruche Chère, no less. The *sálon*, *entré fixeé,* and *le plafond dans le hall* were overhung by a quaint and *ubër*-expensive plastic milk bottle, empty tin bean can, and porcelain plumbing found-art piece by the celebrated Lonnie Holley (curiously titled *The Sand Man's Revenge*). Plasma ceiling lighting shined through Swervouchski crystal.

In the Swyftbyrd Volange Plutonium Prime galley, the chef enjoyed a highly beautiful and stunningly efficient work space; for *cordon bleu* chefs only, of course, *gardé avec le salaire*. The farmhouse style sink was one-of-a-kind, rescued from abandoned barns across the Midwest and hand spray-painted by Y. O. Ming Studios in Jackson Hole Heights. It was surrounded by custom laboratory-ruby countertops created in Switzerland at the LHC. The cabinets were more redwood veneer with doors accented with a special inlay of to-die-for dyed-in-the-wool neodymium, with the added touch of odor-absorbing activated charcoal. The Plutonium Prime also featured a Spreco Del'Soldi Ridicoli-brand 100% automated coffee center and stainless tantalum dishwasher, full high cabinet with laser-fused glass, pantry, utility cabinet with robovacuum, radioisotope-powered refrigerator freezer and an oryx skin-covered dining table. The galley and dining area came fully stocked with utensils with an international feel, if by international you mean Monaco or elsewhere along the Riviera, and not on the inland side of the Coast Road either. The Überlaufruine-brand placemats were hand-woven by pure-blond virgins in a nameless hamlet in Thuringia. Music system, by Porgy and Bass. *L'pied-à-terre pièce de résistance du l'cinéma vérité au l'après-ski.*

But oh, the lavatory. To speak of it required a mute voice and muted organ music in its immutable, divine presence. Porcelain was a mere pot compared to the altar at which one's tush worshiped therein; gold, pure 24 carat gold it was, engraved with orchids and cherubim. Gold down to the bolts that secured it to its titanium undercarriage. Gold, soft and cold, for the proper, pampered pufflesnuffs that would own and enjoy the Swyftbyrd Volange Plutonium Prime.

This was all in stark contrast to the billowing funeral it left in its wake, a noxious toxic trailing cloud of diesel that, if not outright murdering those exposed to it, at a minimum reduced their coveted lifespans by a few minutes per exposure. Now, it made an especially darksome, irksome reek, crawling up the mountain, mile after mile, gallon after gallon after gallon of burned fuel consumed and exhausted, groaning, straining under its load of gold and redwood and lapis and laziness.

In fact, the Double-P had the dubious distinction of producing more cubic meters of pathologically phosgenically puking waste per minute at velocity than a Mack, Hummer, Superfund site dump truck, and Shanghai on a sparkling cherry blossom festival afternoon, combined. Well, perhaps that's an exaggeration: depends on when the oil in the Hummer was last changed. What was certainly true was that no Wall Street bonus in existence could pay for the carbon credits necessary to offset the existence of just one of these evil, flesh-eating internal combustion dinosaurs. And with the rate of Brazilian deforestation being what it was, that seemed as likely to change as human nature.

Short answer: the thing was a big, beautiful killer. An un-silent, un-fast, un-invisible, un-needed one. If the NSA had pointed its satellites in the right locations, and followed the things, and had the right computer programs looking for just the right patterns, they would have seen a trail of slowly withering, browning plants all along the edges of the roads the things travelled on, and grooves, a multitude of parallel grooves in the roadways where the monstrous phallic tailpipes of the basking basilisks had ejaculated liters and liters of sulfuric acid and worse on the asphalt and concrete. But of course the NSA didn't follow the things, or have the computer programs, or look for the right patterns, or watch the right locations, because it's not like these were Muslim beasts or anything. They were mere *recreational vehicles* for Mannon's sake, and nothing says America like *recreational vehicle*.

And what's wrong with that?

*****

I'd just finished my *eight* tongue-twister -- discarding my original *eight great apes ate eight grape crêpes* for the alternative, much more difficult, and newsworthy *Eight Crate's Gates Gaped; Eight Great Apes Escape!* -- when I found the trail veering back up by the road, a road alarmingly producing big black smoke through the trees. *Forest fire*, I thought, from a careless (was there any other kind?) cigarette most likely. But as I got closer, what I smelled wasn't burning spruce and fir, but rather higher aliphatics and aromatics, heterocyclics, and good old reliable tar, with a finishing note of ablated aluminum. Car engine fire. I parted the branches and peered out at the thin ribbon of civilization that passed me by.

On the road was the largest gol-dang vehicle I had just about ever seen outside of a gravel pit or Cape Canaveral. It sprayed and spewed its life essence into the surrounding wood like a deathbed Fidel Castro exhaling his flaming Cohiba Corona Especial backwashed *generalissimo-bravura*-style back through a second flaming Cohiba Corona Especial, despite the fact that *bravura* ended in an *a* and therefore was technically feminine. Up the road ten yards away from it stood two equally gargantuan actors in the drama, male and female. The female wore a royal purple thing, draped like a impregnate Easter, yelling at him, with her arms outstretched and gesticulating, while the male yellee wore a life-affirming, broad flat-brimmed hat with a single, large band, and a belted bush jacket with patch pockets and a buttoned shoulder loop. When the jacket is accompanied by pants, the combination is called a "safari suit". Typically these items are khaki-colored, and this one was typical, although its wearer did not seem the type to gut wildebeest in the Kalahari with a Bowie. He seemed more the type to, well, purchase its skin at Sotheby's via an anonymous phone bid, or have his Bushman porter do the gutting and skinning and scraping and tanning and any other actual work for him.

But then my attention was diverted back to the monster on twelve wheels by the gesticulations of the woman. The man seemed ambivalent, seemed to wave down at the ground, away, as if to dismiss, or deny, or.... But she seemed adamant, almost....

When I grasped what was happening, that someone may be in trouble, I stopped interpreting and bolted towards the bus, pushing through the overgrowth and brush, then up and over the low stone shoulder of the road, and running right in front of the startled pair I ran around the front of the bus to the door. It was automatic, a trained medical reflex. By now, I should have known better. I caught a partial inhale of death, and coughed it back out as a violent reflex of rejection. Suspending my remaining inhales for later, I dashed around, up, and inside.

I stopped, stunned. It was as if I'd stepped out of the wilderness and infernal fire straight into the Taj Mahal. A golden radiance suffused the perfectly chilled and filtered air. There wasn't a microparticle of soot anywhere at all in the interior: not a flame or a smoke or a misplaced dream. It was like a Second Spring sprung from heaven, with angels, and harps, and countless viols, sighing in aspartame sweetness purchased with sweet platinum cards. Rainbows cried. My diaphragm gave, in shock, astonished, irresistible, and I sucked in the perfume and the presence, and after a moment, as I slowly exhaled, all perdition left me, and I expressed the inexpressible with the only words that came to mind.

"What th…."

I stoned, looking at the same woman, the same man, sitting *inside* this temple to vanity, in plush impossible chairs, the man smoking a Meerschaum pipe and reading the WSJ, the woman watching *Fancy Lissom* on a flatscreen in the wall, as if nothing had happened. I realized I'd been fly-papered, hooked by a worm, insert other lower life-form metaphor here. I should have known better, by now. Oh well; *que sera sera*. After a few seconds, they still hadn't noticed me. I realized the TV was shouting, and shifted my eyes to it.

Fancy was out-acting her typical acting-out self, self-righteous, self-serving, self-centered: a lugubrious, puissant pulchritude (a.k.a. large, putrid pussy). "People, we have got to *do* something!" she concluded, evidently not in conclusion. "Where are the men in this? Where are the *fathers* of these children? Let me tell you," sandbar-driven to answer her own question, "I just don't think I can let that go right now. I... just do not think I can... Well, let's unleash the lawyers. Let's see the lawyers, please, Ted." An off-screen male voice attempted a few initial syllabic interjections but was wiped out by the mop-headed star intent on cleansing the room of stain. "But YOU all know that *fact* can be argued at trial. YOU know the *law,*" she rolled out of her eyes via the side of her sarcastic snarl, as the male voice died off in submission. "In many jurisdictions, it can be given as the law to the jury by the judge, and the prosecutor could argue forever, for nothing. All it takes is some sympathetic jury and some Al Sharpton press conference and before you know it...."

"Yes," the woman murmured, mesmerized. "Oh, yes."

"Falderal," I said abruptly, catching the woman's attention for the first time. She started, staring at me for a moment, then continuing as if my presence were....

"Falderal?" she said, "Don't know what you mean."

"A showy but worthless trifle, " I said, defining the word for her, adding, "as always." Looking around, I multiplied, "As opposed to this showy and highly *expensive* trifle."

It sailed like a peregrine right over her head. "Why thank you," the woman said, brightening, "the Volange is our pride and joy. It took Phil here six years, six *whole years*, behind a trading desk at Bunco Mountebank to earn enough to buy it. Isn't that right, Phil?" She dug a plump and multiply-jeweled finger into his side when he failed to respond. "Phil, isn't that RIGHT ?!"

"Wha...*ooooooffffff...*" he said, jumping as the digit digitized his diaphragm. His head jerked towards her, a huff of air forced out of him back through his smoldering pipe, spewing a chunk of choke into the air, right in my direction. I stepped back automatically, tried to wave it off, as Phil caught sight of me and pushed his paper to the side. Too late; the toxins caught my mucus membranes, *badda bing*, I coughed. Its taste instantly adhered itself to my bronchial passages, a parasitic cancerous worm made of burnt popcorn and mass transit vehicle oil pan. I'd be hacking it up for hours now, that god-awful flavor. Fuck.

"Why you should have told me we had a guest Meg!" Phil said; the woman just rolled her eyes, something clearly learned from the Fanster.

"Dr. Durant Allegheny," I offered along with a hand to each of them in turn, hard-pressed to restrain my instinct to hack it all back up. "At your service and your family's. You must be the next peck of pickled peppers in this piper's peter." They gripped it with large damp paws in turn, with me doing the shaking for them.

The woman seemed puzzled, sort of chuckling but uncomfortable at my *non sequiter* and making it sound more like a bison wheezing. "Ah...

oh, well, OK, well, yes, the mountains are sort of, um... fairytale like." Her attention seemed to wander then, back to the plasma screen. *A place of comfort for her*, I supposed. I noted the man was back to ignoring me and reading his WSJ.

"You a big Fancy fan then?" I asked pointedly, wanting this thing to move on and get itself over with. At that, her husband -- I imagined that's what his role was supposed to be -- peered up at me over the edge of the paper with chilly discreteness, as if I'd just produced a large flayed fish in his presence.

"Ooooh," she said, exhaling and touching me on the wrist. "She's just... a champion, that's what she is. A champion. Like that Mary Lou Retton, or Judge Judy."

"Judge Judy," her husband huffed, eyes returning to text as his interest evaporated.

"Well yes, Phil, Judge Judy!" she said disgustedly, poking him again, or trying to, an act he dodged this time. She turned back to me. "Never you mind ol' Mister Legless here, how can we help you Doctor... what did you say your name was again?"

"Just call me Doc," I said. "Actually, I thought I could help you."

"Eh? Oh... oh.. " she laughed, nervously. "Well... I don't know."

"I thought I saw a fire in here," but looking around, ventured, "but I take it I was in error."

"Fire!?" the man plumped, throwing down his paper. "Fire!? Son, tell me: what do you know about recreational vehicles?"

Hubris? "I know these mountains can wear out the meanest of men and machine," I said calmly.

"Well son, *this* is the Volange Plutonium Prime. If it does give out, and it *never* does, " poking his wife back, with his flaming Meerschaum, "I'm one satellite call away from a two-hour helicopter rescue." He slaps the side of the bus and an ornate handset drops like a stone airline oxygen mask from the ceiling; a few seconds of clicks and tones occur, followed by a professionally-sexy female voice on a speaker saying, "Mr. Legless, this is Angelina at Volange Customer Care. How can we help you today?" "Oh, it's nothing," he answers, "I'm just showing the system to a potential buyer," he said, grinning from ear to ear and wielding the phone as if it were a Special Oscar for Lifetime Achievement -- something he clearly felt he deserved.

The line went dead instantly I noted: no *Thank You*, just cost-cutting. Mr. Legless didn't notice, didn't care.

"Those to whom evil is done do evil in return," I said quietly, quoting Auden.

"Excuse me?" asked Mr. Legless.

I spoke up, looking around again. "I said, those who zoom in fun like Evel Knievel burn." That made him laugh.

"Well, we won't be zooming around in this." He stood up, gesturing. "This baby is for *cruuuuuuuuusing*." His hand dipped low then up as he said it, like an emerging surfboard. He laughed again. "Can I get you something, Doc? A show of appreciation for your professional concern. Beer? Or something stronger? It's not like you're on duty."

I almost said something else, but then I thought, *What The Limbo*. "An ice-cold beer would be spectacular, Phil. Something foreign, unwatery. Can I call you Phil?" I slapped him on the arm. He stopped short, grin disappearing. *No, I guess not*.

"It's in the fridge there," he said icily, pointing to a featureless vertical expanse of grained veneer, inlays of silver metal and pearl and crystals of something, and, damn, some kind of animal skin. I took a step up close, examined the wall where he pointed. He may as well have said it was in the Vatican Archives: I had no idea how to get in there. It was just a wall, albeit clearly a highly-leveraged one. I turned back, looking at them. He had returned to his seat and his paper; she'd never left Fancy. I sighed, turning, and leaned against the wall. There was a beep; then, a feeling of warmth, almost immediately turning into genuine heat.

"I think I just cut on the ov...."

"Aaaaah!" Meg said loudly, back to ignoring me in favor of the TV and applauding with fat hands. "Oh, that Fancy gets it right every time."

"Mmmmrm," said Phil, or other consonants to that effect, yawning perhaps, snapping his paper hard and fast in displeasure.

"I think I cut the oven on," I forced myself to say, speaking up, looking in bewilderment for the controls.

Phil didn't look at me; he just slapped the wall again. The phone dropped from the ceiling again. *Click, beep-beep, click.* "Hello Mr. Legless, this is Christina from Volange Customer Care. How can we help you today?"

"Can you kindly cut my oven off?" he asked, eyes never leaving his paper.

There was a brief pause, then the voice asked: "Excuse me?"

He looked at the hanging phone and spelled it out for them: "CUT MY OVEN OFF."

There was another pause, then an almost-laugh only stopped by proper customer service training, then a few beeps from the wall behind me, and the heat vanished. *Zooop*, up went the phone into history.

"How's that beer?" he asked from behind his paper, without looking at me.

"It was great," I said. "Thanks so much." I swallowed dry saliva, wondering what to say, what I was supposed to say, next.

"Uuuuuurrrm," said Meg in response to something Ms. Grace said, approvingly. I took it as a spiritual prompting of sorts. "Guess I'll be going now," I said, very loudly, trying to push events.

"Mmmmmmrp," said Phil, reading his paper, smoking. Meg said nothing, mouth somewhat open. Someone on the TV, not Fancy, was railing. "You know, Fan, I had read a report that Debbie (*my mind drifted*) did with a reporter for a British newspaper, went in depth saying that she knew, according to her, that Michael Jackson was at least not the father of (*what is that weird art thing on the ceiling?*) she was artificially inseminated, just as she would inseminate horses on her ranch, Fancy. So it could be that, at least in Debbie Rowe's case... (*I yawned, big and long*) but we don't know yet. Haven't had that confirmed." A caption appeared, identifying the speaker as one Fortuna Charon, of *Gloss n' Glossy,* a checkout rag. *Wow,* I thought, looking at it speak, *that's a GIRL.*

"Poor, poor Michael," Meg muttered, shaking her head.

Apparently I was supposed to remain. I sighed, decided to play by the rules, and interacted. "Michael Jackson?" I said. "Poor nothing."

"I can't believe you'd say that Doc, of all people!" She pulled off then threw a big fuzzy slipper at me in one motion, which hit the wall behind me, causing more beeps and another round of instant heating. I ignored it this time.

"Why's that?" I asked, only half-pretending suspicion.

"Ohh... he's dead!" she said. "DEAD! Poor Michael..." and she began sobbing. Hmm, Michael Jackson, dead. Phil just threw his paper down, disgusted. "Oh pet, give it a rest honey…." but she wailed and wailed, blowing her not-insubstantial nose in a not-insubstantial hanky.

Fortuna droned on. "And it is just absolutely not the case. You look at them, they look nothing like him, or like he would have looked before all of his medical problems and everything that has been very well documented. But not only that, you know, the sources are very accurate.

And we, actually, at *Gloss n' Glossy* uncovered this week through various sources, multiple sources, who the actual father is."

Fancy bit the bait. "And THAT would be?"

Triumphantly, Fortuna pounced, ready to earn her paycheck. "That would be his long time dermatologist. We are the first outlet to actually reveal this. A lot of people have known and a lot of people actually have reached out to me today, saying that they also knew about this and were very surprised it never came out earlier...." She beamed as she spoke, a lighthouse of knowledge illuminating a safe sail through the insipid darkness, or at least acknowledging the *cha-ching* sound coming from her wallet.

"What did he die of? When?" I asked.

"How could you not know about Michael Jackson? Where've you been the last three days, in a..." She looked me up and down. "... cave or something?"

Excellent question. Didn't have a clue. Most likely I was dead, but I thought it best not to theorize. "I'd rather be in Philadelphia," I said. "Three days ago?"

"Three days ago. They don't know why," Meg sobbed, "but they're saying all sorts of horrible things about drugs and suicide and such. Ooooh, what's this world coming to?"

"Discussions of how the children of his still-warm body are bastards, apparently," I said. "I'm sure his kids love that. I guess at the end of they day it's just another dead black man and ratings to Fancy."

Meg's tears froze with a hard gulp and she whipped her head towards me as if I'd poked her with her husband's flaming Meerschaum. I thought she was going to ask me to leave, but Phil broke the moment.

"Hrrumph!" he stated, throwing the paper down. "Damn markets. Down thirty-four yesterday, gold and natural gas were up but oil rolled over in the afternoon," he said. "How you doin' in the markets these days, doc?"

Jeez I hated that. Everybody always thinks doctors are rich and geniuses at finance. Family always asking for advice. Friends always asking for advice. Patients always asking for advice, and meds. (Truth be told, family and friends did *that* too.) Fact was that after the divorce I was worth far more dead than alive. Hell, even before the divorce I was just a penny stock.

"I'm up ninety percent on the year," I lied. "One word for you Phil: *plastics*. Plastic dolls, plastic plants, plastic surgery for plastic people."

He hrrumphed again, said "You doctors and your investment clubs. You know, I used to handle some accounts for... for... what was that doctor's name, honey?"

"Mengele?" I suggested helpfully. "Moreau? Kevorkian?"

"Don't know them," he said distractedly as his wife waved off his question, slapping his hand with hers several times accidentally in the process, eyes never leaving their Grace. "Oh!" she said, annoyed; "Mrrrm!" he responded, annoyed. For a moment they were like swaying, sybaritic bonobos fighting over a piece of sugar cane gripped in one hand while holding onto their respective trees with the other. But only for a moment. Within seconds, their energy supplies depleted, they turned from *Pan troglodytes* to mere troglodytes, a devolution visible in their hard breath, that pathetic hardness that comes from softness.

Phil huffed and puffed. "Umm, hmm, can't think -- hhhuuuh -- of it right now. Done a lot of it --- huuuh haaah --- investment management I mean. Your club turn a good penny?" He coughed like he'd lost a prize fight. Meg blew her nose again in her hanky, a molting goose-honk.

"Yes, my club," I said as they both phlegmated themselves. I was a doctor; I'd seen worse. "Two or three pennies. The real zinc-clad stuff." *Dang it's warm in here*, I thought.

"Yeah, I still do some myself. M&A, that's my *reeeal* specialty. Whip it and flip it," he said, trying to laugh as he cleared his lungs, "and it's --- hhhhhruuh! --- always a moneymaker. Best thing about retirement now is, with the Internet now, see, I can do it from here. You know, some of the guys on the Wall said it stood for *Money and Attorneys*."

"Or, *Madmen and Ass*," I said. He laughed harder, coughed again.

After a moment he produced: "Yeah, OK, so... you really make money in plastics?"

"Well, you know...." I realized I was sweating quite a bit now. "I think the oven's on again, Phil. So what's it like laying all those people off?"

"What? Dang it." He slapped the wall half-heartedly again, *zlorp* came the phone, *BARK!* went the order, *chortle* went the laughter at the other end of the line, *zoop* went the phone back up into the ceiling. *Zlorp-bark-chortle-zoop.* Then, *beep-borp*, and the heat disappeared again; and again, no *Thank You* from either end, just *zlorps* and *borps,* effluents of a digestive process of sorts, without the post-processing dividend of farm-bound fixed nitrogen compounds. Phil ignored my question, turned and poked his wife again. "You gotta quit turning the heat on Meg!" he said.

"I'm not the one who..." she began, and off they went, at each other. Their fight turned into a barrage of consonants and sharp vowels, no longer words, more an invasion of pigs into a second-grade classroom. I turned to the TV. This was a surprise to me: normally, the idea that *Fancy Lissom* would be more attractive to my attention than pretty much any discussion about anything else would be, to say the least, abnormal. Alas, like a doctor examining exquisitely large and breakfast-fresh new breast implants, nothing was normal anymore. "Well that just tears it," Fancy was saying with complete disgust, betraying her east Texarkana accent. "I've had it with all those MoJos and FloJos and, you know, TJs and MJs that think they can just moonstep, you know, a few numbers and forget a, you know, a, um, glove one day and make a million dollars. I had to work, you know, HARD to make MY first million and get to where the tabs want my photo for a buck. You know, and I was so fast, you know, they couldn't catch me half the time, but when they would catch me, oh my god. It was bad...."

Wah wah wah. As always it was about her, and who gave a rat about that? I mean, what did she do? She sat in front of a camera and railed. She incited the passions of morons and got a paycheck for it, just like all those TV political pundits. Blah blah blah. What kind of talent is that? Just exactly how does that add to society? To distract myself from the schoolyard conflict in front of me, I imagined Fancy at a job interview. "So, Ms. Lissom, what is it that you *do*?" "Me?" she'd respond, indignantly. "ME? I'm a goddamned hero, Mr. Hiring Manager, that's what I am. I'm golden. I'm ratings. I'm ad placements. I'm America's Fucking Sweetheart. I'm Your Worst Nightmare. I'm...." Then like any man, he'd make the male mistake of interrupting. "Yes, yes, Ms. Lissom, but... what do you DO?" That would shovel all the coal in at once, the bad, high-sulfur-content hellish stuff, roil the boiler to full pressure, shake and bake the piping until at almost the point of blitzkrieg explosion the valves would give way in a scizure-like spasm of apoplexy, spewing, "I'm a TWICE-CENSURED FORMER STATE PROSECUTOR WHO IGNORED JUDGE'S ORDERS BECAUSE I KNEW BETTER THAN HIZZONOR DID, MOTHERFUCKER!"

My pickled peck were still pecking at one another, screeching, yowling, generally acting childlike. It was true love: you could tell from the pink valentine color they each left behind after a slap. But then they began heaving again, then rasping, then coughing, deescalating and finally sitting down. It made one wonder what good ever came of love. I thought of an old syphilis-treatment reference I'd learned in med school: *A night with Venus means a life with mercury*. These two were certainly mercurial.

Ahem, time to move things along again. "OK, so, I guess I'll be going now, thanks." and I turned to leave. They undulated, chests pumping, eyes closed, still recovering. Phil rolled open one eye eventually, continuing the conversation as if nothing had happened.

"Put a lot of our money in oil, myself. Drilling, production, consumption. Though I had to unload all of my GM and Ford this year, ehhh, what a waste. I like energy, good old petrodollars, I mean, everybody needs it. Black gold, Texas tea, you know, hah hah hah! That's where it's at. Gotta grow the economy, you know, not just here of course, but, you know, look at China, India, look at those places. All ready to bust out. Brazil too. All ready to bust! Gonna be some gold comin' out of the ground there. Petrobras, you know, drilling all around South America, just put some of my money in a venture in Cuba they're doing. Gulf of Mexico, yeah. Hot stuff, *reaaal* hot stuff there. Get a Republican back in the WH, we'll get some drilling going again, you know, "Drill baby drill!", hah hah hah! And that Alaska, yeah, that Sarah Palin needs to, well, she needs to get that going and you know we'll get some action back you know, not be run by all those middle eastern states and doin' what they want, you know, being the victim of *them*." He made a face like a nauseated weasel. "Yeah, gotta put an end to that, right? Yeah, safer world all around. Gotta get back into the oil, and you know, not just that, but natural gas. And coal! Yeah, coal and tar sands. Gotta dig, gotta dig and drill. Black gold, Texas tea!"

"Yeah? Yeah, a real Texas tea party," I said, meaning it sarcastically. But he took it somewhere else.

"Yeah, those Texas tea partiers irk me. The GOP needs all the help it can get right now, and what do these guys do? Bah! They all want some independent you know, something between a Bush and a Barack, something homey that speaks well to the cattlemen and farmers and doesn't sound too educated or urban. I don't know, maybe... maybe a tea party is what we need. Anything's better than *this* guy and his idea of *fair*, Jeez. A little more fairness will kill us and our jobs. In all this talk coming out of his White House, all you hear is fair *this* and fair *that.* It's like kids debating the rules of the game they're making up. I say so what: who gives a rump if it's fair? Kids just like to argue. It's a way to make-believe they have power. They ain't got nothin' but a lease on a house owned by you and me and the rest of the over-taxed top-half of Americans."

"Yeah? The bottom half can always sleep on the Mall I guess," unsure of what he was talking about. Sounded like developments in my absence.

He chuckled. "Yeah, while they wait in the Free Health Clinic line going into the Oval Office!"

"Yeah? Yeah. So... what does this thing get?"

"Huh? Oh, uhh... well, it's always driven me nuts that this thing is turning some pretty high revs, uhh, for a, let's see, twelve-odd liter diesel that redlines at four thousand, I do, oh, three thousand rpms at seventy mph to be exact. I can spend a chunk fixing it and still turning those revs at seventy, or I can spend a chunk more and drop the revs at seventy to twenty, maybe twenty-five hundred. Which might be a bit much. Dunno. It's just barely off the power band there, but I'm not sure by how much since peak torque happens at twenty-three, twenty-four hundred rpm."

I just stared at him for a few seconds.

"Oh, um... say, two, three miles per gallon."

JEEEEEEE-zus! I'D get further if I drank a gallon of gasoline! No way, that had to be.... "Diesel?" I asked.

"Of course!" he said.

I let it sink in for another second, then I ventured, quietly, "That's a lot of diesel, Phil." *Yeah, and Canada is a lot of cold.*

He missed my point. "It's got quad fifty-five gallon tanks," he said. "A fortune to fill of course, but I have a fortune. Good thing I don't have to work for it anymore!" He suddenly coughed in a fit again, eventually producing a large yellowish-gray mass. Fifty bucks said he had at least the beginnings of emphysema, if not out-and-out small cell. He regarded it the way one regards their elderly aunts when children; then, producing a large ornate hanky he wiped it from his skin, held the hanky to the wall, and an invisible vacuum vent materialized and sucked the linen and its contents into its beryllium bosom. There was a brief sound underneath us like the flash and clang of a furnace, and I knew it had been carbonized, vaporized, and exorcised into the outside air. Something beeped behind me, then a second later, two short tweets overhead as if in answer. He took a long draw on his Meerschaum, making more of what he'd just shipped to consumers, and continued.

"But speaking of diesel, my concern is those environmentalists," he said. "I mean, you can't really trust scientists, right? They live off our tax dollars, those damn grants they get and all. They need problems, want problems, you know: new diseases, or mountain topping, or polar bears having to swim a bit too much." He laughed. "Eh, who knows? I don't know, maybe they're right, or a little bit, but who cares? I'M seriously dubious that there's going to be a climate change catastrophe anytime soon or 50 years from now or ever for that matter. Hell, it seems to me these weathermen can't predict the climate for the next month, let alone the next century. You know, all the fear surrounding climate change is nothing but a magic bullet of an excuse for governments to increase their power. Greenie weenies often think that all the taxation and regulation they propose will hit those large corporations which they accuse of being the biggest polluters. Umm, no. Money is power is influence. It's not going to be large corporations which will be taxed and regulated up to their eyeballs, but ordinary plebs like you and…." He gestured at me, but couldn't bring himself to say the next word. "Well, folks like you. When I hear these Professor Sweaters claim that their work will stand up to scrutiny, they're just arrogant and trying to get more of our tax dollars, umm. The government needs to instill fear in the masses, and impending environmental disaster is a very effective way to do this. I wonder for how much longer government thinks it can continue to bullshit people and use climate change as an excuse for ever greater authority." Then he jerked back, observing the look on my face maybe, realized he might be speaking to the enemy. "Eh, Doc: you're not one of those environmentalists, are you?" He soured, shoved his Meerschaum in my general direction as he said it.

Excuse me? Here I was, fresh off the Trail. I *was* the goddamn environment; all browns and grays, fungoid in appearance and bacterial in content. I was Dead Man Hiking. I looked like Conan the Barbarian. I *smelled* like Conan the Barbarian. Conan's author once said that civilized men are more discourteous than savages because they know they can be impolite without having their skulls split, as a general thing. So, I was generally impolite.

"Damn right I am Phil, and... I'm an independent voter, no Reps, no Dems, over my dead body any Libs. Progress is great, growth is great. Problem is man created shit, Phil. Man created asbestos and put it in our buildings which put it in our lungs. Man purified the mercury and put it in our batteries which we then put in our landfills which we then put in our water supply. Man made tar, nicotine, and a delivery system. Man gave man cancer, knew he did it, and took their money anyway. Man doesn't care, Phil. Man created strontium-90 and plutonium-239; helpful and dangerous, just like man himself. And man doesn't stand by his man; woman, maybe, but man, never. Much more of this progress and growth and we'll all be dead. Mind if I take my pack off?" I didn't wait for an answer, popped the hip and chest buckles and slipped it off. It landed on the self behind me, *beep bleep*, suddenly the surface lit up, red, hot, and I yelped, pulling my pack off and dropping it on the floor. On the way down it hit the wall, *dleep bleep*, the wall lit up, I cursed, then yellows and reds, and a churning sound like a dryer spinning started. Gosh darn it was hot in here.

Phil shivered, puffed, plumped, prumped, fluffled, frumped, flabregated... then he hit the wall again. After a moment of prumpfing and flumpfring on the phone, remote control did its thing, *brump bump bleep,* all the lights went off and sweet sanity returned, if not the chilled air.

"Thanks," I said sheepishly, then: *Wait, you're not real... or, are you?* Some oddball sense of guilt hit me then, and I offered a plum from no internally generated conscious fruit tree of mine. "Sorry about that," I said, carefully shouldering my pack back over one shoulder.

He just looked at me, huffing and puffing, a breathing blimp. He sat back down, but not really since he'd never really stood to begin with. My mind was wandering again. Maybe I needed to write myself a prescription for Ritalin or something. Luckily for me, there were only three pharmacies on the whole Trail, two of them behind me in Damascus.

Then again, who knows where I was?

Phil was staring at me. I realized he'd asked me something. Time to pay both attention and piper. "Sorry, Phil, I'm tired and my mind was wondering. What did you say?"

"Meg wanted to know if you wanted to stay for lunch," he said, disapproval and hesitation in his voice. Guys like him liked to talk and lecture and order others around but not much else, especially those who disagreed with them or showed the faintest signs of the disfigurement that was liberalism. Wives tried to humanize these Type A's; too bad that like many public works projects such efforts often failed in the long-term maintenance phase.

"Sure, Meg, thanks," I found myself saying but not really meaning it. Guys like me, the Type X's, just wanted to be left the hell alone. If we had managed to obtain wives via some fluke, we only wound up dehumanizing them.

"Oooh, that's wonderful Doc!" she said, two-thirds smiling and walking to the kitchen three steps away; she didn't mean it either. Nah, best we all git' movin'. Hmm. It was only then I realized I hadn't seen or heard from my companion in some time.

"Ah... excuse me, but did anybody see someone else come in with me? Little fellow, about yay," I said, gesturing, then turning behind me as I looked towards the front entrance to the bus and took a step, Meg screamed.

One circle had remained red on the counter-top, and a piece of Phil's WSJ he'd laid there at some point in the fracas was a-smoldering. Just as Meg had reached to retrieve it, it had burst into flames. Phil leaned over from his seat without getting up, quickly fashioning the rest of his WSJ into a club-like instrument, began to beat the fire with it. Bad move. The paper in his hand caught fire. He dropped it, they both screamed. A lot of things happened at once. Phil slapped the side of the bus, Meg the other. Two phones dropped from the ceiling on either side. A confusion of voices filled the air with the smoke. I tried grabbing a Nalgene from my side pocket, had trouble reaching back in the small space, swore, and turned sideways and leaned over slightly to get a grip on the water. *Help!* shouted Meg to the voices in the air, *Fire!* shouted Phil more specifically, *Hire!* and *Felp!* being the combined effect. The gods of OnStar replaced those of old, asking what they could help with, and not understanding the garbled mishmash, typical of gods. A red light descended from the ceiling, began rotating, lit up, and a siren began wailing not just for unwary sailors but anybody else in hearing range. "NOT THE FOAM!" Phil screamed piercingly, looking up, around, as large copper nozzles started to lower from on-high. I finally freed my Nalgene, whipped the top off, and in one motion tossed the contents onto the fire. Steam briefly replaced smoke, the red light turned off, the nozzles retreated, and something resembling normality returned.

There was a long frozen pause. Two phones went *zloooop* and back up. Another second, then another. Then Phil yelped; in the commotion he'd dumped the contents of his pipe on his shoe. Helpfully, his wife stomped on his foot, he cried out, jumped up, slapped her, producing a loud *OWW!* from her. They stood there, staring at each other, heaving once again.

I burst out laughing. In unison they turned to me. "Sorry, hmmm, hrrrm," I said, clearing my throat, then a very low and externally serious, "Sorry."

I just looked at them as a large blank spot descended in the air between all of us. It sat there, bloated, unapologetic, an Arctic silence. Phil grabbed up his half-burnt paper, sat back down, snapped it in front of his face, hrummphed, began to read what he could. Meg opened the fridge, stuck her head inside, and hibernated; after a long bear-winter moment, she started throwing out meats and greens on the counter with a flabby fitfulness. There was a matching hard thump outside with a slight vibration though the floor, a long distant scraping along with a weird sound like a choked, distorted *quack*, then, silence again. "Duck," said Phil, from behind his paper. It took me a blink or two to realize he didn't mean it as an imperative verb.

A minute passed, the Arctic silence turning bipolar into a colder, Antarctic one. I no longer existed, or didn't matter. My thoughts rotated. The Volange Plutonium. It forced a memory of Cécile de Volanges in *Les Liaisons Dangereuses*. To be reduced to mere social concerns, the slight of one's character, cruelty for the sake of coolness aforethought, standing, charm, and powdered, fake hair worn to some forgotten opera of no historical consequence and barely more in its moment stage center. Boredom, it seemed to me, was the real device that vice devised here. A yawn so wide it stretched from one end of life to the other. Only the most dangerous of liaisons eased the sheer maniacal thumping of one's pulse in one's ears, ticking off the seconds wasted at the humidor or the harpsichord or some other bullshit thing not necessarily starting with an "H" but bullshit nonetheless. Sipping tea from a cup of fine Wedgwood Jasper. Trimming the verge. Stamp collecting. Epistolary novels. Manservants. Country estates. Adherence to tradition's rules. Expectations. Shawls.

Or, hiking, another bullshit thing starting with the letter "H". Hmm... funny how free association works sometimes.

Again I felt the urge to move events along. I seemed to be the only one steering them, although events had already proven themselves steered by... others. I wondered again who was puppet, who was puppeteer. I spoke then out of fear, just to hear some sort of soulless words in the air, filling the unfillable. Meg was staring at the countertop, now covered in greens and meats, heaving again from the mere act. "Can I... um... help you with lunch, Meg?"

As if a 911 rescue squad had arrived in sirens and splendor, she cried out her thanks, then promptly fell back into her chair and refocused on her precious TV. Fancy was replaced by *The Crush Twigbranch Show*, sigh, even worse. Simple thoughts for simple people too simple to simply think for themselves. *Lazy is as lazy doesn't*, I almost said out loud.

I felt a gear in the back of my head turning. It was an odd mechanical sensation, nagging and persistent. Events began to fit together, a crystalline pattern forming from the chaos. Yes, a yawn so wide it stretched from... from one end of this monstrosity on wheels to the other. What was it about that thought that....

"But that's how it is," Phil was saying warily, realizing once again that I had drifted away. "To be something, one must do something. Except for investors like me, of course. We supply the demand: dollars and donuts for dreamers. No offense, Doc."

"None taken. All with little or no effort on your part?" I said, beginning to guess how to shape events for myself, attending to the meats and greens and building on the beginnings of a genuine insight. *Where's the bread? Ah, there it is.*

"Ideally, silent partner. No fuss, no muss. Let others do the actual work, take the risk, while we just reap the harvest. It's what we did in M&A." He was frowning at me, sounding suspicious. "But... eh... you sound like you wouldn't approve of that, Doc."

I sighed. "Somebody has to do it I suppose," I said after a long thoughtful pause. "No, Phil, no, I'm not really anti-capitalism or anti-market. I guess... I guess it allows the greatest number to live in the most comfortable lifestyle possible. I don't know. If human nature were different, if a truly objective and just distribution system could be created without the baggage of totalitarianism and centralization that such things breed historically, I might think diff... no, I would think differently about it." I was feeling lethargic, sleepy. It was hard to focus. God DAMN it was hot.

Evidently he was going to take it all personally. "Guys like me keep the wheels turning, Doc! Guys like me are necessary!"

"Yeah, I know," I said sheepishly, agreeing with him, albeit grudgingly, inside and out. I decided to steer it away from him. "But I find that most everyone is necessary to somebody, even if it's only to their mother or their child. The need doesn't necessarily justify the means. Take your oil for example. We drill for it and pump it out and refine it and burn it. We don't really look for alternatives, in the investment sense. Unless there's an immediate quarterly benefit to the bottom line, corporations won't spend much on changing what they do and how, so they're out. Startups won't start on it since investors want quick ROIs too. And the government?" I laughed. "Shit, Phil, you and I probably totally agree on what the government can accomplish when it sets its collective Neanderphallic mind on things. You want bombs? Government works. Food stamps? Government works. Minimal maintenance of the social order and big defense contracts are what the government is all about. They can do the machines of war and the farm like nobody's business. But not R&D. Nobody's investing in humanity's long-term, Phil. Maybe the artist does, a few futurists and philanthropists, the philosophers, but that's about it."

He drew back as I spoke, slowly shaking his head no, then more rapidly as I finished. "Well, the government is shit Doc, you're right there. We just need less regulation and...."

"*Less* regulation? Less regulation is what got us into this economic mess. People don't care about others, Phil. We fill the sky with carbon dioxide and people say there's no global warming just to keep doing it."

"Ehhhh!" said Phil. "Now there you're wrong! It's all money and politics…."

"That's the problem with guys like you Phil. You're trained to think conservatively, in terms of the quarter and the four that make a dollar at the end of a year. You want profits, profits matter to you. Therefore, anything that stands in the way of profits you're against. Here's the real problem, Phil. Suppose you're right about global warming, that it's all baloney. Problem is Phil, it's only baloney *for a while.* All you need is four basic facts. Fact one: carbon dioxide absorbs more heat energy than it emits. Fact two: we're pumping more carbon dioxide into the air every day. Fact three: there's more going into the atmosphere than is absorbed by life or rocks or oceans. Fact four: *none* of the other three facts look like they're going to change anytime soon! Sooner or later, Phil, *sooner or later*, the planet will heat up due to this activity. But nobody's allowed to do anything about it, and nobody who would be allowed chooses to! *Nobody* is working for the long-term of humanity at a global scale in an empowered role with which the majority agrees. We're all petty and selfish and primitive Baptists. The hell with our children; science or God will save them. Hell, most Americans believe Jesus will return in their lifetimes! Why should *we* be responsible for picking up our underware after ourselves? We're preoccupied with sinning and Fancy Lissom and gays in the military and dancing competition eliminations and other falderal while the real problems we face as a species go unchecked. We say we'll let God sort it out. Phil, maybe the point is that God wants to see if we're grown up yet. Nothing wrong in acting like adults for a change."

I'd left Phil speechless. Hmm, the edges of the lettuce were brown. And slowly browning in real-time, right in front of me. Hmm. "Falderal," I repeated, sighing.

"Excuse me?" Phil asked, shaking in anger.

"Blehhhhhhhh, I've had enough of this! I can't watch any more! These people get me *sooooo*... oooooohhhh!" Meg declared, slapping the wall and asking the subsequent customer service rep to turn off her TV. The clearly-annoyed rep did that, after a moment of arguing and making the mistake of thinking that Meg was asking for instructions on how to do it herself. After the phone *whooshed* back up, it hit me why the reps never said thank you or goodbye: they were sick to death of these lazy sucking-lamprey bloated bastards, and for good reason. They were sloths of the worst kind: obtuse, entitled, and judgmental. Had been, would be.

And that's when I finally had my first real sure-'nuff, somna-bitch, well-I'll-be-n'-mercy-me moment. Ah-*HA! Sloth!*

"Falderal!" I said, loudly straight at Meg, then looking back at Phil, pointedly. They looked confused, Phil still wearing his anger, drew back. I poked my head at them like Phil poked his Meerschaum at me. That weirded them out.

I started off with an obvious statement. "You a capitalist, Phil?" He just stared at me, the looked at his wife, who looked back at him. "John Maynard Keynes once said that capitalism is the astounding belief that the most wickedest of men will do the most wickedest of things for the greatest good of everyone. He was right. It's absurd. Capitalists do nothing for anyone except themselves. If you're not on the board of directors or a preferred stockholder, capitalists don't care, and even then, once the cash is in the Caymans, hey, screw everybody. Maybe marginally, maybe afterwards, after they get theirs, they live the white dream of having and being able to give back to the little guys, the less fortunate. Hah. How can you have more or less fortune? It occupies neither length nor breadth nor width. It simply *isn't*. Fortune has nothing to do with the real differences between the little and the big: ambition and naked raw aggression. By which I really mean fear and response, predator and prey. Somehow we expect a utopian civilization to emerge butterfly-like from this, that the good of capitalism can be produced from the evil of capitalists. Of course it's a lie. Then they say, *you have your freedom* while we enslave ourselves to the likes of the Boss because the dream that we could be him someday, or at least have the same or better stuff that he has. Meantime, the world dies around us... and since the world is ours for the taking, why not?"

The Bibb in front of me accelerated its browning. The meat began to wither and dry up into jerky, in seconds. It was supremely hot and growing hotter. Meg huffed, sweating, and grabbed Phil's burnt paper, began fanning herself with it. I became aware of an orchid in a flowerpot in the corner, wilting, shriveling, turning into dust, as I spoke.

Yep, I got it now. I continued. "Oh, in the short-run, we all gain: bigger homes, faster cars, better eats, bigger breasts. But it can't last. If you burn and burn and burn, you're eventually going to make a lot of smoke. It's as simple as that. At some point, you have to breathe again. Know what the worst part is? There's no better way that doesn't involve totalitarianism. Man won't help his fellow man unless he gets something out of it -- a seat at the right hand, ninety-nine virgins, daddy's approval, good blow... or *a* good blow. Or unless he's made to by the business end of a weapon: a gun, a smart bomb, a wife's vitriol, a 1040 form, the sound of demanding bells at Christmas. No, Fancy's right: we suck. I hate to say it, but Fancy is right. Man needs manipulation, deserves it, asks for it. Otherwise the six billion of us will going on making more of us and eating and consuming and burning and killing and destroying everything around us in the process, until it's just us, and that's when we'll turn on each other in a *serious* way. Unless someone stops us now, somehow, we won't stop and the whole world's going to drown. A benevolent dictator, that's what we need. A benevolent dictator who…."

I stopped, as stunned as if I'd been struck. Silence as I shook my head, in wonder at what I'd almost said and what it implied. I chuckled, filling the air with my fear. "Damn Padma, is *that* what you meant?"

"What's gotten into you Doc?" asked Meg, hopelessly lost.

“Do you know what real boredom is?” I asked by way of explanation. “Real boredom is knowing you are better, stronger, smarter than others, and doing nothing about it. Real boredom is living the non-dream. Real boredom is accepting yourself and your situation for less than what you could be; not what you are, or have been, but could be. Real boredom is letting the wash and the dry and the goddamn fucking spin cycle get in the way of living and making a contribution. And mark my words, mark my words: the day you are really bored, down deep in your soul, when you let someone else call the shots, make the decisions, when you wall yourself up to stop the innate knowledge that what you and others are doing is wrong, or worse, nothing, when you accept it in silence, motionless, like a deer on the wall, glassy-eyed, indoctrinated, programmed, reverently obeying, when you cease even ceasing, *that*, my friends, *that* is death."

They just stared at me, all eyes. In unison the eyes on the countertop came back on, as if by themselves, staring too, staring with hellfire. Then, slowly, more red lights, in the walls, the ceiling, the floor. I backed away from all the glowing eyes, towards the front of the vehicle. Whatever was going to happen was going to happen now.

Startled, Phil and Meg looked around at the bewildering display, both sweating profusely now. Phil hit the wall. A phone dropped. A voice materialized, but a different voice this time, sounding authoritative, decisive, and in its own way, deadly familiar.

"Hello, Phil, this is Mr. Plutus at Customer Care. How may I help you today?"

"I... I don't know, it's very hot in here, everything came on all at once: the stove, the oven, the dryer, the heat."

Two loud hair dryers, his and hers, lurched to life in the back of the bus, causing Meg and Phil to jump.

"Yessss Phil, sounds like they're might be a short somewhere in the wiring. Possibly a meltdown of some sort. Those things happen, to machines and markets and men. A terribly unfortunate situation. As unfortunate as the state of your account."

"Excuse me?" asked Phil, looking at Meg.

"Well, Phil.... Can I call you Phil? Ah, you see, it appears that you have depleted your service account. Let's see... yes, according to our records, you've used up all of your pre-paid lifetime service calls in, let's see, that would be... seven months. A spectacular run; in fact, it's a brand new record-breaker. Of course, privacy laws prevent me from disclosing *from who you stole it*."

There was writhing sarcasm in his last words. Shock filled the faces of the lambs. Their slaughter would undoubtedly follow.

"Yessss Phil, it seems you have used up what help we could offer. Like all assistance, it came with a price. Well-managed, properly controlled, it could have lasted you a lifetime. It could have been given to your children. It could have been your treasure and theirs. But you chose to wear it all up and out. Truly unfortunate."

The silken air was shimmering from the heat. A large red light descended from the ceiling, began rotating, then lit up. Large copper nozzles followed just afterwards. Meg and Phil looked upwards, slowly, mouths opening.

A slight laugh, disdainful, from the ethereal voice. "It appears that the automatic fire suppression system has detected your plight, Phil. Hopefully this will resolve our crisis. Then again, one never knows what the future will bring."

Overhead, a loud gurgle, the rodent sounds of liquids pumping through pipes, a clang, two sharp clanks. The nozzles began belching loudly, rude farting exclamations, gases making way for baby.

Meg grabbed Phil, and vice versa. "Not the foam," they whispered, pleadingly.

"But, really now," said the voice, "*shouldn't* they?"

The nozzles exploded. A torrent of fluids, cold, very very cold, drenching everything, everyone, in a brutal, relentless, stinging onslaught. And in its own way, other than the obvious and despite the forewarning, quite unexpected.

"*WATER?!?*" screamed Phil above the roaring. "*WATER?!?* I pay good money to these people and THEY can't even get the right kind of...."

"Ah, I must apologize for not informing you ahead of time," said the voice, much, much louder this time, overriding the Legless. "You see Phil... can I call you Phil? Ah, the foam system is not *per se* part of the vehicle's purchase price, *ahem*, you understand, your *Advanced* Fire Protection Plan is part of, *ahem*, your service contract, which I believe I mentioned has unfortunately expir…."

"I DON'T CARE YOU!!" He threw a dripping fist in the air, shaking his soaked arm, while Meg moaned and cried, dropping to her knees in the pool on the floor. "LISTEN HERE BUDDY, YOU SHUT THIS OFF THIS VERY INSTANT OR MY LAWYERS AND I WILL SOAK YOUR HIDE IN YOUR OWN...."

"...so unfortunately we must revert to the *standard* protection system, which of course is just your run-of-the-mill water-based system," the voice continued unswervingly. "Of course, *that* system is entirely manual, couldn't shut it off from here if we wanted to. *And we don't want to*." The voice finally laughed out loud, long and hard and cruelly. "Oh, if you really want, if you even care to try, you can find the shut-off valve yourself," it said, "it's just inside the third cabin storage manifold bin…."

Phil and Meg scrambled, twisted, turned, looking around, desperately, but without so much as a drop of a clue. A minute passed as they scrambled and panicked while the disembodied voice tried to tell them how to save themselves. By then were already three or four inches of water in the cabin, and it was accumulating, very fast. I backed my way to the driver's cabin, sloshing in the wash that washed away sins.

"...so to release that, you disengage the red release bar and twist it upwards a quarter of a turn, then…."

They thrashed, ran into each other, shoved each other in panic, angry, terrified, yelping, slapped one another, shouting like dispossessed children at each other, the only convenient victim of their rage. Clouds of steam rose in the heat, where the water was slamming onto still-red-hot burners.

Cacaphony. Screams of desperation. Animal skins -- was that really *giraffe?!* -- soaked and ruined.

"... releasing the inner pin the cover will lift, and you'll find the piping valves, you want the green spigot, turn it to the left until...."

Fine grain woods warping, cracking, blackening and smoking, even in this Niagara of a spray. Inlays melted, ran like wax. Sparks, showering in frenzy and fireworks. Sizzles. *Bleeps* and *blorps*, but distorted as systems blew and electricity found shorter, more convenient paths. Crazy blinking lights, out of order, a peyote disco in a late 70's hurricane.

I'd backed myself into the stairwell. The door was closed. I searched for a level or handle to open it with, There was a foot of water now at least, and growing deeper by the second.

"...so hopefu... you*uuuuu* k-k-k-an *fnnnnnnnnd....sffffftttty... frrrrr yrrrrrssssllffffs....*" The voice became static, a buzzing, distortion, and finally lost. But I understood his last words. *Finding safety for myself* was what I was all about. I searched the flooded dashboard desperately, but it was like the goddamn starship *Enterprise:* all graphics and touchpads, nothing was labeled. I pounded at the panels, finding them either possessed by random electrical shorts or dispossessed of power entirely.

But then....

A kind of calm overcame me; not the real thing, but that substitute distilled from dopamine and adrenaline and molasses-thick blood sugar produced when you know you have to think, think fast, *right now*, or you will die. It was an adequate substitute. I displaced my fear with it, forced myself to turn towards the door, closed my eyes, and *perceive.*

I was to have faith, and deal. Which meant this hand was almost over. Which meant there was only one card left to play... but the deck was fixed. The House knew the outcome, invited the players, chose the game, wrote the rules... and, enforced them. Which meant the marks on the cards were there to read for those with wits to read them. So... what did the cards say?

If the deck was fixed, and the House however inexplicably on my side in this one, that could... that could only mean that....

"Get help, Doc!" Meg shouted. "Go get help!"

So just like that, eyes still closed, as the water rose up above my knees I took both the hint and a step forward and down towards the Maelstrom's bottom and....

VI

3645 feet, 1261 miles to Katahdin

There was a night of rain, when the stars were hidden behind the gray utterances of the Word, where I lay awake and listened to the noise in the darkness, with only the fleeting walls of my tent separating me from the tears of the angels. The patter of their sadness made a sludge of this mere earth, splattered and splayed randomly, drowning soulless ant and spider and mole and mouse alike; yet, replenishing the oak and ash, fir and spruce, weed and wildflower. Death and life, seemingly at random. I wondered how they could stomach it. If the smallest fall of a sparrow mattered, if the meek truly inherited this mud, what of those out in that night dying right now in that rain? Who swam to save them? What life preserver preserved their life? None and none, it seemed; but now, for the first time in my life, I wondered at the logic of it, wondered as to the logic in it. Was there a point? Death was what life must do in the service of life, but, if death was a mere invention.... Well, that changed things, didn't it? Didn't it? If God spent the time to invent nine billion names for Himself, couldn't He have come up with a better solution to the limited resources problem than entropy and death?

There was no answer, only the wind and the rain in it, and the patter of puddles. Of God's creatures drowning therein, there was no sound. Perhaps if it was daytime, we could see. We could all see. But it was night, or we were blind, or both. The clouds rained on us, even in the dark, a mockery.

Even so, it'd given me an opportunity for stillness, stillness to consider. These events began to crystallize in my mind, commonalities, trends noted. I plotted a regression, fit the dots. Emergent from the ruins of the day was an architecture of examples constructed in the form of allusions. Interpretation led to an externalization of facts; just another day's work. It sounds like a lot, but it wasn't. It wasn't hard, once the pieces of the puzzle had begun to suggest the puzzle's existence. When art speaks, the Artist speaks. I'd purchased the art, abstract, but now it solidified into forms practically semiporous in the solvent of meaning, transiting from the metamagical to the mathematical, even becoming... almost predictable.

All of which meant that at last I was beginning to understand. *Vices.* Lust, gluttony, greed, sloth. *Vices.* And the next one is order was... was....

Well, it depended on the list, didn't it? Lust, gluttony, greed, sloth, wrath, envy, and pride. Or, extravagance, gluttony, greed, acedia (combining despair and sloth), anger, envy, and vainglory (putting one's self before God). Or, from Proverbs: haughty eyes, a lying tongue, hands that shed innocent blood, feet swift to run into mischief, a deceitful witness that uttereth lies, him that soweth discord among his brethren. Or, Gandhi: wealth without work, pleasure without conscience, knowledge without character, commerce without morality, science without humanity, worship without sacrifice, and politics without principle. All had their sources, their merits, their inconsistencies, and their sins of omission. Human behavior could not be summarized into bullet lists. Then again... then again, someone seemed to think it *could.* I found that strange. Categorically I'd rejected the category, considering it a bucketful of nonsense and simplicity in a world that was anything but.

I was beginning to understood the what of it; I did not understand the *why.* Why this, me, now? Why all the goddamn drama? Was this really necessary? I knew of the *amor fati*, but I wanted everything different: the past, the future, I rebelled against them, not to bear the necessity, but to conceal it, a mendacious idealist, hating them all and myself in it. If a million angels could dance on the head of a pin, could they converge to a point, and if so, what was it? Just what the Hell was it?

My night of rain and sleeplessness was over, at any rate. I was in Shenandoah now, playground of American history. The tumbled hills of the Piedmont occupied my right side, and the wide, verdant valley of the Shenandoah River some miles distant to my left. Up the crest from me was the Skyline Drive, terminal end of the Blue Ridge Parkway I'd shadowed for so many miles now. It shared historical similarities with the Smokies: once one of the poorest and remote areas of the country, in the 20s and 30s the government acquired the land through a combination of purchases, some more rudely than others, and eminent domain, the rudest of all. A terrible drought in 1930 had helped pave the way, so to speak, for the displacement of the apple-growing families whose livelihood no longer provided a life in the 'hood. A few stubborn steadfast stalwarts remained entrenched, immovable, like the hills themselves; and being the days prior to the FBI and the ATF, were allowed after years of rangling to remain, in desolate communities which were never very solate to begin with. A few were removed at gunpoint, by force.

The mountains had always produced real men: me who were accountable to no one save themselves and theirs, their land, their hands, and their stomachs. These men had known the value of an extra hour of sunlight, an extra inch of rain. My ancestors had been those men, lived those lives: hard, harsh, poor; yet, vivid, irreconcilable. I'm not romanticizing it; I merely admire it. Men these days give their lives to their fellow man, to subjugate and rule them, lay them off, tax them, tame them, produce for them that they may grow fat and rich and avoid work themselves. It's the American way nowadays; but once, this was. Those men, those women, lived truly free. They had nothing but themselves, and these unforgiving mountains. Once, we were free; once, we were truly American, and not mere double-double half-whip decaf two-raw macchiatos living for the next paycheck.

The first European settlers had arrived here in the early 1730's. They crossed the improbably-named Cohongoroota River and founded the town of Mecklenburg, later renamed to Shepardstown. Scotch-Irish Presbyterians mostly, as I'd been, once. They settled in old Fredrick County, which was much later split into the current counties in western Virginia making up the narrow, hundred-mile-long park. In 1748, a sixteen-year-old George Washington came here, as a young surveyor for Thomas, 6th Lord Fairfax of Carmeron, for whom Fairfax County outside of D.C. would be named. By later, some would say revolutionary, accounts, Fairfax considered all of Virginia as his personal fiefdom, a matter which aroused the natural ire of natural settlers seeking lands to conquer and claim and inhabit, settlers who felt their allegiance was owed, taxation-wise at any rate, to no one. But Fairfax was peculiar, even as British nobility went; he petitioned Charles II for grants and received them, and was the only British noble to make his home not just in the Colonies, but in the wild west of the Shenandoah Valley. For this, he was much maligned and ridiculed in the London papers of the day. But it was a poor man, Joist Hite, who in 1732 is credited as the first European to live in the Valley. In 1736, Robert Harper arrived, building log cabins and a ferry across the river, which gained notoriety over a hundred years later when John Brown led a pre-Civil War raid on the Armory there in 1859.

But now, their bodies all a-moldin' in their graves....

Suddenly as I walk it hits me again, a bolt from the blue.

...leavestheimpairedselfwiththeability...
...tomaterializeitspotentialintoactualities...
...theprocessofreintegrationbringswithituniquerewards...
...newselfawarenessisthegrowingrealizationbytheindividual...
...thattheyhaveafundamentalinternalneedforcontact...
...andintimacywithothers...
...onlyschizoidpatientswhohaveworkedthroughtheir...
...perceptionandfeelingsoflossandabandonment...
...willcometotheideathatthecapacityforintimacy...
...andthewishforintimacyarewovenintothestructure...
...oftheirbeingsyetovercomingtheirdistancetoseek...
...helptoovercometheirdistancecanseemanimpossiblecircle...
...perhapsneedlessperhapsdangerousperhapsimpossible...
...tolearntoswimonemustfacetherealityof...

...drowningfirsttoavoiddrowning...
...drowningfirsttoavoiddrowning...
...drowningfirsttoavoiddrowning...

I slammed my fist into the tree, still wet from the previous evening, and bled. But, the thoughts slowed. "Best git'...."

"I know, I know," I interrupted. Another tongue twister might help. What was I up to now? Fourteen? Fifteen? Strangely, I couldn't remember exactly.

...whichthoughunderstoodtherealitytobethatwhichis...
...ofnecessityacreatedartificebywhich...

Oh, screw it. "Fifteen fitful fireflies fly five furlongs flying fruit flies!" I sputtered. "Sixteen seasick sailors sail six seasons seeking sextants! Several teens save seventeen, save Steven tasing Sven!"

And on and on. I spewed my mantras, trying to force my consciousness to disengage its obsessive thought patterns into pure linguistic computation. *Eighteen, nineteen, twenty....*

...whichthoughunderstoodtherealitytobethat...
...whichisofnecessityacreatedartificebywhich...
...thepossesprmaintainsasenseofcalmandcontrol...
...stillapproachestheneedto...
...drowningfirsttoavoiddrowning...
...drowningfirsttoavoiddrowning...
...drowningfirsttoavoiddrowning...

I felt a Loop coming on. Those were deadly. I gasped for air, sank to my knees. "Twenty-one won twine, twice twenty-two, wine; two, whine tons!" Could a million angels converge to a point? *JUST WHAT THE HELL WAS IT?!?*

Suddenly, the silence of the wild descended, wind and leaves, underbrush, inside and out. I realized by my empty lungs that I had yelled that last stanza out loud. I rapidly exchanged dioxide of carbon for dioxide of oxygen, a loss by both mass and volume but a blissfully welcome gain otherwise. I looked at Virgil; his head was cocked to one side, seemingly confused, but not much else. "Twenty-three," I said to him as I struggled upright again, "makes you and me, one more, twenty-four." I looked at my bloody hand, swore, and spat.

"Twenty-four," Virgil said.

"You got it," I answered as I relocated my *digitus annularis dexter*, biting my *lingua loquax* in the process. I spat again, this time with a little blood mixed in. At least the day was turning out to be more exciting than a grand opening at a miniature golf course. Not getting the ball past the windmill was never this painful.

Just then two blue jays landed on a twig next to us and honked, probably attracted by my shenanigans. Virgil cocked his head up, then sideways, then 30 degrees down angle on the bow planes, giving them a look as if to torpedo them. The blue jays squonked again, not knowing what to make of the odd-looking one, twisting sideways with rapid short movements all in blue and white like an Argentinean Prix pit crew, balancing and rotating their tiny bodies. Virgil answered with a *glissé*, a *jeté*, and a bitingly vicious *snap-é*. Outmatched, the jays shirked, squealed, and scrammed.

"You're a meanie, you know that?" I asked him. He just puffed up, indignantly, a proud *effecée elevé* with which to end the performance. Always the impresario.

I wished I had his pride, and courage. I had neither. Oh, not that I'd ever let him know that; what would the point have been then? To admit the obvious? No; he knew who wore the pants in this tribe of two, same as I did. I flexed my fist, closed, then open again, slowly, and looking at it in annoyance, I gradually resumed something resembling a healthy pace and pushed my cowardice back down. I was no real man inhabiting these parts. My parts were less manly than that. The settlers who seeded this land spoke to me from their graves, quiet in the surrounding woods, penetrating the roots and rising with the dew only as a woody fragrance on the breeze, ghostly, their disdain present in my mind though old and conferring only a slightly darker tinge to the shadows of the trees. If Virgil could accept me, if their shades could accept my passage through their shade, I could accept me too.

He'd been there of course, when I'd landed face-first into the gravel and detritus by the side of the Parkway back on Apple Orchard Mountain. Right there, waiting for me, staring at me, sitting on a stump the road maintenance crews had left behind. Dazed, drenched, I'd looked up, hearing him call. He'd been waiting for me, just outside that monstrosity of a vehicle and the twisted-inside-out morality play reenactment of Noah inside. He'd looked at me and laughed, as I spat the dirt and pine needles from my mouth, sat up, and looked around. Of course, there was no actual vehicle there when I turned. It was gone, or it never existed. But I was wet. Soaked, in fact, head to toe. The ground around me wasn't. He wasn't. So he laughed, sort of, and, truth be told, I did too.

So again we begin again. The clatter of shifted stones, rudely disturbed. The sweet spirals and sprains of a long, labyrinthine climb. The sounds of ghosts. The colors of the sky. A heart, bleeding all that words are. Soon enough the trail smeared itself into so many gnarled footsteps and ragged breaths. The throbbing in my hand gradually dissipated with my sweat into the surrounding air. It was replaced by the throbbing of my heart and muscles, up, down, up, down, a familiar two-step beat in common time for a simple man. Snowbells bloomed alongside, out of season, but in time with us. Butterflies fragmented the blue between the trees.

But I had to occupy my time with something, lest time occupy me. I felt burned out when it came to tongue twisters. I tried some old Japanese poetry:

In the awakened eye
Mountains and rivers
Completely disappear.
The eye of delusion
Gazes upon
Deep fog and clouds.
Alone in my zazen
I forget the days
As they pass.
The wisteria has grown
Thick over the eaves
Of my hut.

Somehow that wasn't satisfying. So I tried:

In the silence of my heart
I remain a place of forgetfulness

Others laugh and tell me
I should come out and enjoy the snow;
But why should I?
For while I remain here by the fire
I am like the snow,
Desolate, a desert.

Which only depressed me. I tried some song lyrics: *Polly Wolly Doodle, Jimmy Crack Corn*, a couple of other old-timey nonsense numbers. Those didn't work either.

I was tired of thinking. I didn't want to do this anymore. I figured I'd left my body to science fiction and been buried alive there. It made me. Why couldn't the message or truth or whatever it was be pre-printed on holy scrolls that everybody was given? And why couldn't everyone be given the same scrolls, so as to avoid needless cruelty and bloodshed? If one was just supposed to accept this, well, that wasn't what I thought acceptable. Acceptance is not weak submission or cold apathy, but the recognition of the facts of the situation. It's the difference between pretending to think with a piece of beating meat versus actually thinking with your head. So why give us a head if we weren't supposed to use it? Just to memorize the hymns we'd sing for all eternity after we croaked, hymns in praise of the master who required our enslavement? Maybe one trait I and the Supposedly Good Lord shared was passive-aggressiveness. That was comforting, if not to the pain still coming from my cornbeefed hand.

So we were just all supposed to have faith and believe and never be sure. It was as empty and deceitful as any political slogan. *Solemnly condemn the capitalist-roaders who use the fear of an earthquake to sabotage the denunciation of Deng!* Or poisoned baby formula. Or imprisoned students. Or Tibetans. Or whatever. America was practicing the same thing now: *The war in Iraq is over.* Whatever. Politics is about power and death, pure and simple. Maintaining power, and avoiding or causing death to do so. Americans had learned that in the utterly unjust wars we spawned in Mexico, Vietnam, and in Iraq with President Bush; the Chinese with every government they had ever had in history. Blame it on the Lin Biao and Jiang Qing Counter-Revolutionary Clique. Criticize Lin, Criticize Confucius. Control the mind and the heart follows. Shell games. Three-card monte. Whatever. Faith was believing just because… because, if you don't, you'll be punished. Then, you're told that faith is a virtue. How can something backed up by fear of punishment ever be a virtue? Real faith is the faith of a gambler. Real faith requires, needs, wants risk. *Ipso facto*, the necessity of the risk-taker. The ace in the hole exists; have faith, and deal. How the cards fell could always be rationalized later. The nature of the dealer: whether a Dealer, or Nature? That, too.

Sigh.

So maybe next trailhead I'd just head out and go into town somewhere and have a big cheeseburger with an even bigger ice cream sundae and a truly enormous root beer, and drown myself in caloric, fatty bliss. I started salivating at the very thought and....

That's when I started to hear the music.

It started as a slight background pulse, an *um-ummm-um-um um-ummm-um-um* through the trees which swayed chaotically with a sudden wind, and emancipated with the music and the wind was a light rain, the first daytime rain I'd had in ages, the first one I could remember since all the way back in Fontana. It seemed a prophecy, a cup of tea leaves served with a plate of entrails, cold and chilling. Matching it was a heartbeat, throbbing, a witches' pulse, an undertow pulling me outward towards the abyss. I realized clouds had moved in with the rain, as if materializing on command; the sky grew dark, sinister. But it was not a gray sky of rain that now greeted me, but a different kind of dark, a live thing throbbing and pulsing. A whorl of wet leaves struck me in the face, like a slap. I brushed them away out of reflex, and the wind howled at me in return, angrily. A primal, porcine fear seized me then, and I stopped.

It changed slightly, *um-ummmmmm-um-um*, a drawing out of the second beat, divining the air for a sign. It was ahead of me somewhere, not far, or perhaps infinitely so. I tried distracting myself with facts. I knew I was close to the next shelter; excuse me, *hut.* Here on the Virginia stretch they were called huts. All the same thing to weary travelers like ourselves. Rock Springs Hut, 3465 feet, highest hut in Shenandoah. Huts here were smaller than the shelters in the Smokies, but more enclosed, and often with picnic tables due to their proximity to the Parkway and the popularity of the park.

Then the cymbals entered, *crash-bang*, and I perceived that the music was a march of sorts, but there was something odd about it lost in the twists and turns of the switchback I was on. Then I came out on top again, and it was much louder, and much clearer. I stopped and listened, wary and full of suspicion, but just as I stopped it did too. I stood there for a full minute, and nothing. I told myself it was a passing vehicle on the nearby road, just tourists, and ignored the fact that it was coming from another direction entirely. The weather remained ugly and growing uglier. A strong gust pushed me backwards, reviving my will. I resumed walking, struggling against Natures both external and internal.

The next two to three miles passed in twenty-five, maybe thirty minutes, silent but for the ever increasing howl of the wind. I hoped I'd get in before all heck broke loose and save myself and the pack from another drenching. I'd had enough of water, at least on my outsides. I pushed it, hard. Finally I arrived at the shelter. Like every other shelter I'd hit since Tennessee, it was vacant, an impossibility due to the popularity of the Trail and its surrounding mass of humanity, a very few of which actually enjoyed what I enjoyed, not many but still far too numerous for my liking. Yet here I was, alone. Terribly alone. Except for Virgil, of course; he was as alone as I.

I threw my pack off with a loud exhale. There's no moment like that: taking your pack off at the end of the day, when you blood resumes its normal course through the body, back into dry veins and barren arteries not seen since lunch or perhaps breakfast. While my calves and thighs were more Greek than *spanakopita* in their godliness, my shoulders were battered and fried practically Southern. I took a good long stretch just to prove I could still do it, regardless of the inning and my current position in the far left of the outfield. Virgil regarded me in silence, then asked for some trail mix. I obliged, and threw in some dry oats for good measure and proper fiber maintenance. I was too tired for a real hot meal, so I boiled some water and made some polenta with a few wild blackberries I'd picked in-stride in the last ten miles. Simple fare; but, the gift to be simple is the gift to be free.

We talked mundanely about the wind, the weather; observed the shelter and the signs of a lack of rodents, which spoke to a healthy population of predators. Mice were ever-present in most of the shelters along the AT, but not this one. No droppings, no nests, no chew marks on the wood, nothing. Virgil liked the mice, making friends easily. He didn't bother them; usually he'd just watch them play then inform them that they'd "best git' movin," always a laugh riot. I knew he'd be disappointed this time. Night fell as we ate and talked, a darkness on the face of the churning deep. I tried not to look at it or think about it.

After dinner I rinsed and wiped everything off, loosely packing it back in the pack. I grabbed it up, to go outside and hang it up on the provided cables, away from the bears. But just as I stood up, behind me, behind the shelter, the music roared to life again, loud and immediate in presence. I froze, and Virgil cried out in surprise. There'd been no one there when we'd arrived. Listening in fear, the music blared, strident, other-worldy and weird, and I knew our time had arrived again.

There was a certain salience to this music, an ambiance, like a Philip Glass string quartet played upside down and backwards, resulting in a sonic wave weirdly like the original, but in harmony a hemiola, in rhythm retrograde, its intent inverted. The notes opposed and clefs reversed; but still, the diminished chord remain diminished. This was an utterly astounding fact. Four minor thirds, anyway you looked at it; but, did two wrongs make a right? No; that would be three lefts, unscribable by any transcriptionist. It had to be interpreted, improvised. I imagined a transposition that left the current chord progression to move to some higher, astral plane; a music of the angels, harpsichords and viols, and trumpets, and divine retribution, Wagnerian trash metal. Gotterdammerung and grunge all rolled up into one chord higher than the Firmament, deeper than the Abyss. Yet, the pulse of my heart remained pure Glass, shattered, with a beat that yet repeated, endlessly. Primal throb, no crescendo or decrescendo, yet all ups and downs. No resolution to this suspended dissonance, just a V7 sus sharp 9 flat 11 who-knows-what 13 with microtone additions that passed out of all knowledge into the upper harmonics, unplayable, and thoroughly, thoroughly unenjoyable by any listener of taste and style. The Eleven-Fingered Man might attempt it willingly, but I was no willing participant to this music. This wail in the air was born more of a Lygeti, or Lutoslawski, woven with a lot of insistent Sousa military bellicosity. Throw their scores in a blender, and hit the whip button. Smooth and creamy the results were not.

So of course I had to go see what all of the fuss and muss was about. I told Virgil to stay put, and he obliged, with no objections to Your Honor.

I stepped out of the shelter leaving behind my half-open pack, pots and pans dangling out. I walked around the corner, turned towards the back of the shelter. Behind it was a short rise to the ridge top only fifty or seventy-five feet back, and a trail leading up and over. On the other side of the ridge a flickering bright light rose, a mystic red and orange fire, and the music was coming from there, just out of sight. I walked up the short barley-discernible path that led over the rise towards the light. I rose over the top to a short steep descent, surrounded by enormous old-growth oaks and hickory. The path came to a dead stop at an enormous tree, twelve to fifteen feet in diameter, stretching upwards into the blackness. It was one giant in a wall of giants, packed tightly together, with barely enough room for one person to squeeze through. The light and the sound seemed to radiate from behind them, brilliantly, almost blindingly, between them. I dropped my pack and toothpasted myself through the gap slowly and carefully, using the bulk of the trees as protection... as if it would have made any difference. A moment's exertion, and the loving caress of the rough bark gave way to open air again, and I emerged into the strangest scene yet.

There was a flat circular clearing perhaps a hundred-eighty or hundred-ninety feet across enclosed by a thick ring of trees that seemed to bend inward towards the top and open only to a small patch of sky. In the center of the circle was a bonfire, blazing, consuming shapes resembling large logs and branches, flames reaching over man-height. But there. There. There, around the fire, closer to the ring of trees than to the fire itself, arranged in a semicircle facing me, were....

*****

Many of the worldborn see belief as a held thing, a beloved trifle with which to while away the hours. Alas, poor evidence. It requires strenuous effort, that; to learn, understand, retain, and pass on. So much easier to sleep, perchance to dream. Aye, there's the rub. Fear rules the hearts of all, especially fear materialized as its opposite: confidence, unshakable and unquestionable. A paralysis of righteousness inhibits the nerves, despite conscience making cowards of us all on the inside. But when confidence passes all self-reflection, darkening all mirrors, silencing the questioning tongue, it becomes a danger, and a weapon. High Purpose gives birth to high explosives, and those who would deliver us from evil with a backpack full of them. Why the Higher need such amateurish, crumbling intervention on our part is anyone's guess. Who knew They were so weak? Regardless of the needs of the Many, such soulless bravado does give the self-immolating a great power: the power to kill without guilt. Just like at Nuremburg: *I was only following orders*. But dreams differ from land to land and cot to cot, naturally adding to the confusion, and God forbid we question. No; that would be disrespectful, and we can't have that. No calling a spade a spade. Such Ones Under God are mere cards, each to be delt and played. It is a sin to question. One must have *faith*. One *must*, or burn. Easy to guess who made up that rule. And pity those with white-washed brains led to the front lines to enforce it.

When the U.S. dropped the bomb on Hiroshima, it was neither a military target, nor a particularly valuable one to the Japanese war effort. It's only value was in its relatively large population and the psychological impact that population's destruction would have on both countries. It's hard to think about, I know. The denial is almost automatic -- I've most likely angered you by even mentioning it. Apologies. I'll do like everyone else does. I'll repeat the standard school-textbook mantra: *it saved lives*. There. I promise I'll do it, over and over. Cross my heart, hope to... to... something, I forget what.

Nowadays even thinking about what we do is frowned on, let alone discussing it, let alone criticizing it. Criticism isn't the American Way anymore; Fox News is. Diatribe for its own sake. A kind of mass-driven avalanche of freshly powdered ignorance directed at us by our own power centers. And ignorance is what fuels wrath. Get to know someone, understand their position, learn, mix the blacks and whites together to a Middle Way grey, and what do you have? Compassion, understanding, acceptance? Perhaps; although, one can understand a thing, and still kill it. One can always smother Grandma with a pillow and rationalize it as "what's best for her." Who knows? Maybe that's what Grandma wants. Sometimes it's the right thing to do.

So we talk, and talk, and talk, and talk. Channel after channel, show after show, pundit after pundit. Who's listening, exactly? Both those with ears and those without. But who adds, and who merely repeats in a twangy mouth-harp simpleton's *D.S. al Coda* what the guy on TV said they should believe? Repetition is at the heart of all music; without it, we'd have no themes, no melodies. For if they weren't repeated, how would we ever know what they were? The simplest music is always the more popular, or at least the most marketable. There's a reason for both.

Hence, terrorism. The ones the terrorists want to coerce aren't their direct victims: they are fodder for the newsclips and nightmares of others. No; terrorism is about sending a message to a leadership and a population that *You Can't Win*. Meaning this: even if you win the war, you will lose its battles. Japan learned. We taught them. Manhattanites have learned. They taught us. That's give and take for you. That's a melody, a melody with primal rhythm, dispensed down through history and bequeathed to our children, and to theirs, and to theirs.

Who can find the cause? This death because of that one; this perceived injustice because of that one. On and on, rolling through the years, across seas and continents and religions and politics. And in every case, at least one leader on each side, rich and relatively unaffected, afflicting their power on the masses. All in the name of *wrath*. Oh, concealed as something else, named as something else: a god's crusty grumpiness, a flag's kitschy colors, a bumper sticker's simple slogan. But bred and spread, like butter made from blood, generation after generation, nonetheless.

Our individualism is both our strength and our weakness. It defines us and separates us, like a good bra should. Helps us hold it together. At least until it tears us apart.

The Cherokee tell a story. A grandfather is teaching his grandson about life. "There is a fight going on inside me," he tells him. "There are two wolves there. One is evil. He is anger: full of sorrow, slow to regret, reeking arrogance, hiding self-pity, forgetting guilt, remembering resentment, spreading lies, feigning superiority, fearing inferiority, and projecting a righteous ego." He continued, "The other is good. He is joy, and peace, and love; he has hope, he has serenity, he has humility, he has kindness, and benevolence, and empathy. Generosity, truth, compassion, too; and he has faith. The same fight is going on inside you -- and inside every other person, too."

The grandson, wide-eyed, asks him, "Which one will win?"

"The one you feed," says the grandfather.

*****

There was a grim woodsman right out of the 18th century, in old musty leather, musket battered but strapped a-shoulder, and a squirrel-head embroidered with a flag out of a Northern grandfather's yellowed history book, but no uniform, no insignia of any kind, only his Brown Bess, and playing a fife. There was a young man, less grey and more gaunt, in a Union's blue but a Confederate's grey felt cap, missing an eye and a leg, but strumming an old-timey three-stringed Washburn. There was what appeared to be a bandito, complete with sombrero, dual bullet belts in an X marking the spot, playing a *vihuela.* Next to him....

From the waist up, they were men, dressed in uniforms: on my left Revolutionary Army, then Civil War, both Union and Confederate, then Spanish-American, Mexican-American, followed by World War I doughboy, then World War II, Korea, Vietnam, and finally Iraq on my close right, ten all-told. Each was holding and playing a musical instrument: fife, banjo, fiddle, some kind of small guitar, then a much larger one, then accordion, trumpet, tenor saxophone, electric guitar, and finally a rapper's turntables and sound board. But they weren't entirely soldiers, entirely... men. Their lower halves were… gone, replaced, transmogrified. From the waist down they were trees, wood with bark, rooted in the ground. A chestnut, an oak, impossibly a mimosa, others, native and anything but. They were half-man, half-tree. Even worse were their faces: bandaged, maimed, bloodied, as they blew and plucked and strove in time playing their march to nowhere. The Confederate was missing the upper right third of his head. The Vietnam vet was burned and charred, horribly so. Behind the semicircle of players in the far darkness and barely visible in the glare of the blazing fire was a set of percussion:

drums, cymbals, and sinister cannon and small howitzers, menacingly unmanned, though I had heard the cymbals crashing before.

“No, no! Punch it! *Fortissimo*, Charles. Not you, Charles, the other one! Ok, yes, that’s better… you’re late Karl. Tempo… TEMPO…”

Little Napoleon's arms beat the air, a tornado of insistence, grinding the fluids and sinews of these apparitions into their music, twisted and violent. The players sweated, bled, moaned, and the little man would grunt, frown, yell at them, curse them. At one point, Vietnam simple dropped his instrument in mid-flight, slumping over in exhaustion and crying out, a horrible writhing wraith of a cry. But Napoleon would have none of it; with one loud shout and a thrusting gesture of his arm, to my astonished horror Vietnam was torn from the stump that was the lower half of his body, blood and viscera splaying across the players, and flung high into the air. Then, falling down into the bonfire in the center of the circle, the fire leapt upwards at the contact, with a burst and fountain of flame like a hundred kerosene-wet logs, as his body exploded, showering the fire with the molten fragments that once perhaps had been a soldier, a mother's son, a human being.

The others played on, terror in their eyes, at least the ones who still had them. They reached for a sort of climax as he shouted on, beating tritones with augmented seconds with piles of fifths, retching up attack and embouchure, coming at last to a noisy dissonant cluster chord that seemed to serve as a tonic of sorts.

They'd stopped playing, illuminated by the fire, and looked at me as I pondered all of the above. They stared, and the small man in front of them turned around. He was a boy, a child, no more than ten or so in appearance, with wide eyes and a odd shine, as if one unruly schoolmate had held him down while another applied a glue stick to him. He regarded me for a moment without expression, and I had the unnerving, intestinal impression that he was made of paper-maché. I recognized a half-bemused look on his face, turning moreso as he recognized the terror on mine.

"*You* are interrupting our performance," he said to me in tinny, high-pitched words, "which under normal circumstances would be unacceptable. Unfortunately in your case it seems I must make an exception."

I am being protected in some fashion, or I am supposed to think I am. "So it seems," I said, carefully choosing my words, slowly. "Dr. Durant Allegheny, at your service and your fam…."

"Yes, yes, yes, I know who *you* are!" he flung out. "As I said, you are inter-*rup*ting our performance!" He stressed the pause and the accent on the *rup,* impatient, angry. He turned back to the musicians, tapped his baton on the now-visible stand in front of him, then looked over at the stump that had been Vietnam, but was now moving, changing, and impossibly groaning. "Are you ready yet?" he asked, dripping disdain.

There was a shape, a figure growing out of the stump where Vietnam had been. In gruesome, maggoty moments it became another Vietnam growing back up out of the stump, unfolding and crying in pain in the process. He screamed as arms emerged, extended, forming fingers, new skin melting down and over. As he reached full blossom he was forced to reach down and pick up a guitar, groaning in pain. The others winced, looked away.

"That's more like it!" said the director. "Now, from the top!"

The men all cried out mournfully, but the director would have none of it. He pounded on his podium for silence.

"ENOUGH!", and a perfect quiet fell. "If any of you persist in your futile efforts, you know how it will end for you. We expect your best, at *all* times. Now, we WILL begin again, from the top…."

So they started up again, a frankenmash of melodies in conflicting times, keys, and pseudoharmonies. There was a distinct lack of bass; everyone playing the same two- or three-octave range, a combination of barrel-rust and boot-smell, grievous and painful. It twisted maniacally in the air, a mescaline dervish of wail and clang. Two or three players would take up a pretender to a melody, or a fragment thereof, but after a few sonorous moments the process would devolve into one going up the scale, one down, the other impossibly sideways into a toxic dimension somewhere near 1847 or Charles Ives or whatever seemed to strike their mood. A lot of modern improvisation and free interpretation from the right side; literal, statuesque, 18th and 19th century delineations from the left. Folk, classical, hip-hop, Golden Age Flamenco, and psychedelic machine gun fire, all at once. Call-and-response, if by *response* you mean hysterical screaming. Or was that me?

Throughout it all the little man in the hat would wave and gesture and implore, yell and spit, a schizoid Stokowski amongst his insanely free bowers. And every now and then one of them, Spanish-American or Iraq or Revolutionary, would seem to provoke his random wrath, starting as an evil dictatorial fixation, devilish, eyes squinting, teeth baring, as the little arms drove harder and harder, faster and faster. Then in mid-flow little paper-maché man would yell, stomp, scream, and another of them would be launched into the air out of nowhere, screaming, flung into the bonfire in the middle of the circle and instant consumption, only to reappear almost as instantly right back where they were, right up out of the ground, reformed, moaning, dripping blood and bile and bits of bark, only to pick up the instrument where they'd dropped it in bewitchment and endless, endless pain, forced to play and be played, consume and be consumed, reweaving the harmony of their Hell back into the shared one of their damned blood-brethren.

As I watched and listened.

After a shapeless amount of frenzied time, somewhere between a minute and an month, the little man had enough, and hurled his baton to the ground, waving them off. "Oh just stop, just stop it!" he cried, and the players quickly died off, so to speak. "You're all such... such... *ammmaaaateurs*." The word rolled around languid in his mouth, oozing a prolonged contempt. The soldiers huffed and puffed, groaning, exhausted.

Reality and I, never being the best of buddies, had finally parted ways. None too amicably; my dearly departed simply seemed, well, crazy now. Takes one to know one. "What do you call that?" I asked, in words not originating from me.

"It's an original piece," he replied. "I'm very proud of it. It truly captures the moment, don't you agree?"

"And what moment would that be, exactly?" I asked, finding my own voice again.

"Why, the moment of their death, of course." he said. "Allow me to introduce tonight's players. On the left we have Charles Waxhaws, fifer, from the Santee north of Charleston, hewn down by Banestre Tarleton himself. To his right on the violin and banjo are Charlie Fort Donelson and Charles Fredericksburg, born in Virginia and Maryland a mile apart, but divided by a million more. On the *vihuela* we have Carl Monterrey from Texas, and on the *guitarrón*, his half-Mexican grandson, Carlos Tayacoba. Then Carl Verdun from Brooklyn on the Chemnitzer concertina, Karl Ardennes from Chicago on the B-flat trumpet, Charlie Chosin on the tenor sax, Chuck B. Kontum on the Stratocaster, and finally C-Phase Line Bullet from the city of *angels*." He spat, expelling the distaste of his last word from his mouth.

I managed eye contact with most of them, but only a few met it. Revolutionary did, Chicago actually nodded at me. Donelson didn't acknowledge me at all, in fact didn't seem to be capable of movement or expression when not playing. Vietnam just stared at the ground, shaking. WWI and Iraq had wet faces, and not from any rain. No one spoke.

"Where's... where's the percussion?" I asked, just to fill the air with something other than a burning soldier's smoke.

"Percussion?" asked the little man, cocking the edge of his mouth upwards.

"Percussion," I repeated. "I heard it... before," jerking my thumb back whence I'd come.

"Percussion?" he said, pretending fake ignorance, looking around melodramatically and reaching in his pockets. Then he feigned an over-the-top *Oh! Ah-ha!* expression, retrieved his hand, and snapped his fingers.

"Percussion!" he said, ready to pull a rabbit out of his hat, all Spring-Heeled Jack of face. "Ah, you must mean... *this*."

Space twisted around me. Instantly I was in a broiling trench filled with dead servicemen, shell bursts and bullets screaming past me, mortar fire left, right, in front, behind. I instinctively dove, landing on a dead corporal, face concealed by a gas mask. Flames whipped over me, around me, through my soul. Inchoate shouts of command from distant sources in the nebula pried through the smoke and screen. Moans from the dying. Screams from those who wished they were, or very soon would be. A bullet grazed my right arm, shredding fabric and scorching my skin. I cried out, grabbing it with my left hand. Then, the clamp of chlorine on my nostrils, and a yellowish-white wall of death rolled over the lip of the trench down into its pureed heart, as I choked and screamed in one last heave of air out and....

Then it was over, and I was back, and the little man was standing over me, and I hacked and coughed on a darkness of dry leaves and scrabble. I reached for my sleeve; it was undamaged. I looked up at him, standing between the fire and I. His face had turned an ocean-night's black, all folds and shadows.

Except for his eyes: like twin neutron stars.

"You mean," he hissed, "like *thaaaaat*." I felt his unseen smile grip my throat to still it, full of serpent tongue.

"Yes," I struggled to answer, whispering it and shaking. "Y-Yes, just like th-th-that."

His head tilted back, and he laughed, long and hard, an echoing cannon fire booming down the ages. "Bravery is an excellent quality to have in this outfit," he said, looking back at the fire, "yet you serve not. Why is that?"

"I s-save lives, I don't take them," I said, hesitatingly, unsure of his meaning.

His head, blackness with burning eyes, slowly rotated back towards me. "*Reaaaaallly?*" he said, sardonically devilish.

I didn't know what to say. It was as damning of a judgment as I'd ever received. I sat up, brushing the forest's detritus off me.

"I'm... I'm not judging anyone," I said, loudly this time, looking past him deliberately at the men.

"Yes you are!" the conductor yelled back, mocking.

"Doesn't seem fair," I said, meaning them, and he knew it.

"Ah, you think they were only following orders," he said sarcastically, a nod in the dark.

"Is... is that was this is supposed to be? Following orders?" I asked. "Them, you... me?"

"We all have them," he said, then looking back at his men, spat again, and added, "whether we *like* them or not."

"They're a necessity," I said, trying to maintain control, or pretend power, or just to engage in order to end this engagement as soon as possible.

"Necessity?!" Napoleon shouted. "*Necessity*?! They are fodder, nothing more. Good for dying. Good for rotting." He tilted his head back, laughed, a hot, gravel-like sound.

"I'm saying that a military is a necessity, that brutality is necessary to overcome brutality, madness to conquer madness."

"Were the poor Mexicans mad to fight for Texas and California?" he asked, pointing back at Carlos. "The Spanish?"

A history lesson? Is that it? "The Indians?" I responded. "It's frivolous rage I'm against, fraud and manipulation and propaganda inciting anger producing needless destruction."

"I wasn't needless," Revolutionary responded in a British accent. "I fought for my home, my family, freedom." *So, they can speak.* It horrified me all the more, to make me think of them as still men.

Iraq countered,. "Shit, I fought because they told me to, you know, they said there were weapons of mass destruction."

"Then it changed and it was about *other* people's freedom," said Vietnam, looking at Iraq. Iraq nodded in agreement.

"That's what I mean by needless," I said, standing up. "Not you, Charles," I said, nodding to them, who all nodded back. "We can't go fight everyone else's battles for them, and there are plenty of battles to go around. And, some people.. some people like things the way they are just fine."

"Enough, all of you!" the little man shouted angrily, striding around the fire back to the podium. "No talking! Follow the rules!" Instruments flew into position, as he grabbed his baton and rose to his full short stature, tapping insistently to get their attention. "Now, where *were* we?" he asked, puffing up and looking around.

The veterans I'd seen in my practice were shocked, through and through. PTSDs, one after another, making them sick, or suicidal; a few, homicidal. Then I'd look around, at our grateful country that sent them there in the first place. I'd tell them I was sorry. I didn't tell them why. And I knew they were the ones who'd been saved, and that there must be others: others who had hardened instead of softened, others to whom a Muslim, any Muslim, or perhaps anyone in a turban, or perhaps just plain *anyone*, was a beast deserving of death. After all, God in His infinite powerlessness had ordered it, ordained it, anointing them as His messengers, His prophets, His latter-day saints. I felt an instinctive protectiveness then, from the doctor in me. I knew there was no point, that none of... this... could be... real. On some level, by some definition, it was all illusion and allegory-play. But still. I'd had enough of brutality, whether fiction or non. I decided to take initiative, take his attention away from the others.

"Why bother," I said, "when the composition is such shit?" *See, that's why you never make friends.*

Gasps from the group. Little man slowly turned around. "*What* did you say?" he asked.

"You heard me," I said. "It's noise. Monkeys on Mister Microphones could do better."

"Do you have some kind of *problem?*" he asked sarcastically.

"Be careful, Doc," said one of the men, low and scared, a few others murmuring in agreement.

"Here's the problem I have with...," gesturing around. "Uh... this. Why? Why this charade? Why the drama? Surely the allegory isn't lost on you. Well, guess what? It's not lost on me either. Know why? Because I'm all grown up now, that's why. I get it. It's wrath, right? RIGHT?" I shouted now, looking around. "This is supposed to be wrath. I get it. I'm supposed to be appalled and say something profound and be amazed and deeply changed and...." I yawned, big and long, an actual impulse, not acted out. "Jeez," I said after regaining control of my mouth. "What a frickin' waste of time." I looked up in the air, shouted. "I GET IT! I GET IT, PADMA!" Not even the wind responded. I looked back down at the men, around the men, revolted at what I saw. "Shit," I said, averting my eyes and turning around, "what a frickin' waste of time. Hell is one big frickin' waste of time. Punishment achieves nothing, it just causes pain and psychological disturbance. I'm sorry, I just can't reconcile that with a god of love." I started back towards the way we came in, Virgil following. "I'm outta here little man!" I said. "I need a good night's sleep, not more schlocky sock puppetry and bad John Carpenter special effects... even if they're from a different kind of carpenter." I reached the ring of trees, shoved an arm between them squirmed sideways, seeking escape from the visions.

"You can't go just yet!" yelled the little man.

"Like Hell I can!" I shouted back, body wedged fully between the trunks now. I twisted my head sideways as much as I could and hollered, "Free will's a Craigslist bitch, brother."

I pushed through, scraping my knee; Virgil yelped loudly in my right ear; I'd nearly crushed him against the tree. I pulled my right shoulder back, hauled my upper body through, forcing my head sideways, away from my direction of motion. I kicked up with my right leg, pushed forward with my left. The I was through, but falling out while looking back. My foot snagged on a large root; my momentum carried me forward turning a half-second later into downward, and I fell hard but out. I landed on my knees, facing back at the ring of trees, slamming my already-scraped knees into the root I tripped on. I barked something Sunday-school-inappropriate, but suited to this awful schooling whatever day it was. I paused for a moment to get my ship back together, then, hearing the all-too-familiar crackle and pop of burning wood, still on my knees, I turned around.

Aw, crap.

Paper-maché Napoleon was there, facing me, smiling. As was the bonfire. As were the others.

"You can't leave just yet," Nap said, very quietly, walking up to me and brushing the dirt and bark off my shoulders. His touch was both real and unreal, solid but plausibly deniable.

"It's *still* shit," I said.

He exhaled, hard and short, looked at me, face to face. I could see it now, close up. It wasn't real. It wasn't unreal. It was some other modification to *real* I'd never conceived of before.

"What's the point of this?" I asked. "Why can't you just *tell me* what I need to know? Why all the drama?"

"Because," he said, stepping back, then hissing the answer at me. "*Words don't mean a thing.*"

I gulped. "Words make all the differ...."

"Afraid?" he interrupted, saccharine.

"You already know the answer to that." I looked him straight in the eye as I said it.

"DAMN STRAIGHT you're afraid!" He slapped me hard across the face. "Now GET UP! Enough whining! Stop running and take your medicine!"

I got mad then. Fuck this animatronic escapee from the Hall of Midget Idjit' Presidents. I jumped to my feet, poked my finger at him. "Now you wait just a second there, Leopold! I'm sick of this and I'm sick of you! Doesn't the Heavenly Host have something better to do like praise or pray or kill the firstborn or some productive shit like that? Go save someone who needs it!"

"YOU need it!" he shouted back at me, undaunted.

I seethed, ignoring that. "Doesn't the shit flow both ways in the sewer? Why do you or your theater manager need me to play by the rules? If I'd wanted to go to the movies I'd have gone to fucking mall first and walked around *that* with the Buckhead blue hair club! Doesn't your boss have anything better to do than ruin my vacation?"

He really flamed out then, advancing again and pushing me with his fake little Napoleon stubs-for-arms. "ENOUGH! When the Boss says He wants and needs...."

I shoved him back, pushing him backwards, with a look of surprise on his face. And nothing happened. No bolt of lightning; no skewering on a pitchfork. That instantly empowered me. I turned my filters off and let go, kept shoving him as I went. "Wants? Needs? What the fuck? Maybe others. Maybe others, but not me! Most of the other hairless fearful apes still seem to want to remain children, believing in Santa Claus and the ability of the incense smoke to drive away the demons and really crazy stuff like those snake handling verses. Stand up, sit down, kneel, stand up, *latria est* and all that. Wouldn't a just Power rather us all be tending the sick and dying and malnourished and downtrodden, rather than socially networking in some church cafeteria wallpapered with chipped-cork bulletin boards while downing hard-water chicory coffee and a holy eternity of women's circle's tunafish-mushroom soup casseroles? You know, skip all that crossing and bowing and transsubstantiationalism, all that exhibitionist confessing of juicy-goosey tidbits of sins, and -- My God! -- all that hymn singing, all that loathsome, terribly afflicted hymn singing, and go out and actually do something for the terribly afflicted? I mean, why waste time on God? Surely He doesn't need anything. All music is a waste of time, after all. Just distortions and pressure waves, especially during the homily. Isn't there real work to do, other than reminding God for the ten thousandth time that the All Mighty Me still hasn't memorized *Amazing Grace* past the first stanza because I recognize institutionalized Madison Avenue hype and manipulation when I see it?"

I stopped to breathe, chest pounding. This was worse than any uphill slope. A drift of wild infernal smoke washed my nostrils; they flared slightly, as did I. The moon or something meant to resemble it occluded another millimeter of sky overhead, illuminating the tension.

"It seems conflict is in the nature of Man," he said, unexpectedly quiet.

"How can one know justice without its absence?" I asked, exasperated.

"Good requires evil!" he shouted triumphantly, throwing his hands up in the air as if he'd won something.

"Only in the schoolyard sense," I proposed. "One cannot teach a thing without demonstrating its opposite. That doesn't make war any less or more just. Conflict maybe, but not war. War is the punishment for being an obstinate fool. All war is unjust. A few playground bullies think they rule everybody else and drag their populations into death and chaos, without realizing that their whole job as leaders of the playground was to prevent that in the first place. Soldiers kill people who have done no harm to them or their families. They in turn are killed by others equally detached and remote. Children die in war. Children are *armed* and die in war, by adults too cowardly to do it themselves, for their own perverse game. And like any vicious cancer, more die as a result of the side-effects of war than the war itself: disease, famine, fallout. Infrastructures restructured to rubble. What environment remains gets bequeathed to cholera, orphans, and landmines. Those who wage war arrogate to themselves the divine prerogative to decide who will live and who will die. So answer me this little man: Cain killed his brother, Lamech killed a total stranger; hell, Abram almost stuck his son. The Good Lord intervened every time -- or so it's said. War and its side effects kill thousands, millions: so where is God? Is He too busy minding the fall of a single sparrow to be bothered?"

He shook, seething. "You... *you* will fall," he said, barely able to contain himself.

"I *have* fallen: before I was born, or so they say. Born that way, and not my fault. Right off the bat we're told we're unworthy, while we're still wallowing in our own diapers. Pisses me off if true, frankly. So go to hell, little big man." I poked him dead center. A chuckle escaped the men behind him then, from one or two.

He twisted, screamed wordlessly, and all of them, all of them, shot upwards in a mushroom cloud of blood and entrails and agony, all thrown into the fire, which exploded underneath the cloud and *whooshed* upwards in a roar of death. I threw myself on the ground, terrified.

"*YOU WILL ALL FALL*!" he roared, animal, rabid.

Moans, agonized moans as the men sprouted again, all of them, all at once, reborn into a world that was not a world. I found a molecule of courage, pushed up, hunched on my knees.

"Enough," I gasped.

"Or what? Or you'll what?" he said, striding back over to me, grabbing me by the scruff of my neck like a dog.

"Stop it," I insisted, losing my breath, trying to recapture my heartbeat in its genie's bottle.

"I said ENOUGH!" he shouted at me.

I got quieter. "Stop it. You can stop...."

"I SAID ENOUGH!!" he bellowed, stomping the ground, which made a booming sound, an unholy tympanic rumbling earthquake of a sound.

I shook myself free of him, stood up, finding my feet, then quieter: "You can stop it. You don't have to do this."

He looked at me, cheeks bellowing in and out, huffing, unable to speak in his apoplexy. *So, he breathes, too. A nice touch; great CGI effects. I was right to begin with.*

I spoke directly and lightly. "There is always choice. You always have a choice. No punishment, no threat can force you to do anything, ever. You resist, succumb, or fail to decide between the two. Only the hallucinatory, the utterly irrational, have any excuse. There may be a price, but there is always a price in this universe: a price for breathing, moving, blinking, and a price for resisting. There is a price for everything. It may be barter, an exchange of accounting goodwill: but still, a payment and a loss."

He could take it no more. He reared back and let out a horrific banshee's screeching wail, a Purgatorial mix sounding like all the percussion instruments on Earth going off at once. That's when I knew from where the percussion I'd heard before had come, and just as the realization hit me space twisted around us again, and after a moment's nausea and disorientation we found ourselves in daylight, but only half in the forest with a suddenly applauding studio audience behind us. And instantly, there in front of me was Ervil Creek himself: a vitrolic, incendiary flamethrower of a man, known around the country as a purveyor and salesman of class division, racism, hatred, fear, and conspiracy theory after conspiracy theory. A radio show, two TV shows, syndicated commentator, overwhelming Internet presence: the man had a message to deliver, and saw himself as a prophet of a new Age of Unreason, an age he reasoned should be properly populated by old, Christian, white people serviced by the lesser races and ages with a minimum of acknowledged discomfort and physical contact. Unfortunately for him and his followers, demographics were not on their side. The top name for male babies in Texas is now Jose. By 2012 Caucasians will constitute only 49% of the American population;

by 2050, 65% of Americans will be first- or second-generation immigrants. The America of the Founding Fathers, if it ever existed at all, would never be again -- but tell that to Ervil and his Ervillite following. They weren't interested in the facts. They were interested in fascism.

"What planet have I landed on? Did I fall into a black hole last night and wind up on some Planet of the Apes that looks like America?" he shouted at the audience, then directly at me, "*You* tell *me!*"

After all this time I was too jaded, all bravado. "Which one? Original, Beneath, Escape, Conquest, Battle...?"

"Enough of you!" shouted Uncle Sam, but I pressed it, mocking him with a related and obtusely racist reference.

"Got any grape juice plus?" I asked. "I sure could use some right now."

"Well, right now we have to get to the real story!" said Creek. "And the real story is: the anger of the American people!" The crowd behind him cheered for two or three seconds, applauding wildly, then just as abruptly stopping. "What do you have to say about that, Dr. Allegheny?"

Job came to mind. "Thou renewest thy witnesses against me, and increasest thine indignation upon me; changes and war are against me."

Ervil seemed bewildered for a moment, then catching himself: "Just a lot of Jew-talk from a Jew!" he proclaimed, both correctly and incorrectly. "A big lot of victims and their victim mentality! (*scattered applause and cheers*) Jesus should have come back from the dead and made the Jews pay for what they did (*much greater applause*)."

"The Jews didn't kill Jesus; the Romans did," I corrected him, but only halfheartedly. I was already feeling the boredom seep in and stain the moments. It was just more drama and needless pageantry, sigh.

Ervil overrode me with his voice. "But thank God for the men and women of the armed forces! Thank them for preserving our way of life! They're here today to present us with a little concert, a magical melody to restore our faith and our promise, and *their* faith and *their* promise, to *us*!" Cheers, cheers and hootin' and hollerin'. Ervil sure was popular -- right up there with ritual cannibalism in Tenochtitlan.

But up went Midget Man's arms, waving wildly, as instruments flew into position and their impossible music of disaster and insanity started up again. It ostensibly began in mixolydian with a tritone's bass accompanied by machine gun and mortar, until WWI and WWII entered with a transposed theme in precambrian mode, trilobitic, clawing chalkboards on its way through the air to smash its beat directly on the eardrum. I felt my eyes vibrate, their jelly quivering inside them from the waves pounding on their shore. Then Revolutionary entered on the high fife, with an obnoxious, pecking melody, a cutting *wee-wee-wee-wee* that served its Master only too well. Then at a high plateau of tension paper-maché boy turned to the audience, arms razor slashing the air, and as he opened his mouth a hodgepodge of banshee wails, jackhammer destruction, and explosions, over and over explosions, one loud long ruinous roll of explosions and martyrdom and death, death made sonorous, death made an enharmonic accompaniment, thematic and theologic, death and darkness made semisolid and served hot and proper to an adoring throng. They stomped their feet, pounding the stands with their animal pulse, merging with the madness, consuming the darkness produced, oblivious, marching nowhere in place in a place that was no place.

"This is pointless!" I shouted at Sam over the din.

Instantly the music died. It didn't just stop; it didn't just end. Normally there is an in-between moment when music's echoes die and the breath of the players resume a normal rhythm. There was none of that. There was sound, then there was no sound. It was existence followed by non-existence with no funerary or requiem separating them. It was instantaneous, sinister, physically impossible.

"Excuse me, but did you say, *pointless*?" asked Sam in the quiet. Gasps from the crowd.

"Yes, I did: pointless." I answered. More gasps.

Suddenly the scene changed again, in another nauseating indistinct blur of motion, and I found myself on a stage with Ervil and little Napoleon, being interviewed in front of a faceless crowd.

"So what's your story, Doc? What's your problem? Why aren't you a *real* American?"

I moaned in response, still recovering from the reality shift, finding myself seated suddenly under harsh lights, stomach turning and temporarily blinded.

"That's no answer. What do you think, Sam?"

"Go to Hell," I said, still gasping.

"Then fine Doc, you answer it yourself. Why aren't you for America? Why are you against these brave men? Why are you supporting the failing followers of a failed religion?" Cheers from the audience.

I managed to return to a semblance of stability. "Who? Them? I'd disagree. Sure, the onesies and twosies since have mostly failed. The shoelace bomber may have failed, and even been laughably pathetic, but their strategy has been nothing but successful, and it's our fault." More gasps. I continued. "See folks, the war is over, because there never was a war to begin with. It was all... bread and circuses. Grand theater. Somebody said that. Somebody said terrorism is grand theater. No; wait. No. The war ended in October of 2008, when Al Qaeda effectively bankrupted America. Since then we've seen theater, lots of it. No folks, Al Qaeda did their job. They pulled us into an unwinnable, goalless situation with no clear target or purpose, against no strategic assets, against no army base or silo bunkers or marbled halls topped with strange flags. They hit us once to get our attention, rile us up, begin the churn of hatred and rage and nationalism, racism, theocism, and all they need to keep the snowball rolling downhill is a few half-hearted but heavily-reported attempts here and there, a video or two released every now and then, a kidnapped solider or dead military outsourced consultant here and there. They knew we'd respond reflexively, and we did. We're predictable, and they're smart. They're not mindless, no more so than any other military command. Now the thing drives itself, its own smart bomb, right on vague, nebulous target, incessant and unyielding. We've already lost. We were baited, pulled into a conflict of other's making. We've lost. The politicians will never say so, it's against their very fibrous nature, they can't say we've wasted all these taxpayer dollars acting like the angry jock with the bloody head in the bar fight too stupid to go home and stop letting others smash bottles into the face he's supposedly protecting. Too many jobs to protect now, too many careers, too many election promises. That's what we're fighting for now. It's grand theater all right; we're just the audience, throwing cabbages at kings without realizing they're just actors on a stage, and we're missing the real kings of this thing: Al Qaeda's financiers and host governments watching from the plush box seats funded with our assistance. Those are the guys who...."

"ENOUGH!" shouted Sam. "You're talking about our allies in this!"

"Go to Hell," I repeated.

"Too late," said Sam, grinning his Cheshire cat grin again.

"For you maybe. We'll just see about the rest of it."

"But America's *in* Hell, Doctor!" cried Ervil. "We need rescuing! We need salvation! America needs to turn back to God!" More cheering.

"Why? Because God is punishing us, or would, or would less so than He punishes us now? So, we should do this thing you want out of... out of *fear?*"

"Exactly! Fear! Fear of *The Lord Our God*!" Ervil threw his arms high and wide, and a burst of lightning filled the sky above him as he said the big G-word. Sam cackled and rubbed his hands, gleefully.

I let the moment pass, inhaled, and expelling it in one big long hiss, responded: "*Bullllll-shit.*"

Gasps. Boos from the audience. Perhaps a ripe tomato or cabbage head thrown. Nice touch, though it missed.

"Oh, please!" I shouted, standing up. "Fear? Fear? *That's* the way a benevolent all-powerful being is going to motivate us? *Fear*? I thought it was love. I thought it was about love. What does love have to do with fear? What does damnation and brimstone and all that Hellenic, Babylonian-influenced primitive Bronze Age schoolyard bully motivational science stuff have to do with love? Bullshit. With all the pain and grief and misery and injustice and fear in the world as is already? Bullshit! Does that make any sense? Do any of you think about it? Does it sound *reasonable*? Wouldn't you electrocute or hang or shoot a world dictator that tried to motivate us all by instilling fear in everyone? Wouldn't he be overthrown? Vilified? Demonized? Haven't they *all* been? Isn't that why we *called* them a dictator in the first place? If they'd been great and perfect Ghandiesque leaders, wouldn't they still be our leaders? So why aren't they? Because they sucked? Isn't it because they sucked and failed us? Right? *Right*? Bullshit."

"We fight in the name of our country, founded under God!" Ervil cried, maniacally.

"Thou shalt not kill, Ervil. It isn't qualified. It isn't parenthetical. It's a statement. It ends in a period, not a big long *well, except when this or that or the other*. Jesus said when your enemy strikes you on one cheek, offer him the other. He didn't mention anything about drones or cruise misses or Delta Force take-outs in the dead of night. Consistency please, Ervil. Believe what you believe or don't, but don't pick and choose and ignore and highlight according to *your* desires. And as for the founded under God thing: historically untrue, yet so convenient. We can avoid responsibility for our own actions that way. Of course, that's exactly what the terrorists do too: they're just following Allah's orders, they're just doing what their master told them to do. Following a book rather than a flag -- I mean, *our* flag and *our* book. It seems following orders mindlessly makes one a hero these days: it doesn't take a lick of intelligence at all. At the end of the chain of command it's men -- men that pull the trigger, light the fuse, close the mortgage, sell the stock, arbitrate, arbitrage, and profit righteously off of it all. Maybe what God wants is for all of us to kill each other. At least that theory matches the objective facts at hand. And, no need to waste time thinking it through. Not that you're doing that to begin with."

Cat-calls, hisses, more cabbages. I ducked one or two. Ervil was aghast, or at least faking it extremely well. "WHAT? Have you lost your pride? What kind of American are you? Don't you want to take back America for Americans?"

"Do you mean the Navajo, Apache, Cherokee, Iroquois, Blackfeet? Or those before them: the Mississippian culture, the tribes of the Hopewell tradition? Or before them: the Oshara, the Na-Dené, the Folsom? Or back even further: the Paleoamericans, the Siberian tribes, proto-Indo-Europeans, the Out Of Africans parts I and II, the *Homo Erecti*...."

"WHAT? How can you joke about *America*, Doc? Don't you *care*?" More applause, righteous indignation, several guys standing up behind him pumping the air with their fists Arsenio-style.

"Absolutely!" I affirmed loudly, surprising him and them both. "What's happened to our spirit? Our can-do attitude? I can remember a time when I actually got out of bed before 10 a.m. to fight for the things I believed in. I guess I'm part of the problem now. I've been replaced by a pathetic emotion-less motion-less balloon-boy. Clearly I'm a threat to the American way of life. Why didn't I vote in the local school board election so those liberal give-away homosexual Commies didn't take over and fill our vulnerable helpless children with the virtues of medicinal marijuana, free love, Godless taxation, and evolution without representation? Our precious children! My oh my. What would Benjamin Franklin say about me? Or Thomas Jefferson? Oh, never mind that they were deists; let's just gloss over that for now. Right now we need to reclaim America for Americans! I mean, I need to reclaim it from myself, since when I say *we* I really mean *I* and not *you* since *we're* not victims and *we* can do this... whatever exactly *this* is! They took our honor, our faith away: our faith in God and in ourselves. I mean, the *us* that isn't *them* and the God that's *our* God and not *their* God. I mean, despite the fact they're technically the same God. Uh... anyway my point is that *they* don't care about *us*; *they* care about *them*. No, wait; I mean, *we* gave up, gave it to *them*. I mean... wait. I mean WE can take back what is OURS that THEY took from US. Or is it what they're going to take from us if we let them? Whatever *it* and *us* and *them* and *we* mean.... WAIT! Of course it has meaning! I mean, *it* has *meaning*! No, wait. I mean *we* and *us* and *it* has meaning, to *me*! And, *I* can articulate it! I mean, the *us* and *we* that we agree *is* us and we and not the *us* and *we* we *know* isn't us and we but *them* and *those!*" I cried out in mock exasperation. "See? *See*? This is what THEY do with all of their confusing *facts*! DAMN THEM! Now THEY have me all confused! I mean *us*. No; I really mean *them*. We have to take the Truth back from the fact-mongers, and take it back now from the them that isn't us whoever we are and whatever the hell it means to take back something from someone or someones that isn't or aren't there in the first place!"

Cheers from the studio audience. I turned, taking a melodramatic bow, sweating like a pig from that one. Ervil just looked totally confused. Uncle Sam glared at me, shiny and red-faced. Excellent.

I turned and whispered to Sam, quietly, as he seethed. "Millionaires wish to keep their millions, whites their power, the retired their pensions and health care. Companies wish greater profits and market share, politicians want reelection, drug users a longer and higher high. Meanwhile, despite gross desire, the world changes and grows, every day, confounding us all and our fear-bred need for an impossible risk-free life and history-ignoring non-change. Am I missing something?"

Little Tin Man just grunted, veins or what I was supposed to interpret as veins throbbing, jaw shaking, trembling in anger all over.

I decided to throw down on him. "So what are we holding now, boss? Aces and eights -- dead man's hand? Tony and Cleo? Alabama Pillowcases? A gratuitous pair of Bo Dereks? Or just a pathetic 7-2 whip? What's it gonna be? Fold 'em or flop 'em, boss? After all, this ain't nothin' but a game." I wore a pleased-with-myself-and-eating-it grin. *You know, this really is getting easier.* I went for it, owning my part in the ridiculous plot line. I stood up, addressing the rowdy, riled up, non-existent crowd.

"How about a game of tic-tac-toe instead folks? Did you know the Xs and Os were originally a religious distinction between Christians and Jews? At Ellis Island, actually. Most immigrants couldn't read. The Christians would gladly mark their Xs when asked to sign the forms. The Jews, on the other hand, refused to mark an X, as it reminded them of the Christian cross, and there wasn't an X in the Hebrew alphabet anyway. They made an O instead: and in Yiddish, a big *O* was *kikel*, and a little *o* was *kikeleh*, from which we get the wonderful slur *kike*. Tic-tac-toe was a game of derision created by the employees at Ellis Island to wile away the time, in mockery of the immigrants they looked down on every day. Who would have thought that when our precious kids play it they're reenacting a two thousand year old religious war?"

Confusion. The faceless exchanging faceless looks. Uncle was redder than beets with a sunburn, clenching his fists and trembling.

"C'mon folks; don't you hate the Jews?"

Shock, gasps, whispers, downcast eyes. An encumbering, thickly dripping silence.

"Aw, c'mon. At least be consistent. In the 40's it was the Jews and Germans and Japs. In the 50's and 60's, the blacks and the hippies and the Commies. In the 70's... well, so many of you were on coke in the 70's, who knows? In the 80's it was the Ruskies. In the 90's... hell, so many of you were on coke in the 90's, who knows? Now it's the Mexicans; wait, I'm sorry, *immigrants*, because I can't say Mexicans, that's not politically correct. Oh, and the Muslims, all billion-and-a-half of them. So what's it gonna be, folks? Who do you need to fear... I mean, *hate*, now?"

Sam was vibrating now, shaking so fast that it couldn't be called anything else. Smoke began rising about him, from him. *At least this will be over soon -- one way or another.*

"We send good men and women to die for us. They'd better be given a good reason to do so. A good reason, not just some commandments from some old burning Bush men in a room acting like gods, appropriating the power of life and death to themselves over *personal* vendettas. Odysseus once told Achilles: *war is young men dying and old men talking*. War is also the unborn remaining unborn, nothingness remaining nothingness. It's up to you. Stop *talking* about Washington, about politicians, about the system, about the Man keeping you down, about God's Will when you have no idea what that really is or if it even exists. They're all abstractions." I grabbed Sam by the arm; it felt like I was grabbing heavy, hard, hot cardboard. "*He* is *your* puppet, not the other way around. The only sanction we provide him is the one we grant him through our actions -- and our inactions. We've forgotten that in America... or we've at least allowed it to happen. Allowed the little dictator to boss us around, sanctioned our victimhood from him. Maybe Atlas should shrug. Maybe a little revolution is in order. What do you think, Sam?"

But instead of answering, Sam grabbed his head and screamed in one horrifyingly blare of white noise, bursting into flame from the bottom up. He turned his head upwards, and spouted flame skyward. The crowd screamed, audience and soldier alike. I jumped back, feeling the hair on my hand that held him singed and burnt.

"See?" I yelled over the flames at the assembled minions, defying Hell itself. "There is no America or Washington or power above you other than what you think there is, other than what you allow! Don't you see? There is just *us*." I pointed back at the terrified soldiers. "And there is just *them!*"

A wall of flame roared towards me then, engulfing me, whipping me in a molten tornado, but then just a suddenly it was quenched, and the blackness of the wood's night returned with its equally dark wood, and I was back in the circle of trees, next to a burned-out pyre of logs, facing ten elongated mounds, graves in a semi-circle on the side of a hill open to the stars. There was only a light wind, and crickets, or frogs, unseen. After a moment the circle of trees relaxed, seemed to slump, and most of them faded away, out, and into the blackness of the night sky, like souls arising at the end of days. The graves themselves remained, inviolate, dust to dust.

I stood there for a long time in silence, honoring the unknown, heart churning inside me, calming down. I'd been moved this time; apparently against all logic I remained human. I considered the likelihood of bones actually being present, but the thought turned me cold and nauseous. For once, now was not the time to think; a little feeling was in order. So I stood there, for a long time, feeling, until out of the corner of my eye I saw a snake, a long grey ominous silent thing, moving slowly around the bottom of one of the trees, across the loose rock and towards the graves. I didn't wait for Act Two. Quickly I turned, and returned back on the trail from whence I'd come, back over the top of the ridge, to the shelter and Virgil. I said nothing when I flopped back down on the bench, exhausted in body and spirit, shackled in sweat and an indigo fear, and he didn't ask. God bless Virgil. After a while I stole sleep from somewhere or someone, with no intention of atoning for the crime of it. I slept, thankfully a dreamless sleep. I slept until the stars had fled with the clouds that had mocked us so, hiding their beauty, leading me and leaving me to the fire.

When we left the shelter in the morning, I did not look back. That whole day, I watched my feet move forward, and nothing else. And the next day. And the day after that.

VII

1240 feet, 791 miles to Katahdin

John Wesley Hill once said that patriotism is the religion of the soil. I agreed. I felt America under my fingernails.

Unlike most feelings, this one persisted. Fact was ever since Shenandoah I was twitchy-scared. So, I intellectualized and pondered leadership. What was it to lead that led men to leadership? What was it to be led that leaden men sank in swift submission to their leader? To a man, men usually went one way or the other, early on in life. Some babies cooed, some babies cowered. Playground children knew who to pick first for their teams, and who to pick last. Imagine that boy picked before all of the other boys: that boy who was feared, respected, trusted, counted on, turned to, needed. Imagine that boy who was picked after all of the girls were picked: the kind that after school still colored with crayons, and cried on what he colored. Is there any hope for the latter, to ascend the ladder of manhood, through sheer effort or willpower or raw desire, to displace the former, without losing something fundamental of himself and what he has colored in the meantime? Is that desirable? Is it even really possible, or is the effort to do so just another kind of childish wish-fulfillment, just insecurity and ego, and bitterest falsity?

Is there a point in life when the wheels once set in motion lose their capacity for change, when the sum of our journey becomes a collection of rough aggregate and coarse fill traveling on fixed rails down a path already chosen for us? Or, like the song says, if life is a highway, can we ride it all night long? Do leaders create success because they find it, or because it is given to them? Do those who are led find out they are just another car on the train, just another self-contained self-absorbed collection of dry (or, in my case, dried-out) bulk goods? Still, trains could thunder, and shake the very earth beneath their tracks. Trains could derail, and in their destruction create a moment of magnificence, mangled and metallic. Trains could runaway, like Virgil and I; although, I wondered now where our tracks led exactly. I'd thought I was the conductor of our travels; but now, realizing the conductor was someone, some... *thing* else, I knew I was just a hobo after all, and that my caboose was cooked. Sure as you can steer a train, you can change your fate.

I wanted to believe that, like Hamlet, you can fret me, but you cannot play upon me. A lie, I know. But such lies are the bedrock of the quicksand foundations of our stony countenances. So here I was, sinking in elevation, while being played.

Experienced thru-hikers say that the psychological halfway point in the Trail is at Harper's Ferry, Virginia. The actual halfway point is harder to determine, but is somewhat further along, somewhere early in Pennsylvania. Problem was the actual route varied from year to year, as Nature created and destroyed, or as the portions remaining on private lands (now very few in number and size) changed hands. I'd passed Harper's Ferry and the crossing of the Potomac (definitely a river, not a crick!) days ago and was now in the midst of the least-interesting part of the hike, panoramically-speaking; pretty, but nonetheless dull. The five states until the Berkshires in Massachusetts would be a literal low point for me, the highest point in the five being Burch Run at a petty 1795 feet. Mere hills. The days passed quickly, making 18, 19, 20 mile days in ten hours of motion each, an antihistaminic haze of indifferent pretty sameness about them, like days and days of Olympic ice skating, or that row at the drug store with all of the hair color products with all of the artificially colored women one after another in every shade of human head perceivable, marketable, and stoichiometrically stable at room temperature. I skipped one of my planned off-days, choosing to push on, knowing the real adventures lay ahead. V-Man didn't mind. We hiked up smooth low rises, into and out of small plots of state game lands filled with the doe-eyed innocent. I wore a conspicuous orange, lest an intimate encounter with a crazed woodman's out-of-season lead or bow wood occur. V-Man wore his usual reds and blues.

Virgil. Like the Underground Man, I am spiteful, unattractive, and I believe my liver is diseased. But unlike him I cannot say that I know better than anyone that by all this I am only injuring myself and no one else. That's not true. There's Virgil to think of: Virgil, my companion, my mentor, savior and saint, my philosopher-king, my vassal and knight, my inscrutable wisp of connectivity back to the monotonously classic rock hits radio and deep-fried potato world of the lowlanders. It was a world we skirted very closely to now, here at, oh, somewhere around 900, 1000 feet. Trivial wins, for both sides.

We were in New Jersey now, in Harriman State Park, passing the William Brien Memorial Shelter, heading down to cross the road and head back up the other side to spend the night at the beautiful (by all accounts) West Mountain shelter, a mere three miles ahead. We'd kicked it this day; we'd be coming into camp after 23 or 24 miles, probably our best day yet. It was hot and humid, perhaps 80, 85 degrees. We'd pressed ourselves through the infamous Lemon Squeezer, where the Trail goes between two large boulders a foot apart on a fifteen degree slope, then passed through a rock tunnel with pine trees growing on top of it. Exertion and evaporation argued back and forth for our collective souls, drawing no conclusions save one. The last clutch of days had provided much more ambient noise, growing as I went forward; here in the Garden State, within a half-day's walk or a hundred-fifty-dollar cab ride of the Big Apple, the sounds of the cityfolk were everywhere, a distracting ragweed's pollen inviting nothing but an allergic response.

We'd been alone, utterly alone, all these many days. There had been a comfort in that at first, a numb quietude after the events in Shenandoah, already nearly six weeks and some four hundred miles and change behind us now. Never a soul at a shelter or lean-to or cabin or squathole. Never a passer, right or left lanes, a mathematical and geographical impossibility. Dreading the nights and what might or might not happen, finding their firstborn grey mornings as regular and monotonous as their dead and buried ancestors. Never a late-night arriver to camp, a lost dog, a ranger, a hippie, a hobo. Even crossing I-87 had been an exercise in Buddha-scale emptiness, without even a gurgle of a Mack truck rumbling by. Never a soul; only the soulless, parodies of the solid, damned puppets from Hell. But now the sounds of writhing humanity were faintly growling in the air like an avalanche, aloof, pouring turbulent down a long gorge and spilling into an empty distant valley as a malevolent grumbling of far-off ice and rock. Thirteen thousand taxi horns, blaring; sixteen million feet, marching; eight million throats raw from the clamor, the anguish, to be heard, anything to be heard, and therefore noticed, and therefore valued, a stand-out, important, at least for a mental moment. Throbbing waves in the polluted air, pounding on my distant shoreline again and again, higher and higher, as I approached closer to the edge of the bitter dank sea that was urban humanity. The inexorable tide of Malthus was rising to greet me with a warm and unfriendly smile.

Eventually I came to the pavement of U.S. 6, and stopped as if I'd come to a river of lava. I closed my eyes, sniffed the air. There was an unnatural stillness about things: a lack of cars, no birds, not even squirrels chasing one another in their endless bid to be Tree King. There was only a light breeze carrying the distant rolling murmur of the masses, and I slowly let it fill my sore lungs, feeling the syncretic sounds of mankind grow larger inside of me, a tapeworm of drivel. Finally I stepped forwards onto pavement. But as I did so the sudden blare of a car horn, several car horns, shocked my eyes back open to see a line of cars travelling both ways into and out of the park, a line not present just seconds before. Angry drivers swerved, waving their pudgy fast-food arms at me, shouting Yonkers obscenities. Stunned, I grabbed Virgil, and dashed across the road through a small gap that finally appeared in the line. Yet, when we hit the grassy gravel on the other side, just like that, utter silence fell again. I froze, and turning back, slowly, I saw to my astonishment that even the road has disappeared, replaced with an old, worn, rutted cart path, full of flowers and grass.

I looked down at the largest dandelion I had ever seen. It seemed to take on a ultrasharp, perfect Pixar 3-D clarity as I stared. I gasped as it floated up, out and off the ground in a seeming desire to be blown. I reached out, and it swam into my hand, willingly. I turned it slowly, as the sounds of birds and insects slowly gained in volume. I pulled it to my lips in slow-motion, and blew softly. It shimmered away, a bright golden efflorescence mixing with its thousand tiny pearls as it shown cloud-like in the sunlight. The seeds loitered as if hesitating, afraid to leave their nest. Then suddenly the stalk in my hand slumped, dying, and a strong gust of breeze pushed the seeds upward and outward, tossling my hair. As I watched the children leave, I thought I heard schoolyard-laughter on the wind. I smiled. As I watched them, Virgil took the rest of the dandelion in my hand, tore a leaf off, dropped the rest, and proceeded to snack nonchalantly and slowly on the leaf.

I laughed, a singular expression. For some reason this gave me hope, and up and off we trotted, up the hill to what I now knew would be our next test. At least we were getting some forewarning for these last few acts. Perhaps so few acts were left, the need came to increase the tension, add dramatic flair. I laughed again. It seemed so... comical, pointless. Oh, the drama: maudlin and vaudevillian. But not so far to go now, not so far to the end.

Thinking of it, I quickened our pace. The end, at Katahdin. Not so far now. I could almost smell the Canadian spruce of the Hundred-Mile Wilderness that presaged it: a hundred miles of no roads, no towns, no people, only rivers and bogs and flies and more flies. I longed to be there, the longest stretch of genuine wild land on the entire Trail. I longed to be there. Two accipiters circled overhead, soaring on warm currents.

I consider the reality of the situation. Sanity like love is in the eye of the beholder. I walk a wire high in altitude and flowing with currents electric. What is the lie, and what is the reality: the wire, or the electricity? Perhaps I am lying; perhaps this is all a lie. Your Honor, I really appreciate the opportunity to stand here today and speak a few words. It's been a long few years, a lot of memories. I'd like to apologize to all for my actions, to all in this room, to a lot of folks not here today, and I realize I hurt a lot of people and that I accept responsibility for my actions: and I would do so, but for the fact that Virgil is a witness, speaking truth to the facts. Your Honor, electricity is just gravity operating in the fifth dimension, or so testified Kaluza and Klein. And what of their radion? A mystery and enigma, like Padma. Facts interfered like bands in the photon spread past the slits, mysterious action at a distance, neither wave nor particle, and just as inadmissible as evidence. The conclusion? The solidity of the wire is sure; the effects of an invisible aether just that. Doubt is a healthy thing, as is sanity. Thus I counterbalance on my wire, full of lightning. South pole behind me, north pole ahead. Not guilty, Your Honor.

Don't worry, I'm not certain what I am saying either. There is truth there, I'm sure of it; but it eludes me as surely and as surly as the underlying truth of reality. I'm just thinking out loud, passing mental gas to pass the time, so to speak. Don't concern yourself with it. What's far more important is the girl, or what appears to be a girl, on the trail ahead of me.

I first saw her through the trees, a mile or two up from U.S. 6, ahead and above me on a ridge side, disappearing around a turn. I slowed down at the sight of her, wondering who or what she represented, she and her long black hair. A ghost, a sprite, a demon, an illusion, a succubus, or some combination of all of the above? Oberon carefully observed that neither he nor his court feared the church bells. Why should my midsummer night's dream be any different? So I slowed down, but did not stop. Onward, Christian soldiers.

But I did not see her again, not until much later, and even then, when I did see her again, it was a while before I realized who she was, and why she was there, and why I was allowed to see her here in the *Tir na nÓg*, our personal Fortress of Apples.

Apologies. I'm getting ahead of myself, and that won't do. How I wish I was human, and sane.

*****

Schadenfreude. How all the other passions fleet to air as doubtful thoughts and rash embraced despair and shuddering fear, in the presence of green-eyed jealousy. Then again, as the Muslims say, *maashallah*. For without it, we destroy, envy becoming anger and resentment. When we are reluctant to see our own well-being overshadowed by another's because the standard we use to see how well off we are is not the intrinsic worth of our own well-being, we accede power over ourselves to those others. We cease to become men, and become reactionary robots instead, puppets on the strings of life. *Mudita* is taking joy in the good fortune of others; *schadenfreude* is just taking.

Which one would think the members of the Marching Members of Mahwah would have known. High bred, high class, high minded, and in the main so Ivy League one would think them in league with leagues of ivy. Every couple of weekends spring to autumn they would meet in Mahwah, from places as disperse as the Upper East Side to the MacMansions of Alpine, from the hamlets and hovels of Ho-Ho-Kus to the exotic palaces of far-off Mantoloking, to gather and be manly. The Marching Members gathered, stocked, carpooled, and disembarked, to prove themselves worthy among the pine, to remind themselves and each other that they were men, manly men, as befitted their title and honor arrayed as they were as princes of the land. Fore X. Fucci, the Italian currency speculator, a man of suave means and manly, meaner persuasion. Ulysses and Diomedes Bond, high-yield investors of Greek and British extraction, yielding highly, with little or no return. Bertram DeBourne, arbitrageur *affetuoso*, a giver in markets located in one time zone and a near-simultaneous taker of the same goods in another market, another time zone half way around the world -- and pocketing the difference fortuitously created by "inefficiencies in information flow". Bernard McCool, Ponzi schemer (excuse me, high-yield investment manager) extraordinaire, with homes by the Park, in Jupiter, in Tahoe, in Monaco, and Palm Springs, and matching private bank accounts in Midtown, the Caymans, a wall safe in Tahoe, an underground vault in Switzerland, and a buried water cooler in the desert just outside Tijuana. Adam and Sinon Krappe, brothers of indeterminate origin and less determinate economics; Mediterranean certainly, but to be more precise would be to invite charges of racial profiling, or worse (in the dead of night, emphasis on dead). Piers de la Vigna: in character, part Irish, part Spanish; in word and deed, part usury, part used. Jeff Eleazar, president and founder of Metals2Moolah: Where The Suckers Check In But They Don't Check Out (With A Fair Market Price Anyway). And ruling over them all at all times from his boardroom, at least in his own head anyway, Ronald Rumpe: richelieu, raconteur, ruminant. All rich, and all poor: a strange diversity. But all manly-Stanley enough to be out here in the woods this fine day, the rulers who rule us, with their rulers, judging, and being judged.

Friends and patriots, parasites and killers. But that's what America's all about. Everything that isn't explicitly illegal -- or can't be traced back to you, or can be but the person or persons who can trace it or have traced it can be ignored, bought, killed, or some combination of the three -- everything else is fair game. The world exists for the taking. This is my body; take ye therefore, and eat. And eat. And eat and eat and eat. The problem with predators, though, is that they don't take kindly to other predators in their territory. Two sets of fangs in a hungry mouth are one too many. Then again, an *exceedingly* hungry mouth could always consume them too.

Nowadays the hawk and the vulture circle together, but no one would call them a flock: just a sign of the times. And when the hawks and vultures come, to subdivide the subdivisions even further via the creative financing and investment vehicles of the first decade of the twenty-first century, best to hedge your bets behind the hedges -- before your neighbor does. For sooner or later, when there's nothing left but hawks and vultures, the predators and carrion tend to descend on one another. For example, when the neighbor loses his job, his house, and departs with his few remaining guilders and goodies in boxes and trucks, well, he deserved it, didn't he? His downward-spiraling credit score proves it: clearly, he's guilty of that unforgivable personal character flaw that is *just plain bad luck*. No need to leave your forwarding address, Joe. In America, bad luck is regarded as more contagious than Ebola: it's less treatable, and far less desirable in a neighbor. To each his loss... as long as it's you and not me. Besides, if I put you down in my mind, I bring myself up. It's all relative; and, as long as I don't see you as my relative, I'll be just fine. I deserve it. And you don't. And I'll have power over you, because you'll envy me. And you'll demand my guilt, because I have that power: but who cares about that?

All for one and one for all is *so* eighteenth century.

*****

I woke sometime in the ambient blackness to the sound of several men, eight, maybe ten, all arriving together at the shelter, noisy and congested, a snarled traffic jam, all of them talking nine times louder than necessary, all at once, all at each other and around each other, none of them *to* each other.

"That was AWESOME man!" "Woooo-hoooo!" "*Bellissima!*" "Fuckin' A bro!" "Killer!" "*Markotašnik!*" (*Laughter, entirely male.*) "Fuck YOU, and fuck YOU, and...." Etcetera, etcetera. English, Italian, Spanish, and... Russian?

I roll my eyes in their sockets. I'm going to just *hate* this one.

Virgil squirms to life, pops his head up. The boys, surprised, let out a yelp. Virgil, startled, shrieks, very high pitched. The boys jump back, yelp again, twice as loud.

"Jeez!" says the one closest that jumped the highest.

"No, that's Virgil," I replied. "And we're both exhausted." I lay back down.

"Ah... aw, c'mon dog, I've got a snifter of Glen Garioch here somewhere." He starts digging into his pack.

"That slop? Who wants that twenty five hundred dollar slop? Hey bud, I have some Glenfiddich Rare, 1937, cost me twenty-one-five."

Then they all began to talk at once. "You know, I have a Macallan 60-year-old single malt in the cellar, bought it off my bankrupt neighbor." "Dalmore gave me a bottle of mixed single malts dating from 1868 to 1932 for that legal work we did in London." "How about a Bowmore, 1856 single-vint, original cork? Bought it for my twenty-fifth birthday." "Fuck all that scotch shit. Remy Martin's Black Pearl, sold by invitation only!"

The one said loudly over the others: "You guys and your damn scotches and cognac, give me a break. Vodka is the real man's drink. Brings out the communist in your eyes." They all laugh, loud and long. "I've got a ruby- and diamond-filled bottle of Scottish Diva, a cool one-point-five-mil."

The others all *ooooooed*, except from a rather meek one in the back that adds, "Tequila Ley Point-Nine-Twenty-Five? Platinum bottle and..." but the others all override him with mocking laughter. "Tequila!" one says, pointing his thumb at the guy. "Imagine, tequila," another one mutters, shaking his head. "Next he'll say he owns champagne," another adds, and they practically double-over. When he replies, "But I do own champagne," they stay true to their word, practically gasping for air as they howl.

Another one produced some cigars. "And what better after a long day than a Pinar P-Three-Thousand? Pre-embargo tobacco rolled in the past couple of years."

More *ooohs*.

"How about some Davidoff Cubans? I have some Three Thousands, some One Thousands, and a couple of Number Ones."

Nods, *hmms*, all around.

"*Pshaw*. Auturo Fuente. Period."

Pshaw? Someone actually says *pshaw*? I'd only seen the word in books. Saying it out loud just made it sound vapid.

A mixture of sounds then: unzipping, things being removed, clothes being taken off and put on, the high-pitched clink of titanium, and then smoke, tobacco, simultaneously sweet and poisonous. I couldn't imagine a worse thing after a long day of exertion, but to each his own. Lord knows I had my poisons. I watched them plunk, whack, unpack. Sleeping bags started to be thrown down on the bunk next to me.

"Hmm, Feathered Friends," I said, noticing the tag. "Nice bag."

"Handmade since '72! 850-fill duck."

"*Duck*? I have a genuine Spotted Sports bag, hand sewn in Mendocino, endangered owl feathers and down, rated to...."

"*Owl*? Check out this Ark Antarctic Nine Thousand, that's actual Emperor penguin -- no feathers, ALL down -- with waterproof sealskin. Feel the seal, baby!"

"You guys and your bags." Again, everyone stooped talking, and that same older, deeper voice dominated. He was holding a walkie-talkie, giving a radio order: "Okay boys, bring it down."

And down came a spider. Suddenly there were floodlights and the sound of chopper blades thwacking close to the upper branches. To my astonishment, as he gestured upwards down came what I could only describe as a Quonset hut made of brightly polished metal and ends of a rich hardwood of some kind. Zeus only knew what it weighed, and Jove the size of the 'copter above that had carried and lowered it. Then, just after its cable detached and shot upwards, four more ropes came down, accompanied by four men in high-class tuxedo-like waiters uniforms, unhitching themselves from their rigs the moment they hit the ground in a practiced, delicate dance of violent efficiency.

You have got to be fucking kidding me.

But no, there they were, pulling a banquet table out of the hut, setting it up, with tablecloths, and candelabras, and what-not frill of all sort, Fifth Avenue come right down out of heaven proper like the Holy Spirit itself to impale each of us with the flaming golden spear into the Saint Teresa's Heart inside us all, throbbing and ecstatic. Oh, they crushed a few couple-year-old saplings in the process, but what's a few years of life compared to a night on satins? Then out came a couple of boxes, and lights came on in the hut, and men went inside, and soon smoke began pouring from the hut's bright metallic chimney. Then came carpets, and silver; tiki torches, and cisterns of coffee, and wine, and wine, and more wine, and hard cheeses, grapes, strawberries (fresh!), then lobsters half-shelled and pre-cubed with a fork pre-impaled into each cube, then caviar (the good stuff) (*it was Russian all right!*), and linens, and silks, and embroidered silk placemats, and multiple forks for each placemat, and two knives, and a teaspoon, and a rounder, deeper spoon, and a longer shallower one, and a very long one with almost no spoon at all, and a normal spoon except it had slots in the bottom, and a spoon with a serrated edge on one side, and a spoon with serrated edges on both sides, and a spoon with....

"Dinner will be served in five minutes, gentlemen," said the older man. You have GOT to be fucking kidding me.

By then the men all held snifters and shots of various brown liqueurs, and cigars, puffing and drinking, drinking and puffing. They stood around as attendants (*where did they come from?*) unpacked them, arranged their belongings. I sat back up.

"Guys..." I started, but they would have none of it.

I seemed to be pulled off the bunk, but by who or what, was uncertain. Suddenly I seemed to be standing, *sans* sleeping bag, dressed in... dressed in... a tuxedo.

"Uh-huh," I mumbled, looking at myself.

Even Virgil seemed dressed for the occasion, as we were both whisked to the long table, at which twelve men sat, all inexplicably, improbably dressed. A large stogie was pushed between my fingers, already smoking, as was the large duck sat down on a platter before me. A man was handing me large carving knives. I wondered who was supposed to use them on whom. I declined them.

"Our guest of honor refuses the first cut," said the man, then I realized who it was standing before me, the same man and voice who'd ordered down the hut and table and all the rest of it to begin with. "Guess I'll do the slicing tonight."

"Ronald Rumpe," I said, surprised but not terribly.

"You won't mention this to the press, will you?" he said, only sort of smiling, the others only sort of chuckling. "We like our little home away from home here. Our private place, if you will, for... men, like us." The others grunted affirmatively, but I remained noncommittal.

"I'm just passing through myself," I said. "Dr. Durant Allegheny, at your service." I didn't add *and your family's*, since I knew he was on his third or fourth wife at this point. He just grunted, deigning his tepid and disinterested approval.

The others weren't so distant. "Doctor?" said one. "Where? Presbyterian? Sloan-Kettering? Private plastic practice?"

"Mount Sinai, I bet," said another.

"Nah, he's no Jewish," said a third, in a heavy Italian accent. "You can look at him and tell he no Jewish."

"I see a nice Jewish doctor at Montefiore," said yet another. "Helps me with my migraines. *Oi*, they sure are a terrib...."

"Yeah, yeah, yeah," said the Italian one, dismissively. "Don't go complainin' about you're…."

"Atlanta, actually," I interjected. "Peachtree-Dunwoody Memorial. Emergency medicine, graduated in '91 from...."

"Atlanta!" said The Ron. "Just visiting us here in the Big Apple?"

"Sort of," I answered, "if by Big Apple you mean the woods and if by visiting you mean I walked here."

There was a long silence.

"You... walked all the way here?" he finally said, disbelief edging his tone.

"Sure," I answered. "This is after all the Appalachian Trail, longest trail in the Eastern…."

"The what?" he asked.

"The Appalachian Trail. Longest trail in the east. Two thousand one hundred fifty miles and change, from Georgia to Maine."

He looked around, as if looking around for the first time. "Maine? So... you're not done walking yet?"

"Not a bit. Headed up all the way to Mount Katahdin, Baxter State Park, another four hund…."

"Now why would you do that?"

"Why? Why do you climb a mountain? Build a building? Buy a business? Tear one down? Fall in love? Because it's there, I suppose."

"Hmm," he said, faintly smiling, already looking down-table, disinterested. Servers took the carving knives from him, began slicing the bird, if bird it was.

But the others *hmm*'d their approval as well, chimed in. "Yeah doc," said one. "I know what you mean. I'm Adam Krappe. My father, Gaius Octavius Thurinus Krappe, founded KrappeCorp, finest espresso machines this side of the Adriatic. The best Norilsk nickel, with the added profit from trading the extracted palladium on the market... oh, of course we part-owned the mine too, silent minority partner so as not to attract too much interest from the neo-capitalist former KGB in Moscow (*chuckles*). When he went to Rome on his honeymoon, he fell in love with the Trevi, bought a little cafe directly across from it in cash from the owner there and then. Cost him more than he paid for his small Greek island, but there it is. But he hated their milk, their crème: too common-market for him, you know, socialist regulating hormones and all. *Organic*, he said he wanted; the in-flight magazine on the way over said that how things were going, so he made a few calls, took us out to Lombardia the next day, looking for a quality dairy farm. He got pissed when he realized how fragmented, how inefficient milk production is in Italy. Sixty-eight percent of production went into cheese: Romano, Parmesan, Pecorino, Gorganzola, blah blah blah. Nobody making the liquid stuff owned more than ten cows or produced more than four thousand gallons a year. He got pissed. *Fucking wine drinkers*, he kept calling 'em. Spent the next ten days buying out a half-dozen farms with the *right kind of meadow*, as he put it, though he wouldn't have known his grass-fed beef from his *grillo*-fed (*laughs*). Nah, he just wanted suckers who would take his random price, you know, desperate families and the like."

"So that's how he got into dairy," says his brother (I know because they look identical). "Sinon Krappe, fellow…."

Adam nods, continues, ignoring his brother.. "That's how he got into dairy. Now he practically owns Lombardia, Veneto, Emilia Romagna.... got them all drinking it, ran a bunch of commercials to build the market: *Si Fa Un Buon Corpo, Sai?* That sort of thing. In a land of wine drinkers! Folks who give their kids wine for breakfast! Just like the fuckin' French, them wise guys. Then, whammo, he hit 'em with breakfast cereals. Instead of cheese and wine, talked them into grains and milk for breakfast. Americanized them more than Patton and *Baywatch* put together! Started making *Forum Flakes* in Florence and *Roman-o's* in Reggio nell'Emelia, can you believe it? And the *Caesar Crisps*!? Hah! You can't get a breakfast nowadays anywhere between Trieste and Messina without being offered *Caesar Crisps*!"

His brother jumps in with some jingle: "*E tu, Brute?"* in one voice, then much deeper, *"Così fan tutte!"* Then both of them together, making some sort of stabbing motion: *"Meglio Di Un Dittatore Morto!*"

They both laugh, along with a few others. "And along they went. Changed the face of the Piedmont forever they all said, damn grumbling greasy locals. But, that's how he made friends with the Affrogare-Acido family, the Scarpe-Cementos -- had to, they owned all the trucks -- and Testa De Cavallo himself. Of course I never said that (*knowing chuckles, all around*). And his second wife never forgave him for ruining their honeymoon. Cried all the way to her lawyer's (*more laughs*). Eventually he had the Acidos, er, dissolve her trust, in a manner of speaking (*hearty laughs*)."

My stomach turns over. A roast lamb arrives at the table, with the little paper chef hat looking things adorning its nubs, and other fine accoutrements.

"Ah, our attention span's too short-sold to remember anyway," said Ronald, eliciting more guffaws. A girl poured him more wine. *Where'd she come from?* "What about you, Jeff? Ah... Allegheny, this is Jeff Eleazar. So what's your story, Jeff?"

"Yeah, YEAH! Yeah. OK," and it's like somebody throws a switch that electrifies his eyelids or something. Twitching all over, he races. "Get the gold. Right? In this market, right? Yeah! Gotta hedge. Equities suck. Too many players. Players with information. Damn data. Damn analytics. Gotta get on a level playing field. Gotta hedge! Equities going South! Who do you long? Who do you short? You know? YEAH! (*He spits a little, inadvertently.*) Yeah, so, get the gold. You know, solid, sure, gold's goin' up, up, freakin' UP in THIS market, boy! Yeah! So get some nerds, you know. Real prop heads. Razzle 'em in, you know. Pay 'em a couple, get a web site. Then the hard part: what do we call it? *We Want Your Gold*? Nah! Heh. Too obvious. *Hand Over Your Gold*? HEH! Nah. *Hand Over Your Gold AND Platinum*! Yeah! So what's in it for you little guy? HEY GRANDMA! I'M TALKIN' TO YOU GRANNY! What the fuck do you need that wedding ring for? Gramps ain't gettin' outta bed anymore now is he the useless prick? HAH! Nah, yeah. HEY FUCKIN' GRANDMA! You need MOOLAH baby, yeah! Yeah! Moolah for your BILLLLLLzzzzzz. (*It's a distinctly insect-like sound.*) Youz gots BILLLLLLzzzzzz. That old man needs his heart meds! HAH! YEAH! Don't come cheap! Nah! Here, here's a frickin' envelope. YEAH! PREPAID BABY! Drop it in, mail it. Mail your fuckin' gold and platinum in the uninsured regular fuckin' postal mail like the Alzenheimer you are, Gran! HAH! We'll getcha a check in time for Christmas, or Hanukkah, or Kwanzai, Bonsai, The Fonz-eye, whatever the fuck you believe in, grandma. If we get it at all! HAH! Shit gets lost in the fuckin' mail babe! Hey! Not OUR fault! NO WAY! NAH! Hey! Who's yellin? HEY! WHO'S YELLIN' NOW GRANNY FANNY? HAH!"

My stomach turns over again. He stands up, gets really going. A large fish in capers and lemon sauce arrives. Donald tries to stop him: Jeff, not the fish. "Uh, say, Jeff...."

"YEAH! That's it! Got a lawyer Gran?! GOT A FREAKIN' JEWISH LAWYER IN YOUR PLAN, GRAN? 'CAUSE WE GOT ONE, GOT TWO, GOT THREE, YEAH! THEY'LL PAPERWORK AND PHONE CALL AND DEPOSE YOU TO YOUR EARLY GRAVE GRAN! YES SIR! RIGHT DOWN INTO THE GROUND! YEP! NAH, WE NEVER GOT SHIT FROM YOU BITCH, F YOU AND F YOUR HUNDRED DOLLAR AN HOUR COMMUNITY COLLEGE LEGAL REP GRAN, YOU GO AHEAD AND PAY HIM THAT HUNDRED AND HE CAN TELL YOU HOW FUCKIN' POINTLESS IT IS YOU VARICOSE WRINKLY SPIDER-VEINED ARTHRIT...."

"That's enough, Jeff!" shouts Donald, and he shuts up and sits down, still twitching like he's having a gran mal. "We have a guest here, remember? Someone who's not a Member. Wouldn't want to have to NDA him all the way out *here*." Laughter, and he looks at me, face both calm and sinister, simultaneously, like a crocodile right before it lunges. I get the warning, but I wonder if by NDA he meant the same thing I meant. I couldn't help it; I started to work over the various alternate possibilities. *NDA, hmm. Non-Detectable Alkaloid? Noose Dangled from Ash? Naked, Doused with Ants? Nuts Detached Angrily? Nails Driven up my...?*

I swallow, smile at him. Me and my imagination, sheesh. Two men with meat on swords takes their places at either side of the table. Hmm. At least this one would be *tasty*. Then.... *Hmm. Uhh. They have swords.*

"No worries, Ron. (*All worries, Ron.*) Can I call you Ron? (*Hmm, no I can't.*) So, what brings you gents out here? I'm sure you could have someone trim the verge for you, so why do it yourself?"

The all laugh. It sounds like weasels rotating in a drum with a few handfuls of gravel and some broken glass. Then there is a quiet space for a moment, when they expect Ron to answer my question. Only he doesn't. He ignores me. Six people with various vegetable platters arrive as if from nowhere at the table, depositing their goods: sliced broiled artichokes, roasted eggplant, white asparagus in Béarnaise, what looks like pumpkin or squash stuffed with the most enormous prawns I've ever seen, a tray of roasted purple carrots, and something utterly unidentifiable but topped with gold leaf which I know on an intellectual level is actually edible albeit non-microwavable the day after.

"A toast, gentlemen," he finally says, raising his wine glass. *Actual factual crystal, out here, wow*. "To hard work!" he says. A round of *Here, here's!* goes around. Then plates get passed, real china, gold-edged, and I've no doubt it's actual gold. Duck is sliced and loaded, lamb cubed, fish tonged and meat deskewered, and vegetables slopped.

Ron was the official host, asking his guests one inane question after another. After fifteen, twenty minutes of it, I realized Ronald was on a fishing expedition. I wasn't sure what for, or why, but he was certainly the one asking all the questions. Maybe I should sit out this one. If I was to sideline and act as mere observer, a mere Schrödinger Wave Collapser, Third Class, why, I might even enjoy it. But I didn't think my entertainment mattered so much to....

"So, Fore: tell us about yourself," The Ron ordered.

"Well, ah? Where to begin, eh?" he answered in a deep, thick accent. "Let me see. Well... I believe in America, you know? I was raised, taught freedom... but never to dishonor my family. I got a girlfriend, not Italian. I went to the movies with her, kept her out late. She didn't protest. Two months ago, I took her for a drive, with her sister, eh? Then they tried to take advantage of me. I resisted. I kept my honor. So they...."

"Fore, that's the *Godfather*!" exclaims Ron, and they all groan. "Fuckin' *Godfather,*" affirms Jeff, who rolled his eyes. Moans and groans. Someone did a bad Brando impersonation. It wasn't well received, and they shouted him down.

"OK, OK, OK, OK, fuck youz guys," puffed Fore, indignant. "It's the greatest movie! If Michelangelo himself painted saints and shit on celluloid it wouldn't be bettah! I'm just tryin' to play it up, you know?"

"C'mon Fucci, what's the real scoop?" said another one. "Yeah, scoop the Catholic poop," said yet another. More chuckles.

"Hey! Hey! Do NOT take my religion's name in vain, OK?" He poked a fat finger at the perpetrator. "My *familia* was *esserci dentro* from early on. My Papi was a good man, feared his God but not his neighbor, heh heh. No; put the fear in the neighbors. Except the nice lady in 2B; she was *imboscare*. Drank *chianti* every day, enjoyed a healthy swim, *in se non ha a che fare col legno*, you know? Heh heh. But that's not what she said! She was like a muttah to me.... I grew up in Calabria, and the Bronx. Then there was the Crash of '87! We were left holding the bag, so we ate it. As God as my witness I'll never eat bags again! I vowed to bettah myself; you know, bettah get the money from those punk no-good marks on the lower east side! But they... they tried to hit me. So I went to the police, like a good American. Them two boys were brought to trial. The judge gave them a suspended sentence -- three years. Out they went, the same day! I just stood there like a fool, and those... those two Bonaseras just smiled at me. So I says to my wife, *For justice, we must go....*"

"*Godfather* again!" three or four of them shouted all at once.

"*Fatt' i cazzi!* I told her, *We must go downtown to the church and pray real hard*. And what do you know? Next day they got hit by a Uzbekistani taxi driver with red-green color blindness to whom *taxi* was a kind of dried and pickled salty yak meat. He naively thought his cab company was just advertising it all over the place, like Manhattan was settled by Uzbeks and originally called New Tashkent or some shit like that. But anyway... before you know it, I owned a chain of dry cleaners in the metro area, shook Sinatra's hand at Madame Tussauds, and the rest is history. Well, that and a billion dollars I made basically inventing forex, *sfortunato.*"

Yeah, you're unfortunate all right, I thought.

As I listen to them, I wonder as always as to the reality of it. What's real here? Is that even a pertinent question to ask at this point? They all seem deeply embedded in the world, the world of men and money and the machines for producing it. I feel no connection to them at all. But, the meal is the best I've had out here, so no complaints on my part.

A man the others called DeBourne was going on about some SEC regulation that scuffed his shoes somewhat. He'd made billions trading the same bunch of securities in Hong Kong that he'd buy right back instantly in London or Toronto or Rio or good ol' NYC. Long, short; either way, durationally, very short. There was something special about the Hong Kong exchange -- *magical* was the word he used -- and probably not something homeopathic and herbal, like an ancient Chinese secret. No; it seemed more like a prolonged technological behind-the-times condition that he managed to exploit it for a number of years. That is, until the Chinese took over. *Godless Commies*, he referred to them. *Godless Commies don't play by the rules*, he kept saying, by which he of course meant *they didn't play by the crooked house's (meaning my) rules, like what I wanted them to do for the house's (meaning my) benefit*. He seemed to have an odd innocence born of too many lobster dinners eaten too far from any relevant cold-water coastline accessible by anything other than fuel-guzzling overnight air transport (paid for Net 90 and *in excelsis Deo* by his grateful customers); although, I did have to admit that the lobster provided was pretty damn spectacular.

"Nah," he was saying, "those Godless Commies, they updated all those systems in a heartbeat, replaced it all with good capitalist Silicon Valley stuff, the big iron, added CBOT, NYMEX capabilities, you know, pretty fuckin' funny for a bunch of *let's redistribute all our wealth* mouthers. Nah, those Chinese, they're out to be just like us, only they can't admit it. Whole country of cheats and liars. Liars! 'Course with all that stuff they found us out pretty quick, sentenced and convicted half my staff over there, all rotting now in some political prisoner hellhole doing daily *reeducation* they call it, bah! Well at least I'm safe! 'Course I can't go anywhere near Hong Kong again, not with the contracts out on me!" He laughs way too loud.

Of course given the unending repulsiveness my attention began to wander, me and my attention span and my sense of undeserved, unearned self-righteousness being what they were. Virgil sat next to me, scarfing down what looked like a green bean almandine and ignoring most of the rest of it. He seemed content; I was just waiting for the dinner show. Who knew what would be playing tonight? A nice improvisation? Nah; the things seemed too scripted for that. A stereotypical murder mystery? *Our Town*? *Streetcar*? *The Fantasticks* and its repeated and repeatedly uncomfortable use of the word "rape"; of course, in the old crusty literary sense of an "abduction", but still, jeez, it's the twenty-first century already and the times they are a-changin'? Maybe; I thought these guys might be big fans of rape in a different, more *dinero* salsa sense. Of course I also knew better. I knew these guys were their own story, full of sound and fury and signifying *nada*. I shoveled another fork-full of (*what was this?*) Cornish hen into my mouth, dressed with a lovely lemon and caper sauce. Delicate and refined, unlike these jackwipes, and unlike me. It induced the typical ironic feelings one expected.

And everyone had a ghost story to tell. Tales of nothingness both whispered and shouted, creating a vast and vapid vapor that rose from them, redolent in their power, temporary and fleeting as it was. They shone like suns, glistening in a sweat of self-satisfaction, fusing what was left of a person to create energy: their desires and intellects, their being and their belonging, their greeds, their dreams, their insatiable hunger for the world and the tasties it contained for the picking, ripe and plump and juicy sweet. They ate, glorious, while their servants served, while their minions ministered. Killing, and eating what they'd killed, fat as they were already with their consumed dead flesh, twenty-first century warlords, engaged in a battle to the death, .

I wondered when their dying would start, when we'd bag this brace of coneys.

"Hey Doctor," said Fore, "*scusi*, pass the *fois gras*, *per favore*?" There is a plate of browned yellowish chunks of it in a pile, covered in mustard seed and sliced leeks, and drenched in a *jus* most likely made from the same donator. I reengage with the play around me, pass it to him, noting his politeness.

I considered pushing events, but, to be honest, this one *was* tasty. That's the problem with the gilded, greasy world: it's yummy. An even though I viewed them with a certain loathing, I still ate their roasted carrots and boar and fish cheeks and broccoli rabe with sliced roasted garlic and veal scaloppini and prime rib and potatoes au gratin and sweet potatoes au gratin and....

I burped, very loudly and powerfully. A moment of pure icy non-movement, then the table as a whole howled at me.

"I never said I wasn't guilty too," I mumbled.

"Eh, what's that, Allegheny?" asked Ronald as the rest of them all joked at once to each other at my social *faux pas*.

"Nothing," I lied.

"You're offended by us," he said flatly as the others joked and bragged loudly among themselves. "Don't worry, we're used to it."

"*Offended* isn't the word I'd use," taking this as the opening I was supposed to take. "It's more of an... allergic reaction. That whole easier to pass through the eye of a needle thing and all. Yet I envy you, all of you. To eat like this, live like this, day after day…."

"Yes," he said smiling, "even out here, right? Food is the ultimate expression of wealth, don't you think? It meets the most primal of needs, needs no skyscraper or Lamborghini or supermodel can meet. It fills us, literally. Makes us who, and what, we are, literally."

"It's the acquisition of...." I started, but he waved me off, impatient.

"Yes, yes, of course, I know. We all know. No need for euphemism out here, Allegheny, as you've heard. Yes, we use and take what we can, abuse them, give them loads, burdens, add suffering to them like the stinking desert camels they are, pack animals, harness them to the yoke, and pull. Thus they dig deep for us into the earth for the lime and the iron, smelt and extrude them into the hardened steels and rebar that reinforce the monuments we build to ourselves, at which their better-off brethren enter and try to emulate us, flatter us, outfox us perhaps, to gain a throne in the church and play the idol instead of the idolaters. We suck at them, drawing their precious life fluids into our hidden reservoirs placed away from too close a scrutiny, slowly, over time, as they waste away into an old age supported by the pittances we grant them, enough to survive, or perhaps less. We eat of them, their marrow, their souls, vampires devouring while the sun lies low in the sky and they sleep. Why not? It is civilization we create thus, after all; society, security, warmth by the fire. Otherwise we should all have caves and all starve therein. Instead we build our caves upwards, vertically, away from the riff-raff, reaching to God in Heaven, the new Babel, but speaking in only the one tongue that is of any meaning anymore: that of *commerce*. We soak luxuriously, languidly in its oily, gelatinous riches. It is our blood, our blood that is their blood, ground with the dust of their existence to make the concretes that exalt our own. Greatness cannot be shared, Doctor. It must be taken."

He paused, cleaning a chicken bone, without breaking eye contact. I found no words to reply with.

"Yes," he said finally, regarding the bone in his hand, "we clean the carcass of all usable materials and achieve greatness. Better, more efficiently than the dictators and emperors of old, and far more qualified, we the products of selective breeding and multiple generations of wealth, stored, recharged, electric, growing in power over time, generation after generation, we the Industrialists, we Men of Stature, white and European and better bred for the world as it is. Not as the world is dreamt of by the dead poets or the dead novelists or the dead Communists buried and entombed within their own mediocrity and disregarded history. No; ours is the world recognizing fully the energy potential flowing from the lesser to the greater, a land which proclaims that all men are created equal without actually attempting to fulfill that promise in the least since it knows full-well the stupidity of it. A necessary lie, to instill the necessary sense of hope. Ah, excuse me. *Instill* is such an old-fashioned word. *Install* is more fitting; nowadays, hope is mere software, pliably programmable. Of course, there are *some* few come along to join us each year, but some retire, and some die, and some themselves are eaten. No; we are more efficient than the insufficient leaders of old in who we select for our ranks. We fill their minds with distraction: stock car races, instant breakfasts, Asian massage parlors, newer and shinier gaming systems, phones and pods and pads, and with pornography of every imaginable nuance and perversion and style, every hue both light and dark and in every shade of moral gray in-between, instantly accessible at broadband speeds, downloadable anytime, anyplace. We medicate them, control them, leash them, but sweetly, gently, lest they notice the yoke. Oh, we allow them -- *some* of them -- their ten-day beach vacations, their cabanas, their occasional steak dinners, their mid-scale mass-produced automobiles with cruise control lest their foot fall asleep, their granted thin slices of swank and grated stardust, while we rise above, beyond, living in palaces, cathedrals to Mannon, directing our armies and empires from afar, seducing yet another source of profits, subduing more market share, deforesting, choking the skies, burning, smelting, smashing, adding only the legally required minimal amounts of processed sugars and vitamins and minerals and opiates needed to keep a populace in minimally-acceptable working order. We ignore Clean Air Acts by moving the smokestacks to the Third and Fourth and Fifth and Sixth Worlds where Less is More and More is obtainable by bribery at the appropriate levels of what passes for a government there -- wherever in Hell *there* is. We ignore financial oversight and regulations by buying the auditors and the SEC and the burnt-out bureaucratic faceless with cash, with liquor, with women, and sometimes men. We ignore congresses, courts, journalists, activists, victims. Divert them, dissuade them, dismantle them, destroy them. We ignore them because no one matters to us but us; nothing matters but our hunger. We are the ultimate predators, Allegheny, the crowning achievement of evolution, Darwin embodied at both his finest qualitatively and his ultimate quantitatively. And as for our prey? The ox is more aware of its ceaseless plowing."

He paused again, sipping his scotch and pondering tonight's show, brought to you by the letter $.

"And here's the real beauty of it. *Everyone wants to be like us.* They strive for it, yearn for it, go to business schools for it, start stupid derivative non-competitive badly managed businesses for it, dream the hungry impossible dreams that the ox dreams. Impossible, for we will not allow them to take what is already ours. And, because, even if we did, where would it all come from? We keep eating, and eating, and eating. We have eaten so much. Pretty soon?"

"They'll be nothing left for anyone," I immediately answered.

"Exactly," he said, poking his scotch glass at me. "Can't be. Nothing is limitless; well, merely human desire, and only perhaps the universe. Most likely, desire is the larger. Therefore, at times of necessity, we who sew, we who plow, we who reap, must, dispassionately, weed. For example, like I am going to do right now."

He pointed at a waiter, nodded. The waiter nodded back, walked into the hut, and came back out after a few moments. Wearing goggles, and wielding a chain saw. Every muscle in my body seized at once. *Here we go again.*

"Hey!" yelled a man from then end of the table opposite me whose name I'd missed. "Good idea, Ron! Let's get a fire going!"

"Let's," replied Ron.

The waiter with the chain saw proceeded to yank the cord, and as the thing roared to life he nonchalantly removed an arm from the man who'd suggested a fire. A gush of both blood and screaming erupted from him as he sank to his knees. Presently his torso was sliced in half, fragments of his ribcage and organs whiplashing the air and spraying over the end of the table and those closest to it. As the body fell, the waiter leaned over (thankfully out of sight) and proceeded to quickly slice the poor bastard into pieces, after which the now-blood-soaked murderer backed off, releasing the saw's trigger, as three other men picked up the steaming chunks in white linens and carried them inside, for... for....

The table turned to Ron as one, looking at him. He stood up, glass in hand. "Gentlemen, I'd like to formally announce a... a merger, if you will. The *former* Piers de la Vigna, *former* chairman, *former* CEO, *former* President, and *former* founder of Vigna Financial, has just signed his empire over to us, the Marching Members of Mahwah!"

They stood as one and cheered loudly, applauding. Another one at the end, blood splattered, yelled out. "I want the private wealth division, the hedge fund!"

"What? That's not fair!" shouted another across from him, standing up as well. "That's an unfair market advantage! You already have twelve funds AND the West Coast's biggest wealth manag...."

The first man shook his head and raised his fist. "I don't care what you want, McCool! You're nothing but a scam supported and protected on the backs of the rest of...."

The second man threw his plate full of food at him, screaming. "I have to *launder*, damn it! How do you think I do that? With goddamn *detergent*!? I have to *diversify*! Remember Farquahr? We let you have his banks! And Shumtz? You have his fixed income business! I only got his yacht; geez, what, what do I need with another yacht, what!? Am I supposed to ask my goddamn *family* to invent trades and cook the books? Fuckin' *family*? They're about as trustworthy as the Tong or the Mafia! I have to launder and diversify! How the hell do you expect me to avoid Club Fed, you goddamn greasebag greezer!?"

The first man growled and leapt across the table, snatching a carving fork out of the duck's carcass, and the second one grabbed his steak knife as they attacked each other, falling on top of the table. Shouts, as the rest of the men leapt up and back from the table. Wads of money came out of pockets instantly, as the others bet on the outcome of the fight. Twenties quickly escalated to hundreds, and dropped into the gravy and the gunk, as the two men tried to kill each other. Teeth bared and mouths bit; screams, guttural animal sounds, wolves devouring their own *realpolitik*.

"I'm afraid," Ron said nonchalantly and very, very quietly, as the bodies and their fluids flew, "that by *us* I really mean *me*."

Nails suddenly sprouted on the two fighting men like summer, backs arched, coarse hair shot from their hands and necks, ears elongated, legs bent at the knee, pushing them over. Wolves devouring, indeed.

"So what do you think, Allegheny?" asked Ron, suddenly close into my face, smiling ever so faintly.

"I think Padma outdid himself this time. And... and this, this, I don't envy."

"Ah, not one of us I see. No matter. The wolf ignores the sheep until it is ready to be tasted. Any sooner just wouldn't be proper. It's just business, Allegheny. The art of war."

"Sun Tzu," I said automatically.

"An early adopter, a visionary, a fountainhead."

"Fountainhead? Ayn Rand."

Ron laughed as a turkey leg went flying between us from the opposite end of the table. "I suppose you find her to be... what, a Nazi?"

"Rand? She's too intellectually complicated to be a Nazi. That's just one dimension of it, and she takes another thousand, fifteen hundred pages to explain the rest. If Hitler had done that, he'd have been yawned out early on, maybe caught a couple of tomatoes. No; Rand, she's just..." and after the other matching leg flew past, "exhausting."

He bit the end off a cigar, spat it downwind towards the ongoing battle between two now fully-converted werewolves. He lit it up, leaned back, shook the match out, flung it carelessly into the darkness. He leaned forward, puffing.

"And those movie adaptations! Patricia O'Neil? Ehhhh." The off-on-off flicker of cigar light framed his face as he said it, wicked and detached.

"Neal, not O'Neil. I thought she captured Ayn Rand herself. An emotionless robot, coldly calculating, one computation just shy of fascism. Fits the role perfectly."

"Uh? Oh," he said, releasing a cloud of death but regarding the stogie in his hand like it was an angel anyway. "Oh. I meant sexually."

"Of course you did," I answered. One of the werewolves had his fangs in the others' neck now, no idea whose. The rest of the gang was still coaxing them, cheering, hollering, betting money, completely unfazed by the turn of events. Flying Woodrow Wilsons turned into William McKinleys and Grover Cleavelands.

"I like supermodels, myself," he said just as one of the animals screamed in agony. A second later and we had to jump out of the way as an entire platter of roast beef and someone's recently detached and completely-furred arm came flying our way. "Actually, anything super: models, cars, yachts, property, art, deals."

"You don't say," I politely answered, as I removed the werewolf arm from the top of my plate and toss it nonchalantly off the table. *I really enjoyed that Cornish hen, too. What a waste, sigh.*

"Oh, I do say. I absolutely do say. That's the real power of *power*, Allegheny. You get to *say*. And others have to listen." He stood up, ringing his crystal wine glass with a gold spoon. The others stopped immediately like it was an air-horn blasting for their attention, including the two werewolves. He paused for a moment, allowing the two monsters a few seconds to catch their breath, and one more for the armless one to finally, *finally*, fall over dead. The other one, seeing this, leaned back, and howled in triumph, long and icy.

"See what I mean?" he said as an aside to me.

"What's next on the menu, Ron?" someone asked.

"Oh, more of the same," he answered. "Just more of the same."

In the next moment four waiters appeared with four large silver platters bearing what looked like a whole roast suckling pig. Only, it wasn't a pig at all... not literally, anyway. One platter with an apple-biting head appeared in front of Ron and I. We looked at it, each other, and Ron smiled at me, no teeth and all fangs. It was the most disturbing smile I'd ever seen.

"Dig in," he teased, knowing I wouldn't.

"Why?" I asked him after watching them all chew and slice and fork and chew for a minute or two.

"Why what?"

"Why do you need everything?"

"Why? Why do you climb a mountain? Build a building? Buy a business? Tear one down? Fall in love? Because it's there, I suppose." Again, that smile, unnerving.

"That's not an answer."

"Glad you see that. Eh, Allegheny, why do any of us do what we do? Boredom. Pure boredom, *ennui*, something to while away the hours with. Not all of us can be surfer dudes. Some of us require a greater, more consistent dosage of adrenaline, a finer grain to the wood, a smoother feel to the Corinthian leather. Business is the only sport where the winner's medals are *real* gold. Everything else is fake, a diversion, a game. The only real game is business because the only real sport is power. And by power I mean people's lives. The power to make, break, grow, slash, tower, and confound. Pure gold. Pure absolute hard, cold gold. They even offered it to the baby Jesus, remember? Jesus didn't turn it down the gold; at least his parents certainly didn't. The chosen parents of the Son, and *they* kept the gold! Isn't that amusing? At least no one's ever said they declined: it's assumed, and who in their right mind no matter how blessed would?"

"There's gold, and then there's blood gold." I mutter.

"Oh, please, Allegheny, you know as well as I that it's *all* blood gold. Who makes your clothes? That dry-wick you hike in, those thermals, your pack, your boots? Not Americans, certainly. None of it. But we Americans made the deals that brought those goods here to you. The fact that it came here over an ocean of blood as you'd put it didn't stop you from buying them. Don't be such a empty-headed liberal. You know better."

"Yes, I know better. Some impoverished is better than all impoverished."

"Like the nineteenth, eighteenth, seventeenth centuries, and further. Like the past. Like the opposite of progress."

I burped. "I've got a bit of the heartburn." I observe.

"That's the liberal in you fighting against the realist. You want a better life for the poor. We give it to them, you know we give it to them, no one else, because there is no one else with anything to give. We are the greatest force for good in the world because we are the only real force for *anything* in the world." he leaned forward again. "That's the real power of real power, Allegheny. Destruction always comes with creation. Can't be helped."

"Rock on," I say, verbalizing what I'd thought a long, long season ago.

"Why do you persist in fighting it? Fighting us?"

"It's not you I'm fighting; it's... myself." A waiter brought me a clean plate. Another dumped a load of mashed potatoes on it. Another slopped on some gravy. It smelled like the best gravy every made by humans, or whatever passed for humans tonight.

He laughed. "Please! See these men? *They* fight themselves. *You* fight nothing. You have no power. You're just along for the ride. We're the ones driving. Don't you want that? Don't you want to be... one of us?"

Other waiters appeared, throwing chicken, beef, veal, duck, shredded and sliced and stacked on my plate. Sauces were applied: white with cilantro, a chunky green, yellow with orange and red peppercorns, a searing red picante.

"I want... I want to be a balloon." The smells were unbelievable. Just... just *unbelievable*. "Let the wind blow me where…."

"Please!" Now he seemed almost insulted. "You want what we all want! To EAT!"

"To EAT!" the men all cried as one, raising their glasses and toasting Ron.

"What's next on the menu, Ron?" one of the men mid-table asked.

"Like I said," he replied, "more of the same."

Three waiters appeared with chainsaws, and without a moment's pause drove them straight into three of the men at the table. The others leapt up, screaming, but cheering, unafraid, disconnected as if drugged, aware yet unaware. As the men came apart before them the other cried out: "I want his hotels!" "I get his Lamb and his Maserati!" "Oh no you don't, you got the last Lamb! You can have his majority stake in...." "Wait! Did you say hotels!? Those are mine! I have to expand in...." "Majority stake? That's no majority stake, he sold that months ago!" "Well I get his gold!" "No WAY you get his gold, that's mine!" "No damn you I want his gold, the upside's too big to ignore...."

Hair began to sprout, arms elongate, shoulders slump. Claws replaced fingernails, fangs replaced foul words, guttural grunts overcoming arguments tender and gentle. Ron just picked up his scotch after motioning for a minion to refill it, then stood up and backed away from the table into the shadow and flicker of the flames. For my part I pulled Virgil back towards me, off at an angle from Ron and the table. It wasn't a moment too soon. They flew at one another then, pure animal, attacking, screaming, clawing, chewing, bleeding. They sought to kill: to kill, or be killed.

"Darwin is alive and well, Allegheny," said Ron, a half-face puffing a cigar in the darkness. "Darwin is alive and well. The people pray to a god some call good, but... good for whom? The good is what we create. But an architect must destroy to create. Land must be sculpted, trees uprooted, varmints vanquished, the hot liquid metals poured and cooled, plastics formed and molded and shaped, piping bent and welded, wires soldered, stripped, and all bent to the overpowering, unyielding will of the Architect. We are all Roarks, fussing, feuding, prime movers, and no second-handers!" He took a swig from his glass, pausing for a half-second to regard the doomsday battle raging now across, over, and around his table. "Of course, even that is a lie. We can't all be architects. Some have to serve, and some have to sacrifice. Some have to serve and pay the ultimate sacrifice. And some must be sacrificed, to the gods whom we serve!"

I couldn't watch the carnage, so I was looking at him. I felt oddly safe: I had nothing any of these men wanted. I had only myself, and Virgil. No; I had nothing to fear here. There was no moon in this sky.

"I have a joke for you," I said. "A finch, a wench, and the Grinch walk into a bar at the North Pole."

"I don't joke Allegheny. I never joke," he warned, coldly.

"You're all joke," I reply. "This is all a joke. None of its real."

"It's more real than you realize. It happens every day. This," he gestures, "this happens, every day."

He had me there. I decided to ignore him. "The bartender says, What's you pleasure? The finch says, I want a Nut...."

"Enough! I'm not interested. Don't you want some more of this, Allegheny? Don't you want... *more*!?"

Ah, so that's it. Should've seen that one coming. "So the bartender produces a Nut, and the finch pecks and pecks and pecks at it until he realizes that finches don't eat nuts, but by then it's too late and he's knocked himself out cold...."

"More, Allegheny, more! Imagine! Everything you want, everything you could ever want, yours! For the taking! For the owning!" His fingers grip white and strong on his cigar, only his hand and the flame of it visible.

"Then the bartender asks the wench, What's your pleasure? The wench says, I want Two Nuts. So the bartender...."

"ENOUGH!" shouts Ron, and bored already, I give up.

"Fine. It's a great joke. You should hear what happens to the bartender. And one part of the Grinch grows three sizes bigger! Oh never mind. Too bad you take life so seriously. Or is it seriously bad that you take so many lives? Both, perhaps."

"I do what all life must do in the service of life! Kill it, and consume it!"

"As opposed to nurture it, care for it?"

"Allegheny! You know they're the same thing! What is one nurtured on, nurtured with? The fruits or flesh of the dead, the eggs and extracts of the enslaved! Life nurtures life by feeding parts of itself to that life! Allegheny! Life exists to create life, and not only by procreation!"

"Yes, I know. But do they?" I gestured back towards the table. It had grown silent and still in the last few seconds. I didn't need to look to perceive the truth of it.

Ron smiled wide, stepping forward, back into the light. "Well, they are the Marching Members of... correction, they *were* the Marching Members."

"So... everything's all wrapped up nice n' neat now," I observed, leaning back, putting my hands behind my head. "The lusts, the greed, the gluttony, anger, all of it, all wrapped up good and tight and pretty right here, and just in time for Christmas."

"Ah, you figured that out did you? Good for you. So that would make this...."

"Yes, I know. Wants and desires in conflict. I scream, you scream, we all scream for ice cream. And sometimes there's only one scoop left. Something like that." I was bored and letting it show. I hoped he didn't see how disappointed I was that the dinner was over. At least the dinner show was.

"Don't you get it, Allegheny? Don't you see? All *thissssssss*," he hissed, gesturing across the table and its carnage, "all *thissssssss*, could be yours." He paused, flicking his tongue, firelight flickering in his serpentine face.

I burst out laughing. "Yeah, sure, right. This is what I want. Right. You enjoy, OK? You go ahead and enjoy it." I stood up, ready to hike through the night and sleep it off tomorrow at the next shelter. *Which was, let me see....*

He lunged out suddenly, grabbing me by the arm. I felt a jolt of fear as an instinctual reaction, no choice involved. I'd have to work on that. "Damn it, Allegheny, don't you get it? Don't you get what all this is for yet? Or are you still focused on the basic fundamentals? The technical analysis can only get you so far. At the sale the only thing that matters is the return."

"And the prevailing tax rate," I corrected. "What does it cost you, Rumpe? What does it *cost* you?"

"Cost? Cost? Cost? Whatever it costs can be paid for! I'll pay for it with whatever Piers had, what Jeff and Ulysses and Bertram had, what all of them had! It's all mine now! Mine!"

"Let go of me," I insisted, tugging, but he would not release me.

"NO! What's wrong with you? We're offering you a chance, the chance of a lifetime! Don't you get it? Don't you understand what all this was for?"

"I'm afraid not," I said, finally breaking free. "What you need is a couple of noble truths. Right speech, right action, right thought...."

"You're hopeless!" he declared, throwing his cigar down in his frustration, stomping it out and smashing it as he had many times before.

"On the contrary, I am all hope. But as for food? A little trail mix, some summer sausage, some cool filtered mountain stream water, and I'm good for another fifteen, twenty miles."

"What about him?" Ron shouts, gesturing at Virgil, who'd found one lone string bean from his earlier almandine among the carnage and was enjoying it slowly. "What are you going to do for him? What have you done for him? Or don't you know that?"

I gritted my teeth. "That's too far. Enough. Go back to the penthouse purgatory you came from. I'm done with you."

He lunged at me, grabbing my arm, pressed his face right into mine. "But we're not done with *you* yet, Allegheny. We're not done with *you* yet. You've still miles to go and minions to meet. It's not over. Not by a long shot. You will see. You both will see." He pulled a walkie-talkie off his hip, and commands, "Bring it down! We're outta here!"

Suddenly a brilliant flooding light appeared above along with the sound of a large chopper. The downdrafts tore at my clothes, pushed me back, and down. Virgil and I both hit the dirt. The winds whipped around us, knocked the glasses and plates and silverware off, whipped the tablecloths and linens into the gale, the gale becoming a hurricane, the hurricane tearing at us. Bones, china cups, spoons slammed into me. I grabbed onto a tree to hold myself down, grabbing Virgil and pulling him in close. Then a enormous sucking, pulling the air up, up, up into a vortex, a tornado, and the bodies and gilt and gold and wealth and carcasses fair and foul whooshed upwards in one tremendous gulp like a swallowing behemoth consuming his last, taking the Quonset and all that remained of the Members, as I finally looked up at Ron, last to go, smiling, demonic.

"Payment is due. Payment is due," he whispers, but I hear it crystal-clear inside a space of stillness, in my mind. "Justice will be loosed upon you for your sins." He points a finger at me, and it is wolfen, clawed, red-nailed. "Justice will be loosed upon you." Then he leans back, and howls, screaming, wailing, agonizing. I stuff my hands in my ears and Virgil cries out, but just as we can stand it no longer, he sails upwards with the last of the vortex, a kind of anti-Ascension involving neither Savior nor Heaven, and disappears.

Bang. We were alone again, in the dark, in the quiet still night, the instant come and gone.

But there is a throbbing in my hand, a wetness. I look down, and there is a gold fork, ornate, pronged, embedded in my left hand. I stare at it, my wound, watch it bleed. I pull it from my hand, crying out as I do so. Was it an accident of the Maelstrom, or... was someone trying to eat me?

As I bundle us up, heading back into the shelter and my pack's limited amount of medical supplies, I wonder if I will ever know. And, watching myself bleed, cold fear, Man's worst enemy, returns. Fear, and ignorance.

Days and nights and miles pass. Endless. Dreams. Disillusions. Something removes itself from me. It is time, it is not time. My fear remains. Far down the trail, there is a night that comes, one that seems darker than the rest.

I shiver, but not from the cold. Darkness. Darkness. The nights, endless, reek of it. I lie awake on top of my bag, unable to sleep, staring upwards, into the darkness. The roof could be inches away or light-years, but the distance separating us remains the same. Nothingness layered with nothingness. Barren. Let loose on me the justice, and be done with it. Spiders in the indigo spin their webs, catching their dreams and dismembering them with sweet jaws. Let loose on me the justice, and be done with it. Rats scurry in corners, hunting for the smaller, the less fortunate. Let loose on me the justice, and be done with it. The darkness howls on its haunches, drooling carnivorously, eating the hours the moon carelessly discards in its wake. The darkness howls, proclaiming its dominion and marking its territory with an absence of being, nothingness pouring into nothingness, its pains into an empire of them, regret's cold icy breath rolling across the ground, unseen but buoyant to the darkness that rides upon it, thoughts of evils lurking as sharks within, awaiting the stimulus to frenzy. Nothing, nothing, nothing. I am miles, murky eons, ancient depths and crumbled civilizations away from you, all of you, all of mine that was, gone, gone, somewhere else not here where I am trapped in the night, a fly to the spider's web, a shrew to the rat, a rabbit running aimlessly from the wolf. I am pure animal in my fear, psychotropic, unwavering. There is no moon, and earth? A misplaced dream. There is no sky or smile or sanity in this, only void, and a pull of gravity towards one arbitrary direction, and the beat of a heart that must be mine but for the lack of a desire to beat lest it give away my position. When all have gone, where all have gone? It is a question worth asking. Other dimensions exist where friends slip through the interstices, loved ones fall through a grate forming interference patterns which cancel, the cries of children and the poor and the undeserving in pain and agony in the waiting room and the streets and the poor places in the world, all mixing in the black and bottomless brew. Drink, Socrates.

Ninety-two consuming brew we don't know who died all for you absolves you too as if brand new. Amen.

...Thefuguestateisoneofanumberof...
...dissociative...

...memory...
...disorders...
...allofwhicharecharacterizedbyaninterruption...
...adissociationfrom...
...fundamentalaspectsofeverydaylife...
...suchaspersonalidentity...

...andpersonalhistory...

There is a sound. A sound in the dark. A twig snapping. A branch falling or being brushed aside. Is there someone there? Is there someone approaching? Something? Grindel? Kali? Astaroth? Chullachaqui? Fafnir? Atahsaia? Whoever you are, let loose on me the justice, and be done with it.

...Duringthefuguestatelastingseveralhourstoafewmonths...
...anindividualforgetswhotheyareandtakesleaveofhisorher...
...usualphysicalsurroundingssometimesassuming...

...anewidentity...

Swimming in water which thickens imperceptibly against the skin adhering to the skin replacing it to turn the observer who creates into the observed created which is a fishing expedition baited on rusted hooks of tainted words a forest of them growing surrounding to capture the created by the observer a fisher of men they say filleted or blackened or eaten raw the fisher creator eating his children creating him by the observation of being eaten except for the wide-open eyes observing being eaten filleted or blackened or eaten raw raw raw.

...Oftenthefuguestateremainsundiagnoseduntil...
...theindividualhasemergedfromitandcanrecall...
...theirrealidentity...

Identity? Identity? I yam that I yam. I yam that I yam and that's all that I yam. I'm Popeye the sailor-man, *sans* spinach. Identity? One equals one. Or if you are a Randian, A is A. Personally I lack objectivity. I am all subjectives and grays, and thus subject to premature graying. Ha ha ha ha ha. I divest my identity into lower yield instruments. Lower yield, but higher risk. Which....

A louder snap, closer this time. Shit shit shit. What is it? A what, or a who? Either way, always a why. Why why why why. Meaning is the collection of aggregate experience, distillates of the daily moments we brew ourselves, drunk with power, with fear. Why why why. Who is it? The wolf at the door, here to blow my house down? Little pig, little pig, let me come in.

...Uponemergingfromthefuguestatetheindividual...
...isusuallysurprisedtofindthemselvesin...
...unfamiliarsurroundings...

Unfamiliar surroundings? Familiarity breeds contempt; case in point: how I despise my old friend the darkness. She envelopes me with her parasitic love, hypnotic, and I hate her for it. Surrounding me, approaching closer, closer. I feel her, her breath, her emptiness like fog on a glacier, mercury falling, chilled and contemptuous. She approaches: Tlaltechuhtli, Phillinon, Lamia, Lilith. Boiled with serpents and toads. Unbridled debaucheries whose incubi suckle on cold dead bile. Dancing towards me slowly, oozing mucus, serpent's tongue flicking, smelling the drafts, shape-shifting between the trees and through the bramble. Anything but familiar, everything surrounding me. My heart pounds, aches, exploding with terror. What comes next? What comes next? What comes...?

I shiver, but not from the cold. Whoever you are, whatever you are, whyever you are: let loose on me the justice, and be done with it.

VIII

3220 feet, 418 miles to Katahdin

Crosses borne are meant for the graveyard. There they shall stand, but not for all time. Bearing them thus they say is a punishment, but you have no Pilate for your life's journey save one. What punishment you provide, you provide for yourself. But isn't it amusing that crosses are made first, and then borne? The opposite of men, some would say.

Regardless, at this point I must digress into a discussion of the *lexicon de jour*.

A *tent* is just a *tent,* unless it lacks a side or two or three, in which case it morphs into a *tarp.* That's the easy one; it gets tricky after that. *Shelters* are *shelters* south of Connecticut; to the north, you have *lean-tos* regardless of the actual degree off-vertical, becoming *shelters* again in Vermont unless fully enclosed in which case they are *huts* with the exceptions of the fine Upper Goose Pond *Cabin* in Massachusetts and Smarts Mountain *Cabin* in New Hampshire. Oh, and they become *lean-tos* again in Maine.

Streams are *brooks* in New England; south of Pennsylvania the term *brook* is never used unless extended with the word *trout* while salivating. Further south they are *creeks*, not "cricks", a term nobody uses except for those with a neck injury or those who live in *hollers*, which are *hollows* further north and *pockets* in areas where quaintness retains its virginity. In invirginal Virginia or Maryland *streams* may be called *runs*, depending on whether or not a Civil War battle of substance was fought in the area (now replaced by suburbs and SUVs filled with latter-day soldiers marching as to war over said bones). A *river* may be merely a large *stream*, and don't let current rainfall conditions fool you otherwise. In New Hampshire and Vermont the small *creeks* are *brooks*, but always *streams* once in Maine.

A *valley* leading into (or out of) the mountains is a *cove*, large or small, while a few long narrow ones are *valleys* unless the sides are steep and a *stream* or *creek* or *river* or *brook* or *ticklely-dickely* runs through it, in which case it is a *gorge*, or unless it is a traveled connection between *ridges* in which case it is a *notch* or *pass* or (in the South) a *gap*. Unless of course you keep the company of true Alpinists and refer to them as *cols* just to fit in at the *très chez beret* cafes and lifts in Chamonix. The bottomland surrounding is soothingly called *bottomland*, or among the naughty just *bottoms*. Large, rounded, rocky mountaintops are *domes*, while smaller ones are *knobs*, and grassy or meadow-topped ones lacking trees are *balds*; otherwise they can be *mountains*, *mounts, summits*, *peaks*, or *points*. Unless they're topped with heath, in which case they're called *slicks*. Or with rhododendron or laurels, in which case it's a *laurel*. Or balsam, fir, and/or spruce, in which case it's a *balsam*. All except for Clingman's Dome on the Tennessee/North Carolina line, the Trail's highest point, which is in fact a *balsam* by this definition (although visibly many of them are dead from the adelgids), unless one takes into account the grotesque concrete observation tower on the peak, which arguably legitimizes it as a *tip* or maybe a *point*, or just plain *ugly*. Ridges are carefree and colorful: the Sawteeth, or the Hogback, or a *crest*, or a *view*, or a *line*, or....

With me so far?

One important point of practical value. Between Erwin and Damascus, there are no privies at the shelters. Gotta dig a hole, my friend.

But I was beyond Erwin, beyond Damascus; I was beyond all of Tennessee and Virginia and the South, almost a dream now, as much as the South could be a dream. It seemed less than a figment of my lost imagination -- not even a fragment of a fraction of a figment. It had all happened to someone else, displaced, detached, back before the Schaghticoke of Connecticut and the Berkshires of Massachusetts. I was beyond the Green now; in fact, the Green had become the White. Tennessee was all the way back at the other end of the spectrum for me, a sweltering infrared of heat and sweat as invisible as anyone's yesterdays.

We enter a thicket of sugar maples. Somewhere in Vermont we'd encountered a particularly spectacular grove of sugar maples, just beginning the hint of a turn to the cherry red fire of autumn announcing the churn of sweet syrup within. If I'd had a corkscrew handy, I would not have used it: better red than dead. I remembered it as if it were the present. Time was beginning to stretch out like a lazy afternoon's cat, practically Persian in its luxuriousness. Events merged, forming stalactites of immutable solidity, a sea of Chinese green tea calm. The red merged with the green, making nothing but a coward's yellow. Still, our legs moved, in reptilian repetition, scuttling across the sea of scrabble and shale. Once this was a sea's bottom; now it was a forest of maples. Green becoming red, but time remaining time. Colors abound in my mind.

It had grown truly cooler as I'd gone not-so-true North; yet, I knew the truer warmth of my situation had yet to be. Some formerly anticipated miles approaching me now would be the first above genuine treeline, beyond the Velvet Rocks and aforementioned Smarts Mountain I'd just left this morning (a genuinely wonderful cabin, that). I was past all that was velvet, while definitely smarting; my knee tendons had finally turned to tapioca in the Taconic. The miles were at last wearing on me and mine, enduring all this. I drew in the air, filled today with the odor of wild mint, adding to the growing chill but, like the cheap generic mouthwash in a strip-club bathroom Dixie cup, only marginally soothing.

So, what was left? When one is down to the dregs of the day, there's little left of the rocks in the glass. But -- given all the rocks here in New Hampshire, and at the end Maine, on Mount Katahdin, in Baxter State Park -- the end was the end, rocks or no rocks. Even rocks such as Virgil and I obeyed the laws of thermodynamics. The Second Law of Thermodynamics says perpetual motion is impossible, and I was a stickler for the rule of law. Laws were meant to protect, in the end, despite the damage done in spite along the way in and for and by their name. Laws were meant to corral the seething human horde within the rusty, barbed fences of civilization, to inbreed the herd instinct amongst the hunter-gatherers, lest they gather and hunt us. Best to have a big rock handy, just in case... and Katahdin was one big rock.

Of course, the judges behind the laws both natural and unnatural might be corrupt. If the only end product of a law of the fallible, by the fallible, and for the fallible was the chaos of uncertainty turned into some kind of amoral principle, perhaps the point needed arbitration instead, keeping it out of the Judge's hands. An arbitration, To Protect And Serve, with Hell's own subpoenaed and testifying. I just wish I knew what crime had been committed. No charges had been lain before me, yet. Original Sin, perhaps; a trite and tired concept diluted by Bishop Ussher and countless others across his six millennia (and Darwin's millions) of genetic daft and drift. But eventually the DNA gets watered down: spliced, resequenced, mutated, passed on to future herd members, diluted again and again and again, divided and subdivided until only the least significant bits remain. Whatever Original Sin we'd inherited now seemed at most a pittance, yet the price remained unadjusted for inflation (or so said those who passed the plate to pay for it). Of course, even the judges in the church had to obey laws less seemly than the Law seems; even their pocketbooks' entropy increased to maximum. Cause and effect, for post- or prelapsarian alike.

Not such bad things, then, those laws and thermodynamics, given the choice between beach-front condos or bona-fide cannibalism. I've never been a big fan of defeat. But I'd already drunk a full drought from my spring, and watched it turn into a summer of discontent that was a winter in all but name. I'd given up on the tongue-twisters; I'd gotten bored with them somewhere around fifty-seven in New Jersey. There were only so many words that rhymed with numbers, and *Thirty-Seven Dusty Heathens Thanking Heaven Drank Iced Tea Then* sounded a lot like *Forty-Seven Fifths With Ginger Gave Five-Sevenths Gout, Four Fever,* at least in liquid volume displaced, and *Fifty-Seven Severed Brethren Set Fire To A Seven-Eleven* just didn't cut it for me, somehow. I decided to pass the peace pipe and try a stab back at the nonsense poetry. I'd had Indians on my mind since skirting the reservation of Schaghticoke reservation back in Connecticut; not seeing any, mind you, since I'd seen no one other than the damned the last nigh-on-a-thousand miles or so. Here in the east (or its incredible facsimile thereof), the Iroquois were a dominant culture -- an agglomeration of tribes with a common ancestry dating back to at least 1000 A.D., moving out of the Finger Lakes region into the Ohio River valley. Which made me think of Illinois. Which after a few minutes gave me:

The old Iroquois
Who know of the boy
From North Illinois
Who only ate soy
Loaves loathe to enjoy
Swore oaths in a ploy
To Okie cowboys
In their lowly employ:
Be no oaf, oh killjoy,
Of North Illinois
Boy's beans born o' soy
Nor only enjoy
Your gold troy by troy;
Be bold hoi polloi
Both boastful and coy:
Try soy with savoy!

Which made me just stop and burst out laughing like the total dork that I was. I doubled-over in fact, and as I laughed long and hard being overly amused in completely nerd-like fashion, I overbalanced, bringing the top of the pack down too far forward, losing my balance and falling face-first into the scrabble. I caught a stone in my left nostril, releasing a choked chortle through my right nostril combined with a yelp of surprise and pain as I hit, the combination sounded a lot like a loud "*Ormphdgh!*" on my part. Virgil yelped and sprung left automatically, a proper wood-instinct far more manly than my stupid poem.

I was still laughing as I picked the rock out of my nostril, blowing it clean and letting my mucus run free, a fine and odoriferous beast, finally declaring myself un-unclean again and an in-the-good-graces Sadducee despite my regular consumption of the cloven-hoofed (a *mensch* or a *schlemiel* maybe, but no *tzadik*). Hog-like in both content and odor, I liked my southern barbecue way, way too much.

Crap, there I went again, bringing up the subject of food. "Hey little big man, want a snack?" I asked Virgil. He replied with his typical hungry dance, bouncing left and right and left again, a couple times in a row. I kept on chuckling. After all, why not?

"OK, OK, I get it." I sat up right where I'd landed in the Trail, unsnapped the hip belt (the chest strap having popped open on my fall), and eased my pack off and around. I opened the top pocket, pulled out the snacks, and offered him some water as I cut a hard cheese with a large knife. We ate and drank then, among the thin grass and wayward twigs, spruce and pine swaying in the gentle air.

"You know," I said after a moment, "I don't even remember where we got this cheese. I mean, clearly we resupplied somewhere, with someone, but you know, I can't seem to recall a thing about it." I munched, pondered our water bottle. "I mean, I remember filtering this, filling it back at... where did we cross I-89 at? Was that before or after I-91?" Virgil just ate like a maniac like he always did, making a big mess and wasting a lot of the food. He was quiet, uninterested in my conversation, quietly emitting some sort of repetitive rhythm that wasn't quite a melody, lacking the required minimum percentage of pitch. I wasn't taken aback, nor did I judge him; I just persisted as usual.

"Ah well, doesn't matter. I suppose not remembering should bother me. It should, right?" An intellectual weariness sat in, a sudden hard rain poured cold through a high forgotten gully's bramble. I scratched a non-existent itch from some psychic rash. "I don't know. Don't know the players without a program. *Can't* know the players without a program. Just numbers and positions and relative skin tones. Might not even know the game being played. The field can be as green as grass or bare as pavement. Doesn't mean it's all meant for entertainment, just because you can bring a ball in and knock it around. " I looked around, falling silent for awhile. "That's where us Americans got it wrong. All this isn't meant for anything in relation to us, but rather the other way around. We thought we invented the game, built the stadium, sold the tickets and made a fat full-figured profit. We believed in the Most High Umpire, covering our bases, keeping score, making a list and checking it twice, coaching and correcting behaviors when we littlest leaguers swang and missed, or spat nasty tobaccy, or corked our bats surreptitiously in the dugout behind the grownup's backs. Little did we know He'd left in the early innings, to leave us to referee ourselves. Play nice together, and all. Play nice with our toys. And when we were done, take care and clean up after ourselves, put the playtime things away, and stop playing games and get to the real work at hand, like the grownups we were expected to be."

I watched two beetles emerge from a deep mahogany bark, scuttle around a young tree's truck once, twice. They froze in tandem for a second, then zoomed around the trunk a few more times, then stopped dead again, synchronously. A pageantry, pagan: *zoom*, stop, *zoom*, stop. A few times they'd touch each other's antennae, youthful instinctive caresses. In another moment they raced back down to the earth, and started back up all over again.

I turned my head left, just as the small cluster of cedars there was descended upon in a *whoosh* by a flock of twenty or thirty cedar waxwings. A handsome bird, sleek and refined. Virgil perked up and offered his greetings, but they were more interested in the cedar's remaining trove of berries than in us. We all ate together, taking what we needed, and only that, with us. We shared the fruits of our labors: the waxwings sitting next to each other passing berries back and forth down their line, while Virgil and I split some dried strawberries, real ones not made of wax. Funny; I couldn't remember where those came from, either.

So, where was I? Ah, yes: what was left. *Let's see. Lust, greed, gluttony, sloth, wrath, envy: check!* That made the only one left the sin of *pride*.

"The grownups we were expected to be," I murmured. "Expected to be," confirmed Virgil.

Pride, the worst of sins of old. Vainglory, putting one's self before God. Not minding your place. Well, I had no place, so there was no minding it. At least I didn't think there was anything to mind. I wouldn't leave this for all the tea in Padma's China, wherever or whenever or even *if* that was. I hadn't left it yet, despite him and his damnable Cirque amongst the cirques. Yet I was soon to leave it of my own volition, at Katahdin, the end, in, oh, a month or so, maybe six weeks. I would leave it and return to my past again: my past, and my prideful ways.

Or, would I?

Pride always got the better of me, proving I was American. Pride had always gotten the better of America. We were the Six Million Dollar Man of countries: we could build it better, stronger, faster. Because better is... better. Right? As a physician I understood the importance of vitality, of a driving force that led men on, and out, and through it all; after all, that force had led me to medical school from the depths of Southern poverty, a culture and poverty I'd never been comfortable with, fit in, or enjoyed. I'd wanted more. I'd wanted something... something to mind, drive, control, something to give me a sense of purpose. In my youth I thought in my ignorance that those purposes were external to myself: a title, a job, a big home, a big car, a beautiful girl, all for me, all mine, to mind, drive, and control. It was all about me.

What a goddamnably idiot fool I was.

It was only after years of work and struggle, years of a marriage to a pretty girl who it turns out wanted things and a title and a car and a career and other things of her own to control and mind and drive just like me, years of internecine warfare between us for the pointless generalship of our infinitesimal kingdom, the constant unrelenting political pressures of medical school and then one hospital and then another, that I began to see. I began to see that struggle for struggle's sake was anathema, an unending inflammation of the senses that no steroid could cure. And as I'd dried up, the life force sucked from me, as it all fell apart, she'd left, and so had I. I'd left behind the pavement and the promise, for something more, for something less. It was a dream and a fantasy, but that's when I'd finally found something genuinely resembling hope; something less, and something more. I gave her everything, and what I didn't give she took; but, at the end of our war, when everything I'd ever owned was hers or the lawyer's, without shackles of any kind, I finally found what I'd really been looking for all the years of my now-middle-aged life: freedom. Freedom, a highly-valued thing in America, land of leveraged buyouts and darkened bullet-proof sedans, ostintate walled-off foreclosed mansions and ostentatious breast-enhanced fore-heavy women. Freedom: the one thing that absolutely none of those things can ever, ever give you.

And Virgil. She'd given me Virgil. But I couldn't think about that.

My intent this glorious day was a hard 21-mile day, descending from Smarts Mountain and passing three shelters (Hexacuba, Ore Hill, and Jeffers Brook) and ascending back up to the end of the day at Beaver Brook at 3650 feet. My knees ached, throbbed. I'd popped two Ibuprofen each morning for a long time now, Ibuprofen that like the food I carried I had no recollection of buying and stocking. Although it inhibited my cyclooxygenase and thus my prostaglandin, it did little to clear the muddy mind. Only an agonist of spirit mitigated that. We crunched along through the mild air of... what was it now? August? September? I couldn't be sure. I couldn't be certain about anything.

We turned a switchback heading downward, and came to a pretty little waterfall against the side of the Trail. It was small but full, evidence of a rain in these parts perhaps two or three days back. There were so many waterfalls along the way they'd become commonplace. There was Amicalola, but that wasn't technically on the A.T., just on the way to its beginning way back in Georgia. Laurel Falls in Carter County, Tennessee. Crabtree Falls were nearby in Nelson County in Virginia; there were a few others, all small-ish by global standards. This one was just another fall in a series of falls, of water, and Man. But something about this one made me slow, and eventually stop, Virgil along with me. In silence we listened to the hard smack of water on moss and stone. How many of my brethren could stop and look at this waterfall, so small and pointless in and of itself, and wonder at it, wonder as to the truth of it, in it, and choose a different path, another trail, leading someplace entirely unexpected?

How many of my brethren had we lost along the way? By envy of others with lives we couldn't realistically afford, stocked with toy after toy, leading empty materialistic lives, or in envy of the raw power they held? In unjust wars, by the sin of wrath of lying leaders led to their positions in envy of that power, in response to the wrath of the dictator or terrorist, real or imagined, with their own wrath from injustice or insult causative, imagined or real? By the sloth of those who elected those leaders to facilitate their culture of ease and its easy, quick ways to gain for themselves at others' and now even Nature's expense? By the gluttony and greed of those who would take from us by way of insane financial instruments and consciously institutionalized fraud to stock and feed our sloth and the impossibly gilded mansionary mausoleums we erect to honors our gold and our golden calf gods? Or by our own senses with their residuum lusts, an attempt to medicate the effect of the world we have created on us, a world that deep down we loathe and know cannot last, a world that the better side of us in our greater nature knows is wrong, a cause of pain, and ultimately only a path to death? The death not only of one, or a nation, or of us all, but the Earth and all life on it?

And all for what? Our genetic hubris. Survival of the fattest. Endogenous ego. Call it what you will.

All this time I've served you. I'd put you back together, piece by piece, when you'd run your Suburban into a freeway retaining wall after a night of irresponsible binge Jaegerbombing with the clientèle. Or I'd purge your stomach when you'd swallow an entire bottle of vitamins thinking they'd kill you, and us knowing it wouldn't, but having to empty you anyway because if you're that uninformed and/or stupid then maybe you couldn't tell the cartoon character chewables from the less Saturday morning Dummy Duck entertainment pills in the house. Or sew that digit back on after you wore open-toed sandals while weed whacking with some top-end diesel monstrosity meant for far more than your measly pittance of clover and broadleaf plantain amongst the Bermuda but effectively marketed and sold to you or at least your sense of manly neighborhood competitive yard maintenance nonetheless. Or try to convince you for the fourth and fifth and sixth times that you're not having a heart attack, that it's only the Generalissimo Grande Burrito platter you ate (in thumb-nosed violation of my previous recommendations), until you come in for the eighth time with a genuine Infarction Internationale caused by all the little Tex-Mex donkeys smothered in farmer's cheese now braying loudly in your aorta, which you refuse to believe, insisting it's only heartburn even after I've showed you the blood work that proves otherwise. I've served you: medicated you, de-medicated you, ordered tests, admitted you, admitted nothing to you, and shown you the door... and some of you, I've shown to your next-of-kin, for identification purposes, or worse. In 12-hour shifts, day after endless day, days lit not by the sun but by artificial fluorescents harsh in their glare off your botoxed and blank faces. I'd watched those faces cry, scream, laugh, vomit, bleed, swell uncontrollably, smile unaccountably, and more than once even try to beguile me (the ones who saw doctors as magical mysteries, or just as mysteriously, materially wealthy). The hospital's lights showed you in your true light. Trust me on that.

So few of you were worth it. Maybe none of you were. If you only knew how we emergency room doctors talked about you. We see the stupidest things a person can do to themselves or others, the most reckless things, the most avoidable things. We see the real you (or, the reality of what's inside you, if you've managed to break the skin). People say we doctors don't connect with them, that we fail to show compassion. Well duh. What you do to yourselves is incomprehensible. So much pain for so little gain. So what compassion is it that you think you deserve?

Yet, you have all this goddamn *pride*. Correction: *We* all have this goddamn pride. After all, I haven't done anything differently than any of you. Heck, I'm as adiabatic of a process as they come, and if it's one thing we Americans are, it's adiabatic. Lossless to our surroundings, we sold our souls long ago, to the dream and the promise -- and loss, unfortunately, requires souls.

"Such harshness," said a familiar voice. "Where did all of that hate come from? What happened to you -- really?" I didn't look around; I didn't have to.

"Speaking of reality, what's real here?" I asked the air, the closest thing to a response I was going to make. "I smell brokenness: broken mint, broken paths, and broken promises. All of it trampled and florid. I hope at some point you'll explain it all, provide some bookworm sense for it." But there was no reply, only the wind, though I'd heard his voice plainly enough. Of course there was no response. There never was, never had been. Not a real, unambiguous one.

"Harshness," said Virgil; he'd heard him too. So, I wasn't hallucinating. Hmm, that's food for thought. And, quite a relief, really.

In fact, it perked me up so much that I lurched into motion again, and Virgil with me. Nobody tried to stop us, and I didn't look around for a reason to stop. I knew he'd be following us, on the Trail or off. It didn't matter, like so many things didn't on the Trail. Harshness, indeed.

We turn a switchback.

I judged New Hampshire a very beautiful state. Interestingly, its beauty today was largely the result of a singular and monumentally destructive moment that occurred almost two hundred years ago on the other side of the planet. In April 1815, the worst volcanic explosion in human history obliterated the island of Tambora in far-off Indonesia, leaving out of twelve *thousand* inhabitants only twenty-six alive -- a mere *twenty-six*! -- and leading to 1816, known as The Year Without A Summer. The explosion kicked twenty-five times as much ash into the air as Mount St. Helens had in the 1980's, darkening the skies and lowering sunlight across the globe. Across New England, cold spells in May 1816 delayed the start of the planting season. June began well, but crops were lost in a cold spell between the 5th and 11th. Snow accumulated throughout all but southernmost Vermont and New Hampshire. A warm spell starting the last third of June provided hope that summer had arrived, but a killing frost on July 9th dashed that hope. The rest of the month was warmer, but didn't equal the warmest days of June. A warming trend in August abruptly ended with frost on the 21st and a worse one on the 30th. Some crops did well, apple and pear harvests were very good, perhaps due in part to the cold weather being hard on insect pests. Some people were able to raise a good crop of wheat or potatoes, and they were rewarded with prices that were double that of normal years, a rate of inflation not seen again until the 1970s. After 1816, the weather returned to normal conditions, but farmers had already started emigrating to the more hospitable weather and soil of Ohio and further west. This migration helped accelerate the construction of the Erie Canal, which started construction in 1817 and was completed in 1825. Others went to the mills of Manchester and Springfield, or to Nantucket and Gloucester and Newport and their whaling ships, or to the big cities of Boston or Philadelphia. The populations of Vermont and New Hampshire fell sharply after 1816, and didn't recover until the 1960's. As a direct result of all this, unlike the rest of the country and against all common sense, today's Vermont and New Hampshire are much more forested and pristine than they were in 1816.

All because of a volcano on the opposite side of the Earth at the opposite end of our nation's history.

Oh, there were possibly other contributing factors. 1816 was part of the Dalton Minimum, a period of reduced solar activity. Such periods supposedly tend to be cooler than usual and the years leading up to 1816 were cold and difficult. Napoleon's invasion of Russia in 1812 suffered dreadful losses, many of them due to the early and harsh winter during the return from Moscow. There is also evidence from Greenland ice cores that decreasing salinity in the North Atlantic may have weakened or diverted the Gulf Stream in the Northeastern Atlantic, reducing its warming effect.

But who cares? It's all mere fact. The past exists only where the pudding does: as part of our guts now. Hence, I rise above it all, to avoid the constant agglomeration of glutenized sensation becoming just so much additional brown fat for the memory on which one may chew, savoring, slowly. Like Camus and his Clamence, I never felt comfortable except in lofty surroundings, where I can feel *above.* Claustrophobia has its limits, and not only in the three dimensions of space. Oppressive boredom pens me in on all sides; only the air has ever opened up for me, and the air lies in one and only one direction. A mere fact.

Fact: at the bottom of the incline that takes you to the *Templo Expiatorio del Sagrado Corazon de Jesus del Tibidabo*, just as you begin the treacherous wind back down the *Avinguda de Tibidabo* towards the center of Barcelona, there is a restaurant, *La Venta*, next to which is the *Bar Merbeye*, with a canopy which is yellow on which they have printed their name twice in large block letters. They cut a hole in the aluminum roof to accommodate a palm tree. They serve *aguadente* in bottles but not in cans, meaning that it is a classy establishment. It is run by a family whose father does not know that his daughter is skimming euros from the cash register to buy him a present for next St. John's Day. Correction: three St. Johns Days ago. I wonder if he liked it.

Fact: north of the town of Natal in Rio Grande de Norte, Brazil, but south of Torous where South America finally turns back to the west, there lies the town of Genipabu, famous for its high, steep sand dunes. A man there with a large mustache has three sand buggies, all a chipped and abraded disco-sparkly blue, only two of which run. For fifty *reals*, he will give you his fake name, and take you and three of your closest friends up and down and around the dunes, at insane speeds. You will come exceedingly close to flipping at least half a dozen times. If you do not wear eye protection it is torture to the point of possible permanent blindness. He does not carry insurance. Well, maybe he does now, or maybe he's been dead in the intervening fourteen years.

Fact: the Tour de Mont Blanc takes on average 60 hours with its highest points at the Col des Fours in France and the Fenetre d'Arpette in Switzerland, each at 8750 feet. It is usually hiked anti-clockwise from either Les Houches or Courmayeur. It is of unsurpassed loveliness. Only the silent self in personal reflection can describe the jagged alpine peaks, the air, the meadows, the flowers. A girl works along the trail at the Refuge Elena. She has blue eyes and blond hair. She speaks just enough English to ask you for a kiss after dinner, if she is willing. She smiles at certain things in the flickering candelight, more at others. The blond hair is not natural, which if you tell her will make you both laugh, extremely quietly. I can still hear it, a quarter of a century later and just as faint, though she's hiked down to a family of her own by now.

We turn a switchback.

Spirits supposedly haunt the unoccupied wood, savoring that taste they experienced in life, a memory, dissolute. But ghosts were for children. Nowadays modern man did not believe. Fairy tales were just that. Limited in scope and grandeur, unlike for example the modern business plan with its upward-trending sales forecasts. And spirits had no fingers to point. One cannot hold the dead accountable, yet still fair accountants die. In between walked the undead, so popular in the popular fiction of today, and for good reason. Zombies truly have the best of all possible worlds. They reek of the peace of death, yet pretend the motion of purpose. But what do they seek except brains, that intelligence they instinctively know they lack, only to consume it and be no better off for the effort?

You're all marching toward oblivion. Don't you zombies know that?

The Tragedy of the Commons. Share ten acres with ten farmers, and they will destroy the land. Everyone is incented to take, none to reseed, renourish, or replant. Give each farmer their own acre, they will keep it and tend it well. What we didn't realize was that it was *all* commons. In a complex interconnected world nothing is under the care of a single soul, not even each of our single souls. We all affect. But I grew tired of affecting the afflicted. That's why I left. Or maybe I should say that they grew tired of me. Loneliness both ceases and begins when you identify less with the zombies, and more with the original humanity that led to them. Those who lived in these woods once, who cared for the land and tended it carefully. But that just made me the ghost I was now. Gone, but not yet.

We turn a switchback.

Nature rather than nurture, or was it the other way around? But without the latter, what Nature would there be? And without the former, what would be worth nurturing?

Isolation. A quarter of Americans now say that they have no one to confide in, more than twice the number reported in 1985. In the same time, the number of close confidants an average American self-reports has dropped from three to two. In another thirty years we'll have no one to talk to. This most certainly explains the rise in popularity of reality television. Shows we can watch and point at, laughing, while we smugly nod with wisdom beyond our experience, and assert: "I am not you." Put others down and you bring yourself up. No Like button can fix this, no matter what some Internet billionaire child says.

Isolation born of pride. We segment ourselves into markets of one. We are micro-targeted individuals. I am not you, so customize your message for me. The Good News as texted by my personal Savior? *You are Special.* Why, thanks so much. How could I otherwise have known? Ah, yes; my pride made me this way. I am not you. I am NOT you.

We turn a switchback. We must be near the top, since they're coming faster now.

We chase up the slopes, simulacrums of water. In fact, we oppose much more, not only the fluid, but the unseen: gravity, exhaustion, and scorn. We trace a serpent's tail, Virgil and I, following the clouds, daring to touch the perennial sky, mute but trumpeting nonetheless. My lungs ache, as do my feet, and other parts of me. Virgil doesn't complain; he never complains. He is an example to us all, with his freedom to act within. It parades before us as we parade by. It wounds me, but as I am already wounded one more dull throbbing only pushes me on the more. I sip from my Camelbak as I walk, consuming the fluid; like me, partially visible. It fills me like a religion.

At the crest, an omega-shaped turn in the path routes us around the boulders, and we are around the top, and heading down again on the other side.

One more up, one more down. Just another fall for man. Starting earlier than usual this year, the gift of a dry spring and locally cooler weather. We trotted downhill against an inexorable tide. A hot, persistent flow of air found this ridge somewhere far below, collided with cold impersonal stone, and pushed itself upward, focusing itself and gaining strength in the narrow valley we now descended, to propel itself politic into our faces. I exhale hard, matching pressure and temperature. It's important to fit in. We cross a fault line, visible in a disjoint seam of parallel rocks thrust upward, one of many, very many, we have crossed. The earth moves under our feet. It travels, without constancy; like, yet unlike. As it wrinkles with age, its face twists, distorts, creating the land around us. I refuse to grimace. Despite my desire and the loft of the valley's breath, we skate lower down the slate, ankles bathed in grass and clover. Soon both disappear, signifying the last of the open ridge top for some time.

We turn hard right, descend more steeply.

A return of sorts, also born of pride. To show the way, as an example to all. Hah, an example of thin and emaciated forms perhaps, but little else on inspection. One hoped first impressions meant little... or, that the visions seen took on wholly other forms. We descend as gods, but lack chariots. Poverty stricken, avatars of something better, I hope; some other form, hidden and unglimpsed, underlies our stink. I hope it is a golden form, bathed in light, immanent, and just as false an idol to worship. Man's had enough of idols. The real world's cried out for so much that to let the distractions of the mirror invade seem to invite the heathen inside the temple.

We turn again, left this time, and descend more steeply.

More and more Americans abandon the religion of their childhood every year. Some say we should reclaim what we have lost. I say we are doing just that very thing. Let us raze the temple and melt the golden calf into ingots, hammer the Beast Baal into balls, to then melt and sublime into vapor and dust. That way, we can carry our riches back with us into the dust to which we shall surely return. It's the only way to fly. Amen.

Suddenly I sneeze, hard, and the wind blows it back upon me. I curse. Must've been all the damn dust.

The mountains seem to accelerate, a marginally oiled and dirty carnival fun ride tunnel around me. I continuing thumping downwards, hard boots on hard volcanic rock, intruders among these magma intrusions. Formed by a hotspot in the Earth's mantle, one hundred twenty five to one hundred million years ago, back when dinosaurs ruled. The hotspot was long left behind as North America drifted westward; in fact, the hotspot was no more, long ago consumed by the Mid-Atlantic Ridge. These mountains were a child left behind by its long-dead parent.

But I couldn't think about that.

A tenor. In an opera, one sings. In a conversation, one tries to follow or define it. To a meth head, it's just what makes them who they are; it's what's in their blood, so to speak. But for me, it is the continuance of my general direction and velocity. My tenor in tensor form, where tensor both does and does not mean *of higher tension*. Which I both intend and do not intend as a pun. Which….

Fuck I'm exhausted.

Racing thoughts are a dangerous sign, old friend. They imply the existence of something substantial, like a full-grown Godzilla or full-blown bipolar disorder, for instance. Just who is attacking whom here? I'm no Megatron, after all. Not even a Mothra, and only just maybe a Mothman, even though we were far from West Virginia. Also a pretty state, in places anyway.

We slosh through a stream pouring off bare loose rocks on our right. The water falls across the trail, diagonally a long way down the path, until it turns right around a corner while the water continues straight off the path and down the side. It's how waterfalls are born.

We turn a switchback, and then....

She leaned over, giving me a good long sniff. "You... smell rotted," she observed, puckering up, but not for a kiss.

I beamed. "It's a noble rot, like with proper Bordeaux. The fungus makes me sweeter and last longer on the shelf. May I say you smell like an entire arrangement of flowers native to nowhere near here." I pointed to her. "Carnation, meet, " then pointing back to myself, "the reincarnated."

"Why thank you,' she answered, pulling her boots off. "So how long have you been a smart ass?"

"My entire life, or at least that part of it that involved love of some sort. You know what's funny about reincarnation? It's supposed to be a form of punishment where you learn the lessons of your past life's wrongdoings, yet they completely wipe your memory of it in the process. How can you learn from what you can't remember? Seems like they should do they opposite, right? Remembering is everything. They should make you relive the same thing, over and over, until you get it right or... wait, wait. Was I talking about reincarnation, or love? Ah, yes, reincarnation. Until you get it right or go mad."

There was a long silence from her as I arrogantly chuckled, then she killed both my arrogance and my laugh dead with a blade far too icily close to the possible truth. "How do you know that's not exactly what's happening?"

she asked. Instantly, I felt it sink as deep as any real metal, piercing my heart, freezing my laugh in place. It made for a highly disquieting....

"Aw, would you look at that?" she moaned, holding up a tiny black and greenish squashed something. "I must have walked on him all day. Scorpion, in my boot." My face and mind switched to ER mode at the comment, and I stood up. "Just a poor baby," she cooed, showing me.

"Let me look at it," I said firmly, stepping over and sitting down next to her.

"It's nothing, just a wet spot on my sock. It's nothing to…."

I grabbed her foot, pulled it towards me. "Let me look. Yoda was right, size matters not." I insisted. She stopped, saw my look, and nodded a short OK.

I examined her for stings carefully and slowly. Scorpion stings could be tricky. Sometimes the sting broke off and barbed itself in the skin without fully penetrating, only to push through hours later and send the recipient of the venom into shock or worse. Especially the small ones.

"Foot fetish?" she asked, as serious as a body cavity search.

"Only if they're properly bathed and manicured," I replied, continuing my examination.

"Are you saying I'm not a lady?"

"I'm saying these are cured more than manicured right now, a head cheese kind of way." I checked between the toes. "And, as it just so happens, I happen to be a doctor."

"Eww, a podiatrist with a foot fetish. How stereotypical."

"ER, thank you, as you recall. Watched too much *Emergency* on TV when I was a kid. Used to carry around my dad's tackle kit like it was that big portable phone-in-a-box the actors used." There was the tiniest of red bumps just inside her right hallux. It had a tiny black speck sticking out of it. I gently set her foot down on the ground. "Don't move or stand up or scratch it. There's a wee bit of a barb there on the port side of your big toe. Hang on a sec." I got up to get my med kit from the pack.

She laughed. "I was a *Voyage to the Bottom of the Sea* girl myself. Had a thing for David Hedison, pretty weird for a five, six year old. But the Flying Sub was pretty cool."

"Not particularly aerodynamic."

"Shitty gas mileage," she agreed.

"I'm sure it was diesel. What about later?" I said as I rummaged.

"I'm flattered. Normally I wait until the second date at least."

"Back to reality, stay with me. Favorite TV shows."

"Oh, umm, *Six Million Dollar Man*, *Bionic Woman* of course, loved the Bigfoot episodes.... Do you remember *Fantastic Journey*?"

I paused for a moment, went into lookup mode. That was a tough one. "Bermuda Triangle, right? Something about the Bermuda Triangle." I got the small zippered pouch out, walked back over to her.

"I'm impressed! Wow, nobody remembers it anymore. I kept trying to turn my piano instructor's tuning fork into a Sonic Energizer."

I just looked at her blankly as a I sat back down and gently lifted her foot again, placing her lower leg across my thigh.

"Nice legs you have there, Dr. Foot Fetish," she said, all sparkle and sauciness.

Shit. Shit shit shit.

We turn a switchback.

I stopped. "Did I just...?" Confused, I looked around. But there was only Virgil and I, and the woods, and the Trail. To be expected. I looked at him, sideways.

"Did you just say something?" I asked him.

He just looked at me quizzically, tilting his head. As usual. I felt I'd just forgotten something, or remembered something that had yet to happen. If a promise repeated means a promise made, does its lack of fruition relegate it to a vegetative state? It may bloom, but comes not to seed. What should I then make of his continued silence? It meant something, I felt certain. But I didn't quite know... or, didn't want to. Either equally probable.

We'd just crossed the state line and entered Maine. Maine, the wildest state east of the Mississippi River. Soon, very soon, we'd come to the Hundred-Mile Wilderness. This was Thoreau's Earth, made from Chaos and Old Night. It was his unhandsold globe, definitely of wood, rough and ridden with splinters. The philosopher's thing-in-itself, the fool's gold. Swamps generally held more promise; luckily for us, this was a swamp, dreadful and steeped in wonderful inky muds of alluvial silts, billions upon billions of dead no-see-ums, and black fly guano. And by black flies, I don't mean black flies; I mean culicomorphs of Devonian line, jawed, toothed, possessed by multi-armed Asian or Mesoamerican demons of the cave-wall, syncretic in their disregard for their tormented's beliefs, and every one with a belly as void and aching as the average man's credit line these days. Eyes all razors, a million razors, cutting and slicing. Here, DEET tuned into defeat, with the addition of a mere A and its letter-grade opposite F derived from the school of hard knocks as the state of being *Absolutely Fucked*. I mean, crimeny: what's more fucked than being eaten alive?

Then, on top of that, you could add the real possibility of "beaver fever", aka infection of the intestine -- specifically the lumen -- by one or more species of the protozoal flagellate *Giardia*. I didn't have any metronidazole for it handy, and the side effects made the cure worse than the disease in a lot of cases. Tinidazole was better in that regard, with only a single nauseating dose required. The native Americans of these parts had once used goldenseal (in the buttercup family) to the same effect, and probably better outcome. Cursed with my fine-china Caucasianness, I couldn't have identified goldenseal reliably if I'd tried. We were such helpless babes out here in the genuine wild. A variety of other potential microbiological terrorist attacks presented themselves out here: Lyme disease, an equine encephalitis which turned your brain into mush, not to mention a couple of the sis-es (shigellosis, schistosomiasis, and brucellosis, just to name three -- though the latter was admittedly nigh impossible as we were nowhere near the Yellowstone area, and far more apt to run into a moose than an elk here in the East).

Virgil sneezed, twice in rapid succession. It startled him. I laughed. We kept on walking.

There had been moments like that, a few, where an emotion that was almost happiness emerged from somewhere inside me, butterfly-like. It peered outward at the world around me, at the splendor and the substance, taut with potential energy and fraught with obstacles and distractions. Obstacles, in the form of upward-trending slopes. Distractions, in the form of visions. Despite these, it was a kind of happiness, though I was wise enough to avoid banking on it for a future withdrawal. *Cojones* do not a glue make; *conjeos* perhaps, if you boil their coochey-coo little rodent bones sufficiently. Judgment holds court in the centers of fear in every man's mind, where it finds only self, for defendant and prosecutor. I was alone. We were all alone. Except for this damnable operetta going on around us.

Anywho, back to Maine. Maine was arguably the most beautiful state yet, despite its load of insects and parasites. Luckily for both Virgil and myself, blueberries were blueberries, either in the bush or on the table. Well, blueberries or huckleberries or, every once in a while on the site of some abandoned long-dead European native's farm, what I'd swear were bilberries. I was surprised at how many blueberries there were still in the bush, this late in the year. The deep woods were thick with them, betraying a cool summer's former presence. The witch hobble entangled everything, white flowers long since fallen away into the earth from whence they'd sprung, shooting roots wherever the branches touched ground and generally preferring to make anything off-trail impassible. The lichens colored the stones purple and silver, an odd merger of Christmas and Easter colors.

But none of it made us stop. The real question was why. The beauty of the place, one supposed; but the odd addition of truth had interjected itself some two thousand miles ago. Contrary to Keats, not the same thing; though, the urn was correct in showing that the music is silent and the chase perpetual, especially since its function is to hold the ashes of the dead. But as usual I digress. No; the real issue here was knowledge. Potential energy. A single flake falling at the top of a slope, tipping the balance, overcoming the well in the curve, and with a slow sweetness sliding, pulling along two neighboring flakes, each of those two pulling two more, and each of those two more, and each of *those* two more, and over the course of a few coarse-grained moments the power of the exponent takes flight, a whisper becoming a murmur, a murmur a grumbling, the grumbling a discord, the discord a roar, the roar a thundering, and thundering the mountainside slides off itself into the doomed valleys below. All from a single beautiful bit of crystal, pure order, into raging chaos. At least, that's how it's always been. But now, here was something new: order our of chaos, a reverser of entropy in our very midst. Potential energy solidified in human form. Someone who could answer questions for a change, and oh so many questions. Someone who could order the avalanche; pace it apace, so to speak. Someone -- something -- with real power, not the fake kind they pretend to have in Manhattan or Moscow or Monaco. The real deal. Cat's meow. The bee's knees. The ultimate Magic Eight Ball, and no more *Better Not Tell You Now*'s! Now, there had better be a-tellin'. So I chased him, while he chased me. Two flakes on the slope, racing for the bottom, to find the mountain's Root Cause, or crush ourselves under the weight of it all trying.

Now *that's* pride. But what else did you expect? Like Sean Connery in *Zardoz*, we'd seen better days, and better screenplays.

We turn a switchback.

"Just plain Bee," she was saying, after swallowing a third lead-weighted slug from her water bottle. She hadn't caught her breath yet. She glistened in the amber afternoon, beguilingly beaded, ebony hair long and somewhat matted, with a few stray straws and winged seeds blown in to her spider's-web tress by the wind along the way. She was thin, muscular, and absolutely beautiful.

I just stared. I waited for the star-spangled show to begin. She looked around, caught me staring at her, a wild fawn in my sights, my barrels loaded and ready. But I hesitated, and she took the initiative right out from under me as surely as if I'd tap-danced onto buttered ice.

"Been handling it yourself for awhile now, I take it." She muscled the side of her mouth up and sideways, her weapon now deployed. As she'd said it, I noted her glance down my body to a certain height off the ground and back up in one fluid practiced motion. It only took an instant. She wasn't taking a survey sighting. I missed none of it.

"Hmm," I answered, meeting cock for cock, then allowing the sound of distant birds to meld with the wind. We were attending a meeting of professionals, after all.

She stared at me, eyes on eyes, then the other side of her mouth rose in symmetry and the cockiness turned into outright courageousness. I was still a strange, dirty man alone in the wilderness with her, after all. I wondered what was she thinking when she spoke again.

"Got a name, tall dark and dirty stranger?" She pointed at Virgil. "How about... him? Does the guy in the tropical colors have a name?" Her eyes targeted both of us, darting back and forth, all mischievousness and mirth, like they laughed at everything they saw. A sure sign she was a devil, but the she stopped me with her hand. Against my lips. By actually touching them. She tasted of dirt, salt, and a faint floral, unidentifiable. "*Not* your trail name. Everybody's got the stupid trail name. I don't have a trail name... well, (*grimacing*) I got one all the way back at Walasi-Yi in the Peach State. THEY *(derision)* decided to call me Bee." At that, she hocked a loogie on the ground, a sort of Homeresque punctuation. (*Holy crap! A girl who hocks a loogie as punctuation!*) "It's my fault, really, I shouldn't have told them my real name. What about you, stoic strong and silent?

"Go ahead, Virgil, tell the lady you name," I deflected, gesturing subtly.

"Virgil," he answered, right on cue.

She laughed. It was devastating, musical and complex, a dusky Cabernet swirled in fireplace-illuminated crystal. "Nice to meet you, Mr. Virgil! Think you can get through that?" She gestured at the Notch's entrance.

"So Bee isn't your real name," I questioned, still doubting the premise of the moment. "You want *my* real name but decline to give us yours?"

"Ladies' *prerogative*," she answered, pretending affront in tone but all humor in temperament and posture. *Hmm, my, and what a posture it was...* I shook my head to clear the fog, and at once she mistook my gesture.

"OK fine, so it's Beelzebub, OK? Constance Q. Beelzebub, unconstant minion from Hell, at your service."

At the word *Beelzebub* my heart had stopped beating, and I felt the blood drain from every capillary in my body as I became all acids: hydrochloric, lactic, uric. I felt a twitch in my right cheek, uncontrollable.

"Are you sure you're OK?" she asked, suddenly anxious. "You just went *super* pale on me."

"And I beheld a pale rider on a pale horse." The words just came out as I stepped back away from her. Funny how free association works sometimes. Funny, and lousy. Her smile began subliming in the air, an untimely September frost.

Suddenly I reengaged my brain, reanalyzed the last fifteen seconds, and swore internally. *A referent, provide a referent.* "Revelations of course; sorry, I'm Spiritual But Not Religious, or at least that's what my e-dating profile says. Apologies, sometimes I free associate. I'm used to it, but you aren't. My name's Durant, Dr. Durant Allegheny, emergency room physician, at your service and your families'." I extended a gritty, loamed hand. Slowly, a smaller, cleaner one reached out to meet it.

"Don't... don't worry about it. Real name's Beatrice," she offered, brightening. Her hand met mine then, grasped it, and shook it. We both laughed, all high school lunch room in our uncertain intentions.

"My Dr. Wolf, what a strong grip you have," she observed, staring at the rhythmic up-and-down movement of our joined bodies.

"All the better to handle it myself, little girl," I said in a deep tone. She'd already forgotten her earlier comment, then a moment later in the middle of the faltering shake remembered, laughing more solidly, gripped back more firmly. *Holy Cannoli, I am actually almost flirting.*

She looked up, grasping my hand with her other hand, holding it between hers. "OK fine," she said softly as if to herself, then, slowly, she looked up at me, into my eyes. Still smiles and fear, both of us, but into them nonetheless.

But then, out of nowhere: "So what's the strangest thing you've seen in someone, Dr. Death?"

I felt the clutch grind while trying to reengage. Shoulda driven the automatic. "Pardon me?"

"Anything really scary? Tire iron? Logging axe? Parts of someone else?"

She's using humor to alleviate the tension, dumbass. "Oh, ummm.... That's really... disturbing."

"Takes one to know one," she said. "Guess you're not the only creepy crawly on the trail. How about boob jobs? Anything totally out of control, psycho-huge?"

I actually chuckled. *She's doing this deliberately... and probably for the best.* "Not in Buckhead... that'd be Atlanta. Maybe Palm Beach, Malibu, there's more of that sort of thing. Buckhead is a weird combination, more about botox and lifts and gangbangers with money but capping each other anyway. Umm... as far as scary, freeway accidents are bad, shotguns are bad, power tools, certain common household poisonings...."

"What about cool? Say, a coolness factor of... oh, off-scale?"

Damn. "Oh... that'd be Putting Ned."

Her face scrunched. "Putting Ned?"

"Yeah, a real brainiac: certified accountant, putting in a thunderstorm, hit by a double-strike in a one-two punch, WHAM-WHAM! *(Oops, I made her jump and scared her again.)* Stayed conscious the whole time, breathing, talking, dazed and confused, all his hair burnt off, head, eyelashes, pubic.... Right shoe missing the front half, smoking rubber and leather where the bolts left his body and went into the ground, one melted steel spike on the bottom heel, but *he*.... Well, we admitted him of course, ECG made some really electric kool-aid acid test patterns for a few hours, but he was mostly lucid, though when we mentioned he'd need ongoing neuro tests he turned to the nurse and said, 'So Nurse Ratched, what's your opinion?' *(she gets it! she's laughing!)* He stayed in for six, seven days... On day three, he was sitting up, talking to his family, then just like that, *thunk*, he falls over, his heart stops dead out of nowhere, Code Blue, they shock him back first try, and from then on he's right as rain, like all he needed was a reboot, though the CICU critical-cared him from that point on. Went home then, had babies, which I know because he was back a year later to have them and he stopped by. That's the really creepy part: he had twins. Wife swears it was the double-strike. Maybe they'll develop superpowers, who knows?"

"Scary," she said.

"Babies? Quite a commitment for sure. And you never know what the house will deal you."

"Maybe a big strapping doctor like yourself," she said with a strange tone, looking at Virgil.

I ignored it. "So, what do you do?"

She noticed some moss on her sleeve, wiped it off as she spoke. "I'm an R&D virologist, thank you very much, with V-Strex."

Well *that* required a reassessment of the state of the state. Guess she wasn't just another pretty fat-starved face. "*Really*? They're... a biomed startup in... where was it?" I had no clue, but best to sound informed.

"Cambridge," she chirped proudly. "Harvard, Ph.D., Class of '93, thank you *very* much, Doctor. And we're no longer a startup; we've made some breakthroughs with adenovirsues recently which..."

And on she went as I paid both professional and increasingly unprofessional attention. She talked about memory research, Alzheimer's cures, involving intercalation of manufactured, corrected DNA fragments into a host cell's genome courtesy of an adenovirus transmission vector. Short version: it was incredibly sexy, trust me on that. She went on for some time regarding the impairment of the replication of the adenovirus itself, to autoprogram it to die after several generations, a much harder task than actually injecting the DNA fragment composing the cure into the virus to begin with. Getting it to die at just the right time so as to hang around long enough to effect a cure in all of the host's neurons and glial cells, but not so long that it caused brain damage or tumors or worse, was the tricky part. I was picturing her saying that in a bikini when she caught me.

She'd fallen silent. "You've been on the trail too long, Doc," she finally said, quietly. "I can spot a wandering man a mile away, though I wonder what exactly you're wondering about. Although, it's funny, speaking of wondering," she said, looking up, then back down, the Trail. "I can't honestly say I've seen it this... empty before. I haven't really seen anybody, you know? Since I left the Whites back," gesturing southwest, "*there*. Weird. You're the first, in fact."

That got my full attention. "No one? Seen any strange Asian men, look like they just walked out of Shangri-La or maybe it's equivalent in the Chinese section of Epcot?"

"Ah, friend of yours? No, haven't seen anyone."

"Anything?" I gulped the air for strength. "Anything... unexpected, inexplicable?"

"Other than *him*?" she asked, pointing back at Virgil. He remained stoic of countenance, unfazed and transcendent above her insult.

"This is important," I said, grabbing both her arms in mine, pulling her close. "I need to know. Think. I'm absolutely serious. It's more than you know... more than... you'd believe, actually. But are you... *certain*... you've see no one, no one at all?"

Her eyes met mine, all William Blake innocence and experience. "No... no one, at all."

She felt soft in my arms, and softer as I released the pressure on her arms from my hands. I looked into her eyes, deeply. They held no deceit. I knew eyes, and these held no deceit. They were the first I'd seen like that since....

"Why do you ask?"

I snap back to reality like I've been shot. "I'm sorry... I guess I was mistaken. It's... nothing. I've just probably been out here in the woods too long, me and Virgil here." Bad English and all, I sounded insecure, ironically what I actually felt at the moment.

"No worries," she said, still a faint haze of a confused look on her face. "You... sure there's no problem?"

"I'm... not too certain of much out here, you know," and I attempt an awkward smile, which made it more of a forced grimace than anything pleasant. "Just wondering about... an old friend, someone I saw out here a while back. Maybe I'm just feeling a bit out of it too. Apologies for grabbing you," I added at the end, experiencing a sudden inexplicable shyness, thinking myself overtly forward, pretending to sway from the twisty dizzies or what-not. *What the heck?* I self-reflected.

She tried humor again, injecting a sad pouty face. "That time of the month, eh? I know how you feel. Maybe you have the bird flu, you know, or Lyme disease." She patted me on the back, a series of light thumps like one uses on a herd animal at the petting zoo.

Nonchalantly she planted a foot on a rock, bending the attached knee. Her hips twisted, rotated, slithered, as she retied a boot lace, freezing me in place. I watched her movements, transfixed as if Venus had emerged from her clamshell right in front of me and not in some stupid painting. *Yep, been taking care of it myself for a....*

"We've got to work it together through the Notch," she whispered as she retied it, not looking at me, a vague smirk on her lips like she knew or expected as much.

There was that grinding sound in my head again, of second trying to weld dry, obstinate gears instead of proceeding in a calm and orderly fashion to third. "Excuse me?"

She pointed to her left as she finished her work and stood back upright, at the Mahoosuc Notch trail sign immediately south of the hardest mile on the entire A.T. The Notch was a deep, steep glacier-cut pass through the mountain, with a solid mile of bolder scrambling, ten-foot-plus drops, and several places where one's pack must be squeezed through a gap between boulders, followed by one's hopefully-skinny self. It took the best of us an hour minimum to cross, and most two or more. Not the sort of place one normally met smart, sexy, athletic virologists. As if there even were such a thing! I'd stopped here upon seeing her, the same girl I'd seen so many miles ago, awaiting trial like the fugitive from reality that I was.

But while my mind had wandered away for a second, my eyes had not, and she caught that.

"Get over it, boy scout," she ordered, giving her boobs a grove-picker's squeeze to define *it* for me. "Time to get that field badge you've always wanted." She walked to her pack, bent over to pick it up, providing me an ample view. Not such a bad vision, this one.

Then I thought: *Shit. Shit shit shit.*

We turn a switchback.

Virgil and I are in a shelter somewhere, on a quiet night. Not sure if it's still Vermont or maybe New Hampshire, only because I didn't check the sign or the map or run it through Central Processing, I didn't care tonight. I was tired.

"Sorry pal, no hot food tonight," I'd told him. He didn't complain. I let him rummage through the dry goods, indiscriminately.

Something was nagging at me; something wasn't quite right. I couldn't place it. Hell, I couldn't place *us*. Clouds and churn hid the stars, so celestial guidance was impossible. Fuckin' typical.

At some point there was a loud *crunch*, and I realized I'd sat on my water filter. The broken pump handle and intake housing cracked, then fell apart in my hands. What came out of my mouth then wasn't unique in human history, yet such language has rarely been heard. Certainly nobody else had ever made a comment about the pedigree of my local gravity well with such marital-status-specific information before. Apparently, although the rest of me had possessed married parents, certain irresponsible parts had lacked them, as anyone and everyone within a thousand yards of the shelter learned instantly.

This was a major setback. The filter kept me not just alive; it kept me both diarrhea- and heavy metal-free. It was right up there with boots and a map; pants were lower on the priority list than this filter. *What the hell do I do now?* I wondered.

See, if this was a normal hike, this wouldn't be an issue; annoying as hell, but not a real issue. There was a town or a road within a half-day, almost anywhere, of this Trail. The only exception was someplace I'd yet to enter: the Hundred-Mile Wilderness. Normally, I'd just hike out and get a replacement, lose a day, maybe two if I stayed at a hotel with a jacuzzi and nearby pizza joint offering delivery. But this was different. I pondered the problem for hours, as the evening sank deep into an indigo chill morning, forgetting all sleep. Leaving seemed out of the question at this point. It seemed like... I don't know, like quitting. A challenge was presented. Time to get what you needed from teacher, provide feedback. Mostly I was angry. I tossed and turned, seething at our circumstances. We needed water, damnit. If there's one thing you forgot once and only once when distance hiking early in your career, it was your water filter. Dehydration wasn't a fun experience: it was right up there with chain smoking or meeting your future potential in-laws for the first time. We needed water, *damnit.* And given circumstances, of course I blamed The Man for it.

Where the Hell was he anyway? It had been, what? Seven hundred, eight hundred miles now? More? Something like that. So we were going to be tested with teacher *in absentia*, eh? That was it: *tested*. Well, fuck that lyrical, Biblical shit. We'd show him. We'd show *Him, And* His Orchestra.

Night passed unseen in action. I reverted to a sleepless, unawakened semi-state somewhere between hypnotized and deep-fried for most of the evening. I don't know; perhaps I slept. But the unconvincing cover of our shelter this night bade me wait for a stronger wind to watch and enjoy as it crashed down on us, a gentle high tide of doubt. As luck would have it, no such luck. I stared up and out, watched Orion appear in one corner of the sky, and watched him slide into second base over the course of a few hours. No second base for me tonight. Only postureless form, prostrate on the bunk. Virgil whistled while he slept, slightly congested.

I got us up at dawn, a bare smudge of lavenders and rose on the horizon. We ate dry cereal with a few spoons from the Camelbak before leaving. *Okay, let's see the miracle, miracle-boy. Turn sweat into wine... then back into water.* Or let us die and be done with it all.

So off we went in search of our miracle. It wasn't a thousand yards before....

We turn a switchback.

"Goddamn flies," I was saying as I thrashed at the air, practically an apoplectic Macon Baptist farmer amongst his flock of imminently endangered peaches. I'd disparaged the little flying meat-eaters, commenting extensively on their tendency to procreate with pre-existing mothers, no less rude than what they'd started. It was eighty, perhaps eighty-five degrees, practically Celsius and entirely hellish. It wasn't a dry heat; besides, what was the point of dew anyway? May as well just adhere leech-like to the nearest bare skin. Something bit the backside of my left knee, the thirtieth or fortieth such taste so far today. Forget about the dead moose we'd passed just a half-mile back; at least I'd guessed that what it was. If it wasn't for the smell of naturally Indian summer-cured venison, I'd have mistaken it for a mound of the damnable winged monstrosities with giant antlers poking out one side. But there was no mistaking moose jerky in the making. Bee just held her nose with one hand, grabbed my hand with the other, and pulled with all the might that her steam domes and boilers could muster.

After a quarter mile or so she stops, unclips her belt, and practically throws her pack down, rips the top open. "I'm feeling it," she said. "The burn, the bites, I'm feeling it. I need some Absorbine."

"You mean Absorbine Junior," I auto-correct without thinking about it, the first words I'd said to her in a passel of hours.

"No, bright boy, I mean Absorbine," she says, whirling around, still very angry with me and shoving her finger in my face to emphasize that little factoid. "See? You know too much, and it makes you think you know more than you do. I mean Absorbine. It's a joke. Ha ha ha. *(Flat syllables, low and clipped; gulp.)* You've never owned horses, have you?" I could only shrug, half-meekly. "Ha!" she replies, snapping her fingers. "Absorbine *Junior* is for people. *Absorbine* is for horses. Betcha didn't know that one, bright boy."

She produces a bottle of the green liquid from her pack, inexplicably full. She unscrews the cap, and rubs the sponge top all over herself, and I mean *all* over. I stare at her quizzically.

"It's not for muscles; well, not entirely," she huffs, not looking at me. "It keeps the gnats and noseeums away. They hate the smell. Better than DEET, and far less toxic." She throws the bottle at me without warning, and I barely catch it. "There. Don't say I never gave you anything." She grabs up her pack, and starts walking before she even has it on her shoulders, smelling of wormwood and menthol.

I wait for her to disappear in the woods; best we separate for a bit. After she's gone, I stare at the bottle of A-Junior she's tossed me. No way I was going to use up her goodies at a time like this. Since she still had the cap, I slipped an unused baggie over the top, securing it with a spare rubber band. I sighed and resumed my movement, following her. We weren't really on speaking terms at that exact moment, but as it eventually turned out... well, perhaps I'd best explain first.

We'd left Monson over a day ago, as empty and desolate as any town we'd encountered. When we'd reached town, Bee just looked around, then back at me. We walked through dead streets, devoid of life, mocking us with blinking intersection lights buffeted by gusts of cool Canadian air. We walked all the way through town, slowly, silently. I was imagining Tommyknockers when she channeled me, whispering: "It's like a goddamn Stephen King novel." She was starting to believe. I was grateful; shared insanity is better than no sanity at all. At least then one has some common ground to discuss during the long dark otherwise-lonely nights.

"What did I tell you?" I said finally, letting the winds and silence of the place works its magic on her psyche. "I know it sounds crazy, but you and I can't both be. Something else is going on. Something... not of this world. Or maybe so much a part of it, so much at the foundation, that we missed it the whole time."

"God," she said after a moment, but I wasn't sure if she meant it as an answer. I took it as such anyway.

"I'm... not so sure about that, although the methods... the grandiose drama, the over-the-top symbolism, fit. But I'm not so sure."

"What else could it be?" she asked, her voice trembling.

I didn't want to think about that. "I don't want to think about it." There, that at least was as honest and open a statement as I'd ever made. I guess she'd grown on me, after all these miles. "Anyway, it doesn't matter. We're along for the ride, and we're not in charge. There's nothing we can do about it," although I didn't say that I wasn't sure about that either.

"We probably couldn't tell the difference," she said. She turned, looked at me, with those sharp eyes. I hoped she could see what I couldn't. "You know, whether we could do anything about it. I mean, what if we just walked away? Headed down-road towards I-95 or Bangor. They're only about 50 miles from here. Maybe if we just quit..."

"I don't think I can anymore. I think maybe I could have, once, but not anymore. I think I'm all-in at this point. The cards are on the table and I'm just waiting for the flop. How the money lands isn't up to me, but it's my money, and by God or whomever I have to see it through. But you... you're different," and I squeezed her, gently but firmly. "There's no reason you have to go through this."

"Then why am I?" she asked, now genuinely concerned. "Why you, and why me, and why this? If there really is a point to this, shouldn't we face it together? But then again... why can't we just go, together?"

"You still have a choice," I said, as if I knew anything for certain. "At least, I think so. I don't know. But it's worth a shot. Go; head south-east and...."

She pulled away from me, and I let her go as she pondered the asphalt of the road, the sun in the sky, the last of the empty buildings around us as we approached the edge of the wood again, for a full minute.

"You won't go," she finally said, her face full of effeminate epiphany.

"I can't go."

"How do you *know*?" she wailed, slapping me in a keen frustration right on the edge of anger.

"I don't! I don't know anything," I said, grabbing her arms again, pulling her close again. I seemed to be making a habit of it. "All I know is that he said I was 'chosen', or something equally improbable and grandiose and histrionic like that. I don't know what it means and I don't care to know. Could be anything from Quetzalcoatl to a quantum fluctuation, and I don't have a U on my Scrabble rack to spell it out clear and plain for you. Either way the mystery behind it is the same. It's as unfathomable as anything greater or less than either of us."

She looked at me the same way one would regard a circus fool suddenly apparitioned at the kitchen door on a turquoise Sunday morning. "*So? And?* Is there more, or is that it? This isn't just philosophical B.S., Durant; this is *actually happening!*"

Her face flushed, lips shaking. There was quiver in her left temple. I had to tread.... But then something came up from inside me, something unexpectedly open, perhaps almost honest. "This is... all I have. All I want to have. Out there... out there, I'm not really necessary to what's going on. I fix broken things. I'm a repairman in an assembly line of unending repairs, repairs on the... damnit, the stupid, the lazy! Smokers, overeaters, people who don't exercise, people who stab or shoot one another, or themselves! Jesus! What do I do, Bee? I don't create, I don't add-to; I just patch the lifeboat, over and over, to keep afloat the ones that managed to afford the lifeboat seat and not drown with the damn Titanic like they would have had they been in the unfortunate two-thirds of the rest of the world! Damn Americans! We just drift on and on and on, into the cold dark night over a colder, deeper sea and watch our own drown under a blood-moon sky, expecting me and/or their tax dollars and/or their military and/or their elected representatives and/or their simplistic symbolic God to make it all right!" I realized I'd raised my voice again, regretted it, and tried to defuse it. "That's why I have to go on: because there's no alternative for me anymore. There's no... *place* for me, back there among the quick and the dead. That's why, my little deuteragonist. Like that word? Deuteragonist. Means 'a second important character', right next to the protagonist. I read it once somewhere and never forgot it. Like I wasn't supposed to!"

She looked shocked, and disappointed, and repulsed. I couldn't look at her anymore, turned away. I'd seen that look on women's faces before. After a moment she replied, quieter. "Well what about *him*?" she asked. "What right do you have to put *him* through this?"

For a moment I was confused, then I realized she meant….

"You goddamn selfish bastard! Yes, I mean him! You cart him along, trudge him through the woods like so much baggage! He's got feelings too! Or have you forgotten that, Doctor Poor Poor Me I Never Forget A Goddamn Thing? Doesn't he have rights? Doesn't he count?"

"Ask Padma that! Ask Padma why he's doing this to him, to us! Ask your goddamn god."

"So it's not your responsibility, huh? Yeah, maybe he needs to go home. Maybe somebody that actually gives a shit about *him* needs to take him home." She stomped over to him, scooped him up like so many jelly beans, stood there, looked at me.

"Best git' movin," Virgil cheerily added.

"I can't argue with that!" I said, flinging an arm outward. "See? He's not complaining."

"Not complaining? *Not complaining!?* Durant, have you *lost your mind*? Do you realize what you are saying?" She flung her gaze violently back and forth between Virgil and I. "*He* said he wants to go on? That's what *he* wants? How on *earth* do you know what *he* wants? How on...." Then she stopped, mouth agape and all uvula, gasping, huffing. I may as well have suggested we get married, right then and there.

But the core of her question was interesting, deserving of an answer. I sighed: for once, not for effect, then began quietly. "Suppose... suppose you encountered the Ultimate Mystery. Something that both repulsed and attracted, both positive and negative forces. Don't you see? It's not just about fear. There are answers somewhere, someplace close by, within actual reach! Imagine the questions you could ask, what you could learn! The detailed history of the future. Euclid's *Conics.* The *Gospel of Eve*. A detailed hydrology of the Sarasvati River. Aristarchus on heliocentric theory. The complete plays of Aristophanes. The location of the Confederate *and* Nazi gold. The fully extant *Kublai Khan* Coleridge would have written. What crater Judge Crater is buried in. The Q Document, or the *Arzhang*. A dictionary of the quipu of the Incans. *Love's Labour's Won!* The memoirs of Lord Byron. Whether Flight 19's arrived at Tau Ceti yet or not. Liszt's manual of piano techniques. Fermat's proof in the margin. The original *Book of Lehi*, whether truly golden or mere forgeries. Sibelius's *Eighth Symphony*. *Edwin Drood*, no longer a mystery! Whether your best friend really kissed your high school sweetheart or not. The *Qing Nang Shu*! Imagine the folk medicine it contained! The uncondensed shelves of the Library in their original Coptic, and every other language imaginable! It's not just faith or fallacy now, not just mystery and magic! It's not just about acting and reacting anymore! We can *inter*-act now! We can ask and maybe get an answer this time round! Don't you see? God fears knowledge, because knowledge reduces His monopoly on the truth! And we can break that monopoly!"

She snorted, mouth still open, took a long sideways look at V-Man, releasing him in her anger as she focused on me. "Wh... *WHAT?!* You... you *are* a selfish bastard, you know it? How you could do this to *him* is beyond me."

"Aww, he's having fun! You're having a great time, aren't you, Virgil?"

She snorted and laughed then, utter derision, practically choking. "Oh, fuck you, you bastard! You're too smart for your own good, that's your problem. You think you know so much and it's consuming you from within, got you all wrapped up in your own goddamn...."

"And why is *that*? There, that's as good a question as any. Why am I me? Why am I cursed with this damn jelly? I'm sure when we all stand in the Holy Presence at the end of days all we'll really ask about is ourselves, *maybe* our immediate family. We'll forget all about Ovid's *Medea*, or asking for a definitive dictionary of the Corded Ware culture's original Indo-European, or who made the Venus of Dolni Vestonice and why...."

Her jaw dropped like a stock market, voice shaking with disbelief. "How... how can you be... so.... My God, Durant... how can you be so...."

I decided to push it into the abyss. "Come on, spit it out, we haven't got all...."

And just like that, *WHAM!* She hit me, hard, right upside the head where it was needed. "It's NOT all about you! It's NOT, Durant! Look around you! Don't you get it? If there ever was a time when it WASN'T about you THIS would be it."

I heard the capitalization, plain as day, letters forming solid bricks of her hatred whipping at me through the air. She could do such interesting things with her mouth. Then again, she was right.

"Nope, it's not about me. It's about us. I get it. It's about *all* of us, though: that's what you *don't* get. You haven't met him yet. He can do interesting things with his mouth too. And his eyes. Did I tell you about his eyes? They'll make a believer out of you. Not sure what of, but something. Something not of this world. Or maybe of it; I don't know. There are questions to be asked, Bee! Questions that need answers. Hell, *answers* that need answers. Times a thousand. Times *ten* thousand!"

"Who *cares,* Durant!? Who cares? It doesn't matter!"

"Then *why all the detail*? Someone once said something: *Yesterday we obeyed kings and bent our necks before emperors, but today we kneel only to Truth.* Why do the gods *still* demand of us, Bee? Answer me that. What need does a *god* have of us? And why package it up all in the pretty gift wrap of the world like it's a present, only to tell us to forget about it, that none of it really matters, that the math behind it is mere coincidence and unworthy of study, that all study is unworthy of study: that we should just mind our prayers and table manners and engage in mindless recitation and repetition of thousand-year old revelations, while ignoring the later more reliable ones that utterly contradict them? What's all this earth and air and fire and water *for,* Bee? Just to be forgotten? Just for it to rot all into nothingness in the deeps of moldy inconsiderate time? Is *that* it? Is that *it*?" I paused to catch my breath, then realized who I was talking to. "And of all people! A Harvard Ph.D.! I have to explain this to *you*?"

"You *don't* get it," she insisted, shaking her head. "You need to start thinking about *others* for a change."

"All I did was think about others, for twenty-five years! Sew them, cut them, stick them, poke them, scold them, marry them, and bury them!" I was only incidentally conscious of the fact that I was shouting now, and shaking. "And for what, I ask you? *For what!?*"

She saw something in me snap just then. She saw a deeper darkness, reasons of my own best kept buried. So she stopped, still angry, but more than angry, and I knew it and it was humiliating, and she knew it was and I knew she knew it was. I picked up my hiking pole where I'd thrown it down in a huff, turned, and went. She gave it a few moment's pause, but then I heard her heave her breath out in one shove, expressing several things at once. When she started moving again after a few seconds, I knew she'd made her decision. And so we went, forward, marching on. Nothing like flaming silence to make the Hundred-Mile Wilderness seem cacaphonic by comparison. It would be thirty hours before we actually exchanged words again, regarding Absorbine Junior and its multiple curious uses. It would be another fifteen before I'd admit she was right, that I didn't have the right, and another ten after that before I said so verbally, to her face. And one or two after that before she begrudgingly accepted my begrudged apology.

And rather unimaginably, only another two or three hours after that before we were kissing, in earnest. It seems even pity has its uses.

I have a clear recollection of a moment when she reached up, her face full of concern and a full moon's light shining through front of the shelter. She reached up, wiped a stray hair from my eyes, then touched my face, letting her fingers linger there. Something melted then. Like the stars I pondered her in that moment. I knew it, and she knew it. It was a fusion's heat. It was water turning into wine, fishes and loaves, sweat into substance. We became bound by something, then and there, whether we liked it, wanted, or feared it, or not. I can't explain it. It's crazy. It was the most goddamnably illogical and ruinous thing that had happened to me out here yet.

I also knew in that moment that she was human, as I or anyone else. It was as clear to me as her skin in the moonlight.

Call it an act of faith.

IX

Somewhere In The Hundred-Mile Wilderness

There was mud, and then there was mud. But mud like this? Mud like this did not exist. Maybe places in Alaska, Siberia, Africa had mud like this. The Lower Nile; the Upper Amazon. If Hell was an endless monster truck rally full of Rebel flags and flavorless light American beers then Hell had mud like this. It penetrated my gaiters as if they were sausage casings chittlin'-ripe for stuffing. I swore and swore and swore as I squeezed the mud and filth out of my socks for the umpteenth time this fine rainy day. We had to sit like this every few miles and cleanse ourselves Orthodox-style as we slogged our way through the backcountry perdition of the HMW. Every few soggy couple-thousand-odd feet there was another creek or stream to ford, as violently full and raging as a condemned prisoner after a last meal of pure crack. Repeatedly we'd be forced up and over another creek bank redolent in splendiferous gloop, with the inevitable slip and fall covering us in it again. So we'd stop and sit and swear. Or at least I'd swear.

In the intermittent inopportune breaks in the rain we'd try to dry out and clean up as best we could. Somehow she managed to always find a few extra minutes hidden in a stuff-sack or something, and produced a book whose name I didn't catch at first, carefully protected under the overhang of her ponch's visor: the mark of a genuine professional. She read from it, out loud. "Ever hear of Gene Rosselini?" she asked; I shook my head *no* as I squeegeed my socks yet again with bare soiled hands. "Here you go. *By and by Rosellini left academia, departed Seattle, and drifted north up the coast through British Colombia and the Alaskan panhandle....*" How she found the time to read when all I found was mud, mud, and more mud, I'll never know. "*He became convinced that humans had devolved into progressively inferior beings....*" Well, that didn't sound at all familiar. "*He dined on roots, berries, and seaweed, hunted game with spears and snares, dressed in rags, endured the bitter winters....*" Of course I knew where this was all going, but I knew better than to interrupt a preacher when she's preaching. "*In November 1991, Rosselini was found lying facedown on the floor of his shack with a knife through the heart. The coroner determined that the fatal wound was self-inflicted....*"

I also knew that an occasional interruption to feign interest was required of me. "Loser," I editorialized. She frowned. "I'm sorry," I said, "what is that you're reading?"

"*Into The Wild*, by Jon Krakauer," she said, still frowning.

"Ah, yes; Chris McCandless ventures to Alaska and lives in a bus in the forest and starves and/or poisons himself to death. What a waste," I added, only half-serious. "Was he a romantic or a victim or just stupid or some or all of the above? That's the basic theme, right? I say all of the above; but regardless, he was also respectful... for a dumb-ass." What I didn't mention was that the book had also inspired me to begin this adventure... well, maybe not *this* one, but the one I'd started out on, anyway.

"What?" she said. "Not towards himself. He basically committed suicide by doe-eyed field ignorance. How's that respectful? Of his family or his friends or himself?"

"Doe-eyed field ignorance"? I am starting to really like this girl. "Yep; the lack of proper USFS field maps and a compass and basic survival training, yes. Death by over-romanticizing the woods. Yep, couldn't agree more." I smacked at something nonexistent in my mouth. *Time to add some controversy.* "But he was respectful."

Her face scrunched into a confused, no-way-in-hell look. "What?"

"He had fuel at the end, right? He could have lit a fire, burned the forest, signaled someone, a passing plane. He chose not to. He wouldn't burn a little to save himself even from death. That's respect. (*She starts shaking her head no.*) And he didn't drag anyone else down into his childish romantic fantasy."

"He tried to," she said, thumping her precious book like any *Codex Irrefutabilis*.

"Well, in his fantasies along the way, maybe. We all want companionship. Isn't that right, Virgil?"

Then she gave me that weird *look* again, a look I'd seen and duly noted for some miles. Always when I made a comment about Virgil, or to him. What was her problem, anyway? Next she'll... yep, she looks slowly at Virgil, slowly back at me, as if....

"Is that what you want, Durant? Companionship? Is that it?"

Oh no you don't. We are SO not going there. "I'm going to make mud my god from now on. It demands my respect, and it's as good a god as any." I demonstrated by dumping a giant *plop* of the stuff out of my boot onto the damp stone. "Watch as it transsubstantiates into the Flesh." I stared at it, and she at me, still frowning. A fortnight of seconds passed. "Go on," I said, "the evolutionists all say it happened, once. Could happen again, any second. *Watch* it." I hunkered down exaggeratedly, staring at the shapeless, runny pile of glorp.

"If it's one thing you do know how to do, it's how to avoid things," she said, coldly disappointed, and somewhat disturbed.

"Carnation," I repeated, "meet the reincarnated."

"Practically born again," she sighed heavily.

Houston, we HAVE breakthrough! "Now you're getting it. That's what pride's really for: to mock the gods and test our real limits in the process, for maybe there are no gods, and we therefore are limitless in our pointless power and pride. Who knows?"

"I do," she said, looking at me with sudden steely purpose. "I do." It caught me off-guard, something which by this time, having gotten to know her, should not have in and of itself caught me off-guard. "Whatever's out *there*," she said, pointing to the sky, "I'm starting to get who's in *there*," pointing at me, "whether he wants me to or not. And that probably scares the hell out of him, and he's going to do something about it to push me away, whether he really wants to or not. Oh, he'll engage in a big debate about it internally, philosophize, quote Nietzsche and Spinoza, recite several lines of their more obscure works in their original High German or Low Dutch or whatever, make a tongue twister out of it, relate it to the symbolic works of Chomsky or the behavioral insights of Skinner, but that's all part of the emotional avoidance process, right? You do the hokey-pokey and you turn yourself around."

"That's what it's all about!" I said, agreeing wholeheartedly. Boy was she turning me on right now.

"But despite the fact that I'm turning you on right now by playing into your intellectually-fueled avoidance of reality, the reality remains. (*Oh wow jeez and cheese she's good!*) When it cracks finally, I'm not sure I want to be there."

"I am a rock, I am an *eyyyyye*-eh-eh-land," I sang in my best 60's Queens, New York accent.

"I just hope you know what you are doing," she muttered disgustedly.

"No more or less so than anyone else," I answered truthfully.

"Yeah, you're the goddamn common man all right," she added, hands pushing on her thighs and she stood up, exhaling hard, frustrated with me and at the end of some length of invisible rope she apparently possessed. "Only you're not, you just like to imagine you are... while imagining you're not. Which I imagine is very convenient for...."

"Imagine all the people, living for tooo-*day*, you-HOOO-ooh-ooh-ooh…." Went for a Liverpool accent on that one.

"Oh shut up you arrogant ass," she said, sick of me. "You always have to have the last word. Just shut up for a few miles, OK?" She huffed, throwing her pack back on in one fluid, excruciatingly erotic motion. But then she added after a hard inhale's pause, "I'm just going to have to do you. That's it. That's what you need. A good rock-offing. Maybe that will reattach you to the world of us mere mortals."

My initial reaction was: *Heh heh heh. Yeah baby! Who's your daddy NOW?* It was only after we started moving again, after another quarter-mile or so, when it actually hit me, after I rethought it through again: s*hit! Shit shit SHIT!*

*****

All boots have their wear, and perhaps this means in the end that the path as purchased was bought with appropriate markup. But when the boots are worn through, when the pain of the trail becomes a pain of trial, when those of least worth with no boots at all are forced to endure the harshness of the mountain by those Most High who live upon it, the cost becomes subject to such unjust taxation that the most weightless of masses are stirred to revolution. It is this state we find ourselves in today. Look around you. The poor, the weak, the huddled and befuddled. What Justice looks down and smiles upon this? Only that which if He exists allows it to continue in the first place. Now those of you that consider yourselves as fodder in His army that would speak in His behalf would say that rewards await; have faith, and deal. But I ask you: why must they wait, in sickness and poverty, agonizing year after year, watching their children, their parents, their loved ones -- hell, anybody, everybody -- suffer and die? What Justice looks down and smiles upon this, a dry and thirsty land where the weak get weaker and the strong get stronger? A land where garbage lies in our streets, in our lands, in our seas, and on our tongues; talkin' and takin', as they say? We revile the IRS for exactly the same reason, do we not? We revile the robber-baron for exactly the same reason, do we not? We revile the Hitlers and Maos and Stalins of history for exactly the same reason, do we not? Change the name slightly, a shift of mere symbols, and suddenly one must not even speak the name, let alone question Its judgments and actions. Does He own a mirror? If so, is He so great He cannot see himself in it? What Justice looks in it, and smiles?

He is the vengeful, angry Child. He reeks of His own vanity, lusting and envious of power, hoarding it unto Himself, greedily, swallowing the cries of our young and our old in his gluttony. He, more than anyone, should know better. Perhaps a *posse commitatus* is in order. For those who follow this Thing, woodenly, quasianimatronically, think no more than a stone or a sheep would. Yet these same men are esteemed in society, considered leaders, brothers of the neighborhood. They are more likely to believe a voice on Fox News over the voice in the wilderness -- for the wilderness frightens them. That's why they follow: sheep need a good shepherd. To think for them, guard them, keep them safe. And best of all: is a sheep held responsible when its brother is eaten by the local wolf? The very thought is laughable. My Grandfather, what big teeth You have. "All the better to eat you with, my dear," is the implication in the profound and golden silence. It's His will, we say; it's the wolf's doing. What could we have done? What should we have done? Nothing, and nothing. But fear not; paradise awaits. Have faith in the wolf, and deal.

Fear and ignorance do not a belief system make, despite what you may have heard otherwise. Only the Truth opposes them; and Truth cannot reside with them in the same heart, the same world, the same universe. One must of necessity destroy the other, ultimately. That's history, plain and simple.

Which one is it to be? That is entirely up to you. I know you don't want to hear that. I know it's too much responsibility to bear, too much... work, when all you do is work and work and work, day in and day out. I know it's easier to sink into the Barcalounger and detach what mind exists in the dissolved, dissociative offerings of prime time. And after all, what can you do? But that's exactly it: we are nothing but a collection of *you's*. It can be a war averted, or a war coming -- a choice made, or a choice delayed. It will be one, or the other. When the seas rise, when the animals and plants are gone, when the oil dries up, when ten or twenty or thirty more countries have the Bomb. After the next tsunami, earthquake, hurricane, the next terrorist bioattack, the next cyberhacked takedown, the next hundred or five hundred or thousand million people. Joyously asleep, the Armageddonites march in place waiting for the Day of Judgment and its dispassionate slaughterhouse. Mark my words: without a choice otherwise by *you* and *you* and *you*, they will make it happen. Six to seven to eight to nine to ten billion pairs of boots, singing, holding hands, marching in a terrible forward motion of inertia and ignorance and idolatry, wearing down their soles to their doom. The abject horror is that so much of the world, of *you*, smile at the thought of it. That so many of you want Thy Kingdom to Come: to me, that is more terrifying than any relatively tiny group of terrorists. They're just committed; whereas, you should be.

What Justice looks down and smiles upon this? Who cares? Here's a better question: who looks up and smiles upon such Justice? Maybe pride has its place after all.

*****

Of course she didn't off my rocks -- perish the thought. Instead, the next day we were arguing about cultural origins and that unending trail topic: proper food and drink.

"I could really use an Ex-Girlfriend," I muttered from behind her.

She stooped walking, turned, mock surprise on her face. "That's the most optimistic thing I've heard you say yet."

I laughed. "No, no; the Ex is a drink. It's Grapico mixed with... wait a sec. You... *do* know what Grapico is, don't you?"

She smirked. "Of course I do, Dr. Gump. I'm from Knoxville, remember? Best grape soda *ever*." She curtsies the best she can with a thirty pound pack on. "You can take the neck out of the red states but the neck itself remains red. Genetics, my specialty," she reminds me, wagging her hiking pole at me like a giant finger.

I jerked back. She didn't seem to have any kind of accent; she'd just caught me with my pants down, assuming again, something along the lines of Nebraska or Colorado. We'd never discussed Knoxville, at least when I wasn't paying attention to her foothills. Of course, it just led to a bigger concern. "Did... does that mean you're... (*my voice drops a couple of octaves*) a Vol?" Hell and damnation was one thing; but hanging with a Tennessee Volunteer? Utterly unthinkable.

It was her turn to laugh. "Grapico and what?"

"Absolut Peppar. At first it's sweet and seems like a good idea, but eventually it's going to burn you and make you sick. Hence...."

"The name, yes, I get it. Who came up with that one?"

"My fourth-grade English teacher, God bless her. Went on to become something of a writer and put it in a story of hers. What's your favorite?"

"Funny you should ask," she smirked. "The Happy Hiker, actually. Fresh-picked berries: blackberry, raspberry, whatever you can find, crushed with ice and a squirt of organic honey. Topped with an ounce of light rum and a splash of hazelnut liqueur."

My diaphragm knotted itself, hitching to my spleen. "Sounds too sweet, too over-the-top. And where exactly would you get the ice?"

She ignored the practicality of my question. "The honey makes up for the berries' acidity, and it's chock-full of vitamin C," she pharmacized. "Ditch the rum and add a shot of espresso and it's a Power Hike -- bittersweet, strong, and a tad nutty, and after a while it'll just make you sleepy. Just how I like my men." She smiled perkily, already naturally stimulated quite enough, but squeezing my arm anyway. "Or, leave out the espresso, fruit, and honey, keep the hazelnut and rum, add a shot of apple pucker, and you have a Nutty Pucker. Or just make it honey and bourbon and a slice of orange, and it's Kentucky Cough Syrup."

"A former bartender I see. Honey and bourbon? Crimeny. Can you substitute Jaeger for the honey? It would keep better. Ah... never mind. I'll just have a lager, thanks." I found myself smiling. The sensation was not unpleasant, even if she did wear that godawful shade of DayGlo warning-cone orange every fall.

It was her turn to grimace. "Beer's untouchable out here, Agent Ness. What's your favorite Midol highball?"

I laughed. "How about Tetravalin? Morphine, cocaine, caffeine, and codeine. Very popular around the turn of the last century when drugs were so safe every proper prim London Victoria wannabe used them. Add a shot of absinthe and you've got Hightower Highbrow Hypocracy."

She wasn't amused. "Seriously, Spock, drink, name it."

"Hmm... how about a mojito? Cool and classic, and it leaves your breath minty fresh on the way back up."

We laughed together, climbing up out on top of White Cap Mountain, and suddenly, as if utterly unexpected, there she was, framed in the northeast by the sunlight of a swift late morning. We both saw it, stopped short, sucked in the cool air unconsciously.

"Mount Katahdin," I whispered. Bee let out a long, satisfied, "*Hmmmmmmmmmmm*", then turned, and planted one on my cheek. "How 'bout them apples, Virgil?" she asked, pointing at the distant massif, all laid out in its line, northwest to southeast, Squaw's Bosom to the left on the north west, sloping up to the highest peak on the southeast, to the right, Katahdin proper.

"Apples, apples, apples, apples, apples" said Virgil, who clearly knew the word. Katahdin was to me as apples were to Virgil, practically Platonic in their solidity. So in honor of the moment we stopped to enjoy the view, and I produced three apples from the pack.

"Where'd you get these?" Bee asked between greedy crunches. *Where'd: definitely Southern.*

"I have no idea," I said. "They were just there. Like we thought of them just now, and *abrahadabra* and Aleister Crowley, there they were."

She froze, mouth full of juicy Fiji according to her neurochemical interpretation of the sensation, regarding the object in her hand as one would a live grenade, or perhaps Aleister Crowley.

"Don't worry," I said, "if it had wanted us dead, it would have happened a long, *looong* way back."

She swallowed the chunk in her mouth, but still regarded what was in her hand as potentially psychic poison. She offered a personal insight. "Ever see the original *Snow White*? The old witch scared the hell out of me until I was, oh, twenty or so." She examined the apple slowly, turning, analyzing, weighing her thoughts along with the apple. I liked the way she did that.

"Hmm," she finally admitted, though more of a release of tension than an actual statement of acceptance. "I'm not so sure about this. Seems like purgatory to me, or worse."

"Aww, c'mon love, where's your spirit of adventure?" I asked.

"Did you just say *love?*" she asked incredulously, forgetting all teleology. Now it was my turn to freeze, a lame moose in whitest snow and a hungry winter wolf's undiminished eyesight. "Did he just say love?" she asked Virgil, knowing I would remain speechless.

"Love," agreed Virgil.

"I did not," I mumbled. *Oh goddamn it.*

"Did too," she said.

"Did not," I insisted.

"Love, apples, apples," V repeated, reestablishing a beachhead on his own significant slice and making a mess of himself in the process.

"Did too!" she said, self-satisfied smile shining from her self-satisfied self. I rolled my eyes. Damn obvious trap, didn't even see it coming.

"Did too, love, did too, apples, love apples," testified V, throwing down the gauntlet with this shameless Lancelot-scale switch of allegiances.

She laughed but I just shrugged, a feigned and fetid indifference, and resumed walking down the hill. "DID NOT!" I shouted back from thirty feet later, without looking back. I thrashed my hiking pole in the brush a bit, just to be sure I didn't hear her answer.

"*...something something* apples?" is what I heard instead. *Smart girl, change the subject back to the real issue at hand.*

"Oh, I don't know," I said, stopping again and turning, guessing what she'd asked. "Maybe it's a projection of AdS/CFT, two-dimensional dreams of the sleeping Old Ones at the boundary becoming three-dimensional reality." She looked at me blankly.

"For a doctor, you sure are a nerd," she said, squinting her eyes at me in the sunlight. *Doct-ter*, with an *e-r* on the end.

"Hmm, that time I heard the Knoxville, little lady."

"Good for you Doctor Nerd. Luckily for you I like my men nerdy for breakfast." She walked up and put her arms around me.

"Carnation Instant Breakfast, meet the..." but she stopped me with a long kiss, as Red Delicious as any apple.

"I wish you hadn't done that," I whispered after the moment's business was concluded.

"You kissed me back," she teased.

"Yet our lips still parted. That's love for you." I felt a sudden downcast, apprehension, added complexities.

"There's that word again." Smiling, she played with a strand of my hair near my left ear, and ignoring my warning.

"Words don't mean a thing," I told her, firmly, pulling away.

"I understand," she said. "You don't have to be afraid of me."

"It's not you I fear. It's the *us* part, the Two Shall Become One. I'm not a fan of fusion. Requires too much pressure, makes too much radiation, which can be destructive to living tissues such as the heart."

"Or the brain," she pointed out, unexpectedly agreeably agreeable.

"*Especially* the brain. It rots from the inside, collapses on itself, tending to form a big black hole that sucks everything in around it... or just sucks. I don't know about you, but I've precious few of my wits left to risk in open combat."

"I'm not your enemy," she stated, simply, calmly.

"That's what all enemies say during the negotiations. Everybody wants to like and be liked, or at least pretend to be while they stockpile their weaponry and develop the atomic or biologic or romantic or financial device that will make such niceties thankfully unnecessary. Only the pathological, the rabid, the lawyers maybe, start out as enemies right off the bat. Enemies are usually an emergent phenomenon, like belly fat or time or the nutsedge in the lawn. Shit Happens. All the bumper stickers say so. *Hate* is just two consonants and one vowel away from *love,* and *y*ou don't even have to relocate the *e* to get to there from here. Three letter's difference out of twenty-six possible: a change of eleven and a half percent of two hearts. Just five and three quarters percent per heart! I've lost a higher percentage of my body weight on this trail, and heck, I'm only walking."

"You and your damn wit. Enough," she sighed.

"Not nearly," I tried to say, but then she kissed me again, and my words only half-formed were swallowed up by it.

"I'm not your enemy," she whispered in my ear.

I just muttered something unintelligible, and we resumed walking. No need to plant strawberry trees here and now.

The days passed, memories of magic, both white and black. We genuinely liked each other, but still there was that nagging voice of doubt in my mind, always subtle, and sometimes not so much. We huddled beneath raging storms and still quiet skies and appreciated both. We laughed, forgetting our situation. We slept underneath the distant slow scrape of the planets, charting our fates, planets whose ascendancy we received with respect, both essential and accidental. And as the days went by I told her more and more, about Padma, about Tennessee, North Carolina, Virginia, New York; she listened in near-silence, asking an occasional question usually regarding some trivial fact, but on reflection usually much deeper: what was the color of his shirt? Did it change over time or was it the same shirt every time? Was it clean? Dirty? Wrinkled? Imperfect in any way, like a loose thread or missing button? (An interesting question, that.) Did the subtle patterns on it change? Did his subtle patterns change? How did the light reflect off him? Did he have a shadow? How about a five o'clock shadow? Nose hair? Yellow teeth? Bad breath? Some I could answer. Some had answers. Some just produced more questions. Then, there would be an interval of silence, a pause between meal courses or relacing a boot or adjusting a pack strap, all excuses to avoid what really needed to be asked. But it never was... I mean, she never did. The real questions never came. Normally I would have found that trait annoying, but from her it seemed, I don't know, innocent, or perhaps just practical. After all, what did either of us really know of astrology?

The planets finally aligned for us on a cold day in either late September or early October. Under a deepening sky we came upon Potaywajdo Spring Lean-To, just above Permadumcook Lake. Across from us, there stood a rather large chunk of rock that marked our goal, our dream, our hope, and our hell of the last two thousand miles. In the dark, its presence was marked by an absence of stars in a slice of the night, our arrival being rather late, and the day being as luck would have it the same day as the new moon. Oh, and it was still four shelters away before the peak itself, a good 33 miles distant as the moose flies (and not in anything resembling a straight line). No; instead, just before you entered Baxter State Park, the trail routers threw *another* day or two in by sending you suddenly west for fifteen miles for absolutely no discernible reason at all. It'd seem cruel under any other circumstance, but after all this time, hell, what's one more day? Because there it was, a large shadow you'd been heading for all these many months, and the last thing on your mind was... hell, was Hell. I could taste the success along with the sweat on my lips.

Well well well. Shizzle my bejizzle.

So arriving at shelter and daring the chill to bite harder, I started my first real fire in a long, long time. I filled the iron fire ring with what twigs and debris I could find that seemed reasonably dry, then poured a liberal amount of white gas fuel on top. Where the gas had come from, I couldn't say. A match, and then....

"Jeez!" I shouted as the pile practically exploded in my face. I leapt back, cursing my stupidity. A little more magic frikin' fuel and I'd have sizzled my bejizzle.

"Whoa, easy there big fella," Bee laughed, as she grabbed me from behind to keep me from falling.

"Sorry." The fire blazed with near-white hot intensity for a few seconds, enough to make us both back up some more, chuckling.

"Maybe we need some good last words handy for future moments like this," Bee reasoned. "Something better than just, you know, *Jeez.*"

I considered it for a second. "How about Poe's -- Edgar Allen's? A guy quoted his thusly: *The arched heavens encompass me, and God has his decree legibly written upon the frontlets of every created human being, and demons incarnate, their goal will be the seething waves of blank despair.*"

Bee stared at me for a moment, then burst out laughing.

"I shit you not!" I assured her.

"Sounds like 19th century obituary bombast. What the hell is a *frontlet*?" she said, still laughing,

"I have no idea. Yeah, he probably just said something like...."

"*Jeez*!?"

"Yes, exactly," and we both laughed. We allowed it to linger for a bit; then, as we quieted down, we started unpacking for the night.

"You know," I said after a bit, thoughtfully, "they think Poe may have died of rabies. Big mystery around it. He was found in the street, delirious, and died a few days later at the hospital. Went in and out of it in his last hours, alternating periods of lucidity and unintelligibility -- a classic rabies symptom. At one point when brought something to drink he exhibited hydrophobia -- fear of water -- another classic rabies symptom."

"Rabies, rabies," Virgil sneered.

"Don't worry," I told him. "You've had your shots."

"Where do you keep all this stuff?" Bee asked, patting my rear. "Notecards in your pants?"

"Nah; they'd just get soggy in all these downpours. Maybe I'm telepathically connected to my long lost twin the librarian somewhere, who knows?"

We started cooking a beef stew with quality digs: taters, carrots, a leek. As we watched it start to bubble, warming our hands by the stove, she asked: "Who's *they*?"

"Excuse me?"

"Them. The *they* who think Poe died of rabies."

"Oh, I don't know. Some medical experts I think."

"What?" she asked, surprised. "I thought you remembered everything. Did you bother to find out? Or did you forget?" She snapped her fingers. "Hmm. Did you vet your information to start with?"

It was my turn to be surprised. "What? Umm, eh, I... I don't remember."

She looked me long, up and down. "You don't remember? You either fact checked or you didn't."

"Well, what of it? What does that mean: fact check? All knowledge is provisional. Precision isn't as important as accuracy, and quality isn't as important as quantity. Lots of general things suggesting the same thing mean the same thing is probably righter than other things with less support, even if those things are more precise."

She crossed her arms, leaned back. "Hmm. So you don't know."

They way she said it annoyed me. "Not anymore than the godly do. But at least I'm honest about it."

"Hmm. So a billion Christians can't be wrong, then."

"Nice try. Precision isn't as important as accuracy, but right still beats wrong every time. Everybody used to think the world was flat: precise but wholly inaccurate. Everybody was wrong. Ditto a lot of things folks believe nowadays too."

"Oh, sure. Either a billion Christians are wrong or slightly fewer Muslims are, or about the same Hindus. Who knows? Somebody's headed down the primrose path with a bunch of other primroses. Who knows? Although...." She pondered thoughtfully for a moment. "Maybe it's my upbringing, but I tend to side with the Christian version of reality. It's... it's got to be closer to the truth, right?"

She was baiting me, and I knew it; but, I answered her anyway. "Truth is independent of the observer. Matthew 27:9 paraphrases a quote it attributes to Jeremiah, but it actually comes from Zechariah. Inaccurate and imprecise. I rest my case."

She crossed her arms, dissatisfied. "What? Giving up so soon? Just like that? Is that it?"

"Oh, not by a long-shot. How old was Noah when the Flood came? The Bible gives two different answers. How many creation stories are there in

Genesis? What if I told you there were two of them? The Passion occurs in the sixth hour in John but in the third hour in Mark. Origen, a third century philosopher, deliberately changed a place name in John to avoid an impossibly quick and long journey, a change that's persisted in everyone's copy today. Matthew and Luke give different names and genealogies for the ancestors of Christ. Judas dies by hanging himself in Matthew and by bursting open after a fall in Acts. So much for your all-knowing, all-splendiferous holy book."

"Really?" she said doubtfully, pursing her lips and taking the opportunity for a quick dig in the trail mix. "Sounds a lot like science to me! They're always going back on what they say. Tobacco used to be safe."

"Actually, there's some evidence that smoking protects one from adult-onset coeliac disease."

"Bah, bah, bah. Tobacco *used* to be safe, cocaine used to be safe, nuclear power, communism, sex, our civil liberties, real butter, the Internet, sunshine, Social Security, Toyotas...."

"Toyotas?" I asked, genuinely surprised. "I guess I've been out of the loop for a while."

"Hmm, yes, all sorts of stories about abruptly accelerating cars." She stirred the pot for a minute in silence, both of them.

"There's a difference between marketing and science," I finally said. "Most people just perceive the marketing side of the science -- all they know is what they learned in school if anything, and just how it's sold to them from then on. There's rarely any genuine continuing education that doesn't support pre-accepted propaganda. And, most people seem to think inaccuracy in religion is OK, since science is inaccurate. The ones who use the 'evolution is *just* a theory' argument that somehow makes their case stronger as a result. The If Not A Then B school of logic. Then there's the reprehensible stuff that's A-OK by God. The Book of Kings allows the children of a debtor to be sold into slavery as repayment for their father's debts. Exodus 21 defines rules for selling and keeping slaves. Deuteronomy gives an OK to the Israeli armies to keep their women prisoners as wives. Ain't just the O.T. either. In the First Epistle of Peter, slaves are admonished to obey their masters."

"Hmm," she answered, tasting the stew, checking for errors. "Yeah, hmm." She smacked her lips together, exaggerating, for effect. "I like Tallulah Bankhead's last words: *Codeine... bourbon*. Sums up her whole life."

You learn something new every day, I thought. But I didn't want to let it show, especially since she'd grown tired of the previous topic of conversation. "Abruptly accelerating cars?"

"Yes," she said, after a few seconds of looking sideways at me, both of us wondering where our heads were at.

"If people had faith in their corporations like they do in their religion, far more people would die." She just yawned, big and long, with an exaggerated stretch. I could take a hint, right in the chin if necessary. "OK, OK, I'll drop it."

"Uh-huh," she said, still yawning. "I'm tired. How many miles did we do today anyway?"

"I don't know," I said honestly. "It's all *mise en abîme* to me. Codeine and bourbon, eh? I'd still like that Ex-Girlfriend."

"Who knows?" she asked, annoyed. "Maybe you'll get one any little 'ol day now." She looked up at the rafters, trying to divine divine inspiration I guessed.

Uh-oh. She must be really tired... of a couple of things. I decided to probe. "Why... me?" I asked finally, after a long quiet, in as serious of a tone as I'd ever used.

"Why not you?" she instantly responded, then shook her head. "You're too sour-flower dour. I speak French too, *mon ami*; all that *into the abyss* crap, you know, we really need to work on that. Maybe a guy like you deserves a fine catch like me. And it's not like you got me into this." She grabbed my hand, dragged me out of the shelter's foyer back out under the stars.

"Look, here we are, once again. You see the night, but I see the day yet to come. You feel the cold night air, I feel a nice cool-down after a long day's proper work. You say one less mile to go, I say one more mile accomplished. Half-empty canteen, half-full canteen. Broken water filter, or a chance to share resources? Hard rock or firm support? Unending mountains, or wide-open vistas? On that one I think we can both agree, or we wouldn't be here. You ask why, I ask why not. I wish you could share that one too, with me."

Her answer surprised me right into silence. I had no idea how to respond, which she read in my eyes.

"It's sad. Nobody's ever said anything like that to you, have they? Said it and meant it, I mean. Oh, well. Don't worry about it," she said. "You worry too much. Let tomorrow be. It will, whether you want it to or not."

We ate then, savoring the mystical treats that filled us night after night, morning after morning. We no longer questioned them, just received them at rest as part of our rest masses' Mass, sort of a reverse Eucharist, the holy body of whomever becoming plain Jane schmaltz on contact with our vain and profane tongues, blatant First Law violations of the magically-appearing stuff be damned. We wolfed it down, greedily at times, and didn't even kneel once. As we ate, I watched her with the same sense of wonder I'd felt for weeks now, thinking about her words: *It will, whether you want it to or not.* Too soon we had finished, washed out our kits and hung the packs, and bedded down for the night in our bags. Virgil murmured himself to sleep, while Bee snored like a merchant marine. I was used to both by now.

But the murmuring of frogs increased as the night lengthened, almost a dull roar despite the chill Newfoundland air blown down from the north. They spoke to me not of beginnings but of *ends*. I thought of Bee, and her use of the term *the future* without ever saying it. All these many months I'd held in my heart but one goal. Now, unexpectedly, another presented itself, freely, willingly, and beyond all reason. Oddly this made me feel more alone than ever. It's not like I could spill my guts to the local barkeep over a couple of drafts. This one was up to me, and added up to just one more responsibility to mind. I tossed and turned, finding no comfort on the beams.

As quietly as I could, I unzippered myself out of my bag, swung out and down, slipping my boots on unlaced. I grabbed my fleece hanging on a who-knows-how-old rusted nail, and slithering into it I sneaked out of the lean-to, towards the murmuring frogs by the lake's edge. An army of them sat by the water, not a lot but one called them an army anyway (had they been toads, they'd have been a knot of them, also not a lot but at least in this case rhyming with it). They regarded me the same as they did any other Sasquatch, ignoring my big feet and not the least bit threatened. The fire meanwhile had lost its impetus; improperly tended, it glowed softly, eeking its remaining existence out among us dearly departed here in Annwn, entropy near maximum.

Across the water, Katahdin stood against the sky, mute, impassive, a black hole of uncertainty pressed into the sky. No amount of cajoling would convince her to let us pass. Only our own determination, our will to achieve, to claim and take. A typical human response to stimuli. Very male. I could only hope that the other forces at work would allow us to pass as well.

And just as I thought that, said force finally made his overdue appearance. I heard an unmistakable sound: twigs snapping, leaves being crushed in an identifiable rhythmic two-step pattern. I turned, at first thinking *bear* (a strangely normal thought). But there walking towards me was another beast entirely in dark shape, rustling and ancient. He stopped a few feet away from me, looking at the mountain across the lake. I glanced at him for a scant second more, then turned to regard it with him. I wasn't the least bit surprised, or afraid, which was itself surprising.

"I was wondering when you were going to show back up. I was starting to miss you... and Little Miss Optimist there needs a good preaching-to," I said to the darkness.

"You're welcome," he said. "Thought you deserved it."

That caught me off-guard. I was oddly embarrassed. "Sorry. And, thanks... thanks for the bone," I muttered to him.

I sensed discomfort from him: a subtle shifting, minute changes in posture. After a moment, he said, "You're not a pet. Neither is she. None of you are."

"Aren't we? No; not a pet, but certainly children."

"Much closer to the truth. Trouble sleeping tonight? I take it you have something on your mind?" he asked, very politely I thought, which I acknowledged.

"Thanks for asking. As a matter of fact I do. I'd ask you the same question I asked her, but I've already asked you, and I doubt the answer would be any clearer now than it was then."

"Clarity lies in what the mirror chooses to reflect. When a mirror reflects others, it reflects reality. But when a mirror sees only itself, its obsession leads it down an infinite path to nowhere." I knew he was smiling in the dark, damn him.

"You too, eh? Hmm. Sartre was right: Hell *is* other people. Only, you're not a... ahh... hmm, nah, that's too much, I don't really mean that. Let me be less specific. Why *us*? Hmm. Let me add a little more specificity." I cleared my throat, and recalled my prepared statement. "Why are you here with us?"

"Haven't figured that one out yet? You? The great logician?" *Wow, that was quite informal. Interesting. Maybe we're buddies now.*

"Pride," I muttered, knowing what he was attempting.

"Pride," he said. "All things flow from it, to it. Wants, desires, power, energy, people. It is the mountain and the valley. But not quite yet. Man has dammed rivers and made lakes, controlled the flow of waters off these mountains. But the voices from the mountain, man has yet to dam, and so they flow on to damn the valley."

How's that? Is he saying dammed, or damned? Hmm, I'll be parsing that answer for a week. I proceeded, carefully.

"Words fill merely the spaces between, the ears and books of old, not the soul. We have less of a wish to die of thirst or flood. Fill a man's belly, fill his children's bellies, and you will win his soul forever. So why didn't He do that? They say God is the prime mover, the ultimate causeless cause, the source of everything, and we, being mere beings, are utterly and absolutely dependent on Him. So why didn't He do that?"

I'd said that deliberately, planned for miles on what I'd say when and if *he* showed back up. I paused for a response. Instead, he simply said, "Go on."

Good: he's allowing me to keep control. "Instead, He decides rather unfathomably to engage in the opposite. Instead of convincing us imperfect beings of His love, it is *we* who must give to *Him*. We are totally dependent on our God, and He can destroy us at His unfathomable divine whim. In fact, did so, and often, in the Old Testament. Total dependence means total slavery, and we are treated as such."

Another pause, but no response. I'd expected a response by now. Whole lines of argument would have to be canned, and not for future consumption in a fallout bunker. *It wouldn't be this easy, would it?* I went on.

"Fundamentally, total slavery and ultimate dependence implies we've no rights: no right to self-assertion, to differ on the issues, to alternate forms of belief or opinion. In fact, having them is defined as a *sin*. *Vainglory* in fact, the worst sin of all: challenging the will of God. We can therefore take no credit for anything: no credit for creation or improvement or accomplishment. Only God creates, improves, accomplishes. We are flawed and always will be. So here's the part I don't get. *We get none of the credit yet all of the blame.* We succumb, we fail to resist, or just plain fail. And through it all, for no purpose -- literally zero -- other than to praise Him who put us in this tragic position in the first place. To glorify and slave and believe and trust with no earthly rewards of any meaning or purpose. We must not praise one another, or ourselves: only Him in Heaven. The most important thing about us is that there is nothing important about us."

More silence, except for the frogs, pointlessly croaking. Where was my Guardian of Kallipolis, my debate partner? Sigh.

"More confusion ensues. So we have this free will of which you spoke so eloquently several hundred miles ago. As Augustine said, such boundless, reckless impulse requires both bad and good natures, the sanguine and the sublime. But the possibility of free will -- the merest hint of it -- implies that we *can* do good, things in which we can, perhaps even should, bear some pride, take some credit, feel good about ourselves, or others. Without that, there is no free will, only automation, instinct. So we can do good, and a few of us great measurable quantifiable analytical amounts of it, mountains of it in fact, in one or two cases: say, Mother Theresa, or Gandhi, or Buddha, perhaps even the guys who invented air bags or the smallpox vaccine or securitized mortgage vehicles."

"Agreed," he admitted, finally speaking. "An unfortunately small number."

"But it doesn't matter. God creates utterly dependent slaves to worship Him, installs version 1.0 of a free will so we may choose to glorify Him without the nastiness of coercion or repugnant force, but then, at the first disagreement we have, the first doubt, the first misinterpretation which leads us off the obscure and opaque path, He punishes us, labels us *sinners*, and bye-bye birdie, we're left out in the cold, or in the heat of Hell's damnation, depending on one's personal choice of denomination and demagoguery. So while we can choose to disobey, we really can't. It's not a genuine freedom. God arbitrarily defines evil as that which He doesn't want. God kills a hundred thousand in an earthquake? It's God's Will, which we cannot prosecute. A man kills a hundred thousand in a conflict? It's genocide, and we must execute... preferably with a firing squad. There are two sets of rules. There is no freedom here: there is a marriage of unequals, master and slave, into which we are born with Original Sin fixing the game ahead of time so we'll always lose at the table, no matter the cards delt. Then we are damned, shamed and damned, right smack dab into oblivion, for the way we play those cards, from which only the Heavenly Dealer can *save* us: it's His rules, His table, His game, His house. *And the House always wins.*"

There was a long silence, but I wasn't letting go this time. I waited it out. Finally, he sighed in the darkness, and said, "Please, continue."

"So, what is this free will, then? Clearly, you exist. *Cogito, ergo sum*, or something like that. Clearly, I do too: *mojito, ergo dumb* I'd normally conclude, but this time there's a much more sobering truth at work. Or perhaps this free will we speak of *is* a kind of intoxicant. At any rate, what kind of free will is it? It's the free will to hit or stay at eighteen. It's the free will to pick red or black. It's the *gambler's* choice: the free will to make a choice from a menu of choices predetermined by management, and thus, no real choice at all. Into which an original man was interjected with an original woman, who were deliberately kept ignorant of the whole concept as to how the game was played. Until they played it, and lost. Upon which the Ultimate Umpire declared that all descendents of the first players were found guilty of crimes against divinity *ex nihilo post facto*: sentenced, tried, and spiritually executed. Now we are cursed with a flesh that cannot help to, indeed is born with, this crazy little thing called not love but sin. And the original variant we are all cursed with at birth, according to Augustine, is one that cannot actually choose, really perceive, between good and evil, but is instead one that is deformed and tainted by something called our 'natural depravity', the same way my older kin used to speak of Blacks in the South and their innate inferiority, untrainability, and general piteous state slash untrustful and ungrateful natures. We are incapable of anything more. We are *losers*. Always were, always are, always will be. So naturally, we will be tormented in brimstone and hellfire for all eternity for being this way. How dare we be the way we cannot escape from being due to our immutable natures that our Creator and Judge granted us in the first place. Imagine: the sheer *gall* of it."

I paused for impact and a breath, then continued. "Now the real question: why? What's the point? Apparently, solely for the benefit of the Good Lord's ego. We must attain redemption, through Him. We must strive for salvation, through Him. We must engage: play the game, follow the plan, subjugate ourselves, slaves on the cotton farm, indentured to His Will, with no possibility of freedom or parole. It is what it is. God takes the credit, we get the blame. So I ask you: what's not wrong with that picture?"

Boy was I out on a limb. But I sensed nothing from him now... and heck, he knew I thought all this anyway. Didn't he? We listened to the frogs for another minute, then he said quite unexpectedly: "Ever heard the one about the devil and his friend who walked down the road one day and saw a man pick something up? The devil's friend asked, *What did that man pick up?* And the devil answered, *Just a piece of the truth*. The devil's friend, knowing the devil, smiled and said, *Such a small, unimportant thing in the grand scheme, then.* But the devil replied, *Oh no, not at all. At least, it won't be after I help him organize it.*"

I suppressed a guffaw. *That* was the best answer the Immanent Divine in my presence had to give? *That*? Krishna was far more eloquent at the Battle of Kurukshetra, and he'd had thousands of years to practice in the interim. Maybe he'd come to realize the futility of it, or maybe He had. I let the disdain seep into my tone. "Whatever. We've had enough of parables. Just another non-answer in a five-thousand-year series of non-answers. We're not your children anymore. That's just it. We're on to the game now. We perceive the house, the table, the rules. We've calculated the odds, realized we're in a losing game, a game we can't ever win, and you know what? We're done. We're done, with this, with that, with you, all of you. We've had enough of gods and golden temples and the undying narcissism of the Host. We're not perfect, or subtle, or probably deserving, but there it is. It doesn't matter, because the more we know of the world you've created, the less we seem to know of you, and there's got to be a deep mathematical truth behind that. Truth, meaning concrete, understandable, grown-up. Not coerced, not demanded, not forced, not legislated, not threatened or cajoled or bedazzled or bewitched out of us. The sun is rising, and the night is departing. Allow us our dawn and the true freedom to explore what we are, with all the risk that implies."

"Could you?" he asked. "Many of you need to believe."

"Need? To believe? In what? Fairy tales? A politician's promises? Fat-free cheeseburgers? Healthy suntans? Shooters on the Grassy Knoll? Free energy? The Continuum Hypothesis? Secret reptilian cabals that rule the world? *(He actually chuckled at that. Hmm. He has a sense of humor. He can laugh at himself, and at us. Interesting.)* Ignorance runs deep, irrationality deeper in my people. Part of the price one pays to think freely is that intelligence and rationality and education and fear and all the rest of it span the spectrum, just like our tastes and skin tones and wagging tongues do. One accepts imperfections in a bucket of sand. It's the resulting sandcastle that's the thing of beauty, as impermanent as it may be, and as identifiable as the child's creation and whimsy that it is. But it serves as a model for later, more adult, constructions. Need? Or *think* we need? Marx said a lot of mostly idiotic things but the idea of religion as opiate wasn't one of them. Addicts always *think* they need."

"Marx? That doesn't sound very American. Do you think... Americans would go along with you?"

"Oh, no one *wants* it. Children never want to grow up: that's why they're children. The fear rules them, rather than the other way around. As for Americans? Americans want odd things. We deify freedom, then demand the freedom to enslave ourselves to whatever baloney we believe in, whatever god Mom and money and the marketing department conspire to provide. We're a weird mix of the twenty-first and first centuries, truly a new Babylon. Temporarily dangerous technologically, but still Puritans and Pilgrims and cavemen hiding in the safety of the cave by and large. Only our caves are wired for broadband connectivity to all the other caves so we can post cave pictures of ourselves on Cavebook that all the other cavepeople ignore because they're too busy posting their own pictures on Cavebook as well.... But I digress. Americans aren't the only ones here. *Nobody's* going to want it: *everybody's* going to hate it. But we're where the transformation has to start."

"Now *that's* pride," he said, chuckling.

"Anyone else in the world would repress it out of fear! Choke this new thought's growth dead before it started. China's leaders would imprison it. Russia's corruption would sell it on the black market. Religious repression in most of the Third World would starve it. Catholic nations, Muslim nations, Hindu nations, all the same. Europe would debate it in endless parliamentary sessions; they can't even agree on their own Union's Constitution, crimeny. I don't know. Greenland? Tristan de Cunha? Antarctica, perhaps. At least those would give new meaning to the phrase *a fresh, cold start*."

"So it must start here."

"Home of the Bill of Rights. And despite recent setbacks, still its home. Oh, and the home of the U.N. If it's to happen *now*, it must happen *here*." I felt something stir in my words, and in the cold night air between us.

"And what is it that you think must happen?"

Well, here we are at last, at the nuts of the fruitcake. I inhaled, letting my words out slowly. "Cascading improvements, an uphill snowball. Evolution." I said.

"In the form and time intended," he replied. I knew he smiled as he said it, though I couldn't see it. An interesting statement, taking us to what seemed to be a real possibility. A kind of unexpected dawn occurred in me then: a hope, a hint of rosebud promise.

I chose my words carefully, slowly. "Are you... actually agreeing with me? Is... that what all this is? Was?" Then I had a kind of internal avalanche of my own, thought after thought. "Is *that* it? *Armageddon*? Just drastically scaled back from the original battle plans!?"

"Ah," he said, and his dark shape turned to me, but no more illumined. "I believe you would consider it a... what did you call it? A phase transition. The next step. Better sounding, more... *rational* as you would say, than Armageddon."

He may as well have turned on a flashlight. "So that's it!" I was more amazed than I'd ever been in my life. "That's been it, all along! You're asking the question! You're actually asking me the question!"

"Many of you, most of you, still need to believe," he repeated, his way of saying the simple truth: *You got it, bucko*.

"And many still will." Then it dawned on me what it really meant: more or less, nothing. Nothing, and everything. The dawn bloomed in me fully, brilliant and frightening. "We will still walk the same high wire, just without the safety net," I concluded, jumping straight to Go and collecting my $200.

"Your earlier words were less kind. I believe you called it 'brimstone and hellfire'."

"Apologies. Not just the prison, but the police as well, right? You'll... leave us alone, completely. Right?" I felt myself tense.

After a few seconds consideration, he chuckled again. "I thought I heard you say you had questions. Questions that needed answers, you said. Answers that needed answers, you said."

Now it was my turn to chuckle. "Well... I assume that to get our dessert we children must eat our damnable veggies first."

"I don't like it when you use that word. The message is... not the messenger. You recognize that, of course. Humans have perverted and twisted the truth, and always will, whether from above or from below."

"We both agree that we cannot change human nature," I said. "Not immediately, not at present, anyway." And that was it, I thought. That's where the fruit dies on the vine.

"But therein lies the key." He said it very quietly, subtly; so subtly I almost missed it. But then, then, what he was implying, what he was really saying, hit me like a ton of trucks filled with a ton of bricks each, and a whole '*nother* dang avalanche hit me, an avalanche of avalanches, bless his soul.

I couldn't help it: I grabbed him by the arm. "Of course! *Of course!* You... you could... *make* it happen!" I realized my affrontry, releasing him, but still excited at the prospect that... that.... "It's the miracle to end all miracles! Literally! Evolution in the form needed, and sooner rather than later!" The scope of what he was suggesting! The audacity, the actual possibility that all *that* -- all the bloodshed, the wars, the pandemonium, the endless conflict, the endless loss -- could be avoided in the process of change!

"And for this... gift, you are willing to give up a greater unknown?" he asked, straightening his sleeve nonchalantly.

"Better a known we can live with than an unknown we kill each other over, century after century, nation after nation, truth versus truth!" This one I would win. This was one battle I was NOT going to lose. I was so close... we, *we* were *so close*.

"That won't change," he rightly pointed out. "The high wire remains. And all of you must still navigate it. That includes you. You want to be a balloon? You will no longer have that luxury. Every purpose needs its purpose: a propeller, to propel."

I considered it, and that's when the rock-bottom thought occurred to me. An obvious solution, and one I found difficult to voice. I could barely even think the word: *apotheosis*. But that's what it would take. A willing transfer of power. The cost to the receiver could be -- probably would be -- enormous, perhaps even ultimate. But every avalanche required its ultimate snowflake. I found myself speaking my thought, out loud.

"How about a wish?"

For once, I threw the Unknowable for a loop. "Excuse me?" he said. It almost sounded familiar.

"A wish. You know, like Major Nelson and Jeannie, only without the ever-shrinking outfit of an increasingly pregnant Barbara Eden in season one. One wish. Call it a... miracle if you want."

"And what would you wish for? Not money, certainly. Power? No, you're not the type. An end to suffering? No... you see the value in that too. Maybe... lo...?"

I interrupted. "For the capacity to make the change happen. The ability to start the phase transition. For a seed to sew, and the fertility of the field in which to sew it. For the ability to win one for the Gipper. To be able to take credit for a human doing something good for once for humanity, to de-demonize humanism, by actually doing it: humanizing humanity, as a whole, all at once. To actually... matter. Back there, in the imperfect world of imperfect Man. To start the change, be a catalyst, be a... be a...."

As I spoke a smile developed on his face. "Messiah?" he asked from within the smile, now in full-blossom.

For once I had an answer, but held my tongue. *Yes, that's exactly what I'm asking for.*

Then his smile disappeared. "So you are asking for power, after all." He sounded disappointed.

"Not without limits, or responsibility."

"Is that so clear? Are you that mindful of yourself? A person throwing a pebble in a stream cannot be blamed if a tidal wave comes back at them. Or would you want the power to stop it if it got out of hand, perhaps even... *amend* it? See? You'll want to. You'll think it's for the best. But others have wants, and desires, and fears, and will append to your work, change it, filter it, color it, and on and on it will roll, and grow, and change, and be different from the thing you intended to set into motion. So you'll intervene to correct, *amend*, and the whole thing repeats itself, again, and again, and again. But others want what they want, and who are you to tell them otherwise? You'll become a despot: a well-intentioned one in your own mind, despised and rightly so by others. See? It's not so easy to be God, is it? Even for the best, even with the best of intentions. Wielding more power means wielding less power. Wielding absolute power means surrendering that power to the chaos of side-effects and inevitable consequences. The tidal wave from the pebble will drown you, destroy you. You criticize, question what and whether God could have, should have. Change of any kind requires a dynamic environment: you measure the *before*, you compare it to the *after*. There must be a difference for there to be a difference. Change requires imperfection, failing, a lessening, for there to be more, for there to be a *better*. Many times -- many times many times -- there is a *worse* instead. Chaos and freedom go hand in hand."

From a human, it would have sounded tired, a bit begrudged. Holy burnout maybe? I didn't ask. "Point taken. Fine. Only the power to set it in motion.

One wish, and one wish only. It won't be for more wishes. If I hate the outcome, it... it doesn't matter whether I hate it or not."

Suddenly the frogs stopped their caterwauling, as if a decision had been reached, or a limiting temperature. I didn't have the heart to ask the one who knew which it was: miracle, or chemical. After a moment, he seemed to reach a decision too.

"Perhaps a Messiah, without the fanfare." A *very* interesting statement, and a humbling one.

"Uhh. Hmm. No fame or fortune, please. Or the Passion. You could leave that one out. And the mysticism. But mostly the Passion. Thanks, but no thanks. I can't stand the sight of blood, least of all my own. I'm happy to fade away into historical insignificance."

There was a long pause then, then he finally said: "I shall... consider your words. Perhaps they will make all the difference in the world." He turned to me, touching my arm for a change. "Just remember this: you are all gifts to one another. Especially, here and now, the three of you. Remember that. Maybe even trust me on it."

A shooting star darted in the sky over Katahdin just then, followed almost instantly by a second and a third. They sliced the night soundlessly and spectacularly, then vaporizing disappeared just as quickly, dissolving into the winds and the past. The metaphor wasn't lost on me.

I turned to say something to Padma, but he was gone, not even breath left hanging, a hole in the luminiferous aether. I regarded the empty space he'd occupied, wondering again what had just happened, and who he really was. *For He has Risen, and His Apostles have seen Him. But what we will report is not His presence, but His absence. And that is what we must report, for the good of us all.* But as to what I can do to make it happen? We shall see. We shall most certainly see.

"*You must still pass the last test*," a voice on the wind whispered, sailing away to its unfathomable home.

"I have a joke for you. A teen, a libertine, and an Argentine walk into a bar in Tierra Del Fuego." I paused, but there was no response. Now it was my turn to sigh. "Fine. Bring it on," I boasted to the air, raising my arm against the impenetrable might of dark Katahdin. "What can you bring that I can't handle, that I haven't already faced?"

As it turned out, just one last thing.

X

Mount Katahdin, 5,268 ft.

"A Messiah, huh?" she gaped, more than a little surprised. More than a whole frickin' fried Friday's worth of surprised, in fact.

Why did the lion cross the road? To get to the other pride. But first, one had to obtain official permission from the lioness. On and on and on and on she'd asked question after question regarding the encounter. We'd discussed it all day the next day and all day the next, while we approached closer and closer to our final destination. I tried to downplay it, which was difficult given that I was also committed to being honest about it. Most of her more pointed comments I diverted with humor, or tried to. Of what he really said, what we'd really agreed to, I said nothing.

"A *Messiah*, huh?" she repeated, a little more ludicrously and doubtfully. I respected her more and more with each repetition. That's my girl.

I grimaced. I could have left that detail out, had I been thinking. Then I lived up to expectations and finally lied. "I'm sure he was kidding, and I'm sure he knew I was. Besides, I'd need more hair, a tambourine, an actual following of some kind."

"I'm following. For the last two hundred miles, if you've noticed."

"More like two hundred fifty, sixty maybe, and over twenty days. And yes, absolutely I have." I stopped, kissed her. Then a not-so-random thought: *you initiated it that time*.

Another pause while she considers her words (and not my kiss, which I notice, disappointed). Then: "What did he say you needed to do then?" *Since you're clearly not the famous rapper JC Mahdi Maritreya*, I heard in her tone.

"Needed to do?" I smirked, ready for that one. "Oh, six hundred forty in Italy, two hundred thirty-one in Germany, a hundred in France, ninety-one in Turkey, and a cool thousand-three in Spain." She just stares, and I know what she's thinking. "*Don Giovanni*," I explain after the appropriate amount of cluelessness. She shakes her head, walks right around me and keeps going. That's my girl.

"*Don Giovanni*," mocked Virgil, unexpectedly and a little disdainfully, I thought.

I threw my arms up dramatically, bellowed in a *basso profundo*. "*Don Giovanni! A cenar teco....*" My Italian was rusty; I'd been a long time since I was in Rome. "*M'invitasti! E son venuto!*" I was no Bugs Bunny in *The Rabbit Of Seville*, but Mozart was Mozart regardless. Virgil cackled madly, and Bee finally laughed along with him. We kept moving, and Virgil and I bellowed nonsense right up to the mountain's edge, echoing into the oblivion of the future. "*La mia pizza! Sta pepperoni!*" "*Don Giovanni!*" "*Don Giovanni! Ed il vino! È terribile! Don Giovanni! Passi la lama! E l'aglio! Sono Il Padrino!*" "*Il Padrino!*" "*Don Giovanni!*" and back and forth we went like that. A mere few thousand vertical feet spread over the final few measly miles left. Easy as pie. Three good spirits, and pie. Too bad the last round of spirits and their hauntings had yet to be.

We'd walked up from the Daicey Pond Shelter where we'd spent the night, serenaded sweetly by mosquitoes. Bee insisted on calling it *Darcy* Pond and I gave up trying to correct her. "Well," she said after the fourth correction, "I'm calling it *Darcy*, OK, bright boy?" as she filled my Camelbak with her water filter from the stillest, calmest, coldest body of water we'd yet encountered. At 6AM, we were eager to be gone, up and away. I offered her my assistance, but she'd refused, saying, "You filled mine last night before dinner, remember?" Strangely, I didn't. Strangely, I didn't care. I wanted to do it, for her. Actual desire, a long forgotten revelation.

We quickly came to the Baxter State Park ranger station, devoid of life, as expected. I was looking for the guestbook, found it, and flipped the cover open, only to suck in the air sharply when I saw it. It met my gaze without flinching: undated, blank, and made from an odd brown papyrus material I'd first encountered back in the Smokies on one particularly eventful and strange evening; a long lost age ago, but not so long, and perhaps ominously not so lost. It reminded me of skin, skin stretched taut, browned and dried in a blistering Great Pyramid of Giza scale of age and UV exposure. "This is it," I told her, staring at the material as I handed her the pen first, intending to be helpful with something.

"Is what?" she asked innocently. Briefly confused, it occurred to me that I might not have mentioned the note. I... I couldn't recall.

"Katahdin," I lied, not meaning that at all. No time to break our mood, meaning not a good time, and no time if we were going to make it up and down today... and navigate the Maelstrom in between sunrise and sunset, the whirlpool we'd surely swim in at some point.

She signed her name, leaning over and thinking nothing of the exotic paper, if paper it was. There were few women I'd known who could comfortably bend over with a full pack on. I wondered if I knew her, at least enough to add her to the list. Up she came effortlessly, handing the pen to me. I almost signed it myself, but she stopped me, saying, "I signed *us* in. Virgil, Bee and Don Giovanni, from the Real World." She took the pen from my hand, placed it back down on the ranger's desk, where she'd expected me to put it. "You know, us. You know, the Real World." She touched my face. For the first time since she'd started doing that, I didn't automatically flinch.

"I'm ready," I said. "Of course you realize, something's going to happen up here."

"No problem, I want to meet the crazy space man that wants to make a fountain of fun like you a *Muh-sigh-uh*." She slaps me on the rear, sashays back out, turns, looks back at me through the window in the door. I actually blush in both places (I assume), then Virgil and I head out to meet her and the Man and our future.

"No time like the present," I tell her, having just been convinced, but she's already walking away, steadfastly uninterested in epiphanies.

"There's only the present, sunshine," she hollers back without looking.

The hike from the ranger station isn't too bad: we circumnavigate two small lakes like Magellan wannabees, head towards the Katahdin Stream Campground, last of the flatlands we'll encounter on this hike. Ever. Well, OK, not counting the ridged mountain top and the wood sign at the roof of the Trail that announces with a sheepish anticlimax that the show is over, thanks for coming, please deposit all waste in proper receptacles and by the way you have to get all the way back down before nightfall, sucker. It has such a finality to it, doesn't it... *sucker*?

It's an odd intrusive feeling one gets at this point in the hike, with the end so close you can literally touch its mineralized roots. After all of it, of this, when you've dreamed day in and day out of bacon-overloaded cheeseburgers and hundred-button remotes operating big screen televisions at a distance and actual paper available in an actual toilet with actual porcelain that actually flushes, not to mention of a time hopefully to come when you'll stop being visited by space aliens showing you people being eaten alive by demons or other people drowning inside their own RV or dead soldiers thoughtlessly killed over and over by their own country.... Where was I going with that? Ah yes. Basically, now that this has become your life, you can't imagine leaving it. The outer world -- with its bicyclists wearing jerseys adorned with corporate logos not because they are some sort of professional cruiser but because the jerseys impart meaningless street cred, its fop pop hip-hop five-dollar download full-on ring tones, its polyunsaturated-trans-fat-infatuated Chicken DeNuggets and goddamn KKK Grand Wizard-level whitest white whitening products ever for both your teeth and coffee (the latter fattening the market of the former) -- seems less real now, somehow less solid, like you saw it one period in high school on a stage acted out by a bunch of kids you shared homeroom with but otherwise avoided and ridiculed in the endless vain effort to retain all-important cool-ocity. You dream of it at night, then wonder how you could have possibly lived in it by day. Like all jungles, the urban one seems safer at night when viewed from one's treasured and defended base camp, I suppose. Yet here we are, living the dream, in full daylight, in nothing resembling comfort and in what only somewhat resembled a jungle. After all, I understand better than she does what is going to come, any moment now. At any goddamn moment now.

The Trail begins an uphill slant. *Here we go.*

Breath starts its heave as gravity begins its work. Boots ravaged by time do what ravaging they can impart, seeking both revenge and steady footholds. The beginning ascent up the west side of the mountain is deceptively gradual, like so many of the ones before it. Five minutes pass, then ten. Hiking poles come out as our breath hardens... along with our hearts. We're here to do a job by finishing one. Few words are exchanged. We move, hurriedly, and not so. We move with purpose and a conditioned conviction. We don't plan on failing, or falling, for that matter.

We pass the 1200-foot contour line.

The brown brush thickens, and shadows lengthen like tall tales among the trees. Hard gusts of wind catch the branches every few minutes, each time discharging the last few tons of formerly flaming red and yellow maple leaves. The woods creak and groan from the whispered temptations of the air. We climb over a few fallen logs across the trail, but we've oodles of practice in that. They are rotted, from within and without, those who caved under pressure. Lacking roots enough to hold onto what they needed, they were lost, amid storm or stream or stone, or collapsing full onto the support of others and thereby weakening their own neighbors to the point of near or partial collapse. It is not lost on me. My anxiety grows, and with it my anger. My determination strengthens me; but steely as it may or may not be at some level I fear corrosive decay and its effects over the many melted miles. Stresses abound, both within and without. A harder gust then, and the tree trunks sway perceptibly, and not in silence. I will not fall. Least of all, on her.

My teeth grind. Why am I so angry?

We are headed towards the first real serious slope of the route upwards. We feel its immediate taste in our thighs and hips, still feeling after all the tested terrain that came before. I slip on a muddy chunk of quartzite, stumble forward, skin my knee. I grunt, but that's it: I will admit nothing else. "Are you alright?" she asks as she turns around, but I just get up and start moving forward. *Damn it, we're finishing this.*

"You're bleeding," she says.

"It's nothing," I mumble, patting her on the shoulder as I pass her. That's when I feel the warm wet trickle down my shin. It is a nuisance, temporary, nothing more. She doesn't say anything else, but I sense her disapproval.

We tread up and around, on the edge the slope, open to the southeast. The view is pretty but not yet spectacular -- and spectacle is the one thing I want to avoid more than anything. As my stomach acids begin to churn on the inevitability of it, there is a rustle in the brush off to our left. I don't really register it consciously, but just enough so that later when I think back I'll remember it as the first sign that something is amiss. What I notice instead is the sound ahead: falling water striking stone, common enough.

We pass the 1300-foot contour line, and turn a little more to the east, approaching the long summit from its southwest.

Skeletons abound in these woods; dead spruce, dead fir, everywhere. Dead from adelgids, from acid rain, from global warming, and other causes. The forest is quiet in its accusations: it went out not with a bang but a whimper. There are so many bones in these woods that from a distance the mountainsides take on a mottled appearance of brown past-fall foliage interspersed with large swaths of grey dried wood. Now the maples and ash and larch join in, shedding their skins for the coming nakedness of winter. Death that I know will be reborn soon enough, but with a little more damage, a little greater wear, a little less health. Rebirth short-term, death longer-term. It makes me angrier, knowing what I know now.

As I ponder death, I turn a sharp corner and stop dead in my tracks. A rattler has raised itself upright in the middle of the trail six feet in front of me, entirely cobra-like and nothing at all like any rattler I've ever heard of. It regards me, and I it, with mutual cold contempt, rattle loudly warning me to *stay away*. I push Virgil off to my right and backwards, and he lands on the slope by the trail, out of harm's way. As I'm considering how to respond, Bee rounds the corner too, moving too fast and shoving into the back of me before stopping. I cry out, falling forward, throwing my hands in front of me to catch myself. They slam hard into the ancient magma, digging in and drawing blood red enough to match the magma's original colors. But the pain deludes me only for a fraction of a second: I snap my head up, and stare right into the body of the diamondback, only inches from my face but towering above me in immanent omnipotence.

"*Shit!*" she blurts out. "Don't move!"

"I don't plan on it," I reply very quietly, frozen in place, wishing I were made of stone, the pain in my hands now matching my re-opened knee. "Listen, whatever you do, don't…."

"Hey!" she starts to shout, waving her hiking poles above her in what's obviously a misguided attempt to draw its attention. "Hey! HEY!"

"*Stop that!*" I hiss. "It's not a goddamn bear for Christ's sake, it's a fucking *snake*! It can't think or reason! There's no forebrain in there! You'll just antagonize it into striking me because I'm its nearest target!"

She dropped her arms, hesitates. The stones dig into my raw flesh, and I wince. I slowly crawl backwards, away, then stand up, as smoothly and calmly as possible. I'm bleeding again, and bleeding more.

"Look, you," I sternly tell the snake, "enough already. We're getting to the top and that's that and…."

"Durant, sweetie," says Bee, a little concerned, a little patronizingly, "it's just a snake. You just said it had no forebrain. You just said it can't think or…."

"Yeah, well, I just said that, you know, just in case. But, nah, it's not just a snake. I've met him before, back down the trail. But I know who he is... or who he thinks he is... or who I'm supposed to think he is," I tell the snake, directly to its face. "Ain't no rattler gonna rear up like no cobra like that. Ain't that right, Old Serpent? Nah, there's more here than meets the eye, and I mean *both* of us. So no way, no how, are you keeping us down, or out, or away. We're getting up to the top, and that's that, and so there, and...."

As I finish my sentence I'm proven right. The snake morphs, growing suddenly into a larger, jet black cobra for true. A cobra with red, glowing eyes. Bee screams, backs up, grabbing Virgil. It's the first time she's made direct contact with... with the Unknown and His showboat spectacular. But to me, it's all old hat and hold-em' by now.

"Shit," I hear matter-of-factly behind me.

"Yeah, V-Man, you're right: shit indeed." My eyes haven't left ol' Scratch. "Nice special effects, very effective as effects are wont to be. I mean, look at us, *woo-ooh-ooh*, we're all a-scared, teeth a-chatterin'. But the Koran says you have no power to do anything other than put evil suggestions into our hearts; well, that and hubris. I'm inclined to believe it's even less than that. I think...."

"Durant! Are you sure you should...."

"No worries, sweet; I have Mister Blister's ticket to ride right here, " I respond confidently, as I poke my hiking pole at him, the one in my left hand, while I drop my other one on the ground "I think you're just an image, a powerless symbol, like a griffith, or a vice president, or a designer handbag. You're just a herald, a sign of the times. An annoyance. A news anchor on Fox News. A congressman. A boss who bullies as a management style. You ain't nothin' but a hound dog, cryin' all the time. Which is ironic, because I'd never do this to a hound dog."

With that, I instantly leap out with my right hand, grab the thing just behind its head, and, with only a moment to express what I'd swear is a look of total surprise on what should have been a standard-issue expressionless, facial-muscle-less face, it goes flying to the right, into the open air, arcing up end over end, out, then down the cliff face -- out of sight, but not out of mind. There is a second when I perceive only empty air, devoid, then another where I exhale and feel my heart beat again. Then, a catharsis, just a touch, a moment of waffle-cone ice cream and candy, a moment like getting that shiny bike on your birthday or that shiny new promotion with its shinier canonization of power under the halo of the you that is you, a moment of utter self-satisfaction, rude, unapologetic, and inward.

I turn and look at Bee, all smirk and testosterone. Her jaw is on the ground, her shock in the stratosphere. "You... you just...."

"Threw the Devil off the mountain, yes ma'am, I reckon I did!" To emphasize the point, I drop my hiking pole and do a little jiggy dance right there. That in and of itself seems to keep her jaw open. Virgil whistled his approval and joins in, bobbing his head back and forth.

But Bee is in shock still; this is all still new to her. She's frozen in place, a waterfall of rationality in winter. I stop my dancing when I see her begin to shake. Just as I grab her she comes apart, crying out in a hysterical wail, dropping to her knees, tears gushing into the dust, no longer frozen in terror but in terror nonetheless, a waterfall transformed.

"Oh my God! Oh my God!" she says over and over, and I can't necessarily disagree.

I remove her pack, throw it aside, cradle her in my arms. We rock back and forth there gently for a minute, perhaps two, the two of us. I slip back into doctor mode, comforting the unwell. Then, shaking, she balls her hand into a fist and slams it into my thigh.

"We're leaving!" she proposes.

"I can't leave. We've been through this. " But, of course there's no reminding her.

"We don't have to do this!" she insists, fists turning into hands, clinging to me, pulling me away.

"I have to. I can't explain it, it's... I just have to." But with that she just grabs me and began screaming, in frustration, fear and anguish. And when she could scream no longer, she sobs.

A human being is a strangely delicate thing. You'd think after all of it -- all the wars, all the hospitalizations, the snide comments, the terminations, the mocking laughter, the curses of our formerly loved ones, the unwanted schoolyard nicknames, all that bad pork, the speeding tickets, the mediocre performance reviews, the videos of our drunken transgressions on the Internet, the 1040 long forms, the addictions, the letters from the creditors, the stake-burnings, the involuntary losses of sphincter control, the morning-afters and the mournings themselves -- that after all of that, the meek would not only inherit the earth, but be it. Yet still we rage in our souls. The fight against ourselves and our natures is the hardest battle of all. Oh, some accept, and crawl back into the dust from whence they've come, to lay down and die. But not all, not by a long shot. Some fight, no matter what. Some get back up off their knees, refusing to either pray or beg. Some struggle against inevitable fate until their last breath. And so would my Beatrice, or so I'd thought, until now.

"Come with me," I say after she quiets down.

"Why?" she sniffs.

"Because... I love you, and I need you."

She shoves me. "It's all about you, damnit. The hell with you and your love."

There can be ice at these altitudes this time of year is what I think. I wonder if and when I will ever be capable of another....

Then I realize I'm thinking about me, and that she's right. I tell her that. There is a long, long silence. We hear the wind rustle the trees. We hear the call of a osprey far off down and behind us, probably scoping the lake we passed for fish to attack. We wait, savoring our discomfort like it's quenched in gravy (milk gravy, both of us being Southern n' all). I repeat what I said before. Again, she does not answer. I don't just like her, I admire her. She is careful, of necessity. She thinks things through. She is wise, also scoping for fishy things to attack.

"Now I am thinking of you," I say, and I feel terrible. She stands up. "Go," I tell her, "go and take Virgil with you. I'll meet you in Millinocket."

Still she says nothing, but after a moment she walks over to my hiking poles, where I've thrown them down, picks them up, and hands them to me. She looks at me for a moment, inscrutable as stone. Then she wipes my cheek, discovering a tear there. A human being is a strangely delicate thing.

Just when I think I've begun to fathom the world, there it goes again. What can one ask for more than a life full of surprises? When she starts walking again, uphill, Virgil clinging to her, I wonder what it is I know at all. Then I realize I'm right back to thinking about myself, and I laugh. Goddamn incurable bastard.

After a bit, we cross the 1400-foot contour line. The trail is noticeably steeper. Regardless, we forge ahead in both senses: to move, and to harden the steel. I pass her. I want this over with.

We pass the intersection of The Owl Trail, a side trip off to the north side of the mountain which we're not taking today. I half expect the *bakaak* to appear from the trail, all skin and bones and chanting in Algonquin. Luckily for us, there's not even a moose. Just past the intersection lies Katahdin Stream Falls, surrounded by mountain ash. I consider not stopping, but, we've come all this way. So, we'll stop and enjoy the view. As God as my witness, we'll stop and enjoy the bloody view.

I'm standing on a big rock doing just that when she trudges up behind me. She's huffing and puffing, and not from any exertion. Oh, OK, maybe a little.

"See? See?" I say, gesturing at the pretty double-cascade.

"See what?" she says, exasperated. "Another damn snake? Another ghostly ghoulie goblin? Not if I can help it."

"*Look*," I implore her.

So we stare at the waterfall for a long time. There is a sound like tinkling crystal, high frequencies and some low, the smell of moss and decaying vegetable matter, a moment of generosity and release. We watch the play, turbulent and chaotic, grace given by the ordinary meeting the stone in a continuous cold liquid slap that surpassed any one of our human lives. The sunlight higher in the day's sky now finds us, peering just above the tops of the trees. We feel a sudden warmth clutch to our skin, a second grace.

To our right and slightly above us is an enormous ash tree; only thirty feet tall or so, but enormous for an ash. My eyes turn to it, slowly following up its trunk. Ants scurry along it, up, down, sideways; some black, some red, some black but with a half-red head, crossbreeds affirming a natural assimilation. Whitecap mushrooms and bracket fungi adorn its hide and gently taste of their host. It is our version of extravagance, and all the extravagance I need.

"Best git' movin," Virgil points out.

"Of course," I tell him. "Moving beats the alternative." I start right back up, tacking my sails eastward and upward. She says nothing. I wonder if her experience resembles anything like mine. Knowing, but not knowing. It's the essence of the coming together, the unexpected improbable miracle of us. Which could blow up like a Roman candle in kerosene at any second.

Minutes pass slowly but inexorably, embedded in the aspic of the world such as we are. We're now crossing the mouth of the Witherle Ravine, heading almost due east. Our climb of the mountain will really start once we reach the ravine's right flank.

"We're going to the top," she says suddenly, with finality, a pronouncement. I ponder this for a moment, then ask her: "What made you change your mind?"

But she does not answer, and I don't look back at her for fear of breaking the delicate spell. We cross the 1700-foot contour. Further up we cross behind the waterfall we passed, across Katahdin Stream itself. Far across the ravine lies an even more impressive waterfall, but we admire only from a distance. The trail has now steepened considerably. The air imperceptibly rarefies. We cross the 1800-foot contour.

Enormous, ankle-twisting blocks pave the trail up and away. Raw megalithic stones, an entire trail constructed of miniaturized Stonehenges one after another, eons of Druidic work and endless weathering. And tree roots like the insane drunken plumbing of trolls. We avoid them like the bloody plague, and she knows to do it without my saying anything. One false step on a tree root, and you find yourself skating on them. And if going downhill, skating, then skiing. And covered with the fall's slick leaves as they were, skating then skiing then pole-vaulting, a wild triathlon of winter Olympian events; and, because you are wearing your forty pound pack and have zero body fat left after all this agony you've chosen of your very cherry free will to put yourself through, it all ends not in the thrill of victory but the agony of defeat. That's why they closed this place in winter, which coincidentally started sometime in the next three and a half minutes, so sharp the dividing edge seems. Or was it three and a half months ago? It was cold enough to believe the latter. We cross the 1900-foot contour.

The lower end of the ravine is strewn with boulders, remnants of an Ice Age's glaciation long ago. Tossed and tumbled, a god-child's playthings. I pick up a fist size chunk as I walk, roll it around in my hand, try to squeeze it. I am no god-child. I push hard up from the mangled tresses forming the ribs of the mountain, feel it hold my weight, feel my weight now in every flex of my ankles and knees. A ligament in my right foot begins a sharp popping with every step, but it's non-threatening, requiring no medical attention. It just makes me push harder into the hardened magma. We reach 2000 ft.

There will be no sleep tonight, I realize. There will be celebration; either that, or damnation. The end-game has been decided, the table set, the knives lain ready to attack at whatever shall be laid at every plate. There will be well-wishers or a well, darkness or a darkness breaking, a curtain's rise or fall. I push harder. Sweat adorns me, rivulets of intention, depossessing me of my much-needed salts, increasing my life's entropy bit by acetylcholine bit. A one, or a zero. Nothing in-between, no grays today. There will be a success or a failure today. Today would be simple. Today would cease to be about the journey, and become the end itself. Today this will transform a piled-up bulky incoherent mass into pure energy, treatable with a mere liter or two of Gatorade. Today I shall reclaim all my salts, and rights, and freedoms, and sanities. Today I shall claim both my love and my desire, and we shall go, and Padma can be about his other business. Today this will all end. 2100, 2200 feet.

"We're going to the top," she states out of the clear blue, "because you're too damn prideful and self-involved to do anything else. So, fuck it."

There's an interesting series of musical pitches embedded in her comment. It's not angry, not sarcastic, not fatalistic, not funny. It's as objective-sounding as any Schoenberg tone-row, but like good opera there's a conflict between its content and its message. Can she really just swallow her fear like that? She keeps impressing me. 2300.

It occurs to me that women are like bears. Bears come in so many shapes and temperaments. Our standard run-of-the-mill eastern black bear, for instance, almost never has a beef to pick with anybody. I've come across dozens in my years out here, and never once, ever, did any of them do anything but either ignore me, beg for food, or turn and walk (or lumber, or run) the other way. About the only time they ever act otherwise is if they're rabid, have young cubs, or realize that you still smell like whatever was in the picnic basket you brought that they got into first. On the other hand, a western grizzly will make a picnic of your face, and a polar bear two picnics: of you, *and* the grizzly. As for pandas? 99% bamboo, and 1% of whatever scraps the grizzly and polar bear left of your clothing. See? Just like a lady. You get ignored, bitten, smelled, snorted at, yawned at, licked, have your stuff thrown about. She might fall asleep in your tent. She might get angry if you try to spoon with her. She might remove your testosterone-producing glands with her claws and predatory determination. Or, her words, and a sizable fraction of your remaining lifetime. She might follow you home. She might like some of your fruit; you might think she's cute, and imagine hers. Just one warning: *Carnivora* may be an order, but it's one that's neither military nor dietary. Women are omnivores, just like sharks or bulldozers or a barrel of boiling acid. 2400 feet.

A dull throb begins in my left knee, on the inside, my fibular collateral ligament. I feel a bump. Ah, my old friend, bursitis. It replaces the pain of my raw hands and my opposite skinned knee in my mind. No matter; it will be iced soon enough. I push harder... although, perhaps I favor my left walking pole a bit more when I bear down. I become claimed by the climb, Newton's inertia at rest and play again. I am all breath, heartbeat, moving muscle, flexing, relaxing, flexing again. I am primitive movements. I am speeding up. I am also ignoring her.

I slip again. This time I roll right, onto my arm. The pack shifts suddenly, throwing me completely on my side, slamming my bare elbow into a pointy rock, my cheek into bare grass and grit.

"Damn it!" I propose.

"Cat got your coordination today?"

I hear the forced tone in her voice. "I suppose." I pick myself up, brush myself off, my anger spilling out wintergreen fresh. Guess we'll both be angry today.

"Someone's trying to tell you something," she says matter-of-factly, not helping me up at all this time.

"Someone's been *trying* for the last two thousand miles," I snap at her. "Someone's always trying to tell somebody something. Can't everyone just make their own mistakes? Aren't we allowed to be imperfect? And what's with a lesson that involves *blood*?" I get angrier, showing her my wounds. "What kind of teaching is *this*?"

"The hard kind one remembers," she snaps back.

"Well I don't have a problem with *remembering*!"

"Nah, the only problem you have is an attitude one," she yells over me. "Enough complaining, enough philosophizing! We're getting to the top, right? We're getting this done, right? Up off your ass, big bright boy. Less talk, more walk! You wanna get it over with, then let's get it over with!"

There's revolution in the air, electrostatic, numbing to the touch. I tremble as we stare at one another, and hear my pulse beating *doom boom doom boom*, wardrums in my ears. It is my heart, and those are my words. She's using my words against me. Just who is playing whom here? It's all whiskey shot coercion, all bravado, hard to swallow and keep down, the realignment of the desires of others to one's own, manipulation by any other name and smelling as sweet. And here she stands using my own goddamn words....

"Inhale," she orders, quietly, and I obey. After all, she's right.

She starts off after a moment into a real trot, almost jogging. I take it she is serious. I haven't seen her serious that often. It's a discomforting scene, rather like suddenly realizing a large nasty spider has descended in front of your nose, and wondering what its sixty-nine-seeming black and blinkless eyes are pondering. I noticed that I'm moving, I'm following her. Interesting how conscious thought is often anything but. Who shoves who around inside the ol' careenium? Ah yes, it's the ol' symballs themselves, hah.

She's pushing it hard and disappears up the trail.

It occurs to me that I don't really know what she believes, what she is making of all this, what foundations in her are being overturned. I see her strength, but I don't know if it's real or fake. I hear the hardness in her, in her voice and in the hard, forced clunk of her boots on the path. It's what I haven't heard that I want to know now. Maybe she wonders whether or not I'll respect her. Lord knows I don't respect the majority. Of course respect isn't the right word; I just *tolerate* the majority. Oh, I can respect those with other attributes worthy of respect: hard working, intelligent, empathetic. But not their opposites. And even then, irrationality, in any form, only detracts from other qualities worthy of respect. At the end of the day I just *tolerate*. Maybe she's afraid I won't respect her. Maybe she's just afraid. Or maybe I am. Maybe I'm afraid that I'm the one who's merely *tolerated*.

I'm not going to ask her about it just yet. I've better sense than that. 2500 feet, halfway there.

I round a sharp S-turn and run into the back of her. She's immovable, a glacier, still and hard. "*Look*," she whispers. Then I notice that she is shaking, and it's not cold.

In the middle of the path there is a large rock, and on the large rock are three rattlers. They are standing up as we watch them, turning into cobras, cobras with red eyes and rattles. I gently pull Bee by the arm, pull her behind me, and Virgil clinging to her.

"*Whaaaaat is iiiiiit that you are fiiiiiinding?*" says an ethereal, malevolent voice. "*A rooooock? A treeeeee? The next tuuuuurn in the paaaaath? It leads only to anoooother turn, anoooother tree, anoooother rockkkk.*" hissed a second. "*But of courssssse, you aaaalready knooooow that.*" hisses a third.

I gulp in the air. "I am finding... finding...."

"*Yoursellllllf?*" all three spit with forked tongues and brimstone's breath.

"Durant," Bee manages, low and hard.

Somehow I know. This is Padma, and this isn't Padma. Something deep, an undercurrent, a river, lava and glacier at once, speaks to me of *hate, hate, hate*, hate unending, an odd juxtaposition of timelessness and recklessness, a billion million hates chained together into an eternal aeon of hatred, a perception of limitlessness that is itself without bounds, utter fearlessness, blindness to all but self, self, self, and hating, hating, hating even that. Somehow I know. I feel loss like a open pit filled with ash and bleach, loss like blood drained to fill the oceans red, loss like the thing It missed never even was in the first place. This is something new. This is Padma, and this isn't Padma. Somehow I know. If you took infinity and painted it black and blood-red and black again, coat upon coat, and baked it in heat upon heat until it rose on the third day and filled the world, the sky, the universe, until it crawled down your very throat and choked the hard-earned dog-eared life right out of you, cell by cell, atom by atom, crying out as it did so *hate hate hate* to the cold empty blackness that was itself, reflecting the words back and forth and back again in a trillion echoes that had nothing to reflect off of except themselves and their own incombustible incomprehensible *hate hate hate*, it might, just might, approximate the cavernous maw of nothingness that fills my thought. Somehow I know.

"*Eeeeeven when weeeee are alooooone, we are neeeeever alooooone*," the demons spoke as one, mocking. "*Fear creates lussssst, greeeed and gluttttttony, laaaaziness and selfishnessssss, aaaaanger and sssssullennesssss, heresssssy, murrrrrder and sssssuicide, beeeetrayal and treachchchchery, and worssssse. Are you afraaaaid, Duraaaaant?*"

An answer escapes me. I do not know what I am. I ponder the maw, and its words.

But then after a moment I realize I *am* pondering them. And then, still pondering them. I realize time is passing, or an illusion of time is passing, either way the same thing. I breathe in, out, just to be sure, and just to be sure I still can. And another moment passes, and another. Then I realize It is letting time pass, allowing me to feel, true, but allowing me to think as well. It is allowing me to exist, to continue, to be, and I realize that It, whatever It is, is waiting, wanting, needing. And I understand. I get it. I know where Its weak spot is. One that wants everything, needs everything. And that everything includes *me*. It *needs* me, to react, respond, to dominate me, control me, to feed off of, to obtain feedback off of, like every parasite: hungry, and hungry still. *It* needs *me*. *IT* needs *ME*!

"You are an illusion, *maya*, *sol non invictus*. You are only my own fears turned against me. You are not real." The words come from me, but they are not mine, or at least they surprise me. "Out of our way. We're getting to the top."

"*Duraaaant*," one hisses. "*Duraaaant*," says another. "*Are you AFRAAAAID?*" "*Are you AFRAAAAID?*" Then all at once and chaotically: "*AFRAAAID, AFRAAAID, AFRAAAID...?*"

I summon all the courage I can find, and look them right in the eye. "I have a joke for you" I answer. "A hen, a djinn, and a Finn walk into a bar in Norway. The bartender asks the hen, What's your pleasure? The hen says, I'll have a Cock. The bartender produces a rooster, and..."

Suddenly the ground shakes under us, and the snakes grow larger, and larger, and larger, becoming vast, tree-sized, filling the trail, rearing over us. Bee screams.

But it means little, then less than little to me, because then I am sure. It is just demanding more attention, a spoiled child, a schoolyard bully. "You are an illusion! You are not real! You are my fear! And my fear is no one's but MINE!" And with that I pushed myself forward, forward towards the demons, and past them.

They vanish instantly like the smoke and futility they are. I absorb the moment, turn to Bee. "*Look*," I say, "Do you see?" But she is occupied with comforting Virgil, who is still shaking, and looking at them I wonder what I feel, what they feel. The source remains elusive. She isn't looking at me, which I interpret as an intercalated hate; spurious perhaps, but hate nonetheless. Still, I plan on having a ding-dongy day today.

"Halfway there," I say. "Best git' movin."

"Best git'..." Virgil starts, but Bee interrupts him.

"Why?" she asks.

"Because it's there," I answer. "I thought you'd already agreed...."

"Oh, please, Durant! Agreed? Agreed? I was trying reverse psychology, but since yours is so stubborn I may as well have…."

"Have what?"

"Left Durant, left, that's what! Left you here to your own devices. Left you here to face this... insanity!"

"Exactly! See? See? Doesn't make sense, does it? Despite it all, we're still here. We're still here! Don't you see it yet? Despite its power, it *needs* us, Bee, more than we need it! All this drama, all the world a stage, all the history and myth and war and bloodshed and loss and confusion. Mostly the confusion. We don't need any of that, but He... apparently, He does.

Don't you see? And finally, finally, after all the meddling, all the tinkering and playing around, all the games and passion plays and goal-line stands and visitations and salvations and damnations, now, Bee, now, finally, He gets it. He's matured, grown-up. And so have we, or at least we're starting to. Now it's time for some sanity, some real garden-variety pruning to occur, better to reap the rewards later on."

She is flustered, tired, exasperated. "What... I don't get it."

"We're still here, Bee! You and Virgil and I! He wants this, Bee! Wants us to go to the top! Wants us to succeed! Because a higher power who didn't want that doesn't make sense... because we're still here! He *wants* to be delt out of the game, because He knows not that He's failed at it but that the very nature of the game is unwinnable! Free will, Bee! He got his chocolate stuck in our peanut butter and they don't go together and he knows it!"

"But... but what about... what was that, Doctor? Goddamn talking snakes? What the FUCK was that?"

"Oh." That stops me short. "Well.... " Then my words fail me.

"I felt it," she answers. "In my head, in my heart. I felt it. It felt like a cold hole in the earth that went down forever, down and down until there was no ground anymore, not even the far side, just nothing and nothing and more nothing until it had absorbed and swollen and swallowed and frozen everything, forever." Finally, she looks at me, and I breathe again. "Jesus, Durant. It was... it was...."

"I felt it too," I admit. "I suppose some will be upset by this change of management. Some will be expelled from their Eden they've worked so hard to pollute. Some handymen will be out of a job."

"You mean...."

"You know what I mean." I didn't think it was wise for her to say it, so I stopped her. I put my fingers to her lips. "But It's powerless. It's just a servant, same as us, but we're getting promoted to management today, Bee.

We just have to get to the top. Isn't that right, Virg?" He bobs his head up and down at me. "Best git' movin', right?"

But this time he doesn't respond.

"Trust me, just one more time, just now," I beg her, whispering, adding a kiss at the end, long and hard and open and wonderful.

"They can't take that away," I tell her.

"Maybe," she answers, "maybe not." But she takes my hand, and we possessors of time are held in the moment we create, sharing, illuminated. I love her. I love her enough to face anything.

Therefore, just to set an example, I start moving again. No time for kibble, or water, or a pee. We're getting to the top. We're *getting* to the top.

We push on, heading up, and up, and up. The trees begin to slowly fall away, thin out. We are approaching treeline, another 400, 500 vertical feet or so. The slope steepens, winding back again to the northeast for a bit. Omphalina and Angelica's lace start to appear on and through the rocks, juncos jumping and chirping on the ground around and in-between them. We're definitely higher up now.

I begin racing up the Trail. I turn and enter some brambles, bushes that stretch far out and into the path· They scratch me, tear at me: my face, my arms, a few thorns penetrating my shirt. I wince and move faster. She's keeping up with me like the fine filly she is. I'm pushing it. I'm getting to the top, damnit. I'm ending this. My breath comes hard and cold; I feel pain in my solar plexus, my diaphragm. It pushes me onward.

Then I sense movement in the brush around me. Not just wind, not just juncos or squirrels or other small things. This is different. It starts as a kind of longitudinal pulse, small waves of up-down motion parallel to me on either side in the ground between the trees and overgrowth. At first it is ever so slight, then there is more, then more. A half-mile passes by, and my pain has doubled along with the steepness of the trail. My knees both start to throb, my thighs start to burn. I hear Bee breathing hard behind me; we are taxed to nearly our limits. We drive forward.

But the waves around us increase in number and intensity. At some point there is perceptible movement of the rocks and brush, then larger boulders begin to be pushed upwards, then the smaller trees begin to sway. It seems as if the wave will pass us, so I grunt and turn from a sprint practically into a run, pulverizing my body to its absolute edge. I'm *getting* to the top. She keeps up, right behind me, as we begin openly struggling for air, our lungs trying to keep up with the demands of our bodies. The waves fall behind us a little, stay there, but still moving, and slowly growing in intensity.

"Durant," she gasps from behind me, and I know she has noticed them too. In response, I just accelerate more, turning my hike into a full-blown jog, a slow run, best I can do with 35 pounds on my back. I push my poles brutally into the eroded scrabble in the path, slipping here and there, twisting my ankles several times, and once or twice hard enough to make me wince and stop for a moment. But when I stop I hear a low rumble around me, the sound of rocks turning in a drum, catching up, and just behind us. And knowing what this meant and not knowing I burst into speed again, ignoring the pain and my drained form, running running running all the way up, and up, and up.

Onward we sprint like elderly racing time itself, as the rumble becomes a bedlam becomes a roar. Now it is a lithe, long, continuous avalanche, sinuous and dangerous as a feline, pandemonium full of Chaos and Old Night, seething, writhing, as the waves paralleling us now seem to foam at the top with gravel and sparks and earth disturbed, and somewhere in the black bottom of my tested, terrified gut I know without looking at what I dare not what the waves really are, and what horror they contain is about to crash on this high and blackened shore. "Durant!" she cries out above the tumult, but I know only the prize within our very reach now, only a mile or two distant. I suck in only desire, finding no usable oxygen on the wind, nothing that replaced the waste products in my lungs or blood, if blood it still was. But desire was enough to burn and propel me onward. I would not be daunted. I would not be denied. I cry out and throw my poles down, unbuckle my pack, throwing it off to the side without stopping, and suddenly the weight of the world is gone and I am born anew, surging forward.

Trees are tossed like toothpicks into the air by the onrushing tide around me, but I defy it, both demon and demand, weight and wanting, hell and throbbing heart. It's close to bursting, exertion broiled with lust and greed and gluttony and anger and all of it pumping, beating, hot and fluid through me, pouring out of my very pores. Another half-mile dissolves behind me. Still she keeps up with me, unable to stop me, unable to stop. The trees thin around us, becoming fewer, smaller.

Then the last of the trees disappeared, and the famous Boulder Field lay before us. Treeline at last. Only rock now, rock against a sea of sky, all the way to the top. We could see it now, the summit standing alone in the light. We could actually *see* it. But this sight was too much, and the desire raw and searing stopped me, heaving chest bellowing air in and out, as if I was stunned into stopping by the simple, inescapable, incomprehensible, miraculous, beloved and despised sight of, finally, finally, finally, *The End.*

But it was not to last. For even as the trees ended, the tidal wave of rustling shapes and forms roars up from behind us, beside us, racing up the slopes on both sides waves of power swept us, under us, throwing us up, then down again, as it passes us, faster and faster, and as we stand there in shock the wave crests and breaks from underneath the ground in front of us, and the earth and dirt and rocks open into innumerable fissures, filled with fire and smoke and furnace heat, and erupting the cracks disgorge the contents of their wave: *snakes*. Thousands upon thousands upon thousands, becoming millions, diamondback rattlers so numerous their rattles shake the very earth, and an ocean of hardened and fresh lava churn with them, frothing the surface until it is nothing but a ball, a hill, a mountainside of snakes entwined and enwrapped together, seething, snapping, shaking, until the whole top of the mountain itself is not rock but reptile, billions of them, with the Trail clear as day routed atop them, through them, all the way to the top, where small but clearly visible still stands the marker at the summit of Katahdin that marks the end of the Appalachian Trail, the end of my journey and our struggle and this Hell, the end of the nightmare, the end and the beginning. Immovable, we look down on what we stood upon as our breath finally slowed, at the last patch of rock and reason left on the mountain. But no! Looking back, the Trail behind us remains as it was, reasonable, disappearing back down into the trees from whence we'd come.

"Durant, no," is all she says, gasping, feebly, sensing me slip away from her, sensing the end had come. But the end to what?

"It's a test," I tell her over the roar of the rattlers and the churning of their bodies like boulders falling forever. But I feel new, refreshed, ready.

"But not the one you think it is," she replies. "Don't you see?"

No I don't. There is the end. Right *there* is the end. Visible, in *this* world, right *there*.

"Don't do it. Turn around. For me," she pleads.

"But..." was all I manage. I am transfixed. Everything I had sought, everything I had wanted, everything I had ever wanted and lost, now redeemable in the sunlight, in this place, in this time. It is right there. I can taste its splinters on my tongue, piquant and piercing. I cannot look away. It is the most beautiful goddamn thing I have ever seen in my whole useless pointless life.

"Then do it for him," she says, with a sigh of resignation so strong that it penetrates even the ignored sunlight.

"Him who?" I ask her, dazed. "Padma?" My eyes stay fixed on the peak ahead. What is she talking about? Didn't she know that....

"*Him*," she answers, firmer, tighter.

But I am blind to it all now, blind to the snakes, the danger, the air, and her words. A stillness has come over the world, a world turned all blue and gold with a single maroon-painted wooden sign at the center of my vision carved *MT KATAHDIN* in big beautiful all-cap white letters followed closely underneath with the gorgeous wonderful terrible agonizing dreadful brilliant blinding murderous statement *NORTHERN TERMINUS OF THE*

APPALACHIAN TRAIL. All I know was the end has come. All I know is that *we are THERE*. "I don't care what Padma wants. I...."

With a shock like lightning the world turns around me, and I feel myself rotating in space, an impossibility. Then I find myself looking at her, feeling her hands strong and unyielding on my arms, realizing she's turned me around.

"Virgil," and it's so quiet, as if her words were made out of moonbeams. "Do it for Virgil."

It feels like withdrawal from a drug, or the administration of one; I shiver as the adrenaline and serotonin and dopamine find and release new and old receptors alike all at once. "What about Virgil?" I snap a bit too quickly, telling her that she has me off balance. *Damn.*

Her face presses itself into mine, a mouse looking my last into the face of its final friendly neighborhood owl. Slowly she asks, "Yes, Durant, there's a question. What about Virgil?"

"What... what do you mean?" All of a sudden I'm confused, anxious. Gravity seems oppressive, confining, my pack gargantuan, a gorilla on my back, loaded with burdens even though I'm not even wearing it, or I don't seem to be but I'm not even sure of that. Where did I put…? What was I...? Who is she that...?

"Tell me about Virgil," she almost whispers, low and calm. "You never say anything about him. Not once. Ever."

"Wh... about..." I am lost suddenly, trapped, closed in on all sides, claustrophobic. "I'm sure I don't know what you m...."

"Durant, who is Virgil?" she murmurs, touching my face.

The sun seems to explode then, and I shout out, falling, stumbling backwards. Stimuli overload, electric on my skin, every star a scalpel, every wisp of cloud howling anguish aplenty. I scream, and then just as suddenly all is silent again, only another day, only another hour in another day. I find myself sitting on the ground, cold and hard, shaking, staring at my hands, also shaking. They seem to be the same hands I'd worn all these years. They whisper to me of where they'd been, what they'd touched. And they don't want to remember.

Ninety-nine nuns mind guns nights at nine,
A hundred hunt dread Huns.
So how many nuns mind huts on the Rhine?
Nuns numbering a hundred and one!

Truth is independent of the observer. But what about the observed?

...apartialseizureduringwhichthepatientmaintainsonlya...
...semblanceofawarenessoftheiractionslocationandevents...
...duringthistimethepatientremainconsciousbutlacks...
...profoundexecutivefunctionsthatnormallydistinguish...
...realityfromthebackground...
...orfactfromfiction...
...orselffromtheselfsownactions...

"Stop it!" I gasp, grabbing my head.

A hundred and two tie knots tight (not too)
A hundred three feed the twine;
But who's at the door, hun? A hundred and four Huns,
Huns hunted right down 'round the Rhine!

The problem is that the cat cannot be both alive or dead for the environment is hopelessly tangled with the box whose constituents are themselves tangled with the table on which the box containing the cat sits whose constituents are entangled with the surrounding air and audience and the linoleum on which it sits and so forth and so on and such like until every atom of the cat like a grain of *mandala* sand extends to the limits of the observable universe meaning that it is all connected and directs the spin in one direction corresponding to a single imaginary vector on the Riemann sphere which being imaginary causes the multiple vectors corresponding to the impossible mixed spin states of three-halves or five-sevenths or the square root of two irrational despite its denial by the ancient Greeks on one particle in one cat irrational in one box on one table in one nation under God irrational to affect all other particles in existence simultaneously magically mathematically miraculously through a D-brane or S-brane or four-space or n-tope or E8 or similar simple quantum unit of irrational mysticism therefore there is no paradox never was a paradox cannot be a paradox for the limit of the vector is one-half times the orthogonal intersection of <I AM THAT I AM $_{\text{dead}}$> *minus* <I AM THAT I AM $_{\text{alive}}$> being subtractive not additive like the food-grade silicon dioxide in one's non-dairy creamer added to prevent untimely caking on the shelf irrational and contrary to all sense and reason and constant speed of light in a vacuum averaged across all Feynman histories where it may exceed *c* nay will exceed *c* on an infinite number of paths irrational which in reality never occur because they simultaneously cancel themselves out to nothingness by virtue of their existence which never actually occurs because they occur and cancel out irrational irrational irrational. *Ipso facto.*

"Who is he, Durant?" All calm and soothing, glass ripples on the surface echoing down to nothing. Nothing, yet observing.

Fire seems to form around the edges of my vision, igniting the raw fear inside me again, motion induced in the swirling black oily depths, heavy, cumbersome. It creates an unlight, a light that wants more than anything to extinguish, to blind, to burn away the combustible sensibilities of everyday life into a bonfire of id, but the water rises around me, around me and in me and through me. I float and drown simultaneously, merge and separating with my senses and their blindness, not wanting to hear, or see, or touch, mere taste only, and that of bitterness and regrets.

A hundred and five find five hundred alive
A thousand feet under the floor
Ten thousand appear and the thousand-plus dear
Are sacrificed sliced thin for Thor!

...researchersstillhavelittleclueasto...
...whatactuallyhappensattheendofafugueepisode...
...whatstimulusorreactioncausesthepatientto...
...finallyreengagewiththerealitysurroundinghim...
...orwhatcasuesanalmostinstantcaseofamnesia...

...tosetindrawingacurtainovertheepisodesevents...
...evenmoremysteriousarethemuchrarercases...
...wherethevictimcanrememberwhathashappenedtohim...
...butresearchersspeculatethesuddenrealization...
...ofsuchultimatelossofcontrolmaybe...
...toomuchformosttobear...
...toomuchformosttobear...
...toomuchformosttobear...

I never forget... forget... what was it I was supposed to forget?

"Who is Virgil, Durant?" She touches him, and he responds.

"Best git' movin'," says Virgil.

I never forget a thing. Except the things I forget. I forgot birthdays. I forgot promises and appointments. I forgot where I put the car keys. I forgot to pay the bills and I forgot other things too. I forgot about life, until it walked back into mine.

"Virgil," I manage to whisper. Then like a wall of concrete and steel holding back a thousand foot deep of cold dark, something internal gives, something like girders or hard unyielding stone, something that formerly supplied a false sense of unseen strength and structure, and with a distinct *pop!* in my head like overpressurized champagne the onslaught washes across me and over me, a tsunami of images: images of home, of family, of hope, and promises, lots of promises, promises over and over, and one more thing, one more face, one more... *person*.

I see how I've been pondering the silence. I had no real issue letting go; the doing of it was a flick of a switch in my mind, automatic. Not a word, or even a thought; I just turned and left, like any exhale would. That was love.

Emotionally, I raged. I was selfish and angry and resentful and hurt. I grieved. I lacked all empathy. I understood the what of it, but facts are easy, facts are just math and logic and cruelty. This was not about facts. She believed in one set of them, I another. Disjoint sets cannot intersect; a union? Downright paradoxical. Uncountably full of points they were, points made and debated and rebuffed in their uncountable need to be unaccountably right, and all without word or comment or discussion. Interpretation and hallucination. False. The truth made untrue. I raged. That was love.

Love, for... for....

"Virgil," I whisper, sounds which must have been mine but for the draining of the words from me as I sank to my knees. He walked over to me, hugged me.

"Papa," said Virgil.

That was love. Or, more precisely, a fugue state. Welcome back to reality, old friend. Long time no see.

Autism is never an easy thing to bear: not in a marriage that was bad to begin with. But for no one, no one, more than Virgil. Virgil, who would never really know. Virgil, who was blissfully unaware. How unwanted he was. By his mother. Who'd left him with me. And of course by me. After all, I'd tried to escape down the trail, escape the inescapable, escape the only person who gave my life any meaning. And I'd succeeded, to a very large, very, very horrific, degree.

If there'd been a cliff nearby, I would have taken it's shortcut to judgment, right then. If he hadn't been right there, hugging me. Someone else inside me appeared then, thank God, and taking control of my arms that person hugged back, realizing how lucky he was, how lucky Virgil was, for having made it this far, together. Somehow I'd made it to the brink, and backed off. Somehow, he did too.

"He's my son," I tell her, through something that must have been tears, though unrecognizable as such to my old self. "And you are my Lady Necessity, the one who waits by the openings of heaven and earth. You judge me aright." I look back up then, at the mountaintop. "Keep your secrets," I tell them all. "I get it now. I get it. Pride. I understand. I can walk away. If I expect You to, then I'd better be able to myself, right?

Right. Mission accomplished. I get it. Was blind, but now I see." I turn, taking Virgil and Beatrice by the hand.

"And thanks," I add, looking at Bee, who smiles; in tears, but smiling nonetheless.

And as I lead them back down and we retreat, we hear a last grumbling, a rolling sucking sound, and we know without looking that the snakes have transformed themselves back into rock, back into normalcy, back into the real world we hiked into so long, long ago. But we did not look back, only forward, like we would in the days to come. Forward, truly forward, finally, at last.

Eli, Eli, lama sabachthani?

But there was no answer to my age-old question, on this wind or any other.

XI

Millinocket Municipal Airport, 408 ft.

On some nights when looking up at the stars, I've wondered if they are aware of each other. Do the stars look out across the night sky, profound in its emptiness and distance, black and cold, and feel anything? Is their only warmth to be found on the inside? Do they ask as we do when we look up at the stars, *Is there nothing more?* Do they ever wonder if through a combined act of gravitational bravery and mathematical impossibility they could reach out and connect, meet their own kind, and gaze in wonder and the majesty of being that their very being made manifest? Trade thoughts? Mysteries? Desires? Long together, want and need, together? Ponder the sadness, the sameness, of it all? Perhaps it does happen. There are more double and triple star systems in the universe than single stars. Perhaps that means that the universe is... perhaps that means more, that there is more, than meets the eye.

Perhaps, just perhaps.

I'm watching them from a distance as I'm waiting in line to buy them coffee. They've become fast friends. She's produced a deck of cards, teaching him how to play Crazy Eights while we wait for the charter plane back to Boston. He's still not getting it; he keeps taking the cards from the discard pile and putting them into his hand and laughing. She laughs too when he reaches over and takes the cards from her hand, and both of them practically fall over when she takes them back. Then it degenerates into the two of them just swapping cards back and forth.

I'd never really seen him interact with anyone before. She knows when to dial it up, and when to tone it down to avoid upsetting him. She's a natural. In so many, many ways, she's a natural. She can even touch him, which no one had ever been able to do. He actually likes it. She's a natural. Almost as if... as if it was preordained.

There's no going back.

I have a plan. I have a plan. I have a wish, and a plan. One wish only, and I know what I must do with it. One wish, and what a doozy it will be. It won't be for me. I already know what I am going to do. I won't be a Messiah, but I will be a catalyst for change. A change right up there with the invention of fire or the wheel. A fundamental change. A change to us all, forever. I won't wish for fish with my childish Ish wish dish. No; my plan involves the opposite in fact. The total opposite, as in, *to oppose*. Wish I may, wish I might. Oh yes brothers and sisters, this convert, this believer that testifies before you today does indeed have one wish coming, one wish for all of us. And I will use it, soon.

There's no going back.

She hasn't said a word about what happened. She hasn't mentioned it at all. She's put it out of her mind. I of course cannot. She stands on a rooted ground I never have, a ground absent of faults and fault lines, a ground that does not belch forth vapors on a whim or spout superheated geysers overlying deep chambers of violent magma. At least she wants to convince herself of that. The earth does not move, change, grow old, or grow too strange to understand. All things are known, and if not those *other* have no bearing on everyday life. She has deep roots, and despite the recent uncalled-for shaking of her foundations, she will continue as she always has. Of course I know too that this will all change soon, that the questions will coalesce, condense, solidify into substance, becoming words first thought, then asked. She won't be able to help it, not while it's all still in there somewhere, in that pretty and pretty brilliant head, bouncing around like so many shiny chrome marbles on a rush-hour-busy freeway. Sooner or later one will pop up and bust her windshield, and I'll be needed to help her through it to avoid the accident. Because it won't be an accident, no sir-ee -- not after I'm done with my plan.

Some say that peace and understanding are the same thing. I used to be one of those people; and understanding little, I found no peace. Funny how events teach – sometime even after-the-fact. I found a kind of strength instead of a long-sought understanding, a kind of happy medium between question and answer. Too many questions of course, and too little time before it all changes and produces new questions. I forgot that it's the journey, not the end. Imagine that: I forgot. Ignorance ain't quite bliss, but it ain't too shabby when there's compensation enough. The trail goes on forever, whether we're on it or not. In the tenuous grip of tempered ridges Mother Earth guides, peddling flesh temporary and transparent, spinning night into day and night again, dividing the hours into what we have and what we do not have, by slow erosion or by sudden avalanche dissolving even the mountains themselves sooner or later into the fine washed sands on the shores of the sea of deepening time. And you stand on the shore of that sea, looking back, looking ahead, and you realize the scale is all the same, and how far you've come, and how far, how very very far, you have to go: if you go, or rather, choose to go on.

Sure there are missing pieces of the puzzle. That's what makes a puzzle fun. You can't ever finish it if a piece is missing. Try it yourself: throw one away sometimes. Or, just turn around and walk away. Liberating like a heart attack, baby. I think that's ultimately what faith is all about: *wu wei*. Action through non-action. Letting go.

And speaking of going, we're going with her to Boston. There's nothing left for us in Georgia, nothing left for us anywhere but here, nothing left in the volume of space and time allotted to us except what we share and create together. There is only us and the innumerable stars, and they are both glorious and fantastic and as much of a miracle as anyone can expect to find these days. I look upon two that I love. And I know what I must do.

I'm a virologist, she said. *Studying Alzheimer cures*, she said. *Cures delivered by viruses*, she said. I didn't forget. I never forget a thing. Not in the end. Not in the end when it mattered and my pride was tested. Not in the end. In the end the love won out. In the end, I remained human, yet more so. I know what I must do. In the end, it's love.

Which is why I'm going to contaminate her virus culture with my DNA. Specific, known, targeted segments of it. Pieces related to memory, pieces she knows about already from her research, pieces she knows how to isolate. I'm a doctor, she's a doctor, we're both smart. I'll get the information I need from her, a little work on my own with some isolation equipment, a centrifuge, the right protein and enzyme mixture to pull them out, then, when her guard is down, when she's not looking, I'll contaminate her culture. Spice it, splice it, pump up the jam. I'll give her an Alzheimer's cure. I'll give her a cure she'll never forget. I'll give her a cure none of you will ever forget. Ever.

My wish? That the virus becomes airborne. Unstoppable, immutable, worldwide. I'll give you a cure, all right. I'll give you a cure that will cure everything. A cure that will be passed on in your genes to all of your children, and theirs, and theirs. A cure for the banalities of the world, the stupidities, the illogic, the evils that all come from being unaware, forgetful, fearful. When the worldwide IQ of every single loser, chooser, poser, peon, and king is jacked up by 50 or 75 or 100 points, when everyone's a frickin' genius because everyone remembers everything the first time they read or hear or learn it, well my friends, then, then, you will see. You will all see.

Especially Virgil. I'm looking forward to talking to him. Actually talking to him. I'm looking forward to meeting the brand new person he'll become. I'm very, very, very much looking forward to that, yes indeed I am. I believe. I believe.

She looks up at me, smiles. I smile back. Our eyes lock, that wonderful sweet mixture of heat and tranquility racing between them. Little does she know. She doesn't realize it yet, doesn't see it yet, doesn't know what's coming. Little does she know that she's the real Messiah here. She will cure all of you from your own humanity. Evolution, in the form and time intended. It was meant to be, when we were ready.

Time to grow up, kids. Time to put the toys away and act like adults. Playtime's over. We're on our own now. God is dead and we have killed him. Or He may as well be. We're on our own now. Except for my one last wish.

And as for Bee and myself? We began as travelers between sunsets, lingering nowhere and everywhere, wanting for nothing and something and everything, outpacing only the tempered desires of our restless hearts, driven by the wind and rain from one end of our modestly sane country to the other, migrating souls who have left our high-country winter behind for a valley of springtimes, our journeyman's journey ended, and the long, long loneliness endured and overcome. Only now the way will not be quite so lonely. Not by a long shot. Not for either of us. Us, or Virgil.

Of course, we sure could use a little less adventure next time around. There's always next year. Maybe I'll mention the Pacific Crest Trail when I walk back over. Remind her the season starts in five months. Maybe I can keep from laughing while she just stares at me and tries to resume her breathing.

Naaaaah.

But now comes the purgatory of change. Same as all the old change, true, but we'll be better equipped for it this time around. Like Bob the Caveman, we might burn ourselves at first with our newfangled, newfound fire, but every fire has its uses. And this fire will burn very, very brightly indeed. Enough to see by. Enough for all of us to see all of it by.

What will become of us? Not worse I'm sure. I can't imagine how it could possibly be worse. Maybe a purgatory's to come, but it certainly won't be the inferno we have now. And who knows? It just might be a paradise, by some standards.

Were blind, but now... well, we'll see.

ACKNOWLEDGEMENTS

The staff and volunteers of the
Great Smoky Mountains National Park,
for keeping the past alive in the present.

Guy P. Raffa's beautiful *Dante's World*
http://danteworlds.laits.utexas.edu/

Tom Dunigan's *very* comprehensive list of
Appalachian Trail shelters
http://web.eecs.utk.edu/~dunigan/at/

The Works and Words of:
Bill Bryson
Umberto Eco
Horace Kephart
John Krakauer
Krishnamurti
Roger Penrose
Thomas Pynchon
Lisa Randall
Richard Smullyan
Henry David Thoreau

Amber and Anita, for, shall we say, inspiration.

That other person who said I shouldn't mention them
because they'd be *soooo* embarrassed… so I won't.
(Personally, I think the whole world should know about you.)

And, last but not least, Dante Alighieri (your loss, Beatrice).

ABOUT THE AUTHOR

Bret Lowery was born in Birmingham, Alabama in 1965, and is an avid hiker of many years. American Inferno is his first novel.

3/12

Coleman Northwest
Regional Library

CPSIA information can be obtained at www.ICGtesting.com
Printed in the USA
LVOW061639201211
260339LV00005B/7/P